The Lady and the Tomcat

When Devon sat next to her, she looked up at him in time to catch his kiss full upon her mouth.

He licked his lips. "Cats are inordinately fond of cream, I perceive." He bent and whispered in her ear. "And I'm inordinately fond of Kat flavored with cream."

He eyed her so sensuously that she had to do something to break the intensity of the moment. She picked up her bowl, poured some cream in it, and set it on the floor. "Here you are. A bowl all your own. You don't have to make do with leftovers."

That regal nose lifted into the air. "Are you implying, madam, that I have stripes or spots?"

"No, but at times I've thought I've seen the beginnings of a tail." She glanced disparagingly at the lean hips encased in casual breeches.

He leaned into her face and purred, "You could be right. I've only to look at you to feel myself growing horned." When she blushed and looked away, he smiled. "Ah, Kat, I don't think you know what you want. Would you really have me be beast or demon instead of a man who desires you? What have you to go back to?"

"Nothing you would understand, but something vital to me: the right to choose my own fate."

He gripped her shoulders in strong hands. "Then choose. Choose me. Willingly. Gladly. You know you want to. . . ."

SURRENDER THE NIGHT

Colleen Shannon

JOVE BOOKS, NEW YORK

SURRENDER THE NIGHT

A Jove Book / published by arrangement with
the author

PRINTING HISTORY
Jove edition / July 1992

ISBN: 0-515-10730-1

Jove Books are published by The Berkley Publishing Group,
200 Madison Avenue, New York, New York 10016.
The name ''JOVE'' and the ''J'' logo
are trademarks belonging to Jove Publications, Inc.

PRINTED IN THE UNITED STATES OF AMERICA

10 9 8 7 6 5 4 3 2 1

To Jason and Devon Jeske, my own two little
heroes, with love.

"Weeping may endure for a night,
but joy cometh in the morning."

—*The Holy Bible*, PSALMS 30:5

Surrender the Night

Part One

"When lovely woman stoops to folly,
And finds too late that men betray,
What charm can soothe her melancholy?
What art can wash her guilt away?"

—OLIVER GOLDSMITH,
"An Elegy on the Death
of a Mad Dog"

Chapter One

AWARENESS RETURNED SLOWLY to Katrina Lawson. Blackness. Constriction. Suffocation. It seemed a bottomless well had swallowed her, or . . . a coffin. The burring in her ears quieted until she heard sounds other than her own heartbeat. Voices. Dripping water. Her gusting breaths slowed. She was not alone, entombed alive as in her nightmares.

Relief was short-lived as she realized two things: why she couldn't move, and who had brought her here. Oh God, now she knew why the tea he'd insisted on fixing her had tasted bitter.

"My offering is a worthy vessel, quality in face and form, though not in birth. I shall display her to you all very shortly. You've never seen hair so gold, or eyes so blue," Viscount Sutterfield bragged.

Katrina strained at her bonds. To be trapped, used and discarded like a soiled handkerchief . . . no, not now. She'd fought too hard, suffered too much to keep her self-respect intact. When her struggles only tightened the silken cords, she went still.

The past three lonely years had taught her to depend upon no one but herself. After her father's death she'd gone in and quickly out of a succession of households, her dismissal each time owing more to her looks than her ability. That she neither sought nor wanted masculine attention didn't signify to the worried mothers and wives. They sent her on with lackluster recommendations, forcing her to accept work where she found it, no matter the dispositions of the males in the households.

Exactly so had she met Sutterfield. The son of her last employer, he'd lulled her, at first, with friendly smiles. She'd hoped that finally she wouldn't have to bolt her door at night and avoid dark corridors—until he accosted her one day in the salon, proving he was like all the rest. His prudish mother happened upon their embrace. She believed her son's tale of Katrina's flirtation and dismissed Katrina without a character. Katrina had subsisted on her meager savings until, a few weeks ago, she'd finally found an old harridan so disliked that she'd been desperate for a companion. She'd hired Katrina despite her lack of references.

Now it seemed all her struggles had been for naught. If Sutterfield had been describing her a minute ago, she could think of only one reason for his fulsomeness. She was sick unto death of being preyed upon. She owed her uncertain existence the past few years to men such as Sutterfield.

Her thoughts shied away from the first and only enjoyable position she'd lost because of a man. Only in her dreams did she allow herself the luxury of his name. She'd sent him away, and part of her had regretted it ever after. But rake though he was, even he had not stooped to kidnapping.

After Sutterfield explicitly extolled her beauty, other men gave raucous calls of "Let's see the ware!" and "By Jove, take that dashed hood off!"

"All in good time, gentlemen, in the proper place during the ceremony," Sutterfield replied.

Katrina stiffened with dread at the word *ceremony*. She scanned her memory frantically. All Londoners knew of the existence of the respectable clubs, like the Dilettanti, who shared a love for travel. But clubs devoted to debauchery, like the old Hellfire Club, had no purpose in a modern society, she'd believed. Thus she'd dismissed the recent newspaper accounts of a new club that had arisen devoted to the "worship of feminine pulchritude," as the *Times* had coyly put it. The article had then gone on to hint of the vile ceremonies performed there and the use of innocent girls by men masked as mythological figures. Several members of the lords were rumored to be involved in this club, which the *Times* named as the Grotto of the Satyr Society. After reading the article, she'd thrown the paper down in disgust, not believing the *Times* would devote space to such drivel.

Now she wished she'd paid more heed. Her panicked thoughts settled to hard fury. Virtue had bought her misery, perhaps, but at her choice. She'd not lose it now to a worm like Sutterfield, nor would it be wrested from her while she had breath to fight. Hooded, cloaked, and bound though she might be, she was still not helpless. Men didn't expect a beautiful woman to be clever; they'd soon learn otherwise. Sutterfield first. Swallowing her revulsion, she strained to hear. She'd need all her wit to escape.

"Lord Pan, I salute you! May this vestal offering make me worthy to join your revelry."

Katrina heard the rustle of clothing and deduced that Sutterfield had knelt before someone.

"Is the grotto sealed?" asked a voice Katrina didn't recognize.

"Like a locked door that awaits only thy great key, O mighty Pan, to open for the pleasure of us all."

"Display thy offering," Pan ordered.

Soft footsteps approached. Katrina had been propositioned and importuned too many times in the past years, sometimes obscenely, for the meaning of the exchange to escape her. She began to shake, fear and fury battling within her.

Hands fumbled at her waist, untying the cords holding her to the wooden bench. She was hauled to her feet, where she swayed, her hands bound behind her, her ankles tied together. The hands then went to her hood, loosed it, and ripped it off.

Cool air and blinding light assailed her at the same time. She savored both, breathing deeply and blinking, uncaring of the male gasps of pleasure. Moisture still glimmered in her large, slightly slanted eyes. The blazing chandelier illuminated the unusual peacock-blue color ornamented by thick, dark, and curling lashes.

If the eyes were the windows of the soul, then Katrina's soul was both pure and courageous. Diminutive she might be, but she stood straight, her chin high, her gaze clear and steady as she looked about. Her oval face was cameo perfect, her cheekbones high and delicate, her nose small and finely modeled. Her complexion was smooth and pale as Devonshire cream, tinted with strawberries at cheeks and lips. She would have had the face of an angel, but for that mouth. Wide, full, sensual, it both reassured and aroused the men, proving she was not only real, but all too human. She was an unschooled but promising temptress, strong yet weak, selfish yet magnanimous, wise yet reckless.

One last quality, blatant and untempered, was conveyed by that mouth: determination. Though she trembled, her mouth stayed unwavering, willful. It sat atop her pointed, obstinate chin like an unconquered peak, taunting every man present to seize it and claim it for his own. Her thick hair, loosening from its prim bun, capped her astonishing beauty like a heavy golden crown. It shimmered with highlights, brown, red, and every shade of gold devised by artist or Creator.

Escape her only imperative, Katrina ignored the hungry stares and looked about. Her heart pounded harder. She was in a cavernous, stone-lined room evidently close to the Thames, for water dripped down the walls. The stench of the polluted river was not disguised by the incense issuing obscenely from the satyr figurine burners behind the stage. The oval-shaped room had been painted to simulate a grotto. Romantic it was not, however. Every boulder, every cave formation, from stalagtite piercing down to meet stalagmite thrusting up, was painted to resemble two human forms in the act of copulation. Naked statues of cavorting gods and goddesses were strategically placed and lit, making the room seem a favorite trysting place for the gods.

Which was exactly what it was for these men who thought themselves divine. She glanced at the score of seated men masked as mythological figures and night creatures. The feel of their eyes made her skin crawl, and she looked quickly away. Her cheeks burning with contempt and embarrassment, she skimmed the room again, but could see no exit. She forced her attention back to the brightly illumined, red-carpeted platform, to the two men proceeding with this mockery of a religious ceremony.

"She is doubtless not as young as some of your offerings, but have you ever had a fairer one?" Sutterfield asked, preening.

"Not of face, perhaps. But there is more to a woman. . . ." Pan's words seeped into the ambience, foul and insidious as the dripping water.

Katrina knew what would happen as Sutterfield reached out. She stayed still and submissive until he came close enough.

When he reached around to unfasten her hands, she swooped down and latched onto his wrist like a rabid dog, putting all her fear and hatred into the bite. Despite his howling and struggling she didn't let go until he boxed her ears with his free hand. When he backed off a step and tied his handkerchief about his bleeding wrist, she spat the residue of his blood into his face, then wiped her lips off on her shoulder.

Appreciative chuckles rippled through the audience.

Their humor fanned her ire. She turned her scornful gaze from Sutterfield's furious face to the membership. "So, my fine lords, your estates, your mistresses, your horses, your cards, and your drinking are not sufficient amusement. You must needs make sport of those less fortunate than yourselves who wish only to be left alone—"

"Silence!" Pan roared. "The unholy ceremony is to be interrupted by no one!"

The watching men leaned forward in their chairs like leashed hounds straining after a bitch in heat. Her spirit, far from shaming them, seemed to have whetted their interest. She looked back at Pan, who was eyeing her sternly from his seat on the great red throne capped with goat horns. Very well, these men truly lacked human decency. But one characteristic they had in surplus: pride. That, surely, would be easy to wound. Wound it enough, and they might even let her go. If they didn't kill her first. Iron will alone allowed her to subdue her rising panic.

She tailored her snide smile after every lady who'd ever snubbed her. "Not even if it's based on a lie?" she asked softly. She felt Sutterfield's ominous stillness, for he knew that tone in her voice.

"Huh? What's that you say?" Pan demanded.

"This, er, novitiate"—she looked Sutterfield up and down—"is perpetrating a falsehood upon you all by foisting me off as a virgin." Deliberately she paused, letting the suspense build, before concluding casually, "I've been his mistress for the past quarter and more." She looked down to hide her satisfaction at the angry rumblings of the membership.

Sutterfield sputtered, "But . . . but that's not true! I offered her my protection, but she refused."

How she hated that word. It conjured up memories of the

first man who'd made a mockery of its definition when he offered it to her. The thought bolstered her determination. "Toby, why didn't you give me my congé instead of ending our . . . association in such a way? Wasn't what we shared worth more than this?"

His wide brow gleaming with sweat, Sutterfield looked at Pan, who was conferring with his attendant, a man in a horned-owl mask. "I tell you she's lying to save herself." He advanced on Katrina, menace in every step. "Tell them the truth, you bitch, how you tormented me with your flirtatious glances, then froze me with your scorn when I took the bait."

The unfairness of the accusation stung her. A fool she might have been to accept his offer of friendship, but how dare he fault her for her human need of it? She put all her acting ability into her whine. "The truth, my lord? Such as your niggardly gifts of garnets instead of rubies, muslin instead of silk?"

Pan waved Sutterfield into silence as he began to interrupt. "If this is true, then you've seriously breached our rules."

Katrina kept her eyes lowered, but her heart thrummed with hope.

"She lies, I tell you. . . ." Sutterfield's voice trailed off. He turned on Katrina too quickly for her to react. Her wrists were free, her cloak untied and wrenched off before she could do more than flinch. Too late she lifted her tingling hands to scratch him, but the movement unbalanced her. She fell into his ready arms.

Chortling his triumph, he set her upright and held her struggling wrists behind her back, turning her to face the audience. Katrina looked down at herself, her gasp mingling with a score of masculine ones. From somewhere came a muffled curse, but Katrina was too mortified to care.

Nor did she see, far back in the audience, a man surging to his feet, only to be jerked back down into his chair by the member in a Neptune mask sitting next to him. "Be quiet," Neptune hissed to him. "If you interrupt the ceremony, you'll be evicted."

Katrina didn't hear. She was too busy trying to free her arms to cover herself, but the viscount was far stronger. Katrina swallowed bile at the knowledge that he must have dressed her so while she was drugged. She closed her eyes and went still, hatred and fear building apace within her.

"Do you still not want her?" the viscount demanded. He unpinned her hair with his free hand and brushed through the glittering strands, bringing them forward and back so that they shielded then revealed the full bosom almost bared by the scandalous bodice.

Sutterfield's voice grew husky with lust. "Even if she tells the truth, isn't she worthy to be your consort, for one night, at least?"

The silence was broken only by heavy breathing as she was coveted by the score of rakes who'd thought themselves too jaded to be stunned by a female. Beautiful women were commonplace in England, especially in London, where many a comely country lass had come to make her fortune. But not a single member, even the wealthy ones who'd had a parade of mistresses, had seen a woman so rare. It was unusual indeed to behold a face so exquisite; it was unheard of for that face to be matched by a body Venus herself might have envied.

The blush-pink, tissue-silk night rail fell in sheer folds to the floor from the high, gathered waist. Her long, perfect legs were plainly visible. Her hips were full but not wide, setting off the glories of her tiny waist and flat, smooth abdomen. And those breasts . . . A universal sigh of longing whispered through the room. The fact that the tips of her breasts escaped their eyes, as did the apex of her legs, only whetted their appetites. Panels of pink velvet had been strategically inset for just that purpose.

The viscount smiled at their reaction.

After an anticipatory silence Pan came slowly to his feet. He turned to the membership. "Shall we put it to a vote?" he asked throatily. "Shall we this once bend our most sacred rule?"

"Aye!" came the reply. The echo bounced from ceiling to floor and back again.

Only one man didn't answer. He clutched the arms of his chair so hard his nails scored the velvet. Then his hands relaxed, as if he forced himself to patience.

While the men stared, savored, and salivated, Katrina kept her eyes closed. She trembled, even the sharp pangs of fear dulled by immobilizing despair. To come so close, then lose . . . but she should be used to losing by now. She was so tired of fighting. What had it won her? Scorn, contempt, and ridicule. Meaner employment every time she was released from a position.

The loss of the only man she could have loved . . . How much better if she had succumbed to his dark fascination and known the joys of the flesh, however brief, than the pain and humiliation this night would surely bring. She blanked out all thought of Devon. After tonight she'd be fit for no man. Let them use her as they willed. They could chain her body but not her spirit. In the end she would be free, even if she had to fling herself into the Thames.

"Your offering is accepted," Pan said to Sutterfield. He gestured to the horned owl. "Take the unholy scroll to the novitiate." Pan retook his throne and fingered the flute he'd left on the chair arm.

The horned owl went to a long, ornate table that had huge silver bowls of fruit and heavy crystal wine decanters on both ends. In the middle a gilded cylinder was displayed like a holy book on a red, fringed velvet pedestal.

As the man brought the cylinder to Sutterfield Katrina could see its engravings. The realistic renderings of female and male genitalia made her blush, then pale. Both the owl and Sutterfield caressed the cylinder, eyeing her all the while. She didn't need to look at the membership to know their eyes glittered with the same lust.

The owl withdrew an ornately inscribed roll of parchment from the cylinder and handed it to the viscount with a ceremonious bow. Sutterfield kissed the parchment as bade, then read: "Venus, I am thine! Receive me with thy bountiful charms and crown my wishes with excess of pleasure. No more shall virtue reign. I, by thy amorous self do swear, will abandon all that is chaste. Nothing shall share my favor while in thy presence but my most libidinous desires. I further swear I shall keep silent about this night's proceedings and shall not admit knowledge of this society to aught but another member."

"Hail, Brother," the others intoned. The owl returned the

parchment to its cylinder. With a last leer at Katrina he retreated.

She watched dully as Pan rose with slow majesty. He strolled toward her, his features masked, his eyes alive with intent. Katrina tried to back away, but her bound feet made her awkward, and she would have fallen if Sutterfield hadn't steadied her. She was too numb with fear even to flinch when his hand dropped from her shoulder to her breast.

Pan frowned. "By the rights vested in me this night as Pan, no member touches her until I've had my fill."

Sutterfield's mouth tightened, but he nodded and backed off, seating himself in the chair the horned owl indicated on the corner of the stage.

"You shall be second, in accordance with our laws," Pan assured him, then he closed the last step that separated him from his prey. He was reaching for the bodice of Katrina's gown when an authoritative voice spoke from the rear of the dimly lit audience.

"Hold, Pan!"

Pan turned slowly, stiff with outrage.

A tall man wearing a unicorn mask with a gilded horn issuing from the forehead brushed aside Neptune's cautionary arm and strode down the aisle. Neptune adjusted his mask and shifted under the members' disapproving stares.

"This is his first visit, dash it. He has the right to interrupt."

If the unicorn sensed the disapproval emanating from every quarter, he gave no sign. He stopped at the foot of the stage and looked up at Katrina. One white hand clenched into a fist, then slowly relaxed.

The murmurs of the membership roused Katrina from her apathy. She saw a man hovering at the stage steps who was severely but finely garbed in black brocade coat, black knee breeches, and black-and-gold waistcoat. His mask was realistic, and she wished with all her heart that he really were a unicorn, that symbol of purity, protector of virgins. Why had he interrupted?

"As your laws have been stated to me, each potential member has the right of challenge upon the completion of the ceremony. Is this correct?"

At the sound of that deep voice Katrina froze in recognition. Could it be? She stared at the arrogant tilt of the head, the finely shaped hands, and somehow, she knew. The heart she'd thought dead lurched within her breast. Feelings she'd not known in three years rushed through her, strengthening her crumpling spine. Gladness, hurt, confusion, yearning. And, briefly, hope. If anyone could deliver her from this conclave of rakes, surely it was he, king of the rakes. But . . . Why was he here? His very presence, "potential" member or not, made her worry.

And yet . . . How she'd longed to see him again. Now, when her very life was in danger, she could almost believe her despair had conjured him. Even masked, he aroused all the old unseemly yearnings. Those exciting, distressing months three years past flashed through her chaotic thoughts. She latched onto their welcome respite. The stage dissolved beneath her feet and became grass wet with dew. The heavy incense became roses heady with spring. And the dim chamber became the Kentish countryside, rolling like a carpet flung far and wide to welcome the sunny arrival of God. . . .

The early mornings were cherished moments in her busy role as governess to two unruly but lovable little boys. Her charges rose late, and these contemplative times fortified her for the busy days. The pain of her father's death a few short months ago had dulled to an ache. These walks in the rose arbor made her feel close to him. How he had loved roses. Katrina paused to pluck a yellow bloom, its petals partially unfurled, but the secret heart of the flower untouched by sun or dew. She inhaled its pure scent.

A deep voice made her start. "What a charming picture. It makes me want to take brush to canvas, but I could never capture the proper hue of that glorious hair."

Katrina went beet red and brushed ineffectually at her unbound hair. She usually completed her toilette only after her walk. Today was the first time she'd had cause to regret her daring. Slowly she turned to meet the admiring gaze of the tall man who stood just within the gate. She sucked in a stunned breath. She'd seldom been susceptible to male handsomeness, but never had she met a man such as he. . . .

Glorious. His face and form were glorious. He was dressed in riding breeches that clung to long, lithe thighs, and his thin shirt stuck to the perfect symmetry of his broad chest. But it was his face that riveted her.

Every feature seemed one part of a harmonious whole. His eyes were brandy brown and flecked with gold that sparkled now in the sunshine. His black brows and lashes were a pleasing contrast to his eyes and golden skin. His hair, unpowdered and tied neatly back at his nape, was also a surprise: it was dark gold, streaked with bands of primrose silk. The mobility of that full, sensitive mouth attested to his frequent, ready smile. Deep creases curved on each side, moving like wind gauges, she suspected, with his mood. They were in evidence now, and she knew he sensed her fascination with him.

She mastered her composure, looked down at the rose in her hand, and walked slowly toward him. However, when she reached the gate, he didn't move aside.

"Stay. Tell me your name." He didn't touch her, but the soft, sensual timbre of his voice wrapped about her like silk.

"Katrina," she whispered. She tried to step around him, but he sidestepped neatly.

She looked up at that. The breeze lifted a heavy curl of hair and flicked him in the mouth. He caught the tendril and tugged gently, bringing her closer until her skirts brushed his breeches.

"My name is Devon. I came to see about purchasing a horse. I intended to leave this morning, but perhaps I'll stay a bit longer."

Gently Katrina pulled her hair away and stepped back. He'd not introduced himself fully, but somehow she knew he was a lord. That nose set upon him too regally, and his air of confidence was too assured for him to be less than a nobleman. "My lord, I am only the governess here, and this conversation is most improper. I doubt we shall meet again."

Resolutely she flung the rose away. To her surprise he caught it neatly and brought it to his lips. He brushed the petals back and forth, holding her eyes all the while. Her mouth tingled, and she felt as if she'd been kissed. Making a strangled sound, she brushed past him.

Her ears burned with his promise, "We shall meet again, my lovely. Soon."

And they had. That very evening Katrina was invited to

dinner for only the second time since she'd been employed. She accepted with some foreboding. She'd not been surprised to find seated across from her the man the other servants had, that afternoon, referred to as the Earl of Brookstone.

Katrina looked at the fawning expressions on the faces of her host and hostess. She knew the earl had not had to use much persuasion to get her employers to invite their governess for dinner. They were agog over their good fortune in having an earl sit at their table. He'd not find her so amenable, she resolved. So she ignored the fast cadence of her heart and answered his conversational gambits with monosyllables. She escaped as soon as possible, but she was to find that her distance only made him work the harder to bridge it.

He soon became a fixture in the house. The boys even took to calling him uncle. No matter how firmly she tried to put him in his place, or how desperately she tried to avoid him, he always popped up, as cheerful and charming as the jack-in-the-box she'd adored as a child. He sent her posies, he asked her opinion on the current affairs of state. Rarely had she met a man who enjoyed a woman's brain, yet he seemed genuinely interested in her responses. They had more than one invigorating political discussion.

Even her employers began to look indulgently upon his time with her. After two weeks, when he was at their house more than at his lodgings at the village inn, they invited him to stay, giving Katrina meaningful looks as they did so. Katrina knew their thoughts. What a sensation it would cause if their governess should make the catch of the year. They were simple country gentry who'd seldom been beyond Kent's borders, and they hoped so perfect a gentleman would make their educated, innocent governess a proper offer. Katrina suspected otherwise, but her fears didn't bolster her defenses, which grew weaker under the barrage of Devon's smiles.

He moved into a guest chamber, "to enjoy rusticating after the hectic pace of town," as he put it. He went on rambles with her and the boys, acting as both protector and tutor. He helped her teach the boys to fish; he escorted them on long, invigorating rides about the countryside.

Almost six weeks after their first meeting he took her and the boys on a picnic. After eating, the boys went to the stream to skip stones while Devon stayed behind to help her pack the remains of their hearty fare. All was put away when silence ensued. Katrina started as Devon lay back on the blanket and pillowed his arms under his head.

"Do you ever make pictures in the clouds?" he asked lazily.

She glanced up. Puffy white clouds drifted overhead like enormous cotton wads. She pointed at one. "That one looks like a frog squatting on a lily pad."

"Ribbet . . . ribbet . . ." Devon croaked. A frog lazing under a tree nearby gave a startled leap, catching their attention. Katrina could have sworn the look in his bulging eyes was offended as he hopped majestically off, croaking in a firm way, as if to show them how the thing should really be done.

Devon's deep, rich chuckles joined her musical laugh. When he laced his fingers with hers, it seemed natural to lie down beside him. She followed his pointing finger.

"There. A unicorn. See it leaping over a hedge?"

She squinted, then nodded. "How often did I dream of them, as a child." How happy she'd been, serving her father's parish. How hastily had she been evicted from the parsonage by the new vicar . . .

Devon propped himself on an elbow to look down into her misty eyes. "And do you dream no longer?"

Wordlessly, she shook her head, moved by the tenderness in his gaze.

"What a shame. Did you know the unicorn is the protector of virgins?" His tone went even softer. "How easily can I see you, hair streaming down your back, fairy wings beating behind you as you ride away to your hidden kingdom. Let me take you there."

How she longed to believe his fervency, but she did not dare. With an effort she reminded herself of the difference in their births. She was not so naive as her employers; if this lord had an offer to make her, it would not be a proper one.

Even so, she thrilled to his touch when he brushed her thick hair away from her brow. "I can make you happy again, Katrina mina. You'd never know need, nor want, nor loneliness in the kingdom we'd make together."

Wide blue eyes stared into darkening brown ones. His

endearment drifted away on the breeze, but the power of it had already lodged in her heart. Katrina shifted, not quite able to move away from the soothing pleasure of that hand. Oh, to be loved again. But no matter how heady his touch, she suspected what he felt had little to do with love.

The morals that were her bedrock stayed firm. "There is no such place on this earth," Katrina responded quietly. "Nor has been, nor will be, since God evicted us from Eden."

"How do you know? Come, let me show you that a little bit of Eden can be with us always. . . ." He finished the last word against her mouth. Maidens dreamed of such a first kiss. His mouth was gentle, soft, and sweet. Entreating rather than demanding. Hinting at what joy his warm hands and hard body could offer, if only she would accept. Every tender slide and silken caress made her yearn for fuller knowledge. When he deepened the kiss, she arched beneath him and ran her hands through his hair, loosening it from the queue. It fell, thick and soft as her own, about his shoulders.

She felt his heartbeat accelerate to a drumlike cadence that echoed somewhere deep and empty within her. He broke the kiss only to slide a fiery trail down her neck to the soft hollow of her throat.

"Ah, Katrina mina, come with me, let me cherish you as you deserve. Horses, servants, a house, jewels, whatever you desire. I've never wanted a woman so."

His words ripped through her sensual haze. She pushed him away and sat up, brushing her own loose hair back over her shoulders with a shaking hand. "You know my background. My father was a vicar. I'd not dishonor him, much less myself, so." She tried to rise, but he caught her wrist and pulled her back down.

"It dishonors you to be offered a more secure, easier way of life?"

"Secure? For how long? A month? Maybe even only a week?"

He thumbed the throbbing vein in her wrist until she wrenched away. "You do yourself a disservice. I'd want you much longer than that. You're different to any woman I've known." He cocked his head as he studied her, and had it been any other man, she might have believed the bewildered uncertainty in his gaze, as if he didn't understand her power over him. "And even at the end I'd see you were cared for—"

"Like an old dog. No, thank you." She laughed harshly and rose, calling for the children. They spoke little on the ride back, and the brooding look about his mouth made her glad to escape upstairs to her room. She pleaded a headache that night at dinner, but a servant knocked soon after and told her she was requested below. She considered refusing, but then she straightened. This would be the last time she'd have to face him, she sensed. She'd do so with all the courage of the convictions she knew were right. She marched downstairs.

Devon was in the study, nursing a glass of port. He straightened from staring out the window at the sunset and turned to look at her. He tossed back the dregs of his wine and snapped the glass decisively down on a table. The servant discreetly closed the door, leaving Katrina alone to face the greatest temptation of her life. Conviction suddenly seemed a poor substitute for the passion she was rejecting.

He seated her courteously on the settee, then sat beside her and took her hand. "Would it do me any good to go on my knees?"

"What do you mean?" she whispered, her heart leaping with hope.

He looked puzzled, then uncomfortable. "I regret any . . . misunderstanding. I plead for your favors, but I want you to know I would keep you safe and cherish you under any circumstances."

Her heart settled back like a lump in her breast. Delicate as it was, the disclaimer was still an insult. "If I were of your world, you'd not offer me a slip on the shoulder." He shifted his feet, but did not reply. She looked down at their twined hands and droned, "I know you don't intend to insult me, but you do. My blood may not be blue, but I have just as much pride in my name as you do in yours."

"Pride is a poor substitute for companionship. Take it from one who knows." He lifted her chin to delve into the resolute depths of her eyes. "What happiness do you think you'll find as an outcast, neither servant nor family member?" When she flinched, his tone gentled. "You deserve better, Katrina. Your strength of conviction only makes me admire you—and want you—more.''

He eased his arms about her waist and pulled her face against his waistcoat. "And you, my dear, want me. Come, kiss me. Deny then, truly, your longing to accept my offer, and I will bother you no more. You have my word, as the Earl of Brookstone.''

When he lifted her chin to lower his mouth over hers, Katrina didn't turn aside. She owed herself this last memory. . . . But at the touch of his lips, she forgot to store up images for the lonely future and reveled in the present. This time his passion was bare, so raw that he quivered with it. He bent her back over his arm and urged her mouth open. She was shocked at the sudden hot probe of his tongue, but the deep exploration made her long to open every secret place for him. Somehow she knew she belonged with him. His lips fit so perfectly over hers, his chest shielded her from harm, his arms cradled her like a treasure beyond price.

For minutes on end he kissed her, his mouth and caressing hands proclaiming in the age-old way his yearning. There was a fine edge of desperation to the way he clutched her so tightly, as if more than lust drove him. In response her own muddled emotions surged beyond her control. What else mattered but this? She moaned under his kiss, then shyly answered the demanding thrusts of his tongue.

He broke away, his chest heaving like a bellows. "Oh God, Kat, tell me you don't want me and condemn us both to perdition.''

Her eyes fluttered open and fixed on his flushed face. Her lips, tender from his passion, tried to form the words, but could not. She shook her head and buried her face in his shoulder, no longer able to control her tears.

He petted her back and shoulders, making soothing noises. "There, don't cry. I'm not worth a single tear upon that lovely face. Shhh . . . I'll torment you no more.''

When she hiccuped, he set her away and dried her tears with his kerchief. "So . . . you do want me. What are we to do about it?''

Wearily she leaned her head back against the settee. "Nothing. I'm not meant to be a kept woman, Devon. If I thought I would be happy, I'd accept your offer. But my shame would eat away at me, until there was nothing left but regret. Is that what you want?''

He gritted his teeth, but shook his head.

Feeling as if every bone would crack, she forced herself to her feet. ''Then there's nothing left but good-bye.'' She turned to leave, then whirled and flung herself into his arms for a last wild kiss. When he tightened his grip, she wriggled free and ran toward the door.

His harsh tone stopped her after three steps. ''I'm letting you go, Katrina mina, not for my sake, but for yours. I believe that *you* believe you can never be happy as my mistress. But . . .'' He strode around her to meet her eyes. She had heard whispers about the exploits that had earned him the nickname Demon. She'd doubted their veracity, but the look in his eyes now made her wonder if she should have given them more credence.

''I may be the first to offer you protection, but make no mistake, I'll not be the last. Your beauty will tempt every man who meets you. If your resolve stays firm, then you will be safe in your ivory tower, your unicorn protecting your chastity.'' His tone hardened. ''But know this: If you succumb to another after rejecting me, I will consider you fair game. Then, Katrina mina, one way or another, you will be mine.''

Their eyes held for one last time. She read her own confused feelings in his: yearning, regret, desire, resolve. She nodded her understanding. ''Good-bye, Devon.''

''Good-bye, Katrina. Be happy.'' After a last long, encompassing look he was gone. Leaving her alone. She was glad, she told herself—but tears trickled down her face as she listened to his receding footsteps, then the gentle closing of the door.

Katrina blinked and found herself in a present that was even more distressing than the past.

Be happy . . . How very little of that she'd known after sending him away. Sometimes, in the quiet of her lonely heart, she'd regretted the choice; now, finding him here, she knew she'd been right. And to see him dressed as a unicorn when he was a menace to every comely female's virtue—he desecrated all the romantic dreams she'd wove about him.

The thought did not occur to her that he'd worn the mask to help her identify him, and to reassure her. That he'd come to save her, believing in her virtue. That the length of his strides attested to the anger that he felt at hearing, from her own lips, that she'd been another man's mistress, after refusing him.

Katrina's emotions were too muddled to allow for clear thought, but the shock of his presence had been cathartic. Fury bolstered her. How wrong she'd been about him. He was not here to help her; he was here to get at last the only thing he'd ever wanted of her. In any way he could. Had he not warned her as much three years ago?

Watching him now as he strode up and down, arguing with Sutterfield about his understanding of their rules, she wondered why she'd not recognized him forthwith. She knew that fluid, arrogant stride; the walk of a man born to conquer. She knew that splendid physique; the build of a man who relished a fight. She knew that inimitable style; the garb of a man with too much wealth to bother flaunting it. And yes, she knew that voice; the arrogant timbre of a man who'd never known defeat.

"Enough! The right of challenge was plainly explained to me, and I exercise that right now. I usurp the role of Pan." Devon stood casually, one foot propped on the first step, one long, white hand caressing the wooden banister. The membership muttered resentfully, but quieted, one by one, as that glittering horn was turned toward them like a bared dagger.

Oh God, it was true . . . he only wanted to be first. He'd not come here to save her, as she'd at first thought. Indeed, how could he have known she'd be here? She hated him, she told herself, yet her heart quickened when that horn was turned to her. Even behind the mask, the hungry sweep of his gaze made her breath catch. Three years dissolved into mist as she felt, full upon her lips, that last desperate, arousing kiss. She looked away. She'd not respond to him. Never again. Over and over she told herself she despised him. Aided by fury, she almost believed it.

Pan stiffened and glared at the unicorn. "If you know our laws so well, you know of my right of refusal." He swung about and raised his hands to touch Katrina's breasts.

In a single bound the unicorn leaped up the three steps. He

drawled suggestively, "Then we shall settle our dispute as decreed by your laws."

Pan turned to face his challenger. Tense silence prevailed in the chamber. Only Katrina was close enough to hear Pan's quickened breathing.

"I don't wish to fight with you—"

"Then step aside." No quarter, no compromise. His way, or none. The demand surprised no one, Katrina least of all. She looked back at Pan and knew that beneath his grotesque mask, he'd paled.

His fists clenched and unclenched as he looked from the unicorn to Katrina, then back. The unicorn's clothes enhanced rather than disguised his broad chest and muscular thighs. With a gnashing of his teeth, Pan swung about and marched back to his throne.

And Katrina was left alone in that brilliant pool of light with the only man she'd never been able to forget. The only man who'd tempted her to forgo the morals she lived by and revel with him in sin. Her eyes betrayed her ambivalence as she looked up at him, but then outrage won.

"You needn't bother with the mask, my lord. My nightmares have left me intimately acquainted with you." She bit her lip as she realized how her words could be construed.

He seemed taken aback at her hostility, then he said suavely, "I'm flattered I figure so prominently in your dreams, my dear Kat. It does my heart good to know that you remember me after such an age." He removed his heavy coat and pulled it over her shoulders to cover what he could, ignoring the protests of the membership. His movements were negligent, but his hands lingered possessively until she wrenched away. She wavered on her bound feet, but she managed to brush aside his steadying hand.

Angry at her contradictory feelings, Katrina refused to be mollified. "Heart, my lord?" she shot back. "You've a molten lump of coal in its stead."

Several gasps came from the audience. Devon Alexander Tyrone Cavanaugh, eighteenth Earl of Brookstone, paused in drawing off his mask. The watching rakes waited for his retribution, acerbically verbal if not physical, for Demon Devon was not known for his temperance. Nor was he known for his predictability, so they were not greatly surprised when he chose to be amused.

Cricking her chin up with a negligent finger, he teased, "Perhaps. But coal is known for its enduring, fiery properties—as I will soon prove to you." Male snickers rippled through the chamber at the implication.

"It's also known for fouling all it touches," she said clearly, her mouth curled in distaste.

The chuckles died. All eyes went to Devon.

He was still for a moment, then, with a smothered oath, he ripped off his mask and flung it aside. "By all that's holy, wench, then you'd best take to wearing weeds, for you'll be black from head to toe soon enough. Besides, it's hard to foul something that's already dirty." He snapped his teeth closed and took a deep, calming breath. His hand stroked her chin with a gentleness that was poignantly familiar to Katrina. "I'm sorry, Kat, but you're making this deuced hard on both of us," he whispered.

If he only knew how she'd longed for him . . . She stared at him, wishing with all her heart that they'd met again under different circumstances. The years had changed him little. Dissipation should, by rights, have eaten at that gorgeous face, but if anything, he'd become more handsome in his maturity. Those lashes were still as lush as a girl's, that mouth as fine and mobile, that hair as striking a contrast to his black eyebrows. He looked what he was, a peer of the realm, with arrogance, pride, and breeding in every patrician line. He did not look like a libertine so debauched that he'd earned the name of Demon Devon before he attained his majority.

However, that hungry, possessive look in his eyes proved the name appropriate. She felt his angry determination to win what he believed she'd granted another. She cursed the self-preservation impulse that had made her claim to be Sutterfield's mistress, but she owed this . . . demon no explanations. Her chin wrenched away from his caress. Whether this night led to a pedestal bed or a watery grave, she'd face the end with pride intact. As long as she didn't succumb to his dark fascination again, she'd naught to be ashamed of.

They stared at one another, the man and the girl, forgetful now of their audience as they battled silently with their eyes.

You'll not reject me this time, he warned; take my body, then, but you'll never win more of me, she replied. Katrina didn't flinch when the earl grew impatient at their soundless contest, fastened his long, strong hands on her shoulders and hauled her to her toes. His soft voice made Katrina shiver.

"Once, I let you go when you claimed distaste for me. I can't help wondering if, even then, you were the innocent you proclaimed. Now, by your own words, you've no virtue to guard. So come, my dear, show me what you've learned. And by God it had better be worth the wait."

Gripping her jaw in one hand, he wrapped his free arm about her waist and bent her backward. She tried to turn away, but he secured her chin and lowered his angry mouth over hers. Three years before, his patient, wooing embraces had turned her bones to jelly. This kiss was a demand, a brand of intent. He was too experienced to be brutal, but the practiced movements of his mouth could not disguise his purpose: to prove to her, once and for all, that he was master.

She was equally determined to prove that no man would enslave her. She didn't waste her strength in struggles. She stayed limp, unresponsive. Only she knew how hard she had to fight the tears of regret for what might have been. . . .

The cheers of the watching satyrs recalled them both to reality. Slowly, Devon drew away to look at her amid calls of "Put it to her, old boy!" and "Get on with it, man. Give the rest of us a chance!"

He glared at the membership, then he looked back at Katrina's flushed face. Her steady gaze showed only disdain. A cruel twist settled about his mouth. "Well, Kat, " he drawled, "what's it to be? Slow or quick? A thing of art or an animal coupling?"

She swallowed when he turned her toward the bench with a courteous hand at her elbow, but her tone was even. "Why, do what you do best, of course." When he paused to shoot her a surprised look, she concluded nastily, "Wallow in the dirt like the animal you are."

She watched in fascination as his expression grew black. She almost expected horns to sprout from his head, so appropriate did his sobriquet seem at that moment. Perversely she was glad that her actions only made what was to come more brutal. Far better for him to act true to form as the knave he was than to weaken her resolve with that spurious tenderness. When they stood beside the bench, she clenched her teeth so hard her jaw quivered. She waited, sick in body and in heart, for what was to come.

Only she heard his soft curse and his "By the saints, Kat, you tempt me to treat you as you deserve."

She frowned, but her confusion was dispelled when he turned her to face him, her back to the audience, and lifted his hands to her breasts. With both forefingers, he traced the seams where velvet met silk, his touch so light she barely felt it. He watched the white flesh above quiver as her heartbeat accelerated, then he slipped one hand beneath the jacket to cup her buttocks. Instinctively, she tried to shrink away, but he pulled her closer, closer, until her breasts crushed against him. He lowered his mouth to warm her lips with his breath.

"You'll not send me so handily off this time, Kat, and leave me yearning for more." When she looked at him disdainfully, his cheeks flushed with the fury that she sensed was driving him. "Ask me nicely, and maybe I'll get you out of here."

She bit her tongue to keep the plea back, but the atavistic fear she could not control was stronger. "Please, take me away."

His tense muscles relaxed a bit. "Go on."

"I'll not beg, damn you!" she spat, even as she trembled.

He lifted a negligent eyebrow. "No? We shall see, my dear."

He pushed her away, and she closed her eyes, fearing she'd feel her gown ripping. When his fingers instead closed the coat and buttoned it, her eyes flicked open. He met her confused stare directly, and for the first time she realized that more than fury was motivating him. Emotions more complex than lust roiled in those harlequin eyes of light and dark.

Yes, there was anger there, and revolted pride, but was that sadness, too, and yearning? Before she could be certain, he felt in the pocket of the jacket she wore, then turned to fling something at Pan's feet.

"My considerable winnings for the night are yours, my fine satyrs. A thousand pounds is recompense enough for one female, I believe, no matter how lovely." By the time Pan's stunned gaze lifted from the purse at his feet, the earl had hefted Katrina over his shoulder and started down the stage steps.

"See here, Cavanaugh, you can't just make off with another man's offering," Pan shouted over the angry mutterings of the satyrs.

"No? Then fetch the magistrates to stop me. I'm sure they'd find this little group most illuminating." The protests stopped midspate.

However, Sutterfield was not so easily intimidated. He overturned his chair as he leaped up, then he vaulted from the stage and ran to block Devon's path. He snatched the cane he'd propped against the base of the stage and wrenched out the concealed sword.

Devon halted. Katrina dangled from his shoulder, limp with shock. Relief followed, and finally came jubilation. He was saving her! Despite the angry words she'd hurled at him he was saving her. Was she wrong about him after all? Her exuberance muted as she heard the scrape of steel and realized why Devon had paused.

"Demon or no, you'll not take what's mine without a fight."

"Yours, Sutterfield? I've wanted this woman for three years and have yet to taste her. You know enough of me to realize I don't share. Now I suggest you stand out of my way." Devon's voice grew hard. "Lest you learn firsthand how little I like having my possessions handled before me."

"No, damn you! She'll not leave this chamber until I've pounded some of those saucy airs out of her."

Devon sighed, then he set Katrina down on the first stage step. Katrina shuddered at the insane rage in Sutterfield's usually benign blue eyes, but Devon just shrugged.

"She's a jade, I agree, but I found her long ere you did, and if the only way I can keep possession is by pinking you, then gladly I shall do so."

Someone handed him a sword. He folded his sleeves back, revealing his corded forearms, then climbed the stage steps, taking slices out of the air with the weapon as he went.

Katrina shrank back as Sutterfield followed him, but he ignored her. She looked at the membership. All watched the two men assuming the *en garde* position. Her fingers steady now, Katrina bent to untie the cords about her ankles. As Devon had just said in his exchange with Sutterfield, she was merely one more woman to him. She didn't dare risk that he'd let her go, not with the past between them, and present events egging him on. She cast a stealthy glance about the room, seeking the exit.

She heard the rasp of steel sliding against steel, and compelled, she paused to look over her shoulder. Most of the light in the gloomy room was trained upon the stage. Weaving candle flames reflected upon shiny, twisting blades. The viscount thrust, the earl parried. Sutterfield lunged, Devon blocked. While Sutterfield was a tall, strong man, his small paunch testified to his leisure activities. Devon, on the other hand, showed in each liquid move what an avid sportsman he was. His fencing had the mark of every master swordsman: He made it look easy.

The end was soon apparent to all but Sutterfield. Devon's hair glittered under the lights. His muscles moved like well-oiled cogs grinding toward one purpose—victory. Katrina saw the ease with which he parried Sutterfield's craftiest stabs, and her lurching heart settled back in her breast. No, she had naught to worry about but getting away. She waited until Devon made his move, slashing where he'd been tapping, lunging where he'd been retreating, then she eased around the corner of the stage toward the door she'd spied between two statues.

When several members glanced at her, she leaned her elbows on the stage as if seeking a better vantage to watch. When they looked back at the duel, she darted for the door.

Devon turned his head at the flash of movement. Grinding out an oath, he slammed Sutterfield's weak parry aside with a riposte that found its mark. Sutterfield screamed and fell to his knees, clutching his wounded shoulder, but Devon paused only long enough to fling the sword away. In four strides he was off the stage, landing on his feet at a run to pursue Katrina.

"She's not worth it, Cavanaugh! You'll find her a block of ice beneath you," Sutterfield yelled.

Katrina flung a look over her shoulder as she touched the doorknob. She saw Sutterfield, grinning malevolently at her, and a bare twenty paces behind her, Devon. She couldn't see his expression since his back was to the light, but she didn't need to. His determined pursuit made his intent clear.

She threw the door open and ran as if the demons of hell pursued. Some other time she might have laughed at the apt analogy, but she was too occupied in fleeing for her life. For without the right of choice, life had no meaning to her at all. . . .

She found herself in a man-made tunnel. She darted a look each way. Blackness at one end, light at the other. She ran, so intent on reaching that reassuring pool of gold that she didn't even notice the rough cobblestones under her bare feet. But she felt *him*. First as a presence behind her, then she heard steps pounding closer, closer. If she could only reach that light, she could scream for help. She was so near. Yet the five feet were leagues, the unbridgeable gap between safety and ruin. Strong hands caught the back of her jacket and hauled her to a stop.

The shock was too much. She began to scream, to struggle, to kick and bite. "No! You foul excuse for a man, let me go." Even when he stuffed a handkerchief in her mouth, she still cursed him through it. When he hefted her over his shoulder, she pounded his back with her fists and wildly kicked her legs until an iron-thewed arm squeezed her knees closed.

The laughter in his voice only made her angrier. "Damme, my girl, I never thought I'd be in the position of pushing your legs *together*."

She was plopped inside a black lacquered coach onto a plush red seat. Devon leaped in beside her. She tore the handkerchief away and drew breath to scream, but they lurched away. There was no one to hear, anyway. She closed her eyes and counted to twenty. Then, leaning back with grim control, she played with the kerchief in her lap and lifted her eyes to his.

At first she was puzzled by his good humor. Head tilted back against the cushions, legs sprawled before him, he exuded no anger at her attempted escape. To the contrary. That devastating smile, cheeks creased, eyes sparkling with mischief, made him seem the best of both boy and man. Only her inner insistence that he was the worst of each—spoiled as a brat and ruthless as a roué—kept her impervious to its force. He breathed easily, as if his recent exertions were no more strenuous than a Vauxhall stroll, but she wasn't fooled. Let her reach for the door handle and that laziness would evaporate. Perforce she realized, abruptly, why he wasn't angry. He enjoyed the chase as much as the capture.

She didn't hide her bitterness as she said, "I'm glad I afford you amusement, your lordship. Would that I could claim the same."

His smile deepened into a cocky grin. "Ah, but I've never wanted to amuse you, Kat. I'm determined upon an entertainment of a different sort." His eyes dropped to her legs, which were dimly visible through the wispy gown.

She almost tore the kerchief, so hard did she have to resist the impulse to cover herself. "And if I'm still determined to decline the pleasure?"

He sighed, and the gold sparks flashing in his eyes dimmed. "Don't, Kat. Don't make me angrier than I already am."

Honesty at last. The softer side that had yearned for him for three lonely years longed to tell him the truth. That he'd come the closest of any man to gaining her favors. Perhaps she owed him that much—had he not obviously decided to keep her for himself. That, she could not forgive.

Her bent head reared up. She leaned toward him. "I may be only a vicar's daughter, I may be poor, I may be alone. But one choice I do have, one thing no one can ever take from me—my right to bestow my favors as I choose. And you, my lord, with all your wealth, your charm, your breeding, and your looks, cannot do a thing to stop me."

Her quiet tones arrested the hand brushing back his loosened hair. His jaw tensed, then he slowly lowered his hand. He looked down, his thick black lashes shielding his thoughts. When his eyes flashed up, they were bright brown, lucid as warmed brandy. She saw admiration there, and liking. Her heart thrummed. Would he let her go? She looked down to disguise her tension.

"As you say, my dear. You have that right. I ask you once more to grant me that boon. I'm not such a bad fellow. You'd find me generous. More generous than Sutterfield, I warrant."

She shook her head wordlessly, staring at her lap. Had she been looking at him, she would have been forewarned. Frustration, anger, and desire crossed his face in rapid succession. His mouth firmed with resolve.

But his voice betrayed only courtesy when he murmured, "Very well. You win." He rapped against the window between him and his coachman. When it opened, the earl said, "Peter, I know our direction now. My dear?"

Katrina flashed a disbelieving look at him. He stared back, his regret ostensibly genuine. Her heart lightened, and the terrors of the night began to ease. In dazed tones she gave the direction of her most recent employer.

The crotchety old woman was a sea captain's widow who had been well provided for, but she pinched every penny until it bled and was as parsimonious with Katrina's time. The old woman never failed to introduce Katrina to her friends as connected, if on the wrong side of the blanket, to a baronet. But when they were alone, she treated her as the meanest scullery maid, taking evident pleasure in her position of superiority over one of higher birth.

Katrina had grown wiser, if more bitter, with every lost position. After the penury she'd suffered when Sutterfield's mother dismissed her, she'd vowed to keep this last post, no matter what. If suppressing her pride and accepting menial tasks were the price of security, then she'd gladly pay. While she wasn't happy, she was resigned and grateful that at least her current employer had no close male relatives.

How she'd explain coming home so late dressed as she was she didn't know. Still, maybe she wouldn't have to. The butler was not above a bribe. Katrina was so occupied planning her excuse that she didn't notice the way Devon watched her.

His eyes were alert, eager. His slouch, hands in pockets, nevertheless had a ready air, as if he awaited only the most favorable moment to spring. But his voice was genuinely sympathetic. "Poor Kat. Is the old biddy really so difficult?"

She looked at him in surprise. "How do you know she's difficult?"

"My dear Kat, I could list every sorry position you've won and lost in the past three years. You've left a blazing trail everywhere you've been, you know. Half the young pups in the ton are infatuated with you. They're eager to talk about you. I've made it my business to keep informed. That's how I knew about tonight. . . ." His rough tone evened out again when she looked startled and opened her mouth to interrupt with a question. "Not that it matters now. At any rate this position, I opine, shall be your last."

Later she would scorn herself as foolish. She should have read the true meaning behind his last comment. She should have been warned by the fact that he'd kept himself apprised of her movements. Waiting for her to fall . . . But at the moment, because she was so weary, so delighted that he had, apparently, come tonight to aid her, she squelched her suspicions and took his words at face value. He was not without compassion after all. He was letting her go, even believing the worst.

"I, too, hope to stay here for a time. She's not really mean, just used to having her own way." She smiled at him for the first time that night.

His face relaxed into the old charm that had thrilled her such an age ago. And could thrill her again—if she let it.

"Ah, then, she's not so different from others we know, is she?" He dropped a wicked, suggestive wink.

She laughed. The sound was rich with the enjoyment of life that had once been hers. His hands went deeper into his pockets as he shifted restlessly on his seat.

"Is it yourself you're speaking of, or me?" she teased back.

His reply was husky. "Both, m'dear. Both."

Their eyes met. Something flickered in that steady brown gaze. Hesitation? Yearning? But the emotion went too quickly for her to define it. She spoke then in a rush, before she lost her courage.

"Thank you for saving me tonight. I truly was not there by choice—"

"I don't doubt that."

"And I confess I didn't expect you to let me go—"

"Did you not?"

"But I shouldn't judge so quickly. That's one of my worst faults, my father always said—"

"He knew you well."

"And I shall always remember you kindly for your help this night."

"How gratifying. Can you show me, perchance, this last time how grateful you really are?"

That steady, challenging stare was too powerful. Her gaze

dropped to his broad shoulders. Strong they were. Strong enough to ably bear all her troubles. For one traitorous instant she longed to accept his offer. More between them was unthinkable, for he was not only one of the wealthiest men in England, his title was one of the oldest. In contrast she was not only poor, alone in the world, but her background was only partly genteel. Her father had been the bastard son of a minor nobleman, but her mother had been a baker's daughter. No, the only alliance they could ever have was an illicit one. A rake he might be, but he was proud of his name and cognizant of his responsibilities. He'd wed only a blue blood as wealthy as himself.

The knowledge sharpened rather than appeased her yearning. No, she couldn't become his mistress, but she could share with him a last embrace. Fodder to feed her foolish dreams, she scorned herself, but had he reeked of brimstone in that moment, she still could not have denied him. Or herself.

"Yes, Devon," she whispered, calling him by his name for the first and last time. At least so she thought.

He went still, but she didn't see his longing, for her eyes were closed. His hands cupped her cheeks to tilt her face to his. His mouth brushed hers, fresh, warm, and appealing as her childhood memory of the bread in her grandfather's kitchen. She savored the gentle kiss that was just as hearty, just as addictive, but instead of sating her, he left her hungry for more. When he pulled her into his arms, she went gladly.

The gentle suction deepened, hardened, as he urged her lips apart. He teased the corners of her mouth with tiny nibbles, then licked the tingling nerves. When she instinctively opened her mouth wider, he delved inside, learning all the exotic tastes and textures she'd long denied him. His arms tightened until his waistcoat buttons dug into her bosom, but she didn't notice. Her hair flowed over his arm as he pressed her back against the seat, his tongue knowing every sweet crevice and secret hollow of her mouth. But when he eased back to unbutton the jacket, she came to her senses. She pressed her hands into his shoulders.

"That's enough—"

His pleasure-slurred voice disturbed the hairs near her ear.

"Give me more than a taste. I'm starving for the full course, Kat."

Her body screamed with the need to let this go where it would, but Katrina had been raised to respect the power of thought. She mastered her pulsing weakness and pushed harder, slipping out from under him.

"No, I tell you! I owe you my gratitude, and you have it. Thank you again. But don't spoil my memories by insisting on more." She scrambled to the other side of the carriage, her bosom heaving, her cheeks flushed.

His hands reached out as if to grab her, then they clenched and dropped. He turned to wrench the curtain aside and peer out.

When Katrina had swallowed her tears, she let herself look at him one last time. And for the first time she let herself think of what she was giving up in the name of morality. The feel of him, hard, warm, secure, had aroused so many urges within her. For scented sheets, a dark room, a bottle of wine; freedom, blessed freedom, from right, wrong, morality, or duty. But even more, he made her long for hearth and home, for shared travail and laughter.

This last need, its nobility made ignominious by circumstance, bolstered her. Far better to suffer now at this parting than to grow to care for him even more, then be cast aside when he was bored. She didn't fool herself like so many had done that she alone could be the one to capture his heart. She knew he had one, but she sensed no woman had ever touched it. She was neither foolish enough, nor brave enough, to believe she could be the first to do so. She forced herself to turn away.

She, too, watched as the scenery slowly became familiar. When they were a street away from her employer's house, she mumbled, "Please stop here. It's best that they don't see your carriage."

He didn't move to tap on the window, so she repeated herself, louder.

His reply was most peculiar. "Please, Kat. I ask you once more. Go with me. Let me show you what we can give one another."

"I cannot. Now please, stop."

Again no reply. His shoulders lifted in a weary sigh. Then, quietly, "Very well, my dear. On your head be it."

She stiffened. She jerked the curtains farther back and saw that they'd already reached the respectable but plain brick house. She lunged for the door, but he tugged her back, opened the coachman's window, and pulled a card from his pocket.

"Give this to the butler, Peter, with my regards. Tell him I've come to collect Miss Lawson's things, that she'll be staying with me for a while."

Her eyes, widening with dawning horror, settled upon him. His features had never been more perfect, more ruthless, or more cold. He might have been masked, for he showed no hint of human kindness or remorse.

The night's events exploded upon her. Dazed, she blinked at him, all the more afraid now that her brief reassurance had been snatched away. "No, please, I don't deserve this," she whispered.

"Do you not? Then I shall remember to make my gifts suitable to your sense of worth." When she drew breath to scream, he covered her mouth with his palm. He pulled her struggling arms behind her back with his free hand and added matter-of-factly, "I needn't explain that this will indeed be your last position. Of this sort, at any rate. After word of your new venue reaches the ton, no respectable woman will have you in her house."

When she went limp, his eyes sharpened upon hers. "Don't treat me to these die-away airs, my girl. You couldn't have kept your, er, nocturnal activities secret much longer, anyway. You'll find me more generous than Sutterfield. Just give me the passion I know you stifle. You'll remember how much you want me, after you've calmed down."

His words were a buzz in her ears. She shivered, so enervated by the repeated shocks of this night that she stayed limp, fighting nausea and weakness, until the carriage bounced as her bags were put in the back. Soon they were tooling away, the yellow wheels chattering upon the cobblestones like lecturing voices chiding her for stupidity. On she went, deeper into the blackest night she'd ever known, a demon her only companion. . . .

Chapter Two

THE SHORT DRIVE was an eternity. Even when Devon cautiously let her go and sat back next to her, she stayed curled in a ball in the corner. Her head lolled on her shoulders when he caught her elbows to pull her to a sitting position.

"We've arrived, Kat. This late no one will notice if you treat me to a scene. Please, come along quietly." If she heard him, she gave no sign.

When the coachman opened the door, Devon jumped down without using the steps and lifted her into his arms. He drew a sigh of relief when she didn't protest. A mobcapped maid had already opened the house door to the coachman's knock. In a trice Devon had her up the three semicircular steps, into the small but attractive brick house trimmed with ornate black wrought-iron balconies on each of its two floors.

"Light the candles in the salon, Martha," he ordered.

After she'd quickly obeyed, he carried Katrina into the room that was an elegant blend of blue and spring green. The sprigged silk wallpaper was complemented by flower-embroidered cushions on the indigo settees. The carpet was decked with raised daisies and gold tulips. Knickknacks sat here and there on graceful Sheraton tables. A Sheraton secretary stood opposite the marble-pilastered fireplace. After seating Katrina on the settee, Devon went to the secretary and opened its central door.

He said over his shoulder, "Fetch Billy to me, please, Peter. Tell him he's to stand guard in the hall throughout the night. No one is to enter—or leave. Then you may retire here in the quarters. Martha, see that the gold room is prepared for the night, then you may go back to sleep. I'm sorry to so abruptly descend upon you."

Martha dipped a curtsy, holding her full robe back from her slippered feet. "Yer ludship, 'tis a pleasure to see this pretty 'ouse used at last—" Those keen brown eyes cut her words off. She bobbed another hasty curtsy and fled.

Devon turned from the secretary, two quarter-full brandy snifters in his hands. He sat down next to Katrina, who remained where he'd put her. He stuck one glass under her nose. "Drink, my dear," he said gently.

When she didn't respond, he set his own glass down carefully on the table next to the settee. His concerned eyes grew dark and moody. He tilted her head toward him and lifted her snifter to her lips. "Drink, else I'll pour the whole glass down your stubborn throat." When her teeth chattered against the rim, he set the glass down with an oath and hauled her into his arms.

He buried his face in her hair. "Kat, Kat, what am I to do with you? Here you are at last, where I've dreamed you'd be, and you treat me like I carry the plague." He blew a half sigh, half groan, then he held her at arm's length to look at her. "Come now, don't make me such a monster. I promise not to eat you, or rape you."

Finally her dilated eyes looked at him. "Why do you do this to me?" she whispered.

"I don't offer you a fate worse than death." He flung an impatient arm at the room. "Everything in this house was placed here for your pleasure. I'm ready to sign each candle-stick and brick over to you. You're only to say the word."

She looked vaguely about. "Pretty."

"Don't you know that I'm offering you security at last? You'll never need to fetch and carry again for women not fit to lick your shoes."

How eager he was, she thought sadly. And how wrong. In this pretty chamber the horrors of the night reshaped themselves into dreams of what could be—if she dared to reach for them. Was she too cowardly to take the chance? Or too realistic?

Her voice was stronger when she said, "A kept woman can be certain of only one thing: that nothing is certain. I can't subject myself to that, Devon. I'll not be one of many, in this house or any other."

"And what of Sutterfield? Did you grant him your favors in the back of a carriage? At least I offer you a house!" When she looked at him coolly, he snapped his teeth closed. He picked up his snifter and sipped, then rolled the glass between his palms. "You will be its last occupant, that I swear." He set his glass down and clasped her shoulders pleadingly. "Please, Kat, let me be kind—"

The last of her apathy dissolved under the surge of anger. She lifted both her wrists and flung them outward to slap his hands away. "If your charity is dependent upon making me a whore, then be as cruel as you please."

With a slight narrowing of his eyes he exuded the danger that had won him his name. Good. This man was easy to resist. She preferred him this way. Didn't she?

"Ah, but I shan't make you a whore. You managed that all on your own, as you yourself admitted this night. Your pretended virtue now sits ill upon you. I thought you better than a hypocrite, Kat." When she stared grimly through him, his tone went even more silky. "But hypocrite or no, I want you."

He forced the brandy snifter into her rigid hand and pulled it to her lips. "Now drink. Since you've no use for tenderness from me, then let's have honesty, at least. I warned you what would happen if you accepted another. I've wanted you for three years, and here you'll stay. I'll have you as often as I like, how I like, when I like. And you'll enjoy every moment of it."

He lifted his glass and clinked it against hers. "To the wanton and the wastrel. I'd say we make a fine pair, wouldn't you?" He took a leisurely sip, his eyes sharp enough to draw blood from her pale face. When she stayed frozen, the glass to her lips, he tilted the crystal and poured a hefty draft down her throat. "Drink!"

After she'd taken a large mouthful, he put both glasses down with a satisfied air. His triumph was dashed by a spray of aromatic liquor as she spat the brandy full in his face.

She fled his feral growl. He wiped his eyes off on his sleeve and was upon her before she reached the door. He caught her elbows and hauled her around to meet his blazing stare.

"By God if you'll not sheathe your claws, then you'll sheathe something else. There's more than one way to tame a cat." He caught her wrist and dragged her behind him up the stairs. When she pulled back, swatting at him with her free hand, she almost overbalanced them both. He paused in the middle of the stairs to lift her into his arms. Kick and slap though she did, he might have been carved in stone.

But when she bent to sink her teeth into his neck, he veered his head away and hoisted her over his shoulder. Though tears of humiliation came to her eyes, and fear to her heart at what was to come, rage overwhelmed all else. How dare he carry her as if she were a possession, a bag of bones and hair that he could unwrap or shelve at his whim? As for what he carried her to . . . why, if he thought to make her cringe, to submit to his undeniably powerful masculinity, then he knew less of her than he supposed.

She'd fought this fate for three long years; she'd meet it now with fortitude. And nothing else. No spark of joy, no reveling in his kisses, no longing to be made a woman. For, with his kidnapping, he'd ruined his stature in her eyes. No matter that he thought she was promiscuous; she still had a right to accept or deny him. His feet of clay had spread throughout his body until he was a lifeless, pathetic colossus who could no longer move her to awe.

And yet . . . When he entered a room and flung her on a vast four-poster bed, her heart pounded with more than dread. A glance showed her the luxury of the chamber: gold silk hangings and drapes, wine velvet settee before the fire, rosewood tables. Everything had a pristine look, as if each expensive fixture awaited her, and her alone. Yet she knew better. She bolted off the bed as if it writhed with vermin. While he shut and locked the door she retreated behind the settee and picked up the poker beside the fireplace.

When he turned, he went still. With a weary sigh he propped his fists upon his hips and shook his head. "You've been reading too many gothic novels, my dear. I'm no villain and you're no innocent. Come now, put it down. . . ." He took several slow steps closer as he spoke, his eyes steady upon hers.

"Stay back," she warned, raising the poker above her head.

The slow advance continued, inexorable as the voice that replied, "No. I've waited for you as long as I'm going to. Bash in my head if you must, but that's the only way you'll stop me from claiming what's mine." He gave a wry shrug. "At least my blood will match the furniture."

Oh, how could he? she fumed to herself. To claim such authority over her was bad enough, but to joke even now . . . What was she to make of such a man? He was almost to the settee. She looked at that shiny thatch of dark gold hair and knew she couldn't bear to see it stained crimson. And those eyes. How could she resist them, the secrets shared, the promises of pleasure they gave? The poker wavered in her hands.

His voice grew husky with the same promise. "Please, come into my arms like the woman you are. You know you want to. You've put up a prodigious battle, and I am properly impressed by your strength of will. But we both know we were meant to be lovers. Admit it now. You've no more been able to forget me than I you, have you, Katrina mina?"

"Don't call me that," she cried, her face crumpling at the old endearment. He was but a fine actor, aping whatever emotion he thought likeliest to sway her. The fact that he thought her experienced did not excuse his blatant intent. She'd not let him pretend this was a mutual decision, nor would she let her foolish, stubborn heart make it one.

The weaving poker steadied. "No, I've not been able to forget you." His glad smile faded when she added, "But we don't always want what's good for us. Too much candy makes one fat and shiftless—"

"And too little sustenance makes one lean and mean. Come, sup with me at love's banquet. Sutterfield is too selfish to give you more than scraps. But I, Katrina mina, want to share with you the ambrosia only a few are privileged to know—"

"Stop it! Pretty words can't disguise the truth of what you want to do to me." The hopeful light in his eyes died. He began advancing on her again. Her voice quavered, "P-please, Devon, stop. I don't want to injure you. But I will not be your mistress. That, at least, is still my decision to make."

He stopped, his expression almost sad. "Ah, but you're wrong. I saved you from an hellacious night, risking my life in doing so. That alone surely deserves some reward. Shall I tell you what usually happens?" He ignored the frantic shake of her head and went on dispassionately, "They usually buy their girls from Madame Lusette's house. The members claim most are told fully of their role, but agree because of the generous fee. Quite often they're not even virgins, but that's a little fiction the satyrs find . . . stimulating. I'm told none of the girls has ever been injured, but they're quite often sore after servicing as many as twenty men—"

"That's enough!" she cried, revolted. "Why were you there as a prospective member?"

He paled a little. "I've already told you I heard you would be there. I've no need to resort to such tactics—as you will soon discover. Lie to yourself all you wish, little hypocrite, but don't transfer your own sins upon me." That charming smile that never failed to move her flickered on his lips. "Lord knows, I've enough of my own to account for."

"That, I heartily agree with."

"I thought you might." He was easing closer as he spoke. "Shall it appease you if I admit that I, as are all men, am often guided by my senses? Whereas you, as are all women, are guided by your acquisitiveness. Once you've become used to me, you'll be as eager for gifts as the rest." Yet he looked at her almost pleadingly, as if longing for her to be different.

Each thus wounded the other with thoughtless words. But Katrina was too weary, too raw, to realize that her own behavior incited his. Did he really have such a low opinion of her? "How little you know me. If I were truly so mercenary, I'd accept all you offer. But material things cannot compensate for spiritual gifts. You, my lord, are living proof of that. And any woman who willingly consorts with you subjugates all that is good and admirable in the feminine spirit. And I, sir, will not be degraded. By you or anyone." Resolved blue eyes squarely met darkening brown ones. What might have been pain flashed across his face, but before she could credit it, his purr raised the hairs on the back of her neck.

"For once we're in agreement, little cat. I won't degrade you; you've done that all on your own. When you became Sutterfield's whore, you made yourself fair game to me and all like me. You, who protested such morality, such respect for the memory of your father, sold yourself to the veriest pinchpenny when I would have given . . ." He bit back the words with apparent distaste. "Now, enough talk. Only after you've experienced my touch will you see how enjoyable it is. And degrading or not, you'll revel in it, I'll wager." He put one finely shaped hand on the back of the settee as if to vault over it.

But when she brought the poker down to smash that hand, she found it turned up, grasping. The poker was snatched out of her grip and flung against the wall. The blow left a long gash in the fine burl wainscoting, but neither of them noticed.

Katrina was intent on flight; Devon was intent on capture. The victor had been obvious long ere this moment, but even when he caught her in his arms, Katrina could not accept that. She writhed, she kicked, she cursed, but her struggles only hastened her downfall. When she pushed to the right, he pulled to the left, wrenching off the jacket she still wore. He'd little time to savor the pleasure of looking at her, for she drew her leg back to kick him, and he had to haul her close, wrapping one of his own muscular thighs about her knees to keep her still. As for her flailing hands, they, too, were impotent against his greater strength. He caught her wrists and drew them behind her back.

He lowered his mouth over hers, but froze at the taste of her lips. He lifted his head a hairsbreadth and licked her salty tears away. The anger in his face was replaced by resignation, then tenderness. "This is not what I want you to feel at such a moment," he said gently. "I am different to the satyrs, Katrina. Since you persist in trying to equate me with them, I'll prove it." He released her and stood back, though the veins in his neck stood taut with the effort it cost him.

She stayed where he put her, looking at him through the haze of her tears.

Clenching one big fist, he turned away. "You need rest after the trauma of this night, as I should have realized. I just want you so very badly." At the door he turned again to face her. "One night. The door will be locked, and guarded, so don't think of escape. Tomorrow evening I'll be back. And I want to feel fire in your lips then instead of tears."

The door closed behind him. Katrina collapsed on the bed and wept, both glad and sorry that he'd gone. Then exhaustion claimed her before she even thought to remove her clothes, and left her only troubled dreams as companions.

The next day passed all too quickly. Martha brought her sustaining meals and a book of poetry sent by Devon. Katrina's heart began to pound as the sunset filled the room with radiance, and she shoved away most of her dinner. Pacing up and down, she rubbed her elbows, trying to come to terms with her chaotic feelings. How was it possible both to dread and to anticipate someone's arrival? Devon had always stirred her strongest feelings, as she, apparently, had stirred his. Except for the one feeling she needed from him most . . . The sad smile froze on her lips when a knock came at the door.

The key rattled in the lock. Leaning against the windowsill, she tried to look casual so he wouldn't see how her knees shook. He entered, relocked the door, then bowed. He was casually attired in breeches and white shirt, but he looked like Adonis to Katrina. In that moment she had to admit how she'd yearned for the sight of him. Yearned for, God help her, more. Still, she had to be strong. If she were, he might still let her go.

"Good even', milady. How do you feel this fine night?"

"Better, but still tired." She affected a languid yawn.

That brilliant smile flickered to life, beaming on her as brightly as the westering sun. "Ah, then we shall sleep well. Together." He approached.

Katrina clenched her fists to keep from running. Too late denial rose to her lips; too late her feet cautioned pride. In a trice she was in his arms, his lips upon hers. He consumed her, obviously famished, but delicate, too. As if he were a gastronome dining with the queen. Dear Lord, the hunger he stirred in her. She fought it, and him, weakly, but was powerless before their mutual need. Too long had it been denied. For three years it had loomed over them, and she knew, with a fatalism her heart could not ignore, that she was about to be buffeted by its force.

When she was bent like a reed before a primeval gale, he cajoled, "Kat, this moment was fated from our first meeting. I ask you one last time to let it be as memorable as our bodies long to make it. Please, my darling." His eyes delved into hers as if he would know her, body and soul. We're not using, he communicated with those compelling eyes; we're sharing the finest joy men and women have to give each other.

She understood, but morality and sensuality waged a fierce battle within her. A dozen replies flickered through her confused brain, none, she knew, sufficient to win her freedom. As she stared up into those solemn, waiting eyes she even considered telling him the truth. But the same instinct that had kept her quiet thus far guided her now: pride.

She'd let him see too much of his devastating effect upon her. She'd responded too wholeheartedly to his kisses. Better he think her shameless than know how weak he made her. Besides, if he knew she'd never been any man's mistress, he was likely to lavish on her that tenderness that made her long for the impossible. No, far better that he think her used and use her accordingly. At least then fear and revulsion . . . yes, she told herself fiercely, revulsion . . . would quiet her own unseemly instincts.

Thus she lifted her head and murmured, ''Release me and I'll give you my reply.'' When he did so, eyeing her hopefully, she took a tiny step back for better leverage. Before he'd an inkling of what she would do, she lifted her hand and struck him with all her might across his beautiful face. The slap echoed in the still chamber like the first shot between duelists.

''You have my answer, sir. Now treat me as your instincts bid.'' She didn't bother running. When his stunned look faded and his pupils contracted to two evil beads, she stayed where she was. His mouth quivered, then set to a thin, hard line. Two ruthless hands settled on her shoulders, caught the well-worn cotton dress, and ripped downward.

''As you will. If you'd rather I treat you as a slut, then far be it from me to disappoint you.'' His color rose until the imprint of her hand barely stood out on his cheek. His strong fingers made short work of her clothes until tatters floated down her body to the floor. She stood in the ruined pool like a statue, the air a cooling spray upon her, and closed her eyes to block his triumph.

Triumph did indeed flare in that heated gaze. But other emotions, deeper, truer, imbued it with soft golden lights that chased the angry shadows away. Radiance flickered over her like Olympian sunlight. When he reached out to her, his hands shook. He paused, stared at them in dismay, then wiped them off on his breeches. His touch settled lightly on her strong but graceful shoulders, tracking their curves down to her slim arms, all the way to her hands. He twined his fingers with hers and kissed her knuckles.

He released her and skimmed down her sides, watching her all the while. She stayed frozen, her eyes still closed, even when he molded her from rib cage to hipbones again and again, as if he could believe neither the slimness of her waist nor the velvet of her skin. Next he filled his hands with the rich curves of her buttocks, then traced the backs of her long, slim legs down to her knees.

Still he watched her face, as if the twin pleasures of sight and touch would be too great to bear. His posture was eager, waiting. When she trembled, the masculine hunger in his face was softened by tenderness.

Running his fingers through the fall of hair glittering like hammered gold in the firelight, he said, ''Ah, Kat, you've bewitched me. In truth you're too beautiful to be earthly. You should sit atop a pedestal and have us lesser mortals worship at your feet.''

She couldn't help it; she had to smile at the picture he evoked. ''Now, that I would enjoy, having you kneeling before me—'' She stared down at the lustrous head bent in what certainly *looked* like homage.

''Goddess, bestow on me thy charity. Have mercy on one who trembles before you in earnest desire to offer all I have to thy charms. . . .'' His head lifted; his eyes pinioned hers. Now she could see the conflicting emotions there. Lust warring with tenderness, anger battling joy, need struggling against pride. And because his emotions so closely mirrored hers, she backed away from him, unable to cope with his feelings, or her own.

She retreated to the bed and pulled one hanging partially over her nakedness. He stayed where he was, watching her with that gaze that kept her prisoner as surely as chains. ''No, Devon,'' she whispered. ''You can't make of this . . . tawdry tryst a noble thing. I'm no goddess to bestow my favors on you. Gift me though you might with all your worldly goods after this night, you can never recompense me for what I value above all.''

Slowly he rose. Just as slowly he began unbuttoning his shirt. ''And what is that, my dear?'' he asked kindly, as if humoring her.

''My self-respect.''

He paused, then flung his shirt aside so hard that two of the pearl buttons popped off when they impacted against the wall. ''I see. Still you persist in this fiction that a . . . now, how did you put it?'' He methodically began on his breeches. ''Ah yes, a tawdry tryst is all you can know with me. Tell me, my dear, did Sutterfield fill you with seed so ennobling that he put you above my touch?''

She shook her head desperately. ''No, you don't under-stand. . . .'' She took a deep breath, but the words would not come.

''In that you have the right of it,'' he snapped, kicking off his shoes so he could pull his breeches down. ''I don't at all understand why you would gladly bestow on that . . . man mannequin what should have been mine. And even now, you refuse me, when I see in your eyes and feel in your kiss how much you want me.'' He peeled off his stockings, then slipped out of his last garment and stood, feet braced apart, to taunt, ''So, m'dear, I'm taking pity on your confusion and will make the decision for you. But if it will make you feel more the thing, if you don't gladly participate in all I want to do with you by the month's end, I'll let you go.''

Her eyes stayed on his face as her color deepened. ''Is that a promise?''

''You have my word as a gentleman.'' He smiled sardoni-cally. ''Or perhaps I should give you my word in a manner you'll more agree with: You have my word as a nobleman. Now, enough talk. Come, wench, it's time to earn your keep.'' When her nostrils flared at his deliberate insult, his smile deepened. The tender gold lights in his eyes had been drowned by brandy hot enough to burn.

Compulsively, her gaze dropped to appraise him. He re-minded her more than ever of a great, sleek cat, with his tawny hair, rippling muscles, and long, powerful legs. Yet as he strode toward her she could not ignore the powerful reality of his manhood. His big, rigid member blatantly proclaimed the purpose on his face, homing toward her like a compass needle seeking true north. And her emotional fears became childish under the rush of her physical ones. She knew the clinical details of the sex act, but forewarned was not forearmed in this instance. She dropped the bed hanging and backed away, her hands held out to ward him off.

When he was almost upon her, she dodged, but he caught her and pushed her back against the wall, holding her wrists above her head in one hand. The sensations at her back, of silk wallpaper warmed by the fire and hard, smooth wood, were matched by the sensations at her front. Had she been less frightened, she would have enjoyed the touch of so much unfettered male power, but all her senses were trained on one thing. It prodded her in the abdomen like a warning finger. When he drew his chest back to look down at the full breasts pressed against him and run his free hand lightly over them, she barely felt the touch.

His fervent, "S'truth, Kat, you've a form made for love. These lovely breasts, full, round, and firm, are ripe for a man's mouth," was a cacophony in her ringing ears. Even when he bent and showed by action what he meant, she didn't move at the tender suckling of one blush-tinged orb. When his mouth lowered to the scented hollow of her bosom and trailed down her flat stomach, he still cupped that breast, as if savoring the wetness marking his possession. Groaning, he released her wrists and knelt to press his cheek into her warm belly, running his hands up and down her perfect legs.

She drew a shuddering breath as that ravenous pressure eased and blinked, focusing on that variegated gold head buried against her. So sincere his husky praise sounded. In other circumstances she might have believed the soft endearments, but she knew his adoration was wholly carnal.

If only . . . tears sprang to her eyes. The pain in her heart galvanized her paralyzed limbs. She pushed him away so hard he fell sideways. She ran for the door, uncaring of her nakedness. She was intent only on escaping him, this room, and the captivity that she did not dare welcome no matter how she might long to.

His laughter rumbled low from his chest, like the mating

growls of an aroused lion. His soft steps might have been the pads of that fearsome beast, so quick and tireless were they in their pursuit. He sprang upon her long before she reached the door and, in four great strides, had her on the bed. Still he chuckled, even when she flailed her arms and legs beneath his weight.

"My redoubtable Kat, what a joy you are. You are destined to be reincarnated as a bulldog. Doubtless I'll be a mastiff, sniffing about you, trying to find a step to mate you upon." When she only struggled harder beneath him, he lowered his laughing mouth over hers.

She attempted to turn her head aside, but he wrapped one leg about hers to keep her still, freeing his hands to cup her head in his palms. She bore the full frontal assault then, and surely no army could boast a vanguard so awesome as the power of those warm, mobile lips. They tasted of brandy, of earthy male and the ambrosia he had promised. She tried to resist, oh, how she tried, but her beating hands grew limp upon his shoulders.

Fight though she had, for this, this she had yearned for three long years. For strong arms firm enough to hold but gentle enough to cherish; for warm lips eager enough to devour but controlled enough to sample; for roaming hands ardent enough to bruise but patient enough to caress. The hands that had grown limp upon him began a journey of their own.

Such warm, supple skin. She skimmed his firm biceps and felt the corded strength of his neck, then charted the vast course of his broad shoulders. When he obligingly fell aside, she could touch the planes and curves of his chest. The light brown hairs were soft but prickly. When she curiously touched the small brown nipples, she was shocked to feel them harden beneath her fingers. He drew his mouth away at last, leaving them both panting for air. She might have surfaced then from the sensual pool he was drowning her in if he hadn't lowered that chest to rub it back and forth upon her excruciatingly sensitive breasts.

While she was still gasping those long, skillful fingers skimmed the insides of her legs from ankles to upper thighs, stopping just short of her throbbing center. Instinctively she tried to close her legs, but his knees were there, urging hers farther apart. She stiffened, some of her pleasured haze clearing as she knew what would come next. But Demon Devon surprised her yet again.

He didn't conquer the new territory that was his for the taking. He rubbed back and forth on her body, wrapping about her a tender chain of kisses as he went. When he reached her breasts, he paused, gazing upon those rose-tipped mounds with a male need that reached out to her femininity like a supplicating hand. He pressed those fruits together and bent to sate his hunger upon her, nurturing them both, but leaving them ravenous, too. When she arched herself into his mouth, he obliged with tiny nibbles that sent shivers through her. This time, when his knees pushed gently upon hers, she gladly spread her legs.

The part of herself she'd rebelled against for such an age would have ruled her then had he not made a tactical error. He brought one of her hands to his pulsing shaft.

"Kat, Kat, feel what you do to me. I haven't been so hard for anyone since I was a youth. . . ." He trailed off when her fingers flinched away from the contact. She began to fling her head from side to side, moaning a denial.

His passion-glazed eyes frowned upon her flushed face. "What nonsense is this? Come now, you needn't whet my appetite. I've never desired a woman more." When her muttering was matched by her hands, pushing at him weakly, he grew impatient. "Enough! Welcome me now as the woman you are, and I'll forgive all. Bring me home and help me forget that you've known another." Slowly, demandingly, he eased his narrow hips up into position, but his hands were tender as they brushed the hair back from her face.

Her eyes opened at that first intimate touch. The haze cleared completely, leaving them cold and desolate as highland winter winds. "Forgive all? *You?* It is you who will beg me for forgiveness one day. And I'll have as much mercy then as you do for me in this moment."

The words had a prophetic echo, but his face darkened heedlessly. "Then be my sacrifice, little saint, for I'm one devil who will have his due." He thrust forward on the end.

The stab was swift, well placed, and ruthless. It sliced cleanly through her flimsy barrier and lodged him, heavy and full, within her. She tensed and turned her face into her shoulder to hide her pained grimace. Only vaguely was she aware of his shocked exclamation.

"My God! It can't be. . . ." He pulled gently out, then pushed slowly back in as if to verify the narrowness of the channel no man had charted before him. Once more he pulled out, pausing to credit with his eyes what his member had felt. Spotty but undeniable was the blood dotting both his tumescence and the sheet beneath their joining. He paused, poised at her narrow opening, and closed his own eyes. Had she been looking at him then, she would have wondered at his expression. There was less of triumph in it and more of guilt mixed with joy. The joy of a heart that had not dared to hope . . .

But she wasn't looking at him. She only felt the burning soreness where his ruthless maleness stole what, under other circumstances, she would gladly have bestowed. When he stroked her hair away and turned her face up to his, she said dully, "Pray continue, devil, have your 'due.' By all that's holy I swear that one day I will have mine."

Those golden highlights muted some at her words. "Ah, Kat, forgive me, but I can't let you go now. If only you'd told me . . . but it's too late. Let me show you that I can give as well as take." He began gentle, sliding movements, his pulsing hardness tender upon her sensitive bud. But he did not enter. He tipped her head back to lavish upon her the feeling shining from those eyes. She didn't struggle, even when he coaxed her mouth apart. His agile tongue danced, dipped, and swayed, but lit no answering flame. Still the twin joys of her flavorful mouth and beautiful body were too much for him.

With the passion of a man who'd hungered too long, he cupped his hands beneath her buttocks and slowly, carefully, eased back into the tender flesh. When she tore her mouth away and moaned in pain, his own mouth quivered.

"Poor Kat, I'm so sorry. It always hurts the first time, but the damage is done. After pain comes pleasure. I promise." His words ended on a groan as he buried his throbbing sword full length in the sheath fashioned for it.

With every thrust she grew more pliable, but the easing of her bodily agony increased her mental torment. Why had she been tempted, even briefly, to share in this . . . rutting? The passion that made Devon shake and groan as he took his pleasure upon her was no substitute for love. Had this moment been sanctified by vows, yet not blessed by exchanged tenderness, she'd still have felt used. The only love this man was capable of was here with them in this bed.

Thus, when Devon slowed his hungry lunges to slow, sliding strokes and took her mouth to spear it in a like manner with his tongue, she was proof against his seduction. She was limp beneath him even when he lifted her hips to better position her. That throbbing warmth had died, leaving only cinders too cold for him to kindle.

"Ah Kat, stubborn to the last. But God, you feel good. I'm sorry, but I can't wait—" His words ended in a gasp as, with one last deep thrust, he bathed her with his passion. The potent splashes trickled off as he collapsed atop her, limp with contentment.

She tried to push him away then, but he caught her hands. "I'm sorry, darling . . . I didn't realize. Why didn't you tell me the truth?" When she didn't respond, he pleaded huskily, "Look at me, Kat."

She obeyed, but her eyes were full of the contempt she felt for each of them in that moment.

He kissed her brow. "Don't glare at me so. If only you'd told me, I would have gone slower." His husky laugh stirred the hair at her temple. "I'd have tried, at any rate. You don't understand what you do to me, Kat. But please believe, had I known, things would have been different." He leaned away to look pleadingly into her eyes. His cheeks were a bit flushed, but she couldn't credit him with sensitivity enough for guilt.

"You'd have let me go?" she challenged. When he hesitated, her lip curled. "I thought so."

The softness that made his features more beautiful than ever hardened again to arrogance. "Why do you persist in painting me so black? Did I not let you go once? As for now . . . I'd have tried to let you go, had I known you were still intact, but I admit I'm not sure I could have. The wanting of you didn't ease, Kat. Not for three long years. No woman satisfied me. . . ." When she turned her head away in denial, he forced her chin back around. "At least credit me with honesty. You lie not only to me, but to yourself, if you tell me you don't want me. No, don't shake your head. Only your pride kept you remote from me. Before we're done, you'll admit as much. Would you like me to begin again?'' He thrust his softening length deeper into her nestling warmth.

"No, I'll forgo the . . . pleasure." When she felt him stir within her, like a cat flexing lithe muscles, she forced out a hoarse, "Please."

"Ah, the magic word." He withdrew and vaulted off the bed, put his arms above his head, and stretched.

Compulsively, she absorbed him. Those long, strong legs buttressed the soaring planes of his slim waist and wide chest. His lines were as perfect as . . . Westminster's. She blushed at the thought, but still she admired every muscled inch gilded by the firelight. Something primitive within her was pleased that *she* had given him this lazy contentment. But when her eyes fell to that part of him that was still wet with his pleasure and her blood, her face hardened again. She pulled the sheet up over her nakedness and turned on her side away from him.

She heard the splash of water, then the feather mattress depressed as he sat down. The sheet was pulled away, and she was pushed onto her back. A cool, damp cloth eased between her legs, soothing her burning discomfort. She relaxed under his ministration, sighing her relief. Had she been less angry with him, she might have been touched by his consideration.

She was off guard when he persisted. "Katrina, why didn't you tell me the truth?"

Relaxation fled. He'd obviously not leave her be until he got an answer. Why was he so dogged about the subject? Shame might have motivated a lesser man, but she'd never known a man less subject to doubt than Devon. She pushed his hands away, propped the pillows behind her back and sat up. She tried to cover herself, but he was sitting on the sheet. She sighed at her own instinctive modesty. What difference did it make now? Besides, his eyes were steady on her face.

"Would you have believed me?" she countered sullenly.

He flung the cloth back into the basin. "Perhaps not, but there are ways to . . . ascertain the truth." When she blushed, his smile had a touch of melancholia. "So much the vicar's daughter, still."

She knew he was only teasing, but the reminder of her father sent a shaft of agony through her. She looked from her own exposed flesh to his casual posture, one foot propped on the edge of the bed, an arm on his upraised knee. His satisfied manhood lolled against one strong thigh, but the blood he'd not bothered to wipe away testified to what she'd lost this night.

"Yes, Papa would be proud indeed of his only child if he could see her now." Her voice was soft, but her bitterness was acid enough to disintegrate even his steely control.

Indeed, his eyes flickered away from hers, as if he could not sustain her gaze. "Do you think he'd have been glad to see you run ragged by women not fit to kennel with their bitches?"

"Probably not glad, but I think he'd agree I'd made the best of what could have been a worse bargain."

His face tightened, then he leaped off the bed and went to the armoire against the wall. He ripped open the bottom drawer and brought a velvet case to the bed. He tossed it beside her. "Open it."

She did so, her movements jerky. Rubies and diamonds winked at her even in the dim glow from the fire. She flung the case away as if it singed her fingers. The necklace, bracelet, and earrings splashed onto the Aubusson rug like drops of blood and tears. The one she'd spilled this night unwillingly; she'd never give him the satisfaction of the other. When his breath whistled through his teeth, she raised her head bravely to meet his fury.

"You might consider me a whore, but no gifts, no abuse, no false kindness will ever make me accept that fate. Then, no matter how many times you use my body, I will still be Katrina Lawson, vicar's daughter, in my heart."

Only the crackling of the fire broke the tense silence, then he murmured, "And would your father prefer to see you alone, friendless, joyless? Or as the cherished companion of a man wealthy enough to protect his own? If it hadn't been me, it would have been someone else soon enough." He scooted on his knees in front of her and put his hands flat on the mahogany bedstead behind her back.

"You want the details of why I was there last night? Sutterfield has been bragging for weeks that you were his mistress, you, who had refused me." He moderated his rising voice and went on evenly, "Do you know how that made me feel? And then an acquaintance told me Sutterfield intended to join the satyrs, bringing his own offering, and I feared maybe he was using this ruthless way to end your . . . association. Think, Kat. What instinct led me there? If we're not bound in some curious way that perhaps neither of us wants, why did I know you'd be there? I assure you I've never before associated with such an organization. A man's intimate life should remain just that—intimate. Surely you know enough of me to at least believe that.''

She had to look away from his penetrating gaze, for at the moment she couldn't deal with the ramifications of his statements. He'd gone there to save her, her eager heart trilled. She believed him at last. And her conscience answered sourly, Yes, to keep you for himself.

He continued inexorably, ''I was terrified to see you there, and I risked much to get you away. I bring you to your own house, give you a fortune in jewels, then have you revile me for my ruthlessness.'' He leaned so close that his breath stirred the hair at her temples. ''Katrina, admit it. You're not meant to die a virgin. Don't you understand why every man you meet is soon panting to get under your skirts?''

She shook her head violently and tried to push him away, but he caught her hands and insisted, ''You know it's true. It's not just your beauty, though you are the most beautiful woman I've ever seen. It's the paradox of this mouth''—he stroked the full, firm lines with a gentle finger—''strong and sensual as Lilith's, with this exquisite face and form.'' He lightly ran his hand from her temple to her jaw, then down her body. Only then did he let her go.

''You're every man's fantasy: both angel and wanton. And I have been the one fortunate enough to win you—''

''To steal me!''

''If you like. But I'll not give you up. I'm sorry for hurting you, but I'm not sorry you're here. And here you remain until you learn to enjoy being my mistress.''

The tears she refused to shed roughened her voice when she asked, ''And when you tire of me? What then?''

''You'll have this house and a lifelong . . . annuity. I promise.''

She should have appreciated his honesty, but perversely she was hurt that he made no protestations of eternal desire. She looked around the room, then back at him. "And this . . . bribery with the things I've never hungered for is supposed to replace the one thing I've always wanted above all?"

"And what would that be?" he asked with an eagerness that might have pleased her. Once.

"A happy marriage. Children. A loving husband. What respectable man will have me now?" Curiously, his face darkened. He looked angry at the mere idea, yet why should he care what happened to her when he was finished with her?

"You'll need no 'respectable man,'" he growled. "This disreputable man will be all that you desire." His eyes lowered to appraise her revealed charms. The flesh that had been flaccid a moment ago began to swell.

She couldn't quell the instinct. She brought her legs up and clasped her arms about herself. He laughed scornfully, moved back, caught her slim ankles, and pulled her supine on the mattress.

This time he was patient. This time his passion would not be denied. It was as if her dreams inflamed him, as if the thought of her with another man, any man, made him determined to put his stamp upon her so deeply, so thoroughly, that she could never forget him.

His was a magical skill, learned at the hands of women whose survival depended upon their mastery of that art. He might have been Cellini sculpting the *Nymph of Fontainebleau,* so assiduously did he mold her end to end. She tried to resist, but even the soreness that marked his earlier passing was not distraction enough from his wicked ability.

She told him so, when his mouth was buried in her breasts, his hands gliding over the tremors she could not control. "You are wicked, wicked, please, don't make me, too—" She broke off with a gasp when his mouth singed a trail of kisses down to the secret place she'd tried so hard to deny. He tongued and suckled, holding her weakly struggling legs apart with his strong hands. The intimacy was shocking. Her heavy eyes opened in disbelief to see that proud golden head bent in reverence to the essence of her femininity. The incredible sight made feelings, wicked or no, more powerful than morality.

But even as she arched her neck against the pillow and gave herself over to sin, he laughed huskily, blew on the bud he'd coaxed to full bloom, and left her aching. She moaned a protest, but he'd not even allow her that. He consumed her words with his lips. This time she met his demand. The kiss was deep, hot and evocative, tasting of their combined fluids, and she consumed him as if he did in truth offer her ambrosia.

He broke the kiss to taunt, "Taste how delicious wickedness can be, my innocent temptress. Shall I leave you be and let you suffer in your virtue?" He levered himself beside her on an elbow, but one finger teased her swollen nipples.

She'd never done anything harder, but demanding as flesh was, mind was stronger. Her voice was hoarse but steady. "Yes, leave me be." She turned to swing her legs around and get up.

"Oh no, you don't!" Two powerful arms wound about her waist and hauled her to her knees in the middle of the bed. "Your spirit may be willing, but my flesh is decidedly weak." When she sent him a shocked look at his misuse of Scripture at such a moment, he merely smiled back. His grin deepened to pure mischief as he levered himself behind her and fondled the firm globes hanging ready for him. "As yours will be in a moment."

Her struggles didn't last long, especially when he pushed her knees apart and raked his eager manhood up and down the field lying fallow and fertile for him. Sin was everywhere—in the hands that left her breasts flushed and throbbing to knead her aching, empty belly; in the hard body that titillated her backside; in the seed-swollen flesh that rubbed a smaller, ripening kernel. And despite herself she reveled in it all, as he had promised her she would.

The long, slow slide was welcome despite the twinge of pain, despite her belief that these feelings were wrong, so wrong. He filled her to the brim and paused to let her grow accustomed to the luxury.

His hands, however, were never idle. One fondled the part of her sweet sheath his manhood could not reach, the other caressed every inch of her. By the time he began to move she was so far gone that she pushed demandingly back against him when he left her. He built her arousal to fever pitch, but never allowed her release until he, too, was ready. As he thrust deeply to bathe her womb in the stream of life, he simultaneously thumbed her, delicately, deliciously. They reached release at the same time, her fulfillment enriched by his own.

She quivered at the glory, the wicked, lovely glory. The earth seemed to shake beneath her knees, turning topsy-turvy all the truths she'd taken for granted. Fornication was not a disgusting, animalistic act; it was a heady intimacy for both men and women to revel in. The man behind her was not evil incarnate; he was solid security, hope of happiness. This room was not the site of her ruination; it was the place of her rebirth. Katrina collapsed bonelessly beneath him, body and mind reeling, barely aware of his husky praises in her ear.

But as the throbbing dissipated, that eternal struggle between flesh and mind began anew. This time flesh appeased, reason triumphed. Yes, he'd won a measured victory, for he'd proved conclusively how enjoyable sin could be. But her sight was unclouded by passion now, and she saw that glory as it really was: tarnished. Like a miscast silver urn that decayed from the inside out, so was that passion of surface beauty, yet worthless and flawed upon closer examination. She'd not sell all she owned, indeed, the soul that made her a good Christian woman, for that one possession, no matter how tempting. Then, if he never heard her admit to enjoyment, he'd have to keep his promise and let her go.

The hope seemed feeble as Devon gently bathed her and held her. He kissed her, not with passion, but with tenderness, as if he cherished more than the superficial casing that roused him so. Emotionally and physically exhausted, she didn't resist when he blew out the candles and climbed into bed with her.

"Sleep, little Lilith. In my arms. Where you belong."

Perhaps because she was already drifting off, his possessiveness did not irritate her. Whether he was a demon in a man's skin, or a worthy wastrel, in that twilight moment she knew she did indeed belong here, in Devon's arms. For the first time in many a moon she slept dreamlessly.

That rare peace didn't last beyond the rising sun. She was alone when she awoke, and her conscience was merciless. The new, intimate twinges should have slowed her movements, but instead they prodded her to haste. Now, while he was gone, was her chance. Possibly her only one.

But when she looked around, she couldn't find the two small valises that held all her worldly possessions. Her mouth tightened grimly. She picked up the clothes Devon had discarded over the back of a chair.

When she clumped down the stairs a few minutes later, Devon's evening slippers held on her feet by kerchiefs stuffed in the toes, she didn't see the man sitting beside the front door until he rose to face her. His expression was as impenetrable as the mountain he resembled. He stepped into her path, crossed his tree-trunk arms over his chest, and called from the side of his mouth, "Devvie lad, the little gel's up."

While she was still blinking in shock at hearing the Earl of Brookstone addressed in such a fashion—by a servant, no less—Devon entered the doorway between the hall and salon. He stopped at the sight of her, sweeping her from head to toe with a disbelieving glance. His knee breeches hung loosely past her calves, where his stockings bagged at her ankles. His waistcoat flapped past her hips, and the coat that fit his broad shoulders like a second skin looked more like a misshapen greatcoat on her. His mouth quivered.

The glare she sent him from beneath the cocked hat lost its impact when the hat, precariously pushed back on her forehead, wobbled at her movement. It plopped down her nose to encase the upper portion of her face. Which was just as well, for then she couldn't see Devon's silent laughter.

His voice, however, was rich with mirth when he said, "Faith, what a gallant lad it is. I must commend your tailor, m'boy. He's given you a fit"—he choked when the hat she rammed backward fell sideways this time, leaving one furious eye exposed, then went on—"the like of which I've ne'er seen."

"That's enough!" she cried, stomping her foot. A loose shoe went flying. Devon leaned against the door frame, laughing too hard to stand upright.

He wheezed, "That's . . . my point. It is too much. . . . You need a tuck here and there, me lad." Catching the hat she threw at him, he swept it before him in a bow. "Why thank you, sir, I'm glad you've decided to stay for tea." He caught her arm and pulled her, struggling, into the salon. He pushed her back until her knees bent against the settee, forcing her to sit.

He fixed her tea as he knew she liked it—sugar, no cream—and pressed a plate of crumpets upon her. When she looked as if she might throw that at him as well, he shook his head. "No, Kat, I'm done teasing. After last night you need to eat to replace your, er, strength."

"To give me stamina for tonight, you mean," she snapped. But she buttered a crumpet and took a famished bite, suddenly aware she'd not eaten since lunch yesterday.

He didn't deny it. He watched indulgently until she'd eaten two coddled eggs and a small bowlful of strawberries and cream. Replete, she put her dishes on the side table and leaned back. When Devon sat next to her, she looked up at him in time to catch his kiss full upon her mouth. His tongue delicately rimmed her lips, but even as she lifted her hands to push him away, he moved back.

He licked his lips. "Cats are inordinately fond of cream, I perceive." He bent and whispered in her ear, "And I'm inordinately fond of Kat flavored with cream."

He eyed her so sensuously that she had to do something to break the intensity. She picked up her bowl, poured some cream in it from the small pitcher, and set it down on the floor in front of him. "Here you are. A bowl all your own. You don't have to make do with leftovers."

That regal nose lifted into the air. "Are you implying, madam, that I have stripes or spots?"

"No, but at times I've thought I've seen the beginnings of a tail." She glanced disparagingly at the lean hips encased in casual breeches.

His nose came down to her level as he leaned into her face and purred, "You could be right. I've only to look at you to feel myself growing horned." When she blushed and looked away, he smiled. "Ah, Kat, I don't think you know what you want. Would you really have me be beast or demon instead of a man who desires you?"

"I'd have you be a man compassionate enough to release a woman who doesn't want to be your mistress," she whispered, her fingers clasped so tightly together that her knuckles gleamed whitely.

"It's too late for that, my darling. No regrets on my part or pleas on yours can ever give you back that small piece of skin I broke last night. With it gone, what have you to lose? What have you to go back to?"

"Nothing you would understand, but something vital to me: the right to choose my own fate." She looked at him, her eyes crystal cool and clear.

He gripped her shoulders in strong hands. "Then choose. Choose me. Willingly. Gladly. You know you want to."

Katrina suspected there were many women who would give all they owned to put that pleading, hungry look in Demon Devon's eyes. She was not immune, but she still had courage enough to look away and shake her head.

"So it's a fight to the finish, is it?" When she didn't answer, he sighed and let her go. "Very well, my dear. I've never known a woman with such a strong will. This should be an interesting contest."

He rose and offered her his hand. When she took it, he pulled her up and over to a small pile of bandboxes behind the door. "Now, as to your attire . . ." He trailed off and opened the top box to shake out an exquisite blue silk gown trimmed in silver roses. "These adornments will suit you better than mine."

Her head reared up as if he'd offered her the worst insult. "I'll not dress as your whore. Where do you plan to take me—the cyprians' ball?"

He flung the dress back in the box and dragged her across the room to the long mirror opposite the door. He stood behind her and forced her to face her own image. "There, look at yourself and tell me—which is the more ridiculous? My arrogance or your pretension?"

She glared at him until he took her skull between his big hands and forced her chin down. Reluctantly, she looked at her reflection. Her mouth fell open. The long fall of golden hair, a perfect foil to the severely masculine garments, highlighted her absurdity.

"Very well, Kat, I'll lend you my clothes if you please, but wouldn't you rather look the beautiful woman you are? I assure you I purchased the gowns just for you. They're not some other woman's castoffs."

"Indeed? And how were they made up so quickly?" She was surprised when he flushed and turned away.

"Money in the right hands can do wonders. They worked the night through," he said lightly, sitting down to pour himself another cup of tea.

Why did she get the feeling he was lying? And why would he lie about such an inconsequential matter? Was it possible he cared more for her than he would admit? She kicked off his other shoe and strolled over to him, knelt, and put her hands on his knees. Her heart raced with the gamble she was taking, but she had to try.

He froze with the cup halfway to his mouth when she said softly, "Devon, tell me truly . . . this house, the gowns . . . did you buy them just for me?"

Arrested brown eyes stared into her pleading blue ones. Carefully, he set his cup down and put his hands over hers. "And if I told you yes? That I value you highly, and would give you even more, if you'd let me? That I find your mind as stimulating as your body?" He grinned, a singularly masculine grin. "Almost." He grew serious again. "If all this is true, would I earn more than your scorn at last?"

She sighed, pulled her hands away, and sat back on her heels. "Why can't you understand that it's not you I scorn, but your behavior?" She bent her head, hesitated, then whispered, "I'd give several years of my life to have things different for us. The feelings you stir in me would be honorable were you not a nobleman, or I not a baker's granddaughter. But I can't change reality; I can only deal with it to the best of my ability. And in truth I would rather starve than whore. Even for you."

Restlessly he stood and paced the room. "Dammit, why do you persist in calling yourself that? I don't think of you as such." His eyes narrowed upon her. "If you think to shame me into offering you my name, it shan't work."

She scrambled to her feet. "Oh, I should have known an appeal to your heart is useless! Well, sir, no more will I tell you what's in mine!" She whirled to leave the room, but he caught her from behind.

"Have I ever asked for your heart?" he snarled into her ear. "Love! Hah! There is no such thing. You pride yourself on facing reality, but you'll not admit that love is an invention of poets and fools. One impulse above all rules England, and indeed, all the world: profit. You have a marketable commodity I wish to purchase. Let's not dress up lust as love, my dear, if you truly want honesty.''

Slowly she turned to face him, and his sneer faded at her expression. The look was a strange one for a penniless orphan to cast upon the richest earl in the world's greatest country. ''Only now do I realize how fortunate I've really been. I had a warm, loving childhood. But you—how lonely you must have been in your great manor house. It's true then. When your parents died in that carriage accident, you had no one to care for you but servants?''

Scornfully he looked down into her luminous eyes. ''Don't pity me. You can dismiss any gothic notions that I subsisted on crusts of bread and shivered in drafty attics. I had the best nannies, tutors, and barristers money could buy. By the time I attained majority, I was fully ready to take over my estates. I daresay my tenants would agree that I have been a conscientious master. A libertine you might think me, but I am probably a better landlord, guided as I am by profit, than are many of my peers who quibble at my way of life.''

''Isn't there aught you care about, truly? Some person whom you will grieve for when he dies?''

''I've friends aplenty, my little puritan. And Billy would die for me, and I him. We've been friends since he was a stable boy at my estate.''

''That's all? This is the legacy you will leave when you depart this earth—one man to grieve and orderly estates?''

''It's a weightier legacy than the one you've sought to leave—*virgo intactus*. A childless, friendless servant.''

She bit her lip at the painful truth of his words, but then she thought of the many possets she'd carried, children she'd taught, and lonely women she'd companioned, and her chin lifted. ''I was active in my father's parish, and would be so again, given the chance. Now, doubtless, the good women of my village would spit upon me.''

''Your complaints grow tedious. I'll not let you go, Kat. Virago though you are, I want you. And by God, before this day is out, you'll want me, too.'' He swung her up into his arms and carried her out of the salon. ''Billy, on no account abandon your post," he ordered as he carried her up the stairs. He kicked the door shut behind them. The sounds of enraged curses grew muffled, then gradually turned into moans.

Billy cocked his head and listened. When the rhythmic sound of a creaking bed frame came faintly through the door, he smiled wryly, tipped his hat over his forehead, and leaned back to doze. When Devon came down the stairs much later, Billy sat up and pushed his hat back.

His piercing gray eyes narrowed at the white look about his friend's mouth. "Do ye really think ye'll win the gel by forcin' her?"

"You know me better than that, Billy. I didn't need to force her." Devon sat down on the bottom stair and propped his elbows on his knees to stare moodily into space.

"Fer a man who's known as many women as ye have, ye understand 'em little. At least not good women. To one such as her, makin' her enjoy agin' her will is a type o' forcin'. I heerd every word ye exchanged a bit ago, and this little gel ain't like yer others. She'll ne'er come to yer bed gladly as long as ye hold her agin' her will—"

Devon waved an impatient hand in the air to cut him off. "Women are the same whether they live in the gutter or Buckingham Palace. Feed their vanity promises of love and their greed with gifts and they'll spread their legs gladly."

"And what did the little gel do when ye give her them jewels?" Devon looked away from his piercing gaze. "Don't that tell ye somethin'?"

"Yes, that her price is the lies I won't give. But she'll come 'round eventually. She's a very sensual woman. I've only to make her admit it." Looking determined, Devon stood and went into the salon, slamming the door behind him.

In the hallway Billy frowned after his friend. He'd seen Demon Devon in the worst and best of circumstances: cool and controlled on the dueling field, explosively furious when trouncing a cheating bailiff. But he'd never seen Devon so single-minded in pursuit of a woman. Usually he treated women like a banquet. When he was hungry, he gorged himself. When he was sated, he ignored them.

True, the little blond wench hadn't been here long, but Billy, too, remembered Katrina. Devon had never desired any woman so long or been reduced to kidnapping. Winning her hadn't satisfied him, nor was it like to. Whether he knew it or not, Devon wanted more than the girl's body.

Billy was the only person in the world who knew how vulnerable Devon really was. He'd been the one to hold the seven-year-old boy, himself only eleven at the time, when Devon's parents had died. He'd watched the vibrant, loving little boy grieve himself into a stupor. When Devon recalled himself to the world, he'd changed. The well-meaning servants had not encroached on the barriers that grew higher by the day. Instead, they'd treated the little lord with the respect they believed he deserved and instilled in him the same feudal pride engrained in them and their parents before them.

But compassion, mercy, kindness are qualities only a loving heart can teach, Billy reflected. He'd done his best, but Devon had needed a feminine hand. The few women servants bold enough to try to get close to Devon were gently but firmly rebuffed by the little boy who'd decided that self-sufficiency was a good thing, after all. And the beliefs his old nanny had instilled in him were the legacy of her own generation, not theirs.

By the time Devon graduated from Oxford, he'd fallen in with a wild crowd. Women were fair game to the young rakes who had no intention of setting up their nursery before age thirty. And the type of women attracted to such men perpetuated their poor opinion of the "gentler" sex.

Thus, now that Devon had met a woman truly worthy of the name, he did not know how to react. And Billy understood, if Devon did not, how susceptible is an untouched heart. Other than himself, Devon had loved no one since his parents died. If he should grow to care for this headstrong, moral girl, then heaven help them all. . . . Bowing his head, Billy prayed.

Chapter Three

UPSTAIRS, KATRINA DRIFTED awake. She opened her eyes to the indented pillow next to her; she smelled the evocative scent wafting from the sheets. A few tears trickled out, but she forced herself to face the cold truth: Every value inculcated in her was violated when she shared this bed with Devon, but still she responded to him. Was she really so weak that her body could overpower the mind she prided herself upon? Or was Demon Devon a man she . . . cared for too much to resist?

Katrina shook her head in denial. Her whispered ''No!'' reverberated like a warning bell in her head. She leaped out of bed. Whatever the reason, she must concentrate all her energies on one end—escape. As long as he held her, she'd be susceptible to him. Each time it grew more difficult to lie still and pretend indifference. Soon, she feared, she'd not only respond to those devastating caresses, she'd initiate some of her own in the best harlot fashion. If she took the jewels, she should be able to sell them for enough to get far away from London, where he could never find her. Her mouth curled. As if he would look beyond a fortnight, anyway.

Deciding to air out the room, she went to the window and opened it. She stood for a moment, enjoying the breeze on her overheated body. She sent a regretful look at the sheer drop. Devon had known better than to give her a room with a balcony.

She searched for her bags, but found only the boxed gowns he'd purchased for her. Even his own clothes were gone. She scanned the room again, then snapped her fingers. Of course. The armoire. Perhaps the maid had put her things away.

She looked in the bottom drawers, but found only the jewels he'd given her and scandalously sheer night attire and chemises. She slammed the drawers shut and opened the full-length door on the left. The day was overcast and she was too short to see the top shelf, but she thought she spied some neatly folded clothes. She stepped inside the armoire onto the bottom of the cavity and reached up, standing on her toes. The door quivered as a gust of wind caught it. With a well-oiled swish and a bang the portal slammed shut behind her.

Darkness shrouded her. Her heart leaped in her chest, but she swallowed and fumbled for an inside latch. When she found none, terror engulfed her. She kicked at the door until her bare toes were bruised. Still the heavy wood held firm. Her heart was pounding so hard she could scarcely breathe, so her first scream was weak.

She banged her fists against the iron maiden gripping her and screamed louder. For an eternity she yelled for help, but no footsteps approached. In the last dimly rational part of her brain she remembered the outer chamber door was closed. No one would ever hear her through both portals. She sank to the floor of the compartment, curled her arms over her head, and wept.

When, thirty minutes later, steps approached, she didn't stir. They came to an abrupt stop. A masculine curse sounded, then came the whoosh of curtains being pushed back, and the rustle of lifting bedcovers. Finally the steps came to the armoire. The door was wrenched open.

Devon gasped. "Kat, my dear, are you all right?" He bent and pulled her out of the armoire. She was so stiff that she stayed curled in a ball and he had to half drag, half carry her, to the bed. Her eyes were rolled back in her head, and she didn't respond to his frantic questions.

After covering her, he poured water on a small cloth and washed her scraped hands. He inspected her fingers, then, looking grim, he fetched a small knife from his shaving kit and trimmed her broken nails so she wouldn't scratch herself. He treated her hands with a soothing salve. When she still didn't move or respond to his questions, he flung off his shoes and climbed into bed to comfort her.

He wrapped her in the down-filled quilt, propped his back against the bedstead, and pulled her onto his lap. "Kat, please, tell me what's wrong." He cleared his hoarse throat. "What happened?'' He rained gentle kisses on her white face. He drew back at the taste of salty tears, his strong features unwontedly soft. Her stiffness gradually relaxed in his arms, but then she began to tremble so hard her teeth chattered.

He said, ''It's all right. You don't have to be afraid now. I'm here. You're safe.'' He rocked her back and forth and made soothing noises.

Slowly his comforting solidness and steady heartbeat eased her catatonia. She wrapped her arms so tightly about Devon's neck that he coughed. If the archangel Gabriel had himself warned her off at that moment, she would not have heeded him. This man had twice saved her from ugly ends. It was as natural to take comfort from him now as it was to respond to his kisses.

She began to talk, haltingly at first, then louder. Her face was buried in his chest, so she couldn't see the arrested expression in his eyes as he listened. ''It . . . happened when I was seven. We played in . . . an old deserted monastery. I thought I'd found such a clever place to hide. It was a crypt so ancient that the walls were disintegrating. But I didn't consider the dangers as I climbed inside the end of a sarcophagus where the statue on the outside had broken away. I . . . suppose even my slight weight was enough, for I was no sooner inside than the outside cornice crumbled. I was there for almost an hour before my father found me.''

The trembling that had abated started again. ''The coffin was still sealed, but it smelled so . . . old. I'll never, ever, forget that scent. I . . . imagined I heard bones rattling as the skeleton arose to berate me for disturbing his rest.'' She rubbed her goose-pimpled arms as if that stench still clung to her. She slumped against him, the last of her terror spent in the confession.

Devon stroked her hair for a few more minutes. Something odd happened then. When she tilted her head back for his mouth, he merely brushed her lips lightly with his, then set her away. He evaded her reaching arms and turned to the door. ''I'll fetch you some tea,'' he muttered, walking out.

Katrina stared at the closed door. Why hadn't he rung for Martha? Had he continued to hold her, she would have gladly participated in whatever he desired, for her barriers had been smashed by his kindness. The fact that he'd rejected her when she'd finally been eager for him both puzzled and hurt. Would she never understand him?

By the time he returned holding a tray, she'd composed herself. She met his uncertain smile calmly. "Thank you," she said, nodding, when he set the tray down beside the bed. While she sipped the tea he'd fixed her he left the room and returned shortly—carrying her valises. He set them down next to the door.

He sprawled in the chair beside the bed and accepted the cup she handed him. When she sent a grateful look at the cases and said quietly, "Thank you," he nodded.

They drank in silence, but she caught his surreptitious glances. He peered at her as if he'd never seen a woman before. If she tried to hold his eyes, he looked away. His behavior was peculiar, for it had always been *she* who'd not been able to sustain *his* arrogant gaze. How could her tale of woe change him so drastically? she wondered. Or did she imagine a concern lacking before?

The suspicion was borne out by his behavior from then on. That night, and for two nights after, he did not initiate relations with her. Though she could feel him growing hard against her leg, he merely held her in his arms until she drifted off to sleep. On the third night he finally turned to her like a starving man, but his lovemaking had subtly changed.

Where before he'd demanded, now he asked. Where before he'd taken, now he gave. And that tenderness was far harder to resist than his selfish, wicked skill, but somehow she managed. His gentle loving sent pleasure such as she'd never known coursing through every pore of her body, but even at its height she didn't return his caresses. Only the conviction that she could never be happy as his mistress strengthened her against the enchantment of those long, lazy nights.

His wooing during the day was almost as devastating. He made her laugh, he made her cry, he made her angry, he made her glad. One occasion was especially memorable. They were relaxing before the hearth during a rainstorm, she on the settee, he on the rug before the fire with his back against her legs. He suddenly sat upright, turned, and clasped his arms about her knees.

"How would you like to walk in the rain?"

She looked at him as if he had maggots in his head. "The Earl of Brookstone surely has more dignity than that," she teased.

He quirked an eyebrow at her. "Now who's toplofty?" He stood, took her hands, and hauled her to her feet. "Come along, my lady. You should look forward to seeing me at a disadvantage."

"How so?" she asked, but she followed when he led her to the door. Billy grinned at them as they passed his post, but turned his head discreetly when their banter became suggestive.

"You can hide your *feelings* much better." Devon glanced down at the front of his breeches.

She blushed, but threw back, "And shame on you if you've aught to hide. Twice already today—"

"Ah Kat, as long as you supply such quality, I'll want quantity. In truth you make me feel like a lad sowing his first wild oats." There was that kindling warmth in his eyes again, but something else, too. Something that touched her heart as well as her body.

She looked away from that compelling stare and collected her scattered wits. "Lad indeed! There must be many a field in every corner of England stripped bare from the 'sowing' you've done."

Throwing back his tawny head, he roared with laughter. Then, removing his heavy coat and tossing it over the banister, he took her hand and said between chuckles, "Your wit is rapier sharp, but you've mixed your analogy a bit. One sows oats, not reaps them." When she tossed her head, he leaned down and nuzzled under her ear. "Shall I show you yet again the difference?"

She shivered. When his arms snaked about her waist, she slipped from his grasp, flung open the door, and leaped down the steps. "First one to the park gets to decide what we have for dinner!" She raced off, her feet flying so fast that her hair escaped its pins and streamed down her back. She lifted her face to the rain and laughed, feeling carefree for the first time in years.

Devon loped alongside her, his hair, too, becoming a ragtail mess. She grimaced at him, realizing that he was matching his strides to hers and could outpace her when he pleased. Her eyes narrowed on the park gates, barely twenty feet away. She glimpsed a leashed pug huffing out of the entrance. Deliberately, she turned her head and gave Devon the smile he claimed always drove him wild.

His eyes dropped to her lips and watched as she licked the rain away, so he didn't see the pug that veered into his path. A rotund little woman hurried along behind the dog in apparent eagerness to escape the rain.

Katrina leaped over the leash that would have tripped her; it caught Devon neatly around his ankles. He sprawled across the soft turf, jerking the leash from the woman's hands. The pug, with a triumphant yip, trotted off to his first taste of freedom.

The middle-aged woman screeched, "Come back, Pip!" When the little dog ignored her and began sniffing at the curb, the woman removed her drooping hat and slapped Devon on the shoulder with it when he tried to rise.

"You clumsy oaf! Why, it's a sorry day when a lady cannot even walk her dog in the park." She went on in an aggrieved tone, periodically tapping Devon with her hat to emphasize her words.

Devon was wet to the skin, his hair straggling down his shoulders, his stockings muddy, and Katrina wasn't surprised that the woman mistook him for a lackey. She covered her mouth to stifle her giggles when he sent her a fulminating glare.

"Forgive me, madam," he said, standing to take her hand and kiss it.

The woman's whine wheezed to a stop. She blinked down at his wet gold head, then batted her short lashes at him when he straightened.

Almost choking on her laughter, Katrina trotted down the street, stepped on the dog's leash, then led the panting little animal back to its owner. "Here you are, ma'am. I, er, tripped his lordship, so it's my fault. I apologize for the inconvenience."

At Katrina's reference to Devon's title the woman's tight mouth gaped into an *O* of surprise. She limply took the leash Katrina offered.

She looked so dazed that she didn't even notice the young man who stopped his carriage until he leaped out to call,

"Come, Mama, we'll be late!" He skidded to a stop when he saw Katrina. His eyes widened, then gave her a heated appraisal.

"Well, hel—lo," he said, doffing his hat.

"And good day," Devon snapped, nodding curtly to them both and taking Katrina's arm to usher her away.

When they were out of earshot, Katrina said, "But I thought you wanted to walk in the park?"

"That thin material is clinging to you like . . . like . . ."

"Like a wet dress? What did you think would happen when you brought me into the rain?" She irritably swiped back a sodden curl from her face.

"I have trouble thinking at all when I'm around you," he groused, then snapped his teeth closed as if regretting the admission. Their eyes met for a long moment. Was that uncertainty she read there in this wealthy lord's gaze? Before she could decide, he removed his heavy waistcoat, stopped, and draped it about her shoulders.

"There, you're decent."

She winced, her pleasure in his company spoiled at the unpleasant reminder. "No, I'm not. Not any longer." She pulled away, but he caught her from behind and sheltered her under his arm.

"Yes, you are," he insisted. "This guilt of yours is silly." He hesitated, then murmured, "I've thought a great deal about you of late. I've come to the conclusion that God was feeling beneficent when he created you. Once your heart was fashioned so true, what could he do but match it with mind and body?"

Katrina's eyes stung with tears. The stifling guilt that was never far away began to lift again at his words. Usually men saw only her body. She'd not thought Devon any different. She glanced up at him, but his head was turned as he looked before leading her across the street.

As soon as they reached the house, he briskly dried her off with the linen square Martha brought, then escorted her up the stairs. "Change so we can order dinner. I'm starved." He disappeared into another chamber.

Katrina was left wondering then, as she changed, if he'd meant the compliment, or if his words had been an empty attempt to win her contentment. As usual she found no easy answers. Her only consolation was that Devon understood her no better.

When she arrived downstairs, Billy nodded from his place beside the door. Katrina began to walk past him to wait in the salon, but she hesitated. If anyone could help her understand Devon, surely Billy could. She glanced up the stairs, but heard no movement.

"Billy," she said in a rush, "tell me why Devon has such a poor opinion of women."

Billy tilted his head back against the wall and eyed her thoughtfully. "Ye should ask such a question of him, not me."

"I know, but . . . emotion always gets in the way of our personal discussions." She blushed under his thoughtful look.

"Ye might ask yerself why that be, as a start." Evidently taking pity on her, Billy rose and escorted her into the salon. When she was comfortable on the settee, he sat down across from her, propped an ankle on his opposite knee, and began, "Devvie is a fine lad, with one o' the strongest senses o' loyalty I've e'er seen. Why, he still supports his old nanny in a style that's the talk o' the village. When he's at his estate, he goes to see her once a week for tea despite the fact that she drives him loony. She's deaf, and the poor old dear never did have a peck o' sense. Devon would probably be a different man today if she'd been a stronger woman. She had more o' his raisin' than anyone else, ye see, after his parents died."

No, she didn't see, but she looked at Billy attentively.

He sighed. "I can't draw ye a picture, lass. Devon would not be happy to know I'm talkin' to ye." He began to rise, but she leaned over and caught his arm.

Her voice shook, and her eyes sparkled with unashamed tears. "Please tell me, Billy. If not for my sake, then for his. For I can't stay with him as things are between us." After another penetrating look, Billy relaxed back in his seat. Katrina's arm dropped.

"Very well, lass, but ye may not like what ye learn. His nanny were an old-fashioned woman who believed the gentry had special rights. After Devon kissed his first gal, an upstairs maid, I was teasin' him about it when his nanny come upon us. I still remember what she told him. 'She's a fine girl to teach ye the way o' life, me lad. But just remember, there's only two kinds o' women in this world: them of good blood ye marry and them of common stock ye don't.' I was a few years older, and I admit I knew the maid were a pleasin' armful, so I didn't quibble with her then. Since I've grown in the ways o' the world, I've learned different. But Devon has never forgotten her words. He's reminded me o' them more than once. 'Twas not the first o' many such talks she give him o'er the years.''

Katrina shifted impatiently. "I can understand why an impressionable boy would believe such rubbish, but a mature man should know better. This is the modern age, and feudalism, thank God, died long ago.''

"Ye don't understand. It's not that Devon thinks he's better than ye and me; he just thinks he's different. His estates and title give him more power, aye—but also more responsibility. And he takes that responsibility very seriously.'' When she still looked unconvinced, Billy said dryly, "Besides, the women Devon has known in maturity have been no different to that first maid. In a word, me gal, they was grasping bawds, one and all. Can ye blame him for believin' his old nanny were right?''

When she reluctantly shook her head, his tone softened, "And that, me dear, is why he don't understand ye even a little bit. He's ne'er known a good woman. Every gal he's ever fancied has been his for the askin'—for a price. Until you.''

A flush of pleasure warmed Katrina. "Thank you. I only wish Devon understood that as well as you.''

"Ye must give him time, lassie. But I can tell ye this: He's ne'er waited three years for a woman before. Nor went to such trouble to win her. Certainly he's never kidnapped a wench before. That should tell ye a bit o' how much he wants ye.''

"Thank you, Billy.'' Katrina twisted at the tie on her dress, but she had to know. She lifted her head to look him straight in the eye. "Billy, if he came to love me, do you think he would ever wed me?''

After a long pause Billy said quietly, "I'd answer ye true, if I could, but I honestly don't know. Ye see, even when Devon's parents was alive, they learned him on his heritage before he could walk. And all the old earl's servants knew how important his lineage were to him, so, when he passed on, they saw to it that it were important to his heir, too. Devon's naturally a man o' strong feelin', and when his parents was lost, he turned all that passion toward makin' them proud o' their heir. I've ne'er known a man with better-attended estates, or happier tenants.''

Katrina was unable to speak for the lump in her throat, so she only nodded. Billy's words confirmed her deepest fears. As she'd known from the beginning, they had no future together. Oh God, what was she doing here? She leaped to her feet, but Billy raised a hand.

''Whoa, lassie!'' When she paused, he finished gently, ''I cannot say whether Devon would ever wed ye, but this I know: When Devon loves, he does so like few others. He would die for me, and did, once, take a bullet meant for me.'' When she looked startled and opened her mouth, he waved her to silence. ''But he would be angry if I told ye the tale. Just try to remember that, whether he shows it or not, he's hungry for love. He just don't know it yet. The woman who wins his stubborn heart will be lucky indeed. In wedlock, or out o' it.''

Katrina choked out, ''Th-thank you,'' and fled up to her room. The tears fell in a cloudburst and were as quickly over. What choice did she have, now, but to try to win that stubborn heart? Conscience and practicality could not quiet the hope that she and Devon were meant for one another. So she bathed her eyes with a cool cloth, pinned on a smile, and went downstairs.

In the following days Katrina's hope burned brighter. Devon seemed to genuinely enjoy her company. He laughed at her wit, and teased her out of her sullens. Whatever his feelings for her, somehow he always plumbed her deepest emotions, making the world a vital place she looked forward to each morning. They shared their thoughts on mundane things: their favorite flowers, colors, and foods. They shared their feelings on exalted things: their opinions on politics, religion, and Greek philosophy. And slowly, their topsy-turvy relationship began to right itself as physical enjoyment became enhanced by mental respect.

At her urging, a few days later, he taught her to play chess. Her brightness was abetted by intuition, and she soon became a formidable opponent. Within a week they were stalemated, or they usually played to a tie.

One night, after a delicious dinner of salmon in croûte,

spring peas, carrots, and strawberry tarts, they decided to play a game of chess. Devon had teased Katrina of late by wagering small items on their games—his kerchief, her garter. Tonight, to judge by the glint in his eye, he had something more valuable in mind. Or, she thought to herself with a hidden smile, more scandalous. Why, she wondered, torn between pleasure and despair, was a vicar's daughter so drawn to this libertine?

Whatever the answer, she found herself, yet again, subduing her conscience. She couldn't leave him yet. This velvet night was not meant for thinking; it was meant for feeling. Thus, when he seated her and took his chair, his serious mien spoiled by a wicked twinkle, she lowered her gaze to the chessboard to hide her own mischief.

He'd set out all the pieces—he, black, she, white—as usual. "Appropriate, I agree, that I take the black," he said, beating her to what had become their standard jest. "So I shall live up to my reputation and suggest stakes, er, higher than usual."

Katrina had a suspicion as to what he'd name, but she looked innocent. "Yes?"

"Shall we say, one item of clothing for every piece lost?" He studied his fingernails as if he'd suggested a standard wager.

"Are you not at a disadvantage, sir?"

He cocked his head. "How so?"

"You've fewer garments to lose."

"Then you've nothing to worry about, have you?"

"Very well," Katrina agreed after an appropriate hesitation. "On the condition that whoever loses gets to name the evening's entertainment."

His slow, wicked smile made her toes curl inside her slippers. "Agreed, my pretty."

They began. Katrina made her first few moves deliberately clumsy, and she soon lost a pawn and a knight. She took off one garter, then the other. When she came out with her queen a move later, Devon sent her a curious look, but didn't comment.

He'd taught her in their very first match that the best chess players tended to use the queen later in the game so as not to endanger her early on. What he did not know, however, was that she'd read one of his books on chess and had devised a daring strategy.

An hour later Devon was sitting in his shirt sleeves, shoes and socks off, and she was wearing her petticoats, and no stockings. He was hot in pursuit of her deliberately exposed queen and was only one move away from taking it when she made her maneuver.

She moved her insignificant little pawn, lifted her eyes, and smiled sweetly. "Checkmate."

His mouth dropped open. He studied the board, then ruefully shook his head. "I'll be damned." He leaned back to cross his arms over his chest. "You do have a way of sneaking up on a fellow. What's my forfeit?"

Katrina delicately patted a yawn. "I'm tired. The only entertainment I require is a good night's sleep."

Devon groaned, but he courteously assisted her in rising. "Very well, heartless victor, I shall toss and turn alone." His smile scalded her as she dressed again, but somehow she made it safely to her room. She wondered, as she took an age to sleep, if he, too, were tossing and turning.

And thus the long, lazy days blended into a time of understanding, a time of waiting, for each of them. Escape became something she'd put her mind to the next day, or the day after that. Whether stolen, whether immoral, this was the first taste of happiness she'd had since her father died, and she couldn't bear to end it yet.

She told herself Billy was too alert at his post beside the door, but in truth no prisoner had ever had a more indulgent jailer. He tipped his hat to her when she passed. His approving smile broadened with every laugh she and Devon shared. She could have easily skirted around him and escaped during one of his many naps, but she didn't. Devon occasionally left her alone while he saw to his business affairs, but even then she found occupation. Soon she'd leave, she reassured herself. Soon.

The crisis of their relationship came the day Devon took her driving in Hyde Park. She'd complained about not being out in the increasingly sunny days.

To which he replied, "And here I thought we were sun,

moon, and stars to one another.'' His eyes belied his teasing tone, but when she met that hungry look, he turned away.

She clenched her fists. Nothing had really changed between them. He was still an earl; she was still a baker's granddaughter. She didn't know why he'd said that, but she dared not read a false meaning only because she desperately wanted to believe it. ''For a man who denies love exists, that's a maudlin remark.'' She looked into the mirror and fussed with her neatly upswept hair. The next move was his.

He took it, coming up behind her to catch her shoulders in his hands. ''And what if I told you that I've much to learn in life?'' he whispered. ''And so, perhaps, have you?''

''Why, I'd say that you need sunlight even more than I to clear the cobwebs from your brain. Demon Devon is not a changeable man.'' She searched his mirrored features, longing for him to countermand her, but he stepped away.

''Very well, my dear, you'll have your sunlight.'' He exited, and she heard him ordering Peter to hook up his curricle.

Her steps dragging, she followed. If she'd expected a declaration, she hadn't gotten it. Though what had he been hinting at, then?

She sent puzzled glances at his pure profile as he drove. Was he really so sure of her to take her out in public? By the time they reached Hyde Park, had she contemplated crying for help, the looks she received would have disabused her of the notion. The sea captain's widow glared at her, then turned pointedly away. Three men riding prime bloods leered at her. Only when Devon narrowed menacing eyes upon them did they canter off.

Her pleasure in the spring flowers, warm, scented breeze, and soothing sunshine was spoiled. She drew her wide-brimmed hat lower over her face and looked down at her feet as, with a curse, Devon wheeled the curricle about and hurried them home.

Neither of them noticed the man following from a discreet distance. He rode a big, spirited bay rather stiffly, a bandage binding one shoulder.

Katrina didn't give Devon a chance to help her down. He'd hardly pulled the carriage to a halt before she climbed out. The business was tricky in her voluminous skirts, and the gray serge caught on a sharp edge. She yanked it free, uncaring that she ripped her last good dress, and ran for sanctuary inside the house she'd needed to escape shortly before.

A broken trail of sobs followed her up the stairs. At the commotion Billy rushed from the back of the house to see Devon burst into the foyer and vault up the stairs. He reached Katrina's door in time to have it slammed in his face. Billy watched him knock with a tentativeness that was far out of character. When no response came, Devon bent his head in hesitation. Then, as loud as a slap, came the sound of the bolt being shot home. Billy winced, resignation crossing his strong face.

Devon's head popped up. His curse was more a growl as he lifted his booted foot and kicked the door, once, twice. The crack of splitting wood coincided with Devon's furious shove. The door sagged on one hinge, giving him room enough to squeeze into the chamber. Shaking his head, Billy plopped down into the chair beside the door to listen.

Like a tigress at bay, fingers curled into claws, Katrina turned to meet Devon. "Touch me and you'll get your eyes scratched out," she hissed. Her cheeks were wet with tears, but her eyes blazed so hot that a lesser man might have felt singed.

Even Devon stopped warily—until he glanced from her to the bags behind her on the bed. When he looked at her again, the fury in his eyes matched her own. "Try to leave me before your bargain has ended and I'll chain you to this bed."

"I never should have bargained with the devil. But your spell lost its power the moment I looked into their eyes." She coughed to clear her thickening voice. "Legerdemain can't change wrong into right. You might have turned a vicar's daughter into a whore, but even a whore is too good for the devil." She turned her back on him and wadded a night rail on top of a crisp dress. She failed to see him whiten, but the deadly quietness of his voice made her fingers clench around a chemise.

"For a whore you've much to learn about pleasing men. We like to be touched, too, as you will soon discover." He grabbed for her, but she clambered over the bed. She ran to his dresser and snatched up his razor.

She whirled, clutching the ivory handle in a white-knuckled fist. "That's your answer for every argument. Why can you not understand that compatible though our bodies are, our hearts will always fight? We're opposites, you and I. We believe in different things."

He grunted his disagreement as he inched nearer. "We believe in the same things, as we have only recently discovered."

"Oh yes? Do you say your prayers nightly, as I do, only after I sleep?"

When he made an impatient gesture, she shook her head and mourned, "You have no understanding whatsoever, have you?"

"I'm not the heretic you think me, but my God doesn't condemn the natural feelings of men and women. He believes in celebrating life, not stifling it."

"That's the excuse every scoundrel uses to justify his sins. You might be able to rationalize your selfishness away, but I cannot. Fornication is wrong, Devon; it's that simple."

"Nothing in life worth having is ever simple, Kat. Least of all my feelings for you, or yours for me." He was only two steps away. He held out his hands. "Please, forget what happened today. You don't really care what they think, hypocrites that they are. They indulge in the same sin they condemn you for. Admit it, Kat. Only what we think, what we feel, matters."

The blade that had wavered in her hand rose up again. The glint in her eyes matched that glancing off the sunlit steel. "For once we agree. My feelings matter as much as yours. And I feel only disgust for each of us." When his hands dropped and he closed the gap between them, she backed away and warned, "Come closer and you'll never again touch me—or any woman."

His dark purpose brightened under the ruddy glow of his smile. "Do you mean to castrate me? Come, Kat, versed as well as you are in the arts and sciences, I doubt your father saw to *that* part of your education. Do you really know where to cut?" His smile never wavered as he came one step closer, then another, until he brushed against her.

She saw in his eyes that he didn't believe she'd harm him. And damn him, he was right. She'd just as soon cut off her own nose. . . . She looked over his shoulder into the mirror. She'd flung off her hat, and her thick blond hair had escaped its pins to flow about her shoulders. Her hectic flush and glittering eyes accentuated the looks she seldom thought about. Unlike most beautiful women she avoided rather than sought out mirrors. Her loveliness had brought her naught but plaguey difficulties. She stared at herself, her fingers trembling around the razor's handle.

Devon frowned at the odd look in her eyes and turned to see what fascinated her. His frown deepened as she slowly, as if compelled, raised the blade. Horrified comprehension twisted his face. He pried her fingers open, pulling the razor away before it could disfigure her perfect nose. He flung the blade across the room and caught her shoulders to give her a little shake.

"Are you mad? Do you hate yourself so? Or is it me you wish to punish?"

She gave a funny little hiccup, then began beating at his chest with her fists. Her words erupted in an hysterical burst. He took the physical and verbal barrage stoically. "I hate both of us. You for tangling me in this . . . unconscionable brangle and me for letting you. You have no right . . . I have no spine for letting you. All the beliefs I've held immovable all my life stand on naught but shifting sand. How could you . . . please, please, if you care for me, let me go. I"—her voice broke, but she forced the words out—"beg you."

Her eyes were blurred with tears. She blinked, doubtful of her own clarity of sight. How could any man who held her in even mild esteem be so indifferent to her heartfelt plea? But his face was closed, emotionless. Gently he pried her clutching fingers away and stood back.

"No, Kat. Call me selfish and immoral all you please, but I'll not let you go until I'm ready."

"And what will make you so?" she croaked.

"You're a clever woman. I'll let you divine that. But you know enough of me to realize that I find a clinging woman a bore." He strolled to the door, bending to pick up the razor on his way. "Think about it." He squeezed out the door, then propped it upright.

Katrina caught her elbows and rocked on her heels, so distraught she hardly realized what she was doing. She was basically an optimist and had always believed that no matter how bleak the night, dawn always came. But perhaps she'd been wrong about that, too. This time there was no way out. She was caught, a hare in a hole, and could only escape by letting the fox who had cornered her dine at his leisure.

But the man who paused on the other side of the door to wipe his brow with a shaky hand had no clever, satisfied air. He stumbled down the steps, refusing to meet Billy's searching eyes. He mumbled, "Send Martha to fetch a carpenter to fix the door. See I'm not disturbed, and have Martha take Miss Lawson's supper to her on a tray. After you fetch Martha, on no account leave your post." Devon entered the salon and closed the door behind him.

Billy didn't have to witness the deed to know that Devon went directly to the brandy. "Ah, Devvie lad," Billy muttered to himself. "Ye ain't so different to us common folk. Wantin' what ye cain't have is a bit o' hell, ain't it? When will ye see that only by lettin' the lassie go can ye hold her?" Sighing, he rose to obey Devon's orders.

That night was the longest either Katrina or Devon had ever spent. For the second time since he'd taken her, they slept apart. Rather, they tossed and turned apart, for neither of them slept. When next they met on the following morning, outwardly both were composed. Devon politely seated Katrina on the settee and accepted the tea she poured for him.

Only after they'd both eaten did he broach the subject paramount in their thoughts. "I've thought over your words, Katrina. I'd not have you unhappy because of me. To the contrary, I want to make you happy."

"Then let me go." She took a composed sip of tea, but her china cup rattled against its delicate saucer when she sat it down.

He gritted his teeth and went on calmly, "I'm not the profligate you think me. Honor, too, is important to me. I've yet to break a promise. I said I'd let you go at the end of this month, and so I shall." When her eyes flashed up from her cup, he added, "Providing, that is, that you give me these last three days to change your mind. If you attempt to leave before then, I'll consider our bargain abrogated. If, at the end of that time, you don't gladly accept and *request* my touch, then I'll have my coachman take you wherever you like, with enough funds for you to survive for several years. Until you find your 'respectable' husband. If I can make you admit how much you want me, you stay. Agreed?''

Katrina searched his eyes, but he betrayed only civility as he held out his hand. She put down her cup and saucer and shook it. ''Agreed.''

He sat down beside her, patting her hand when she tensed. ''Relax. I'm not going to spring upon you. I thought we might read to one another.''

She eyed him suspiciously, but he only went to the small bookcase in the corner and fetched a thin red kidskin tome. When he sat back down, she crooked her neck to read the title. *The Sonnets of William Shakespeare.* She relaxed, truly relaxed, for the first time since yesterday. How thoughtful of him to remember her taste in literature. In truth books had been her only passion since her father died. When she'd had time for them, that is. She rested her head against the lace-clad settee back and closed her eyes to listen to the rich words. Which one would he choose? she wondered as he leafed through the pages. She'd noticed that the heavy vellum had already been split. He, too, must read a lot. She wondered if he knew as much English poetry by heart as she did.

But when he began to read, his deep, mellow voice did not soothe her. Every muscle tensed; her heartbeat quickened. Of all the bard's sonnets, why did he have to select *this* one? Her eyes stayed tightly shut as Shakespeare's Sonnet 116 was recited by the one man she longed to hear say these words. And mean them . . .

> *Love is not love*
> *Which alters when it alteration finds.*
> *Or bends with the remover to remove:*
> *O no! it is an ever-fixed mark,*
> *That looks on tempests and is never shaken;*
> *It is the star to every wandering bark,*
> *Whose worth's unknown, although his height be taken.*
> *Love's not Time's fool, though rosy lips and cheeks*
> *Within his bending sickle's compass come;*
> *Love alters not with his brief hours and weeks,*

But bears it out even to the edge of doom.
If this be error, and upon me proved,
I never writ, nor no man ever loved.

His voice grew husky on the last words. After he closed the book and set it down, silence prevailed in the salon. Two children rolling a ball in the yard down the street squealed. A flock of pigeons landed on the black balcony outside, flapping and strutting. Katrina heard only her beating heart.

She wanted, as she'd never wanted anything, to believe him. Yet how could he have changed so in these few weeks? This was the same man who'd stood in this room and told her love was an invention of poets and fools. How could a man who loved her hold her prisoner? Most telling, a man who loved her would offer his hand as well as his heart, no matter the difference in their births. When he gently tugged her sideways to face him, she opened her eyes to search his features.

Yes, there was a new softness in those amber eyes resting so tenderly upon her. But there was a calculation, too, and a hunger. The same hunger she'd left wanting three years ago when he'd asked her to be his mistress. She knew that she was here today because of the past, not the present. He'd not want her now, if she'd succumbed to him then. The apple ever out of reach was always shiniest, and Demon Devon was used to getting what he wanted.

A sad little smile curved her lips. They were not so different, after all. The unattainable had become her heart's desire, too. For, search his features though she did, she saw no sign of the only love she wanted. An unalterable love, a generous love. Love based on carnality was as fleeting as . . . The words came unbidden to her lips, and they dashed the hopeful light in his eyes.

"'Love built on beauty, soon as beauty, dies.' Donne."

This time it was he who stared. She saw denial trembling on his lips, and because she couldn't bear to hear him lie, she forestalled him. "Please, Devon, be honest. If I were cross-eyed, knock-kneed, and horse-faced, you'd not want me for an instant."

"I almost wish you were cross-eyed, knock-kneed, and horse-faced. Then you'd come into my arms gladly."

"How so?"

"You'd be *so* grateful," he tossed at her with a grin. When she shook her head at him wearily, like a teacher chastising the class clown, his face grew serious.

"I, too, love poetry, Kat. What do you think of Pope's 'Charms strike the sight, but merit wins the soul'?"

She rejoined dryly, "If you admired my mind and my morals, you'd take me to church instead of bed." When he shrugged carelessly, as if the point were both moot and picayune, an edge sharpened her tone. "Myself, I agree with Milton: 'Most men admire virtue who follow not her lore.'"

He feigned grabbing at a stab to his heart, but pure mischief twinkled in his eyes. "Again, I refer to a master more eloquent than I, albeit rather cynical about women. As Pope said, 'Men, some to business, some to pleasure, take; but every woman is at heart a rake.'" When she smiled reluctantly at his neat leveler, he brushed her chin with a gentle fist. "Come, little moralizer, as Spenser said, 'Be bold, be bold, and everywhere be bold.'"

"He also said, 'Be not too bold.' Advice we'd both do well to follow." She tried to rise, but he, laughing, plopped her into his lap.

"'All for love, and nothing for reward.' Spenser must have had you in mind when he wrote it, my faerie queene." His merry light grew dim and solemn as he crushed her in his arms. "But reward me you yet will, in these three days, and, God willing, for many more."

She wondered despairingly how he could invoke the name of God in such a lawless quest, but, as usual, he had the last word, for he consumed her protest with his lips. And, as usual, her clearheadedness didn't stand before the tidal wave of his passion. By the time he carried her up the stairs, she was beyond a witty rejoinder; beyond wit, forsooth.

He was patient, he was gentle, he was man embodied. And what he did to her body was as scandalous as it was pleasurable. However, even in the midst of the greatest intimacy women can know, she held some of herself apart. Pride and self-respect dwelt in a lonely aerie, perhaps, but their fastness kept conscience and virtue safe—as long as she did not give him those ruinous passwords of desire.

Though he wooed her in bed and out during those last days,

she triumphed. On the last evening of April she awaited him in her chamber. He'd been grim all day and had not taken her yet, but she knew he'd soon avail himself of a convenience he'd shortly be without. She stood staring out the window at the sickle moon, ruminating on what had preceded its passing. In a few hours the clock would strike on a new day. She'd all but won, yet she felt only sadness. She'd never been able to forget Devon Alexander Tyrone Cavanaugh when he was only a man who'd pursued her. Now he was her first lover, aye, likely her last lover. He could be even more. . . .

Her hands crept to her stomach. Her eyes closed. She fell to her knees and prayed yet again, though intuition warned it was too late. Faith, even one as strong as hers, could not uproot the seed that had been firmly planted, probably within a few days of her arrival. She was overdue now by over three weeks. In the last few days she'd awakened nauseated. But when Martha brought the tray of tea and rolls, her stomach had settled before she'd embarrassed herself—or aroused Devon's suspicions.

If she did carry a babe, then escape was all the more imperative. She'd asked him once, during one of their arguments, if he'd sired any children.

He'd stiffened. "No! I've always taken . . . precautions. I want no by-blows with my face. The only children I intend to sire will bear my name." When she'd looked at him in mute disgust, he'd tapped her cheek with a finger. "You needn't worry about bearing my bastards, my dear. It's unlikely you've taken my seed in this brief time. . . ." His voice faltered, then grew firm again as if he'd reassured himself, too. "And if you stay with me, I'll take the same precautions. I'm certain you don't want a child any more than I."

Those words echoed tormentingly now in the bleak emptiness of her heart. Bastard. By-blow. The only issue he could get on her because her blood was not blue enough. If only . . . Tears bedewed her eyes, but she swiped them away. Self-pity served no purpose. Leaving was the only alternative, aye, the best one. She'd seen in her father's village how isolated the illegitimate children were. She'd not wish that fate, and an unloving father, upon an innocent babe. Far better to get away from London and concoct a story of widowhood. She'd have to remember to buy a ring. Though she'd earned every penny, she hated to accept his tainted money. However, now she couldn't afford the luxury of flinging every shilling in his arrogant face. She had more than herself to think of.

While she stood in anguished thought above, below Devon stared unseeingly into the salon's cold grate. It was getting late. He'd best hie upstairs and take advantage of this last night, for it would be all he'd have of her. Damn her. Damn her willful, stupid pride. For pride alone stood between them. Hers. And his. He was honest enough to admit that.

The price of her submission was a few words muttered in a hushed sanctum, but it was dear indeed. Pride in his heritage had sustained him through too many lonely years for him to forsake it now. He wanted the best for his heirs. While Katrina herself was both lovely and intelligent, who knew what tainted blood she unknowingly carried from her distaff side? He'd be sickened to see the longevity of his name furthered by a crude lout. He'd seen exactly that fate happen to a friend of his who'd let passion sway him into wedding a tailor's daughter. The poor fellow kept his sons hidden at his country seat, but all the ton knew of their common manners and dull intellects. No, wed her he could not. He owed too much to the memory of his parents and the legacy they'd left him. And stay with him any other way she apparently would not. Impasse.

He'd used every wile he knew on Katrina, yet though she responded to him reluctantly, she never gladly reciprocated. He poured himself another brandy, then stared in disgust as his hand jittered decanter against crystal. He set the bottle down with a bang and threw the glass into the fireplace. It shattered with a satisfying clatter, but his frustration only grew. He bent from the waist to clasp his head in his hands.

Why did this one woman keep him enthralled? His affairs usually lasted only a few weeks; he'd never been obsessed with any woman as he was with Katrina. Fusing with that beautiful body had not satisfied him. If anything, he was hungrier for her now that he knew how very different the act was with her.

From the beginning she'd been special to him, but the real change in his feelings had come when he found her caught in the armoire. For the first—and only—time since coming here, she'd needed him. And seeing her vulnerable, afraid, had pained him so that he could no longer deny that he wanted more than her favors. From that time on he'd been as curious about her mind as he was about her body. And he'd discovered, dismayingly, that Katrina would have attracted him had she been as plain as a post.

What a coil she'd put him in. Finally he'd met a woman he wanted for more than a few days, and she was the first woman he'd been unable to tempt. Still, she had two more surprises awaiting her in reward for this night. A night he still longed to be special for them, whether it would be a new beginning or a sad end. And if he could at last defeat that stubborn will, what then? Would he tire of her, too? He stared at his feet, searching his own feelings as never before. "No," he said softly to himself.

He might be confused about much, but one thing he knew: It would be many a moon before he tired of her. Only *she* made him forget everything. He'd not once, in all their couplings, had presence of mind enough to withdraw before he spent himself. He shied away from exploring the ramifications of that. He knew, as none better, that she had not begun her menses since coming here. Still, she was probably one of those women who were inconsistent. Perhaps being a virgin had something to do with it. Nevertheless, if by some miracle he was able to win the words he sought tonight, then he'd have to discipline himself.

He'd not missed the intimacy of blending his essence with his other mistresses. But, with Katrina, he wanted to brand her, fill her with himself until her very identify melded with his. Dread the answer though he did, he asked himself the logical question: Why were his feelings for her so powerful? Could it be that he truly loved her?

He swallowed convulsively. His nails dug into his hair. Why had he selected that particular sonnet to read? He'd intended to choose at random, yet some instinct had led him to one of the sweetest love poems ever written.

He forced his aching back upright and rested his elbows on his knees. This . . . roundaboutation only clouded his already muzzy brain. It didn't matter whether he'd tested her, or his own confused feelings; they'd both failed miserably, in any case. She believed his obsession was sexual. She was probably right. It was better that way, he told himself. Agitated, he leaped up and turned to the door. His eye lit on the brandy decanter.

He grabbed the exquisite crystal vessel. One last night he had to keep her. If he could break that stubborn pride, then he'd have time to solve the mysteries she posed him. He had a final sensual trick to try. An aging whore had used it on him once, and he still remembered her fondly despite her sagging breasts and wrinkled face. That had been the most sexually enjoyable night of his life. Until Katrina. Maybe she'd be affected similarly. Even if she didn't reciprocate, he'd wager she'd never forget this night. Or him.

His movements brisk, his mind clear with resolve, he strode upstairs. He banged the door open. She started and turned from the window to face him. She was attired in her petticoats and chemise. Not once had he been able to coax her into wearing the expensive garments he'd purchased for her.

He kicked the door shut with his boot. "Good evening, my lovely."

She eyed him warily, looking from the decanter to his flushed face.

"I'm not drunk. But you soon will be. On the wine of passion." He approached her, the brandy decanter in one hand.

She backed off, her eyes wide, unbelieving. "No, Devon, please. I hate the vile stuff."

His lips quirked in a semblance of a smile. "You don't understand, my dear. 'Tis not your interior it will warm. . . ."

She cocked her head in confusion.

Her innocence despite the many times he'd taken her both pleased and angered him. Her charms were boundless, ageless. Doubtless she'd wear just that look when a doddering old man of eighty made advances to her spry seventy-three. The vision of that old man bore a strong resemblance to himself, and he banished the disturbing picture in the only way he knew. With action. Action he should have taken long ere now.

He set the decanter down on the table next to the settee, then bent to kindle a fire in the grate. Sensing her movement, he said casually over his shoulder, "Don't. You'll only put me to the trouble of fetching you." When he had a goodly flame going, he dusted his hands against his breeches and stood, turning to face her.

She stood rooted in place, like a small but hardy tree determined to resist the wind's wiles. That obstinate look was on her face. Rather than deterring him, however, her determination set a like expression about his own mouth. Holding her eyes, he pushed the settee away from the fire, leaving a clear space on the thick Aubusson rug. He held out his hand.

She eyed it, then him, distrustfully. "It's over, Devon. Why don't you let me go now? And leave us some good memories—"

"This night will burn brightly in your mind until you're very, very old. Come, wench, to bed. I've one night left with you, and by the saints I'm going to enjoy every moment of it." When she stayed planted, he advanced on her. "Hold that disdainful expression till you might, my girl. It shan't last long."

She turned to run then, but too late. He caught her, quelling her struggles, and carried her to the rug. He followed her down with his long body. When she still writhed, he pulled her arms above her head. He dusted feather-light kisses on every feature of her face except her mouth. She turned her head from side to side, baring the vulnerable hollows of ears and neck. He explored them with lips and tongue. She shivered, but stubbornly kept up her resistance. Her will lasted only until he trailed those gentle kisses to her mouth. He brushed her lips from side to side, then pulled away to buss the tip of her nose.

So passed the long, patient minutes. He lavished attention on every inch of flesh from neck to hairline, but he only touched her mouth in passing. When her struggles waned, then ceased, he let her hands go. She brought them up as if to push him away, but with a garbled sound that might have been anger or gladness, she buried her fingers in his loosened hair and pulled his head down to hers.

The full, flaming warmth of their kiss owed nothing to the fire. They luxuriated in one another, mouth latched to mouth, lips slanting upon lips, as the heat slowly grew. The fire crackled and hissed, but they heard it not. Prometheus' gift was niggardly compared to Aphrodite's rich offering.

Devon was light-headed with the roaring blaze she incited in him, but he tamped it down, thus stoking her own slower fire. When she muttered impatiently against his lips and stroked him with her tongue, he teasingly refused to open. To his delight she caught his jaw in her hands and tilted his head sideways. He opened his mouth to the insistent thrust of her tongue. She delved into him, kissing him more deeply when he didn't answer her caress.

His hands clenched about her waist with the strain, but he stayed still. He was rewarded with her frustrated moan. She pulled away to glare at him, her eyes aglitter with passion. "For a man who wishes a woman to remember him, you're behaving deuced strange."

He quirked an innocent eyebrow. "Am I?"

Her eyes widened. As clearly as chalk against slate, he saw reason triumph over ardor. "No, perhaps not. Rather you're true to form." She eased away from him.

A smile playing about his lips, he caught her waist. "You've many sterling qualities, my love, but this one I admire most: your ability to think under fire. It shall be interesting to see how long you can persist." He set her upright and unlaced her petticoats.

She didn't move, even when he slipped both straps off her shoulders. He saw her nibble at her lip and felt her tension when he bent to kiss those strong but graceful shoulders. "Relax, Katrina mina. We've a bargain, and I don't intend to break it. Only a few more hours, then you're free."

She sighed, shoulders lifting beneath his lips. When he reached for her chemise, she didn't protest. As her garments slipped to her waist he drew back to look at her. Firelight played over her skin, tinging her with a rosy glow that was only partially due to warmth. He tenderly brushed his lips against her red cheeks as he lifted his hands to cup those full, blushing breasts. He trailed his nails ever so lightly around each globe, then tested his effect upon her. When hard nipples stabbed his palms, he sighed his pleasure and bent to bestow his praise with lips. Her breasts trembled beneath his mouth with her struggle against herself.

His own hand shook a bit when he reached for the decanter on the table an arm's length away. This silky mouthful warmed him far more than the now roaring fire. He glanced up at her. Her eyes were closed, her mouth lax and full with passion. But still her hands stayed clasped in her lap. Not this time, my love, he silently vowed. He unstoppered the brandy, dribbled some into his palm, set the decanter down, then warmed the drops in his hands and rubbed them along her arms and shoulders.

She gasped at the tingling warmth and jerked upright, her eyes snapping open to stare at his bent head. Warm lips followed the trail the brandy had blazed, tugging at her skin with suction and occasional nibbles. She blinked in shock. He saw her mouth open to protest and splashed more brandy against her already sensitive breasts. Protests segued into moans as he again bent his head. Never had brandy tasted sweeter, nor woman-flesh more arousing. Her pleasured sighs thrilled more than his body, however. Hope beat an exultant tempo at his temples. When she tugged weakly at his clothes, he decided to test her.

He eased her down, smiling at her protests as he left her, and hurried over to the cheval glass. He dragged it next to the rug, tilted it down, and pulled her onto his lap before it. He splashed more brandy onto her gleaming, trembling torso. As he licked up the glistening drops he whispered, "Look, my love. Into the mirror."

Her eyes flickered open. Her dilated pupils contracted with shock as she stared at the hands molding her breasts, the lips outlining every lush curve with a cartographer's care. He lifted his head to meet her eyes in the mirror.

"Has life ever been sweeter? Tell me what else you want." She glanced at him, then looked away. She tried to squirm off his lap, but he only dragged her loose garments the rest of the way off and left her, nude, vulnerable before him and, more devastatingly, before herself.

She looked from her nudity to his clothing and shook her head. "No," she croaked.

"Yes," he insisted. "You are naked here in my arms. My woman. And you're enjoying every minute of it."

"No!" She tried to bring her feet beneath her, but he bore her back on the rug. The brandy trickled from shoulders to navel this time, and it took many a kiss to lap the residue away. He made every one of them count. Some were soft, some were hard, but all were arousing. Her stiffness relaxed even as she moaned her self-disgust. She began to squirm and pull at his clothes.

"Off," she commanded hoarsely.

"In a moment." He sucked the last drop from her navel, then bent to lick along the vulnerable crease of her upper leg. She gasped. He laughed joyously and rose above her to fling his clothes off.

Her eyes fluttered open to watch. He savored her hunger as her gaze wandered from his shoulders, to his chest, to his widespread legs, to the point between. He stayed still and let her look her fill. When finally her eyes met his, he frowned at the myriad feelings there. Some he could read, some he couldn't, but one was blatant: sadness. She tried to turn on her shoulder away from him, but he pushed her onto her back and knelt between her legs.

His elation had ebbed as her resistance grew. He stroked her thighs, but they were tense under his hands. Only after many more patient minutes did she relax under him again. But when he smeared brandy about her loins, then shared a sip with her, trickling it from his mouth into hers, she rubbed herself against his caressing hand. Only when that little nubbin stood taut did he withdraw his hand to trail his fingertips over her from belly to knees. He touched but didn't satisfy, brushing over the flesh yearning for a deeper caress.

Sweat stood out on his forehead, but he gritted his teeth. Now, or never. This was his last chance. He pushed her legs widely apart to tongue the swollen flesh moist with brandy and something else. When she was rigid, expectant, he pulled away. Panting, he sat back on his heels.

"Tell me what you want," he rasped.

She shook her head, though her neck strained with effort. He turned her over and pooled some brandy in the indentation of her spine, then lapped it away. All the while his hands were wedged beneath her, fingers and thumbs worrying at her hard nipples. She tried to rise up to give him better leverage, but he pulled his hands away with a hoarse laugh.

"Beg, and I'll do whatever you like."

"No, damn you!" Her voice was muffled by the hair shielding her face, and the denial sounded weak.

That weakness was conveyed by the trembling of her limbs as he once more turned her to face him. He brought her hand to his pulsing shaft. "Bring me into you."

Her hand caught him hungrily, but then she pulled away. His eyes glowing with determined arousal, he pushed her legs widely apart and sank into her in one long, slow slide. They both groaned, but she'd scarcely drawn a relieved breath before he'd slipped out again. She waited, her posture still, submissive, but he didn't return. He paused, kneeling between her thighs, until her dazed eyes opened.

"Tell me what you want, Kat, or I swear I'll leave you to burn." The words were soft with threat, but his eyes pleaded with her. When she swallowed hard, he inserted the swollen tip of his manhood into her and rubbed around. That eager little button, he knew of a surety, was impatient of her scruples.

This time, when he withdrew and demanded through his teeth, "Ask me to stay," the words seemed torn from her.

"Come into me, please. I want you." Her voice faded into shamed silence.

He closed his eyes in relief, and when he opened them again, the light of love gleamed from their molten gold depths. Her own eyes were closed, however, so she didn't see.

Still he stayed motionless, his hips poised over hers. In another moment his victory would be complete. She'd be truly his. He whispered, "Pull me in, Katrina mina. Put me where I belong."

With an impatient groan she latched onto his aching arousal. They both watched her dainty fingers pull the blood-engorged member to the dark blond mound. They both watched as it slowly, inch by inch, disappeared from view. Then they both watched their pleasure reflected in the other's face.

"Oh Devon," she sighed as he probed high, pulled back, then reached higher still.

The long prelude had aroused Devon to a quick release, but the happiness filling him as he watched her lose herself in the moment was too poignant to be merely physical. He could admit it now. Now when, at the eleventh hour, the passion she felt for him had granted him a reprieve. She was his, well and truly his. He slowed his urgent thrusts, feeling his member swell in the tight, moist confines of her flesh. He wanted this moment, the apogee of his love life, to last. . . .

The taste of her in his mouth, the feel of her unbound flesh against him, the scent of the brandy all redefined his existence.

Life was suddenly rife with joy. At last he was complete: he loved her. This act, vulgar and expedient with others, was a celebration of life with Katrina. She appealed to the best of him, at the same time challenging the beliefs he'd held steadfast so long.

Independence was loneliness; pride was weakness; prejudice was poison. Only here, with a woman worthy of the name, was a man able to achieve his full potential. As he felt her stiffen beneath him his control was shattered. Gladly he ceded all he had been as he reached for the lip of her womb. But as he shared with her the seeds of life, he knew that it was he, not she, who was reborn.

"My love, my only love," he whispered soundlessly, collapsing upon her. He was limp with euphoria, and her tears took a moment to penetrate his haze. Only when he felt wetness against his cheek did he understand. He lifted his head. "Katrina, what's wrong?"

She didn't reply, though her eyes, welling with misery, did open to meet his. He brushed the tears away with his thumbs, but more replaced them. "Surely I didn't hurt you?" he asked huskily.

Her voice was so soft he barely heard it. "Yes, you did. I feel wounded unto death."

Alarmed, he pulled her upright and ran his hands over her. Finding nothing but perfect skin, he sat back on his heels. "What nonsense is this?"

"I hate myself. Oh yes, I'm so very moral. . . ."

He relaxed. "Is that all? Pride is a cold comfort, my love. As you've made me realize." He caught her hands, willing her eyes to look into his eager ones, but she pulled away and stared at her hands rubbing her knees.

"You'll never understand, will you? Do you refuse to grant me the luxury of pride because I'm a woman, or because I'm of common birth?"

His boyish gladness faded. Devon the rake responded coolly, "Neither. Because you're a fool." Her eyes flashed angrily up to his.

He met them unflinchingly, the last of his pleasure spoiled. How could he mean so little to her after such . . . sharing? Their loving had apparently meant naught to her. She still regarded him as her jailer and resented her body's need for his. Obviously she needed nothing else. No woman with one tender feeling—and Katrina had many, he knew—could look with such hatred upon the man who'd worshiped her as if she were a shrine. Before he stopped to think, he leaped up and went to pull a long box from beneath the armoire. Uncaring of his nudity, he carried it over to her and flung it on the settee, then opened the lid.

He pulled out a full ermine cloak. The fur of royalty, and rightfully so, the delicate white pelts glistened in the firelight. The contrasting black spots shone with an even deeper luster. He snapped it out one way to show her the fineness of the skins, then whirled it around to display the red velvet lining. He saw the reluctant appreciation in her eyes, and his mouth turned down at the corners. Was she really so different, after all, or did she only hold her worth more highly? He'd never offered another woman a fur so fine. And more was to come. . . .

He bent, caught her wrist, and jerked her up. He turned her to face the mirror. Briskly he dropped a necklace over her head and pushed her hair away from her neck to clasp it.

Her lips made an awed *O* as she stared at her throat. A huge deep blue teardrop-shaped stone, the size of a pigeon's egg, was surrounded by round diamonds. More diamonds formed a scallop pattern around each side all the way to the clasp.

"The stone doesn't exactly match your eyes, but I thought the piece too fine to reject it for such a reason. By the by, the central stone is a diamond. Of the first water. To match its wearer."

He watched her look from the necklace, to him, then back again. She touched the stone as if she couldn't believe its rarity and value. He took advantage of her shock and whirled the cape about her nudity. Then he stood behind her and clasped her shoulders.

"Look well, Katrina mina. This is the regard I hold for you. I paid more for this necklace than I have for all my other mistresses' gifts combined. Doesn't that tell you something?" She watched him intently, as if trying to understand. He could have kicked himself for the comparison when her face changed at that hated word.

"Yes indeed, it tells me much. That I'm only the fanciest whore you've ever kept." She tried to pull away, but his hands crushed the fragile fur as he forced her to stand in front of him.

He twitched the cape to the sides and glared at her, his temples pulsing with anger. "Demean yourself if you must, but know this: My whore or no, I have won our bargain. You not only begged for me verbally this night, you made your desire known in the most explicit way." He caught her jaw in his hands and forced her bent head up to look into the mirror.

They stared at the picture they made. His tall body was Man personified, and his stirring maleness magnified his virility. In contrast she was Woman, elemental, wanton, prideful. The twinkling jewels and lustrous fur enhanced the richness of her natural beauty. Lower, the glistening beads of moisture evidenced how thoroughly they'd explored their contrasts.

Devon pushed his hand down over her belly to curl it in the damp tendrils of dark blond hair. Gently he stroked her, murmuring, "You can deny your feelings to yourself, but your body, at least, knows the truth. You bear physical evidence of your weakness."

She took a deep breath. He tensed. His hand went still as his eyes rose to meet hers. His instinct proved true, for her words did indeed have import for their future.

"And if I admit that I . . . yearn for you? What then?"

"Why, then we shall know as much happiness as mortals can."

"Here? In this house?"

"Where else?"

"I, as your . . . mistress."

"You, as my . . ." But his voice trailed away before he said "love," for her face changed again.

Her eyes had hardened to cold blue steel. He felt stabbed to the heart when she spat, "Then you'll pay richly for your pleasure. These"—she touched the jewels disdainfully—"are not enough. I want the full parure, if you have to search the world over. And this"—she flung the cape off—"is only the first of many. I'll have fur trimming my chemises before I'm done."

Devon literally staggered back as if she'd wounded him. She turned to meet his staring eyes. Her mouth trembled, but she firmed it. "I have met your price. If you would keep me, you must meet mine. Else now you've given me a taste for such things, I'll find someone else who values my true worth."

Dazed brown eyes blinked at her. Devon longed to put his hands over his ears to stifle the ugly words. No, not her, too. Briefly, he was too stunned to realize she was trying to wound him. She didn't mean it . . . she couldn't. She *was* different. Then he got a grip on himself and leaped over the short distance between them. He lifted her chin and stared into her white face.

"Why do you say these things? You know you don't mean them."

Her eyes glittered with a chill icier than the diamonds. "Oh no? Every time you bed me, you must give me a present. Tomorrow I fancy emeralds, I think."

For long minutes they stared at one another. He searched for some hint of softening, some regard that would give him hope. He saw only hatred. It was true, then. She was as avaricious as the rest. Devon's pain was all the fiercer for his earlier brief happiness. He swallowed the words he longed to spew at her and traced a desultory finger over the skin beneath the necklace. When she flinched, he bared a predatory smile.

Casually he lifted her and flung her to the bed. "By your own terms, madame, you owe me. Pay me for the cape—" His words ended in a stormy kiss. The taking was quick, efficient, and unsatisfying. When he was done, he flicked his fingers contemptuously at the cape pooled on the floor.

"'Tis a sorry return for such an investment," he goaded. She turned her cheek into the pillow, but not before he saw her quivering lip. He clenched his hands on the need to comfort her and forced himself to seek the other side of the bed. She had him twisted into knots. He didn't understand her, or himself. Why the hell didn't he just send her away? His overwrought emotions had worn him out, but sleep wouldn't come. His hand snuck across the gap between them to catch a tendril of her long hair. Only then did he drift away—just as the clock struck midnight.

Katrina stared dry-eyed into the darkness and listened to the chimes. Her time of trial was over. That she'd failed miserably was no one's fault but her own. She was weak. Never more so than tonight, when she should have been strong, if not for her own sake, then for the sake of the child. But Devon's lovemaking, more emotive and sensual than ever before, had caught her at a vulnerable moment. She'd not wanted to leave him, despite everything. The knowledge that this was their last time together had defeated the pride that had sustained her for twenty-one years.

She stuffed her hand into her mouth to stifle a sob. Then, slowly, she moved. She realized Devon had caught her hair and held her breath as she untangled his fingers. She clutched his hand, unable to resist the urge to touch him one last time. She forced herself to put his hand down. She dared not chance waking him.

She rose. She twisted, she tugged, she worked. Finally the stubborn hasp gave. She flung the necklace onto the settee and quickly dressed. At this moment she didn't care if she starved. She'd not take a ha'penny of his money. The act of defiance was pitiful, perhaps one she'd soon regret, but the little self-respect he'd left her clamored louder than reason.

She resolutely refused to look at the bed. She hated him, she told herself. He'd kidnapped her, deflowered her, tried to bribe her, seduced her, stomped her beliefs and pride into the ground, then expected her to gladly become his whore. She was glad she'd hurt him. She hoped when he found her gone, he'd curse her name, as she did his. If he thought her as worthless as all his other whores, well, he must blame himself. How could she be bound by the honor he'd stolen?

She swallowed the lump in her throat and tried to deny that she wanted him to remember her fondly. How foolish. She didn't care a jot what he thought of her. She fumbled for hairpins and pinned her hair up as tidily as she could in the dark. She fetched her valises and stuffed the clothes she could find into them. Then she opened and closed the door and tiptoed onto the landing, setting her bags and reticule down. Billy was at his usual post. She nibbled her lip, then she walked down the stairs without subterfuge. At the sound of her steps Billy rubbed his eyes and looked up.

"Where ye goin', missy'?" he grumbled.

"I can't sleep and merely seek a book," she answered, walking past him into the salon. He'd already tipped his hat back over his head when she came back out carrying the poker, but he looked up at her under the brim when she stood over him. He brought his arm up, too late. She hit him solidly on his pate. He toppled onto the floor, the hat squashed on the back of his head.

Her heart pounding, she felt under the hat that had cushioned the blow. She'd not add murder to her sins. Her fingers came away with only a few dots of blood. She listened to his slow but steady breathing and decided he'd be all right. She fetched her bags, then slipped down the stairs and out the door. Briskly, not allowing herself the luxury of looking back, she walked down the dark street lit only occasionally by guttering lanterns. If tears blurred her eyes and made her stumble, she was glad no one was there to see them. . . .

Across the street a grubby urchin straightened against the lamppost. He wiped his yawn away, leaped on a spavined nag, and shadowed her as she hailed a hansom and went to a respectable hostelry. The fee for one night was a tenth of her meager little hoard, the only money she'd managed to save, but she needed somewhere safe to hide while she decided what to do.

Decision, usually so easy for her, was beyond her then. This bleak night was unrelieved by a ray of light. No one saw, no one cared, as the tears burst past the gates of her control. Oh God, why? she cried. Why give me a glimpse of how happy I could be with him, then torment me with the impossibility? What kind of life can I grant this legacy I bear? And why, oh why, even when I know I'm right to leave, do I feel so hopeless?

She stared into the darkness, picturing Devon's beautiful features, and knew that whether hatred or love dwelled in her heart with that image, she'd never forget him. She wondered dully if he'd remember her beyond a twelvemonth. Probably not. Yet loneliness was a brutal leveler, as she was already discovering. Different as they were, disparate as their stations in life were, they could have meant the world to each other, had fate not decreed otherwise.

However, acceptance was a learned lesson, and her heart had had all the teaching it could stand. When sleep at last claimed her, she curled her arms about the pillow and whispered his name.

She was so exhausted that she was being carried out the window of her ground-floor room before she realized what was happening. By the time she drew breath to scream, she was hooded and secreted in a coach. The drive was brief, and ended where putrid water lapped nearby, fouling the air.

Disquieting memories were called up by that smell, but this time she was taken into a building noisy even in these wee hours. She felt herself being carried upstairs, then the softness of a mattress beneath her back. She didn't struggle as her hood was tugged off. She opened her eyes slowly, dreading what she would see.

Blue eyes she'd once thought so genial met hers. "How charming you look, even in your dishabille," Sutterfield jeered. "He must have used you well this night. Doubtless you'll find my attentions more pleasurable."

Katrina sank back on the bed, too weary even to respond to the gibe. Tears burned her throat, but she swallowed them. Her bruised and battered pride rallied. Slowly, she sat up and put her feet on the floor. She scanned the room for a weapon.

Chapter Four

"VISCOUNT SUTTERFIELD, WHY do you bring me here?" Katrina asked steadily, her eyes still scanning the room. Nothing. No poker, no heavy lamps or clocks. He'd prepared well, it seemed. Fury was almost powerful enough to overcome fear—almost.

"I'd think it's obvious. This is your new abode. It's a charming place called Madame Lusette's." When she whitened, he smiled cruelly. "Ah, I see you recall the name. I'm sure Cavanaugh has taught you more than enough to make you a fitting occupant." He peeled off his belt, then his shirt. "She'll pay me well and help me stave off my more insistent creditors. But first I've a score to settle." Shirtless, breeches bulging, he rushed at her.

A knock stayed him as he reached the bed. He scowled. "What is it?"

A tall, buxom woman with badly powdered garish blond hair entered the room. "Let me see the chit." She strode to the bed and lifted Katrina's chin to turn her face from side to side. "She's a right un, sure enough, Sutty."

Katrina's face had gone greenish. The woman looked at her sharply. She stepped back, waving at Sutterfield to do the same, but they were both too late. Heaving, Katrina spewed the contents of her stomach all over them.

Cursing, they each backed away. Sutterfield snatched up his shirt and wiped at the mess.

Madame Lusette swiped at her silk gown festooned with full-blown roses, but it was ruined. She threw her soiled handkerchief to the floor in disgust and eyed Katrina, who was reclining inert on the bed. She scanned Katrina's curves, lingering on the slight swell of her abdomen. With a gimlet-eyed glare at Sutterfield, she went to the door and bellowed, "Marty!" Slamming the door shut again, she approached the bed.

Katrina brushed weakly at the hands that forced her gown above her waist, but they gave her no peace, stripping her stockings away, forcing her legs apart.

Sutterfield's laugh was coarse. "Hell, Lussie, if you wanted to share, why didn't you just say so?" When the madam didn't reply, Sutterfield frowned and opened his mouth, but a brisk knock interrupted. "Damme, this place has gone to seed. A man can't even have a quiet lay," he muttered.

"Enter!" Madame Lusette threw over her shoulder. When a big barrel of a woman complied, she flung her chin at Katrina. "Examine her." Then she straightened and turned on Sutterfield. "You fool! I ought to keep the chit and not give you a ha'penny."

"I say, Lussie, that's—"

"It will be weeks before she can work now." When Sutterfield still looked confused, Madame Lusette snorted and threw a half-hopeful, half-resigned look at Marty. "Well, Marty?"

"Yes'm." The gray-haired woman answered, her big, work-roughened hands still pressing on Katrina's stomach. "She's early on, but caught fer sure."

Sutterfield froze as he met Lussie's cold gray eyes. He looked at Katrina's still form. She was deathly pale, one arm flung over her head as if to block out the world. He approached the bed and jerked Katrina's arm down to stick his face into hers. Her eyes fluttered open.

"He must have used you well this past month. Tell me, how was it?" She blinked, then half sat up, forcing him to back away.

Never had her gaze been clearer or more direct. "It was wonderful, but then, Devon never had need to ask—unlike some men." Her gaze raked him up and down.

Sutterfield's slap rocked her head back on her shoulders. "You bitch!" He waved the other two women away. "Leave us!" He began working at his breeches. Her cheek was red where he'd hit her, but she met him glare for glare.

Madame Lusette quirked a brow in reluctant admiration.

"Ye'll need that spirit, gal, so ye'd best not waste it." To the viscount she snapped, "'Tis ye who must leave. We've work to do."

"Now see here—"

"No, me fine viscount, ye see here. Why should I reward ye and let ye lie with the chit when ye've sold me a pig in a poke? The sooner she's free, the sooner she can get to work. Marty, see him out, then get yer potion."

"Yes'm," Marty said, ushering the protesting viscount out with a brutal grip on his arm.

Katrina's eyes followed Marty's progress to the door. "What potion? What am I to be free of?" The madam's hard gray eyes impassively met hers. Katrina's returning color faded, leaving her as pale as the sheet on which she lay. "No," she whispered over her returning nausea. She had only the haziest notion of what they could do, but instinct as primitive as self-preservation warned her child was in danger. She swung her legs around to put her feet on the floor.

But when she tried to rise, the madam pushed her back down. "Ye'd best make this as easy on yerself as possible, gal. I don't want to drug ye, but I will."

Katrina barely heard her through her panic. She slapped at the woman's hands. Sighing, the madam went to the door and yelled, "Ferdie, I need ye!"

Katrina leaped off the bed while the woman's back was turned and snatched up the viscount's discarded belt. She brandished it over her head and backed away from the vacant-eyed but brawny man who entered.

Looking grim, Madame Lusette ordered, "Hold 'er still, Ferdie. Get 'er back on the bed."

Ferdie lumbered over to Katrina, his unnaturally long arms poised to close about her. Without a moment's hesitation Katrina whacked at one bare forearm, then the other.

Howling, Ferdie dropped his arms and rubbed his hands over their reddened surfaces.

"Ye'd best use sense and drop the belt, gal. Ferdie's a mean one in a temper," the madam warned.

Katrina kept her eyes steady on Ferdie. He feinted one way, but she wasn't fooled and whacked his arm again when he tried to dodge the other way. His face grew red, and the vacant expression in his eyes hardened to fury. Growling, he reached out to punch her, ignoring the lash of the belt. Katrina dodged this time, and his fist struck the wall. He roared like a wounded bear, cradling his hand. Before Katrina realized what he was going to do, he drew back a hobnailed boot and kicked her full in the stomach.

Searing pain exploded through Katrina. She fell to her knees under the impact and wasn't even aware that Ferdie had jerked the belt from her grasp and was using it to beat her about the head and body. She crumpled to the floor, her hands over her cramping stomach, but Ferdie landed another brutal kick in her side as she weakly tried to turn away.

Through a black well of pain Katrina heard the madam screech, "That's enough, you fool! You'll kill her." A sharp slap echoed through the room.

Blubbering, Ferdie whined, "But she hurt me bad. She bad woman." His footsteps dragged to the door.

Just before the tearing pain became more than she could bear, Katrina heard the madam say, "Help me get 'er to the bed, Marty. I don't think we'll need the potion now. Throw that idiot out in the alley. If 'e's ruined this gal, I'll beat 'im myself."

When they picked her up, one on each side, Katrina's body bowed as another vicious cramp twisted her into knots. She screamed, once, twice, and cried, "Nooo!" The long wail reverberated in the small room, then died to a pitiful echo. She went limp as they set her on the bed and pulled her clothes away to examine her. Katrina, her face an alabaster death mask, was unconscious, unaware.

But from the apex of her legs gushed blood. . . .

For several days Katrina drifted in and out of consciousness. The first time her memory returned, she curled into a ball and cupped her hands protectively over her stomach.

Too late. Far too late. "Poor wee one," she whispered, "to be scorned by your father, unwanted by your mother. It's my fault, my fault. But I want you now. Please, God, take my babe to your bosom and give it my love. Please." Her whisper was choked off by the sobs that shook her aching body. Darkness gave her surcease.

Each waking was more painful than the last, for guilt was a sorer trial to her spirit than infection. She welcomed the fever, hoping vaguely that it would consume her and release her from this terrible remorse. If she hadn't been so weak to the wiles of the flesh; if she hadn't succumbed to her silly romantic dreams; if she'd hadn't been too proud to take his money.

If, if, if. And the biggest if: If she'd wanted this innocent life sooner, perhaps God would have spared her babe. Her child would not have joined those poor, hollow-eyed urchins starving in the streets, even if she'd had to prostitute herself.

An ugly, choking sound escaped her, but it was the closest to a laugh she could manage. Whoring had brought her to this end; Devon had been the means thereto. He was as much to blame—nay, more to blame. He had held her prisoner if not against her will, against her morals. Morality was not an idle word to her, and she had abandoned it for the transitory delights of the flesh. She paid for those fleeting moments now, and would do so for the rest of her life. Every time she saw a child, she'd wonder—would her babe have grown up as sturdy and lively? Would it have been a rowdy boy or a winsome little lass? And would her mother's love have been strong enough to compensate for an uncaring father?

She bit down so hard on her lip that she drew blood. "Devon Alexander Tyrone Cavanaugh," she croaked, "I hate you. Revel in your triumph over me, for it will be your defeat in the end. You're poor, poor in all your vast estates and manors. One day, I hope, you'll see too late what you gave up when you lost me and your child." Her heart throbbed so hard that she felt light-headed, torn between remorse, regret, and rancor. Finally her mental and physical agony became too great. And as the darkness took her she embraced it.

She didn't feel the gentle hands ministering to her. They stanched her blood. They kept her bandages clean. They bathed her, bringing down her fever. They forced tiny sips of broth between her chapped lips. And slowly, much against her will, they pulled Katrina back to the life she scorned because of the life she'd lost.

When, four days later, she clearly saw that face, it was night and a candlelight nimbus surrounded the fair head. His features were exquisitely formed, almost dainty. "Gabriel? Will you take me to my babe?" she begged.

A gentle, musical laugh answered her. "'Tis the first time I've been confused with an angel," a pleasant, slightly accented voice replied. "My patients tend more to liken me to a denizen of the nether regions."

Katrina looked about the room. Her eyes were lucid again when she wearily closed them. Fiercely she tried to will herself back to that comforting void. A pinch stung her arm. Her eyes flicked open and blinked indignantly. Her brain cleared under the stimulant of anger at someone rather than herself.

"What type of doctor are you to deliberately inflict pain on your patients?"

"One who prefers a live patient over a dead one," came the dry reply. "Besides, your fever has subsided, and you'll only weaken yourself to no purpose if you don't sit up and eat." The tall, slim man fluffed her pillows up behind her back and set a tray holding vegetable soup, soft bread, and cheese upon her lap.

"Eat." A long, authoritative finger pointed at the tray.

Katrina glared at him, but she nibbled on a morsel of bread. "I suppose if I don't, you'll likely force feed me like a goose."

"Likely so."

The first bite tasted surprisingly good, so she took another. "Doubtless your intentions are as ill as everyone else's. What use do I have to you? Will you fatten my liver and sell it for that disgusting French pâté?"

"I've a fondness for gizzards, myself." When she threw him a shaming look, a lazy smile turned up one side of that mobile mouth. "You don't have a gizzard, child, so you needn't cut up at me so."

That word drained all pleasure in their gentle sparring, in the food, in the life he'd forced her back to. She flung the tray away, curled her arms about herself, and wept.

A pithy curse sounded, then wiry arms gently took her to a slim but strong chest. "Forgive my clumsiness, Katrina. I'm not used to dealing with such cases. . . ." He trailed off and patted her shoulder, cradling her against his chest.

When her sobs had subsided to sniffles, he drew away and offered her a clean handkerchief. She took it and blew her nose fiercely, then slumped back on her pillows. "You don't usually physic at bawdy houses, then, doctor . . . ?"

"Will Farrow. And no, not often, but their regular, er, doctor, was, uh, under the weather—"

"Drunk, was he?"

The young physician shrugged gracefully. "So they said. They came to my school, where I'd just completed training, and asked for help."

"So I guess I should be grateful that you agreed to lower yourself to save a whore." She didn't sound grateful. She flung an arm over her face and muttered, "Well, you've done your Hippocratic duty, so leave me in peace." When she didn't hear him leave, she lowered her arm enough to glare at him.

Kindly eyes a deeper blue than her own stared back. "These feelings are natural, lass, but no amount of remorse will bring your babe back. Would you really want to raise a child in such a place as this, anyway?"

Her mouth curled down at the corners. "How comforting that I even look the part now."

"Are you saying you're new to this, er, vocation?"

"Since this month past. Nor am I here by choice."

He frowned at that, then settled more deeply into his chair. "Somehow that doesn't surprise me. You've neither the speech nor the learning of a girl born to this life. But then—how came you here? Why don't you tell me what happened?" When she turned her head away, he leaned forward and tilted her chin toward him. "Confession is good for the soul. And yours needs healing."

Fat tears swelled in her eyes. "I don't deserve to be healed."

"Come, wallowing in self-pity accomplishes nothing but the ruin of a clean handkerchief. You've dirtied my best one, I might add." He waved a chiding finger at her.

"Then take it back!" She looked as if she might throw it at him, and her tears began to dry.

He cast a jaundiced eye upon the wet, crumpled square of linen. "You keep it." When she ran it through her fingers nervously, he leaned forward and covered her hands, soiled kerchief and all, with his. "Please, Katrina, let me help. I can't unless I know what brought you here."

Those blue eyes, that handsome face, were so earnest that

they drew from her a reluctant response. At first she gave him bare details, but he asked pertinent questions and eventually coaxed the entire dreary story from her. When she was done, she felt drained but fully sane again. Her anger at Devon, however, was exacerbated by the telling.

Wrath had transformed Will's perfect features until he resembled an adolescent Mars more than an angel. "Do you think he had you brought here?"

She blanched and shrank against the pillows, dizzily ill at the very idea. "No!" Then, with quiet bitterness: "No, because I was still a valuable 'commodity' to him. He hadn't tired of me yet."

Will slapped his hands upon his knees and stood. "Well, who is responsible for your presence here scarce matters at the moment. The most urgent piece of business is to get you away."

Katrina's eyes showed their first glimmer of hope in five days. "Can you help me? I tried the door in one of my cogent moments, and it was locked."

"Yes, I fear Madame Lusette expects to make a fortune with you. She's also having the door guarded." When Katrina looked angry, Will expounded, "As much to keep men out as to keep you in. Already the news of your presence has reached the other, er, residents here. I've informed the madam that it will be a good month before you can be put to work, so we've time. But you need to eat to get your strength up as quickly as possible. Leave the other details to me." With a polite tip of his hat he was gone.

Katrina closed her eyes and courted sleep, but with no result. Her confession had cauterized the wound of her experience with Devon; soon she could heal, but in the meantime she ached like the very devil. Tears came to her eyes again despite her best efforts. Devon was not the only one who had lost.

With the babe had gone her youth, and, perhaps, the best of her femininity. Never again would she be able to lie, mindless with pleasure, in a man's arms and not care of the consequences. Never again would she sacrifice what she knew to be right in the feeble hope that she could hold a man's wandering affections. And saddest of all, never again would she offer her body and her heart in hopes of winning the same.

Perhaps Devon had been right about one thing: Love was folly. It weakened rather than strengthened, stole rather than gave, ruined rather than built. She was a living testimonial to those truths, her babe a macabre warning of the danger of denying them. As she resolved never again to forget, her tears dried. Peace, of a sort, stole over her. That it was an expedient, spurious peace didn't occur to her. She knew only that she drifted off to her first untroubled sleep since she'd left Devon.

The remainder of her stay at the bawdy house was quiet. Whenever the madam entered to check on her progress, Katrina took care to look listless and keep her voice weak. Once, however, curiosity got the best of her.

"What's happened to Viscount Sutterfield?"

"The slimy blackguard threatened to call the magistrates when I wouldn't let him have ye," the woman returned. "I give him what we agreed upon and told him his coin 'tweren't good here no more. He's too rough on me gals, anyway. I run a decent house. I'll be fair wi' ye, gal, I promise. Just ask any o' the girls if ye don't believe me." With her own brand of kindness the madam tapped Katrina on the cheek with a rough finger and departed.

Will visited her daily and finally, two weeks later, proclaimed her strong enough to travel. After she'd blushed at his usual impersonal examination, he pulled the covers up to her waist and sat on the edge of the bed to take her hand.

"I've all in readiness, child, if you think you're up to trying to get away," he said.

"More than ready, Will."

He played with her fingers, his bent head indicative of his unusual indecision. "And where will you go once you're away, Katrina? What will you do?"

She sighed. "Leave London, I suppose. I'll probably have to take work as a maid since I don't have a reference—"

"You've no family to aid you, then?"

"None."

He let her go, stood, then began to pace the room. She frowned. He'd always been so calm, so collected. His very composure had helped her regain her own. What had put him in such a stir?

Finally he whirled and blurted, "Then come with me." When she looked surprised, he strode to the bed and took her hands again. "I'm going home to Cornwall, where I've obtained a position as a mine doctor. Our way of life is not an easy one, but you'd be needed there. You could help school the children—" He broke off when she paled, then hurried on, "Or even the miners. Many of them are eager to learn." His body tensed as he awaited her reply.

For long moments she stared blindly at their clasped hands. To be useful. To be needed. To be wanted. At this point in her life she could ask no more. Nay, nor did she want more. The decision was easy, in the end. She owed her very life to Will Farrow. If she could aid him and his people in return, then maybe, one day, she could atone for the weighty sins that had almost sunk her to perdition.

She lifted her head and squeezed his hands. "Yes, Will Farrow. Gladly will I come with you. And I thank you for honoring me with your trust."

He looked as if he might embrace her for a moment, but then he returned her clasp and drew away. He went to his physician's case and said over his shoulder, "Dress under your gown and give me whatever essentials you can't bear to part with. I'll put them in my case. We'll not have room for all, I fear, if my plan is to work." He stayed across the chamber with his back turned, repacking his case to make the most of its capacity, while she dressed.

"Ready," she said.

He swiveled and gave her a critical appraisal. Her long, enveloping gown hid her dress, and she'd wisely left off her stockings. "Give me your shoes." He packed them and the underclothes, Bible, reticule, and one good dress she gave him.

He stepped up to her, mussed her hair, then pinched her cheeks until they reddened. He moved back a pace, cocked his head as he studied her, then nodded. "You'll do." After fetching a small bottle that she'd seen him set aside earlier, he approached her again, uncapping it as he came.

"What's that?" she asked, eyeing the bottle with foreboding.

"Blood." He chuckled at her horror-stricken look. "I've not murdered anyone, Katrina. It's only pig's blood that I took from the dissection room at my school. Wrap yourself in the blanket."

Her disgust receded only marginally, but she obeyed, now that she understood what he was going to do. Her nose wrinkled as he splashed the blood on the blanket near her hips. Then he hung his case over one wrist, cracked the door open, and held out his arms.

The little smile playing about his lips was a fine blend of irony and mirth. "Faith, this is not the way I'd choose to embrace you, but 'tis, under the circumstances, the most convincing." When she wrapped her arms about his neck, he flushed, but seemed to lift her easily enough.

"Put your arms at your sides, keep your neck relaxed, and on no account open your eyes. The guard has gone to lunch, so it's now or never." Then, with a deep breath, he shoved the door open with his foot and stepped into the hallway.

Katrina heard nervous whispers and even a titter or two, but she'd counted seven descending steps before she heard Madame Lusette's voice. "Here now, doc, where ye goin'?"

"This girl has got fever again, and her wound has reopened. Unless I get her to a cleaner environment, she'll die. A more experienced colleague of mine has agreed to look at her—"

"Then let him come here. She don't leave."

"He won't come. I've already asked. Do you want her to die?"

Katrina could feel the madam's indecision and sensed her piercing examination. Will's arm nudged her, and she let her head fall back so that her hair streamed over his arm. Finally a heavy sigh came. "Very well. When will ye bring her back?"

"As soon as her fever is gone." Will began walking again. "Please, open the door." The woman complied.

Katrina felt herself being set in a carriage, then the depression of the springs as Will got in beside her. "You can visit her at my school, if you like." Will gave her directions, then shut the door.

As the driver pulled them away they exchanged a triumphant glance. "Well, that was easy enough," Will said. His little smile deepened. "What I wouldn't give to see those fusty old sawbones' faces if Madame Lusette goes to the school."

Katrina's own smile broadened. She flung off the soiled blanket, exuberant in her freedom. Her sideways glance was mischievous. "Oh, I don't know. They might be glad to see her."

When he quirked an inquiring eyebrow, she finished dryly, "I imagine she could teach them a thing or two about anatomy."

Will threw back his blond head and roared with laughter. Katrina joined in, a bit rustily at first, but at least she hadn't lost the ability.

Will gasped between chuckles. "And . . . doubtless in a much . . . more pleasurable . . . fashion. I can see them now . . . upon the dissection table. . . ." And he was off again. Their laughter mingled pleasantly as the hired coachman took them to the westerly road out of London.

However, they'd not gone far upon it before Katrina's laughter died. She kept the smile upon her face so Will wouldn't realize that her tears of mirth had a different source now. She watched London retreat behind her. The houses thinned, then faded to a flat greensward broken only by the serpentine dirt road.

The future stretched ahead. Whatever came in that future, this part of her life was over. No more emotional torment for her; no more joy, either. Every step took her away from Devon. By her own choice, she told herself fiercely, yet the regret only deepened. Try as she did to tell herself she hated him, her heart knew truth from fiction.

Never again to be held by him, to be wanted by him—how would she bear it? part of her cried. Yet the cool, logical part she vowed would rule her ever after assured her that this distance was best. Any chance for happiness they might have had had perished with the death of their child. God intended other things for her. More important things.

She snatched her eyes away from the road receding behind them. She turned, proud and straight, and gazed only forward.

Miles away, in London's most exclusive district, Devon Alexander Tyrone Cavanaugh was reviling her in a remarkably similar manner. He stood in the salon of his town house, one booted foot upon the empty fireplace grate, and rested his forehead on the arm he braced upon the mantel. He twirled a forgotten glass of port in his hand.

"Damn you, Katrina. Damn you for lying. Little coward, how could you throw away all we might have had out of some . . . pusillanimous, false modesty? Pah! You're like all other women—you don't know the meaning of the word *honor*. Promises made are as easily broken. You lost, dammit! You should have stayed. . . ." He clenched his glass tightly.

For weeks now they'd searched for her, but she'd vanished without a trace. He and Billy had combed every street about the little house, looking for someone who recalled seeing her. She was, after all, quite distinctive, but it had been late when she left. Even now Billy was searching. He'd only recently returned himself to change and eat. Dear heaven, what if he never saw her again? His hand convulsed about the glass. He heard a snap, then felt a sharp pain in his hand.

With an oath he flung the glass away, aware but uncaring that the port stained his expensive rug. He sucked his palm, then stared vaguely at the wound, remembering the last time he'd seen blood. Had he known she was virgin, would he have let her be? Nay, he'd not lie to himself. He'd have been more tender, but he'd have snatched what, even now, instinct cried out was his. And still he'd be standing here, wondering how he had gone wrong. Fearing for her safety. Praying sincerely, for the first time in over twenty years, for another.

Not since his parents died had he known such despair. And the fact that he'd brought this upon himself alleviated his anguish not a whit. How could he have known the chit was lying? She'd seemed as rapacious as the others in that last, rending confrontation. She'd *wanted* him to believe her mercenary. And he, like a besotted halfling, had fallen neatly into her trap. He'd awakened, determined to start afresh with her and woo her gently, only to find himself alone, Billy unconscious. The jewels and fur he'd gifted her with were still very much in his possession; the one thing he'd wanted above all others in his adult life had slipped from his grasp. Only now, when she was gone, did he understand how deeply, how passionately, he had wanted her. . . .

So here he stood, feeling a fool. A lonely fool, in truth. Katrina was the only woman he'd ever been able to talk to meaningfully out of bed. He'd miss those exasperating, emotional confrontations. And despite what she thought, despite their differing backgrounds, they were not so ill matched. Their primary contention was his unwillingness to wed her. Given time, he could have convinced her that he could make her happier out of wedlock than in it.

He desperately wanted that time. He'd handled her wrong, he saw that now. She'd frustrated him so because she was unlike any woman he'd ever known. He couldn't bribe her because material things meant little to her; he couldn't subdue that iron will because it was forged more by beliefs than stubbornness; and he couldn't sway her with passion save for brief moments because she was a woman ruled by mind and heart rather than instinct and self.

He slammed his fist against the mantel, so frustrated that he didn't even wince. Never had he felt less worthy than now, knowing he'd lost the only worthy woman he'd ever known. . . .

When the door opened, he turned eagerly. He saw from Billy's face that he had news—bad news. Devon leaped forward and caught Billy's arm in a crushing grip. "Well, man?"

Billy covered Devon's white-knuckled hand with his own hairy paw. "I found a cabbie who described an odd fare he had—said a wee lass with a gray dress was hooded, carried into his hack by a swell. A tall swell with brown hair and blue eyes."

Devon's eyes narrowed to dangerous gold slits. "Sutterfield?"

"I suspect so. The cabbie said he don't remember where he took 'em, but I think he were afraid to say."

Devon strode to the door without another word. He snapped over his shoulder, "Have my curricle brought 'round."

After Billy obeyed, he went in search of Devon. He wasn't surprised to find him in the study in the act of fetching his dueling sword from the bottom of his gun case.

Devon drew it out, dusted off the leather sheath, then strapped the weapon about his lean waist and threw on a light summer cloak to hide it. He whirled and strode toward the door, waving Billy away from his path.

Billy, however, stayed planted in the doorway. He knew that deadly glitter in Devon's eyes. "Murder won't bring 'er back, Devvie lad."

"Come, Billy, it's not murder to defend one's possessions. Step aside."

Billy didn't move. "Naw, but whoever said ye own the lass? Not her. And if ye kill him, ye may be called to account, even if it's a fair fight. And how will ye find her then?"

"Oh, he'll talk, first. And I'll give him every chance to defend himself. Now *move*."

Billy snorted, but he angled his broad body sideways so Devon could squeeze by. Then, his ugly but oddly compelling features drawn with worry, he followed Devon out the front door held open by a wooden-faced footman.

"I shan't need you today, Henry," Devon said to the wiry little man who served as his tiger. Henry nodded, but he held the fractious team of grays until Devon and Billy were settled on the lofty curricle seat. At Devon's nod Henry released the animals and leaped aside. With an adroit flick of his whip above the grays' heads, Devon urged the team into motion.

Upon reaching Sutterfield's lodgings, Devon gave a tough-faced lad a crown to watch the horses, then climbed the outside stairs. Billy, still grimly silent, followed him every step of the way. A sleazy-looking little man with long, stringy hair answered Devon's second knock.

"Wot ye want?"

"To see your master. Now."

"He ain't available." But when the servant tried to shut the door in Devon's face, he found a boot and a curled hand in the way. Easily Devon shoved both man and door backward and entered the cramped quarters. The stenches of molding cheese and an unemptied chamber pot were overlaid by the acrid smell of cheap gin.

Devon's mouth curled down at the corners. He sliced a glance at Billy, who sighed, but blocked the door, stopping the weasely man's furtive movements toward it. Devon threw back the only other door in the small apartment and drew the curtains to let in the late-afternoon sunshine.

The frayed bed hangings had once been pale blue, as was evident in the creases, but wear, dirt, and sun had bleached them to a sullen gray. Sutterfield, several days' growth of beard upon his face, groaned at the brilliance and opened one bleary blue eye.

He blinked, then sat up. He smacked his tongue against the roof of his mouth a couple of times, then stretched, appraising Devon all the while. Bright sunlight glanced off the gold-embellished hilt of Devon's sword. Unwisely, Sutterfield jeered, "What a . . . queer surprise, Cavanaugh. Do you always come acalling wearing a sword?"

"Only when I intend to kill someone," Devon responded, leaning against the doorjamb and crossing one ankle over the other.

Sutterfield started, and his innocent look was spoiled as his yellow skin went pasty white. "What the devil for?"

"For stealing what is mine. I warned you once. Now you'll pay." Sutterfield vaulted from the bed, but Devon caught him before he'd gone two steps and shoved him against the wall with a hand at his throat.

"How lucky that I forgot to take off my driving gloves," Devon said mildly. "I'd hate to dirty my hands on you."

When Sutterfield moved as if to raise his knee, Devon tightened his grip slightly. Sutterfield choked and went from pasty white to pale blue. When he went limp, Devon smiled.

A less intelligent man than Sutterfield would have read the menace in that smile, and it drained the little cockiness the viscount had left. When Devon relaxed his grip, he coughed and rasped, "If . . . I tell you where I took her . . . you have to promise . . . to let me go."

"That I can promise you truthfully. Tell me where to find her, and I'll release you."

"She's, she's . . ." Sutterfield hesitated. When Devon infinitesimally closed his fingers, he croaked, "She's at Madame Lusette's!" Devon went still, then his grip closed in concert with the breath hissing between his teeth. Sutterfield gurgled as his lungs labored for the air that his constricted windpipe could not supply.

Devon stared at his working face impassively, and only Billy's loud "Let him go, lad!" saved the viscount.

Snarling like a mortally wounded bear, Devon let him go—only to begin raining blows on Sutterfield's face and belly. Billy called to him to stop, but in his red haze Devon was blind to the voice of reason. Billy ran across the room and caught Devon's raised fist.

"Listen, lad. His man's gone to fetch the watch." They heard the sound of descending footsteps, then the slam of the exterior door.

"Good, he can wipe this slime up off the floor," Devon growled, jerking his fist away.

It was Sutterfield himself, sliding to the floor and leaving a bloody trail down the silk wallpaper as he went, who stayed Devon's arm. "Don't you want to know if I had her?" he gasped, panting.

Devon froze, his impassivity slipping to show the anguish he'd hidden so well. Sutterfield's smile was ghastly but triumphant. "Kill me and you'll never know."

Devon's arm slowly fell to his side. Just as slowly his hand lifted, felt for, then clasped the hilt of his sword. "It doesn't really matter. You've degraded her whether you've personally used her or not, and for that you will die. Fetch your sword." Devon stood back and allowed Sutterfield to stagger to his feet.

"I've some other news you'll find interesting," Sutterfield said as he stumbled to a curtained alcove. He came back with his dueling sword.

"Save it. You'll need all your energies for this." Devon threw off his cloak, took off his gloves, drew out his sword, and waited.

When Sutterfield would have spoken again, Devon's face twisted. "Damn you, I don't want to hear what happened to her there! She's no bawd, and for treating her as one you die!"

Devon didn't even allow Sutterfield a salute. They'd engaged only three times before Devon's crafty riposte jerked the sword from the viscount's weak grip. That cruel twist to Devon's expressive mouth was marked as he drew back his arm to thrust. The door slammed back on its hinges. In rushed the watch and the constable.

" 'Ere now, ye know duelin' ain't proper, 'specially 'ere,'' the constable said, stepping between Devon and his target.

When Devon looked as if he might thrust anyway, the man paled. But, to his credit, he stood his ground.

Billy averted disaster by snatching the sword away from Devon. "Come, lad. We must try to find her."

Devon drew a shaking hand over his suddenly sagging features and turned blindly to the door. The constable caught his arm.

"Not so fast. Ye've some explainin' to do." When Devon threw him off and hurried out the door, the constable and the elderly watchman followed.

Billy, however, stayed behind long enough to glare at Sutterfield, who had slumped down in a chair. "If you value your life, you'll make an extended visit to the Continent. Especially if the lass has been harmed."

Sutterfield barked a mean laugh. "Oh, she's the star whore all right." When Billy's mouth tightened grimly, Sutterfield muttered, "They wouldn't let me near her. The last I heard, she was sick of the fever. From the taking of her brat."

Billy stared. "Do ye mean she were pregnant?"

"As a fat cow. With Cavanaugh's seed. Tell him that, from me." Sutterfield staggered to his feet, fetched a valise, and began flinging his clothes inside it. Billy walked heavily to the door, closed it, then leaned against it.

He shut his eyes and muttered a quick prayer. "Poor wee lass. Poor babe." Then, more quietly: "Poor Devvie lad. She'll ne'er forgive ye now."

Devon bribed the watch and the constable just as Billy joined him. Night was upon them. Madame Lusette's business was brisk when they arrived and demanded to see her.

"She don't work much no more," said the girl the doorman took them to. She was a voluptuous little thing with bright red hair and vermilion cheeks to match. She sidled up to Devon and ran her hand down his arm.

"But I'd be glad to take care o' yer . . ." She trailed off suggestively, then concluded, "business."

Devon shrugged her off and flipped a guinea in the air. She caught it adroitly. "There's another for you if you bring Lusette herself to us. Now."

With a half-avaricious, half-regretful look over her shoulder

she hustled her shapely little rear out the door, leaving it open.
They heard a knock, then muffled voices.

Madame Lusette herself, looking harried, came into the
antechamber. When Devon tossed another guinea to the girl
behind her, Madame Lusette threw the girl a sharp look that
sent her scurrying off, then turned politely back to Devon and
Billy. "Well, gents? What's yer pleasure? We've a new girl
from China—"

"We *are* seeking one of your new girls. She's about this
high"—Devon held his hand out, palm down, even with his
collarbone—"with bright gold hair and blue-green eyes. I'll
pay you a hundred pounds if you'll take me to her."

Madame Lusette's eyes widened, then narrowed in anger.
"I'd let ye keep her for that. She's been naught but trouble. But
she ain't here. She ran away today with a sawbones who were
tendin' to her—"

"What was wrong with her?" Devon interrupted sharply.

"He said she had fever and could die, but I sent a man to the
place where he said he'd take her, and she weren't there."

"Fever? From what?"

"Why, from—"

"What difference does it make, now, lad?" Billy inserted.
"She's obviously well and this was a ruse to get her away."

The madam crossed her arms over her huffing bosom.
"Shoulda known that feller were too young and handsome to
trust with her. And I wager she was fine as a trivet by the time
she left, too."

Where Billy's diversion had not worked, this one did.
Devon's mouth snapped shut over another authoritative question. Then, almost whispering, he asked, "And what was this
fellow's name?"

The madam shrugged. "Names don't mean much in my line
o' work. We just asked fer a doc and he's the one they sent. A
tall, slim bloke with pale blond hair and blue eyes."

"They?" Billy asked when Devon stared into space.

"The school where he were studyin'. That fancy new one
on . . ." The madam gave them directions. She snatched up
the palmful of guineas Devon vaguely offered her and was
already counting them when Billy ushered Devon out the door.

Seeing that Devon was in no state to drive, Billy took the

reins himself. The school was almost deserted, but they found one instructor working on his notes. After listening to Billy's description, the physician nodded and said, "That would be young Farrow. A most talented young doctor. But as to where he's from, I couldn't say. He kept much to himself. I know only he attended here on an inheritance and planned to return home soon."

Billy pulled Devon outside, throwing him a worried glance. When Devon climbed up beside him and let him take the reins again, Billy snapped, "Wake up, man! This is no time to go about in a daze if you want to find your lady."

Devon finally focused on him. All his frustration, anger, and worry sounded in his soft response. "'Tis obvious she doesn't want me to find her. What did she go through in these weeks, Billy? What did they do to her to make her agree to become another man's mistress when she scorned me?"

Billy clucked to the horses. "You don't know that, Devvie lad."

"Why else would he take her with him? Out of charity?" Devon's scornful laugh was more a groan of pain. "Beautiful women don't incite charity, Billy."

"Perhaps in a sawbones she would. I'll come back to the school tomorrow and ask about."

But the next day, and the day after, neither Devon nor Billy found any of the instructors or servants at the school more forthcoming. They had no way of knowing that Will, suspecting that Devon would try to find Katrina, told his instructors that an enemy of his would be seeking him and that his life was in danger if his whereabouts should become known to this powerful lord.

As time went on, Will's lie became somewhat prophetic, for Devon's guilt and worry soon gave way to fury. He wavered between longing to get his hands about Katrina's throat and yearning to kiss her senseless. His feelings for Will, however, were uncomplicated: He wanted to kill the man who had stolen his woman. For whatever reason. Whether he'd driven her away or not, Katrina was his.

Resolve gave him purpose again. The guilt and grief that had kept him sleepless and joyless began to ease. But their passing, like a scab that has been ripped off too many times, left a scar over the gentle sweetness Katrina had finally inspired in him.

On the moonless night when he admitted she had left him and had no intention of returning, he stared out his window at the lamp glowing beside his drive. Katrina's hair had been just that shade when the sun struck it. And the pain that took him was so fierce that only fury could allay it.

For the second time in his life he handled his grief in the only way he knew: by denying it. His whisper, soft and deadly, was taken by the gentle breeze. "Just you wait, Katrina Lawson. I'll find you, no matter what, and make you sorry you ever left me."

If his eyes glistened on the words, no one was there to see. From now on the world would find in him the scoundrel they expected, he resolved. Katrina had no use for the namby-pamby who had let her slip him so easily; instead she would know the rake. . . .

Chapter Five

LIKE MOST BRITONS, Katrina had a clear vision of what she expected of Cornishmen. She was too realistic to adhere to the wilder tales of cannibalism and brutality. If Will was an example of the Cornish temperament, then Cornishmen were both kind and generous. Still, a bleak, hard land bred bleak, hard men. She didn't doubt that Cornishmen were also as wild and tough as their moors and storm-racked coasts.

Historically, Cornwall had been isolated from the rest of England by geography and language. If the tales she'd heard were true, they would, to this day, prefer it that way. Would they accept her, a girl from the gentle hills of Kent? What did she, a sinner—no, she decided, she must not delude herself ever again if she were to avoid the same mistakes. She was about to call herself a name she despised when Will interrupted her thoughts.

He covered her clammy hand with his. "Come, you've been brave this entire grueling trip. We've not much farther to go. Don't lose heart. The family I'm taking you to is large, their fortunes totally dependent upon the mines, yet it's one of the happiest I've ever known."

"And will you tell them to be good to the little lightskirt?"

He sighed at her bitter tone and released her hand to tilt up her downcast chin. "No, I'll tell them to be good to the little English." He smiled wryly. "A fact some of our people, at least, will have a harder time dealing with than the other. But they'll not hear what brought you to us from me. You have my word as a Cornishman."

Some of Katrina's foreboding waned as amusement took hold. "Which means more than your word as an Englishman, I collect."

"Too true. And I'm an Anglophile compared to some of my people. There is much I admire across the border—"

They jostled together as their hired carriage lurched over a deep rut in the dirt track. "Such as English roads," Will concluded.

Her laughter joined his. His dry witticisms continued for the rest of the journey. As for what she discovered of Cornwall, Katrina found the scenery both more varied and more pleasing than she'd expected. True, it had rained almost every day, and true, even late in May the nights were chilly, yet the south-westerly winds gave a purity to the air that was refreshing after London's fumes.

The countryside immediately bordering Devon was as richly harmonious as any its neighbor could boast. The lovely, deep river valley of the Looe was thick with trees and fecund with the earth's bounty. Even when they'd passed the valleys and inched their way upon the moors that made the backbone of the county, Katrina had seen a sparse, spectral beauty. Stunted trees struggled against the gale-force winds. Scrawny, thorny hedges and scrub dotted the moor. Bogs lurked to trap the unwary, yet there was something compelling about the ancient feel to the landscape.

"We lay claim to Arthur, you know, despite the legends held in Brittany, Somerset, and Wales," Will said as they bumped along a particularly treacherous piece of road. "Was Camel-ford Camelot? The palace of Carlyon, where Arthur held court, can be found south of the river Fal. Its earthworks are still visible. Did you know that close by is Avallen—Avalon, perhaps, where the weeping queens bore Arthur's body along the river, at his request, where the apple orchards grow?"

Katrina smiled. "You sound just like my father did, all the more certain for his doubtful thesis. I doubt we'll ever know where Arthur really lived."

He tweaked her nose. "Spoken like a true bluestocking. Well then, what think you of this?" He banged on the roof and told the coachman to halt, then helped Katrina out of the carriage. Katrina caught her breath at the sight of the cairn glowering against the gunmetal-gray sky.

She climbed to the top of the tor with Will to get a better look at the massive stones. They were geometric in shape and placed with a precision that had obviously had religious meaning to the distant people who'd set them there.

Will let her look her fill while he teased her mind with another reason as to why Cornishmen took such pride in their heritage. "It's not only because we were never assimilated into the Saxon kingdom that we consider ourselves different. While your ancestors over the Tamar were merely tilling soil and grazing cattle, mine near the Land's End were streaming tin to trade it with strange, western civilizations for golden crescents and blue beads. Some scholars believe it is from these that we get so many of our dark characteristics." When she glanced at his fair locks, he added wryly, "Many's the time I've wished that I'd taken the look of my father rather than the look of my mother, who was half-English."

He led the way back to the carriage. He smiled when she stretched her aching back. "There's no carriage made with springs good enough to keep us stable on these roads. But another few hours, and we'll be there."

He kept up his wry, witty commentary over that time, and Katrina was too stimulated intellectually to notice their change of pace until they rocked to a halt. She caught her breath.

He jumped down the steps the coachman had put down for them and offered her his hand. "Come, little English, make your Saxon forebears proud and do what they couldn't do: Conquer us."

His hand was as steadfast as hers was trembly, and he supported her when her travel-stiff legs made her stumble on the uneven ground. Before them was a cottage sheltered by a slope and a rock outcropping to the side. The sturdy wrought-iron gate opened to a dirt path, sweet williams on each side, that led to a rough plank door. A thatched roof topped walls made of some odd-looking stone material that appeared molded. One tiny window high under the eaves was the only evidence that the cottage had two levels.

Will led her to a bench sitting beneath a hedgerow. "Stay here for a moment while I fetch John."

Katrina rubbed her sweaty palms on her wrinkled dress, but then she forced her fidgeting hands to be still. She took several deep, spring-scented breaths and tried to enjoy the pretty aspect. The day had brightened, and the sun struck the outcropping, glittering off the speckled granite. The gently rolling hills in the distance were green, though bare of trees. Close by, she spied a boy at work in the fields, plodding along behind his oxen team, and wondered if the neat rows belonged to the family.

Behind the cottage stood several stacked rows of faggots; farther down, next to a stream, sat a tiny, ramshackle barn. Sheep, goats, and a lone cow cropped the grass in a small enclosure next to the barn. The burbling stream was an odd rusty color, and Katrina deduced that the mine must not be far away.

All in all the cottage sat in its setting like an uncut but cherished jewel. If she were indeed welcome here, would this place have wealth or dross to share? And if a wealth of contentment it offered, what did she have to give in return?

"Does 'ee like our home?" A deep voice interrupted her thoughts.

She jumped to her feet. She saw Will standing there with a strange man beside him. "Yes, it's most attractive," she said sincerely. By a supreme effort she managed not to twiddle with her hair as dark brown eyes appraised her. Instead she stared back.

She saw a barrel of a man of medium height, broad in body and face, but not fat. He wore duck trousers that skimmed his ankles, a tan waistcoat over a loose smock, and low shoes without stockings. His queued hair was peppered with gray, but he had the erect posture and ruddy cheeks of a healthy man.

"Will says 'ee needs a place to staay?"

Unable to speak past the lump in her throat, she nodded and looked at the horizon. How she hated being a supplicant. But the desperate didn't have the luxury of pride.

Her head popped up in shock when that deep voice said, "'Tes not needful to tell a Cornishman about pride, lassie. Ef 'ee staay here, 'ee'll work as one of the family and eat or starve as we do."

Those acute, shrewd eyes softened when she nodded and said, "Agreed."

"Can 'ee learn my bairns 'tween their chores?"

"Yes. Reading, writing, and arithmetic, plus history and—"

"Ais, history wretten by the English esn't what I want my

bairns to learn. Start weth the readin'.'' He turned and strode back up the path to his gate, throwing over his shoulder, ''Along now, an' meet my missus.''

Will smiled at her dazed look and took her arm to lead her up the path. ''John Tonkin is accustomed to ordering about surly miners and boisterous children, but you'll find no deceit or meanness in him. If I didn't think you could be happy here, I'd not have brought you, Katrina.''

They both had to stoop beneath the massive granite lintel above the door. They stepped down two steps and entered a short hallway. Katrina glanced to the left and saw a tiny parlor with two gaily painted chairs, a settee, and a cupboard with several obviously cherished china figurines sequestered behind its wavery glass front. On the right she glimpsed a Spartan bedroom with a hand-carved wooden bed covered in a simple quilt. An ancient lowboy sat on one side of the bed, a rocking chair on the other.

Tempting aromas drifted from the rear, clueing Katrina to the kitchen John led them to. A long table with low benches on each side sat in the middle of the room. An enormous open hearth she could have stood in engulfed one wall, and a kettle hanging over the fire bubbled, emitting the pleasant scent. Through another doorway she spied a churn and deduced that the rear room of the house served as dairy and larder. She'd had fresh cream daily in the village with her father, but little since she'd lived in the houses of the affluent.

A rush of homesickness and hunger assailed her. Katrina's mouth watered, and suddenly she realized how hungry she was. Noon was nigh. Will had explained that John came home from the mine for croust, as they called lunch, and that the children, occupied at their various chores, would soon arrive as well.

A woman in a simple homespun dress, clean white cap, and apron, turned from stirring the kettle. She put down the long wooden spoon on the tall cupboard adjacent to the fire. She was buxom but comely, and a few inches taller than her husband. Several strands of reddish-brown hair escaped her cap. She cocked her head on one side and appraised Katrina with merry blue eyes.

'''Tes a lovely lass 'ee've brung us, Will Farrow. We'll have the lads comin' a courtin' from miles awa'.''

''Tush, Rachel, let the lass set 'fore 'ee start your match-makin','' John said. He nodded his head at a place on the bench opposite him.

Katrina sat, then leaped to her feet again when her hostess began setting the table. ''Let me help.''

John waved her back down. ''Time enou' for that. Set 'ee down and rest from the journey. How were et crossin' the Tamar?''

Katrina and Will exchanged a wry look. Will dropped John a sly wink. ''I fear Katrina thinks our river is more a barrier from England than a border to it.''

''No, more a river Styx with Charon as our boatman,'' Katrina inserted, then clapped her hand over her mouth. Not for the world would she either offend her host if he understood her reference, nor embarrass him if he didn't.

She soon found that John Tonkin neither offended nor embarrassed easily. He spewed his sip of tea into his cup. For a moment she thought he was choking, but then she relaxed as she realized he was laughing.

''An' 'ee expected to be ferried across to the netherworld any moment, aye? Not that I blame 'ee. The Tamar es a spritely river en the spreng.''

Katrina's hand lowered and she smiled weakly into those twinkling brown eyes, all the while wondering how a Cornish miner knew Greek mythology. Again he read her mind with disconcerting ease.

''I were taught readen' by the old owner of our mine. I've tried to learn my bairns, but there never seems to be time enou'. If 'ee'll do that, then 'ee'll earn more than your keep. 'Ee'll earn my gratitude.''

Cheerful, youthful voices preceded the entrance of several children into the rear door off the dairy. ''Ais, wipe your feet,'' Rachel Tonkin called, fetching a large tureen from the cupboard and dipping hot broth into it. She set this on the table along with a plate of pasties, then put down a stack of spoons and rough pottery bowls.

Katrina smiled hesitantly into four pairs of curious dark eyes. ''Ellie, Bryan, Jimmy, and Robert,'' John said, indicating each child with a pointing finger, starting with the eldest. She was a tall, slim girl with her mother's pretty face and full

bosom and her father's dark hair and eyes. She eyed Katrina
with interest, and nodded.

The eldest boy, Bryan, looked to be about seventeen.
Already he was taller than his father, and almost as broad. Yet
he bore no rusty marks on his clothing as his father did, and
Katrina wondered why he didn't work in the mines. Instead his
hands were caked with mud, and she realized it must have been
he working in the fields.

Jimmy was about fifteen, with the pug nose and freckled
face of an imp. When Katrina smiled at him, he audaciously
winked. Katrina groaned inwardly. This one would be trouble.
She turned to Robert, a dark-haired little boy who was a
six-year-old version of his father. His chin was downcast, and
he refused to look at her. She closed her eyes briefly on a shaft
of agony as she realized that under different circumstances this
sturdy little boy could have been her own. But when she looked
at him again, his shyness eased her distress and she knew only
a need to put him at ease.

She stepped up to him and held out her hand. "I'm pleased
to meet you, Robert."

He blushed, shifted his feet, and peered at his father. When
John nodded, he gingerly clasped Katrina's hand, then dropped
it as if she'd burned him.

"Wash up, then set, children," John said briskly, sitting
again.

When all were seated and the broth and pasties had been
passed around, John cleared his throat. "This is Mess Lawson.
She'll be staayin' here for a time. She'll be learnin' you to read
and such." When Jimmy and Ellie groaned, he looked at them
sharply. "I want you to paay close attention. Ef you ever wants
to be more than a miner or a miner's wife, then you must
learn."

"But Da, I don't want to be more than a miner's wife—"

"Enou', Ellie. I'll not have your sass at table. For the last
time Jack Hennessy esn't fittin' for my girl, troublemaker that
he es—"

"He's not a troublemaker. You know how the workers all
look up to him—"

"A drunk braggart es not an example the more sensible of
my men admire." A stern look from him silenced the words

Katrina could see trembling on her tongue. She took a bite of pasty so hard that Katrina heard her teeth snap together.

Jimmy, on the other hand, was less direct. When his father's grim stare settled upon him, he spread his hands innocently. "Whatever you say, Da." He sliced a wicked look at Katrina. "Studyin' with her esn't no hardshep."

His father's lips twitched as he, too, peered at Katrina, who had flushed. It was left to Rachel to impose order. "Jimmy, ef 'ee bedevel the girl, 'ee'll answer to me." When he shot her a wide-eyed look, she pushed back her empty bowl and folded her arms over her impressive bosom. "And for that piece of insolence, *you* clear the table."

Jimmy scowled. "That's woman's work."

"Do as your ma says." John pointedly thrust his own empty bowl at Jimmy. Jimmy snatched it and rattled the crockery together as he stacked the bowls.

"And ef 'ee put so much as a crack en any piece, 'ee'll pay for et," Rachel warned. Then, relaxing, she turned to Katrina. "Now, lass, tell us what brought 'ee here."

Katrina looked helplessly at Will, who'd watched the exchanges at table with silent enjoyment, but he seemed interested in his napkin. "I, ah, wanted to see more of England than London, and since I left my last employment rather suddenly, I had no references. The further I went, the better, under the circumstances." She held her breath hopefully, then let it out when both Rachel and John nodded.

"And where better than Land's End? Though 'ee've a ways to go yet to find that. But now I see why 'ee don't seek work en one of the great houses," John said. "Ais, their loss es our boon. I know an honest lass when I meet one."

Katrina made a show of folding her napkin to hide her sudden tears as she thought, But do you know a virtuous one? She was glad when Will began to talk to John about the mine. When John left to return to work, Will walked him to the door. Jimmy and the others had disappeared as soon as the table was clear, Katrina assumed to return to their chores.

Rachel seemed to sense her distress, for she handed Katrina a clean cloth. "I'd be graateful ef 'ee'd dry," she said, scooping hot water from another kettle over the fire into a wooden tub, then adding cold water to it from a bucket.

When the dishes were done, Rachel guided Katrina to a narrow, uneven set of plank stairs that led off the kitchen. Up above, Katrina saw one big room divided by a wood panel that didn't reach the rafters. On each side were two low, narrow, homemade beds set with straw mattresses. On the chimney wall vents had been chinked into the whitewashed walls to allow the hearth's warmth to escape into the room. Still, Katrina imagined it got icy cold in the winter. The small, square window set with bubbly glass let the brilliant sunlight only dimly into the room.

"Robert's been staayin' weth Ellie, but we'll move him en weth the boys."

"I don't want to take anyone's bed. Perhaps I could sleep in the barn—"

"Tush, don't speak such foolishness." Rachel bent to strip the bed linens as she spoke. "We've a spare bed en storage."

Katrina thought her voice sounded muffled, and when she turned, moisture glimmered in Rachel's eyes. "I'll get Will to breng your thengs up." She hurried back down the stairs, leaving Katrina wondering why Rachel had suddenly looked upset.

The quietness of the house seemed oppressive after the intense family luncheon, and after Will left, promising to visit in a few days, Katrina asked Rachel for something to do.

So began the busiest time of her life. "For Satan finds some mischief still for idle hands to do" might have been a phrase coined by the Tonkins, Katrina often thought in the ensuing days. Each family member gave Satan short shrift.

Robert had the lightest chores of milking the cow, feeding the stock, and picking what vegetables and herbs were available. Jimmy and Bryan tended the fields, fetched the water, and collected the furze and turf for the ever-burning fire. Ellie helped her mother with the baking, cleaning, sewing, and washing. Even in the evenings family hands were seldom idle. While John read to all from the Bible or from one of his few cherished books, the children and their mother carded wool, cleaned vegetables, stripped goose feathers, and sorted grain. Katrina helped with all when she wasn't busy with the children.

She squeezed lessons in between their duties. She usually

taught Robert, who didn't even know his alphabet, in the morning after he'd tended the stock. She tutored the others before supper, when all had collected prior to the meal. As she'd suspected, Ellie proved indifferent to acquiring skills she was convinced she'd never use, and Bryan was eager to learn. Jimmy was the brightest, but wasted his intelligence. He rushed through her tediously devised lessons, missing half. He was very good at staring at her attentively, his chin propped on his hand, while he daydreamed. The fact that he was at the age where, as the old ones said, sap was rising in his young body, made her chore doubly difficult.

Two weeks after she'd moved in she was tired from yet another sleepless night and the never-ending chores. When Jimmy's gaze wandered from her face to her bodice one too many times, her patience snapped.

Quietly, she closed the math book John had borrowed from his landowner and set it on the table. "Jimmy, tell me what a square root is." They were still multiplying and dividing, so she knew the definition would be beyond him.

His gaze snapped up from her bodice to her face. He answered steadily, "It's a . . . root that's square, of course."

"No, it's a factor, multiplied by itself, to yield a number. Now, tell me the square root of four and you shall be free for the evening. No more reading, or figuring—number, or form." She emphasized the last word and was mollified a bit when he had the grace to flush.

When Ellie and Bryan snickered, he shot them an angry look. "I don't know!"

"What a pity. Then you shall have to continue studying after supper until you're ready to go on to something more challenging than multiplication. Ellie, Bryan, that's enough for this evening. You may go." Katrina rose, too, but Jimmy caught her wrist.

"You don't know the answer yourself. Admit it, *teacher.*"

Katrina didn't give him the satisfaction of a struggle. She met his blazing brown eyes and said evenly, "I gave you the easiest number there is to figure. If one wants the square root of four, one divines what number, multiplied by itself, equals four. In this case, the answer is two. Anyone with a modicum of intelligence and willingness to learn could have figured it out. What, I wonder, does that say of you?''

When Jimmy's fingers tightened, she stifled a wince. John, who was sitting with Rachel on a bench adjacent to the fire, turned to look and half rose. Katrina glanced at him and slightly shook her head, then met Jimmy's eyes again.

''It says I've no use for fancy figures nor fancy women.'' He raked her with a scathing look.

Katrina went still. Fury misted her eyes, but she gritted her teeth and counted to ten. She had committed herself to teaching these children, and she was not ready to admit defeat. ''Doubtless Mr. James Watt, whom you so admire, would find your comment ridiculous. I assure you he uses more than multiplication and division to design his engines. Now release me, and finish your work. Then I want you to write, twice, the multiplication table all the way to fifty.'' When Jimmy's fingers tightened more, this time she couldn't suppress a wince.

When his father said sharply, ''Jimmy! Leave her be!'' Jimmy flung her hand away, pulled some paper toward him, and bent his head. Katrina rubbed her aching wrist and went to join John and Rachel. Rachel clicked her tongue and sent Jimmy a worried look.

''That one's a rebel for sure. He'll dangle on a rope's end, I fear, 'less he quits that wild gang he jaunts weth. Ded he hurt 'ee?''

''Not really. And I don't think he's bad. More angry and undirected. He seems to want to work in the mine. Why won't you let him, John?''

''Will should be able to tell 'ee that,'' John replied. ''Ais, he could show 'ee, too. The doc knows better than others how dangerous the work es. My men thenk I'm crazy to let my able-bodied boys earn a pettance workin' in the laird's fields when they could bring in a good wage. But I . . .'' His voice cracked, and he had to steady it before going on, ''I lost my twens en a cave-en, and I'll not resk my other lads.''

Katrina's throat closed at the tears glittering in John's eyes, but she liked him more than ever when he blew his nose on his kerchief without shame. Rachel, with a funny hiccup, rose to serve up the ubiquitous broth, made from fish heads this time.

"I . . . wondered why there was such an age difference between Robert and the others," Katrina said softly.

"Ais, the twens would have been twelve thes summer. Bryan and Jimmy worked the bal 'fore then." When Katrina looked confused, John explained, "Our term for mine is *bal*, lass." He sighed and admitted, "And I'll not pretend I don't need their waages, but at least I know they're saafe. As long as we can keep body and soul together, my lads staay awa'."

The atmosphere at the table was subdued that night. Instead of the rollicking gossip they usually had about neighbors and the doings of the gentry in the area, they discussed the cholera epidemic spreading in the far eastern part of the county. Bitter experience had shown how fast the illness traveled.

"I'm glad Will's back," John said. "Even 'fore hes schoolin', he were the one we depended on. The old bal doctor were drunk more often than not." John passed Rachel the pipe he lit with an ember from the fire, then lit his own. Bryan and Ellie soon followed suit, and only Jimmy, writing laboriously in the flickering lantern light, and Robert abstained.

Katrina shook her head when John offered her a pipe. "No, thank you." She coughed as the rich aroma of the tobacco filled the room, but she was becoming accustomed to the scent.

"Does Will go into the mine, er, bal, with you?" Katrina asked.

"Not unless a man's hurt too bad to breng out. I does what I can to keep the men saafe. That's a captain's job. But the good ore on the top is worked out. We're havin' to go deeper and deeper, and these old pumps just esn't reliable. The water gets to the timber. I've asked the owners many times to buy better pumps, but they saay the bal esn't producin' enou' good ore to paay for them." John clamped his teeth about his pipe and stared moodily into the fire.

John rarely discussed the mine, and now Katrina understood why. He was obviously frustrated at the dangerous conditions, but didn't know what to do to make them better. And since his only skill was mining, he couldn't seek other work. It was hardly surprising that he'd forbidden his boys to work under the same conditions, despite the resulting economies the household was forced to undergo.

The dusk was deepening when Ellie quietly tapped out her

pipe, set it on the ledge above the bench, and rose. Instead of going to the stairs, however, she eased out of the kitchen toward the front door.

"Ellie," John said sharply. "Where are 'ee goin'?"

The closing door was his answer. John leaped to his feet, but Rachel caught his arm. "Et'll do no good to maake her come back. She'll just sneak out when your back's turned. Let her see her beau. She'll come to the truth of his naature soon enou'."

John looked as if he might argue, then he threw his weight back down so hard the old bench creaked. "And maaybe too late. I'll have my only daughter a wife 'fore she's a mother."

"'Ee should have more faaith en your daughter than that. Besides, she's eighteen and old enou' to make up her own mind. 'Ee cannot protect her forever."

Katrina averted her eyes from the parental argument, but her heart ached for all of them. For John's frustration, for Rachel's good sense despite her worry, but most of all for Ellie. They'd become friends in the past weeks. When the candles had been snuffed, she and Ellie had only each other to quieten the wild Cornish winds. Ellie had often told Katrina of her attraction to that bold, wickedly handsome tutworker Jack Hennessy. Katrina knew he'd pressed her to be intimate, but that so far Ellie had resisted. She wanted to lie with him, but in the marriage bed instead of on the moors.

Poor Ellie, Katrina thought now. Katrina knew what it was to long for a man who wasn't good for her. To yearn to quaff the cup of knowledge with a man whose mere presence was heady. But Katrina also knew what a bitter residue that potent brew left. . . .

With a muttered, "Good night, everyone," Katrina leaped to her feet and hurried up the stairs to her straw bed. She heard the boys go to their cubicle soon after. One of them blew out the lantern, but the darkness only increased Katrina's torment, for it was easier then to visualize the face that she'd desperately tried to forget.

An hour later, defeated, she sat up. She rarely slept more than a few hours each night. Perhaps suppressing her memories only made them more vivid. She rose and went to the window, which was open to let the cool night air into the attic.

She'd learned the hard way that the only way to defeat Demon Devon was to face him down. That appeared to be as true in absence as in the flesh. Deliberately, she stared into the darkness and let herself recall the beauty of his face and form. The old yearning took her, but it was muted by pain. She'd been right to leave. He'd have tired of her soon, anyway.

Ah, but you'd still have your babe, had you stayed. The sly thought crept into her mind. She bit her lip to stifle a moan, and her hand strayed to her abdomen. How could she have remained after that last night? He'd used her like a harlot, forced her to face the fact that her morality was weaker than her sensuality, then tried to recompense her conscience with gifts. No, she had to leave then. A promise coerced from her had little meaning, especially after he'd used her so.

The emotional pain of that night became muddled with the physical and heartsick pain that soon followed. She hated him, she told herself. No man could put a woman through such agony and still hold her regard. But if so, why couldn't she forget? She was free of him now, yet the memories still bound him to her. Why couldn't she let go? Could it be—she didn't want to? Despite everything, did she still care for him?

Her mouth twinged, and she realized she'd bitten herself. She licked the tiny wound, and soon the salty taste of blood mingled with her tears. She clenched her fists and whispered, "No. I only need time to exorcise you, Demon Devon. Please, God, help me forget."

The tears dropped faster, but before she could collapse in sobs upon the windowsill, she heard footsteps coming up the stairs. She wiped her eyes on her gown sleeve and turned to watch as Ellie entered the loft.

When the moonlight sparkled on the tears in Ellie's dark eyes, Katrina's own dried. She took a step toward her friend. "What's wrong?"

Her voice shaking with distress, Ellie replied, "Jack says he'll not see me no more 'less I lie with him."

Katrina went to her, and only then was she close enough to see the red marks on Ellie's neck, and the ripped shoulder seam of her gown. "Did he harm you?" Katrina demanded.

Ellie put her finger to her mouth. "Shhh. Let's not wake the boys. He were . . . a bit rough when I still wouldn't give in. But he didn't . . . Oh Katrina, what am I to do?''

Why was it women who always suffered? Katrina wondered bitterly, even as she cradled Ellie in her arms. Men were takers, draining a woman dry until she rattled like a corn husk, then leaving her for the next juicy tidbit. Yet women were expected to be understanding, generous, and loyal, no matter how they were treated. Then again, maybe we deserve what we get, Katrina thought. As long as we tolerate such treatment, how can we expect better?

Feeling militant, Katrina led Ellie to her low bed and sat next to her. She lifted Ellie's downcast chin and used the quilt to dry her friend's lovely dark eyes. ''If you want the advice of one who's been in your position, I say run for your life. No matter how much it hurts now to let Jack go, I can assure you it will hurt more later if you let yourself be used by him.''

''But I love him,'' Ellie sobbed.

Katrina's eyes watered. How well she understood that anguish. Unhappiness lay in wait whichever way Ellie turned. She tamped down her own sympathy and asked sensibly, ''But it's not *your* feelings you question, is it? Perhaps you should ask yourself instead how he feels about you. Would a man who loved you offer you such a choice?''

After a moment Ellie miserably shook her head. ''But . . . I can't just let him go. I *can't*!'' Ellie swallowed another heartfelt cry and cast an uneasy look at the thin partition. When no sound came, she relaxed.

Katrina heaved a sigh. ''Then your fate is sealed. One night you won't have strength to resist. You'll know then the answer to all your questions. Will I enjoy lying with a man? Will he care for me more if I do? Can I win him that way? The reply to the first question is yes; the answer to the last two, alas, is no. I'd not have it so if given a choice, but women have even less influence over reality than men.''

Ellie peered at Katrina. In the dim moonlight, with her flaxen hair and pale gown eerily aglow, Katrina looked like a fairy from the stories of the old ones. ''You speak as if you know.''

A short, bitter laugh was an eloquent response. ''Oh, I do. That's why you should heed my advice if you wish to avoid my mistakes.'' Ellie watched, frowning, as Katrina absently rubbed her stomach. Katrina said nothing further. Instead she lay down on her own bed and pulled the thin quilt up to her chin.

"Think on my words, Ellie. And I'm here whenever you wish to talk."

"As am I, Katrina."

Katrina balled her hands into fists at the sympathy in Ellie's voice. It was a very long time indeed before she slept.

The next evening Will visited while Katrina was giving the elder Tonkin children their lessons. He'd been by several times, but because he was busy at his mine office tending to the minor injuries he'd had to deal with, they had spoken little. This night he set his hat on the peg by the door with the air of a man who intended to linger.

After smiling a greeting, Katrina turned back to Jimmy, who was being deliberately obtuse. He'd been difficult all along, but since she'd gotten the best of him on the square-root issue, he'd become impossible.

Right now he was deliberately transposing the list of figures she'd given him to add. Each time she corrected him, he nodded obediently—then wrote them down the same way. Katrina didn't notice as Will leaned against the back of her chair and looked hungrily down at the shining hair she'd ruthlessly subdued into a bun.

When Jimmy's eyes wandered from Will to her and back, and he ignored her strained but still patient directions, Katrina picked up the ruler and whacked him across the knuckles. She smiled sweetly into the gaze that lit upon her face like an angry bee. "Since your fingers seem to be somewhat maladroit today, perhaps a little stimulus will help. If not, we'll try bleeding next. Will, I'm sure, can tell you that it purges the spirit."

"It's not my spirit that needs purging," Jimmy muttered, rubbing his knuckles. Then he smiled at her slyly. "But if you want to purge my urge, well, that's a horse of a different color."

Katrina flushed. Will sat down next to her, folded his arms, and cast Jimmy a half-amused, half-shaming look.

Katrina lifted her chin. "Indeed, you should be intimately familiar with horses of every shade, resembling one yourself." When Jimmy cocked his head, Katrina concluded softly, "Or I should say resembling part of a horse. The hind part, shall we say?"

Jimmy's siblings and Will burst into laughter. Jimmy reddened, then leaped to his feet. "I'll not take no more lessons from you!" He slammed out the door.

When Katrina sighed and bent her head, Will patted her shoulder. "He'll be back. Just try a bit longer and you'll get through to him."

Ellie agreed. "Jimmy's stubborn, but once he decides to learn, naught'll stop him."

Bryan, as usual, said nothing, but his gaze was worried as he looked at the closed door. When Jimmy didn't return for supper, even Will and Ellie began to wear that worried look.

Finally John slammed down the dish of pilchards chopped up with onions and salt and bit off, "Where's that boy got to thes time?" As if he didn't expect an answer, he tossed a couple of oat cakes on his plate and passed the dish to Will, who sat next to him.

He got an answer anyway, from an unexpected source. Little Robert piped up, "He's gone to be with the free traders at the pub in Truro, prob'ly."

Everyone at the table froze, except Katrina. She started, for even she knew what *free trader* meant. She'd heard tales of the smuggling rampant in Cornwall, but she'd seen no evidence of it in the Tonkin family. Until now.

There was a general clattering as everyone returned to their meal. But Robert, pleased that for once everyone was listening to him, went on. "An' when I went with Jimmy to Truro to fetch supplies, I heerd Jack Hennessy offer to include Jimmy on his next run."

Ellie choked, and Bryan had to slam her on the back to help her catch her breath. John's fist smashed into the plank table so hard the dishes jumped. "I'll not have any of my bairns actin' so lawless, no matter how much money it earns. Jimmy's not too old to whaale into sense."

"Ais, that's done a heap of good en the past," Rachel

retorted. She turned to Will. "Will, what can we do weth the lad? I'll . . . not lose another of my boys ef I can help et."

All looked at Will. He wiped his mouth on his coarse but clean and ironed napkin. "I'll have a talking to him. But I fear Jimmy is the type who must learn from bitter experience." Little was said after that, but after Katrina had helped Ellie and Rachel clean the kitchen, Will stood from his position by the fire next to John.

"I must be going, but I'd like a word with you first, Katrina." Katrina followed him out the front door to the bench just outside the gate. From the corner of her eye she saw Ellie exit the cottage and hurry down the track in the direction of Truro.

After they were settled, Katrina and Will leaned back and lifted their faces to the cool breeze. The scents of hay and freshly turned turf mingled pleasantly with the aroma of the flowers lining the walk.

The silence was a comfortable one, but finally Katrina reflected aloud, "It's been so long since I lived in the country that I'd forgotten how . . . reassuring it is. Nowhere else on earth does one feel the rhythms of life so keenly as upon a farm. Yesterday I saw a lamb being born."

When her voice broke a little, Will gave her a moment, then asked, "And how did you feel about that?"

"Happy. Sad. But sure at last that I've done the right thing. Here, I'm useful. Here, I can heal."

"Well, that answers one of my concerns. As for the other . . ."

Will sounded so intense that she turned from the stars twinkling behind hazy clouds like merry, veiled eyes. His pale hair glimmered even under the quarter moon's dim light. "Yes, Will?"

"Did you know that Jimmy has bragged to his friends of your beauty? Every young buck in the area is curious about you. Only John's calculated warnings to certain of his wilder miners have kept them away this long."

Katrina sighed and rubbed her temples with the tips of her fingers. "So even here, it begins. What did you tell John about me?"

"That you were coming out of a bad time and needed a place

to stay, as I've already told you. But he's a sensible man, Katrina. He knows that any woman with your looks who's looking for sanctuary is likely seeking it from a man. He's also noticed that not once have you ventured off his land in these last two weeks. He's drawn his own conclusions and will do what he can to shield you from the attentions you obviously don't want. Though his task will not be easy.''

"Poor John. I don't want to be a burden on him."

"You're not. After I'd treated one of his men the other day, he told me you're like a daughter to him and Rachel. They already see the difference you've made in their children—''

"Except for Jimmy."

"Jimmy is too stubborn to know what's good for him. He's also quite intelligent. You'll reach him eventually. But I didn't bring all this up to distress you, Katrina. You can't stay isolated here forever, and unless you want to be importuned by the lads for miles around, I've a suggestion to make.''

When he hesitated, Katrina folded her hands tightly in her lap, suspecting she wasn't going to like his idea. Indeed, her heart sank at his words.

"Let me walk out with you. Everyone will leave you alone then.''

Katrina knew how much the villagers admired him, and she was touched at his gallantry. But the mere idea of letting any man court her, even such a gentle one as Will, was repugnant to her.

She was shaking her head before the thought ended. "No, Will. It's too soon. I'm . . . mindful of your kindness, but I'm just not ready for . . . involvement."

"You only have to pretend, Katrina. I'd not push anything upon you, I assure you."

At his injured tone she turned to him earnestly. "I know that, Will. But I've learned the hard way what damage pretense can do. Maybe, in a year or so, we can speak of this again."

"A year!" Will snapped his mouth closed so hard his teeth clicked, but his reply was even. "Very well, Katrina. But I'd be careful about leaving the farm alone. Some of the men hereabouts have unsavory reputations for a reason. Now, if you'll excuse me, I've notes to write."

With a curt nod Will rose and stomped off to his horse. A

few seconds later Katrina heard the sounds of a whip and frantic hoofbeats. For Will to take his anger out on a dumb beast, he must be furious indeed. She dropped her head against the hard rim of the bench and closed her eyes. Now she'd hurt the one man she should be most grateful to. She didn't want to face why she'd found that necessary, but she'd promised herself to be honest.

"Damn you, Devon Cavanaugh," Katrina whispered. "You hold me even hundreds of miles away, even when you've probably forgotten me in the arms of another woman."

She couldn't let any man court her. Not now. Maybe not ever. Entanglement brought more pain than joy. And hate the knowledge though she did, Katrina felt from some deep, instinctive level that letting another man court her would be a betrayal of what she'd felt for Devon. Oh, she owed him nothing. He'd ruined what could have been beautiful as surely as if he'd escorted her to that brothel himself. She hated him almost as much as she missed him, and she despised herself for still longing for him despite everything. But while she couldn't forget and put the past behind her, she had no future to offer anyone else. She liked Will Farrow too much to use him for her own protection and give naught in return.

A strange scraping sound startled her from her dreary thoughts. She sat up and peered into the darkness. She saw a figure wavering up the track, and when the moon caught the shimmering trails down a pretty face, Katrina leaped to her feet.

She ran to meet Ellie. "What's amiss?" Katrina lifted Ellie's chin when she trudged to a stop without a response. She jerked her chin away, but too late. A big handprint was vivid on Ellie's cheek. Before the night was out, it would be a ghastly bruise, Katrina knew.

"Who's done this to you?" Ellie just shook her head and began to cry again. "Come into the house so we can bathe your face."

Ellie jerked away and gasped between sobs, "No . . . p-please. My da will want to . . . kill him. And Jack's a big, strong man. Much b-bigger than Da."

Katrina sighed, but gently led Ellie to the stream and wet her clean kerchief. As she seated them both on the bank and dabbed at Ellie's cheek, she said grimly, "I suggest you tell me truly what happened, or I'll fetch your father myself."

"I . . . went to his house to tell him to leave Jimmy alone. He . . . laughed at me, Katrina." Anger stiffened Ellie's spine and voice. "Told me not to concern myself with men's matters. That I'd see the sense of what he was doing when he gave me some pretty trinkets. As if I was a dog he tossed a bone to. He certainly had no more respect for me than he does for that stray he sometimes feeds."

Katrina rinsed the handkerchief again, then brought Ellie's hand up to her cheek to hold the wet square. "Press that gently and maybe some of the swelling will go down." She sat back on her heels. "Go on, Ellie."

"He'd been drinking, but that's no excuse. When he wouldn't promise to leave Jimmy out of his . . . skulduggery, I told him I'd have no more to do with him. Then he got mad. Threatened to take me by force, but I kicked him and he let me go." Ellie looked at Katrina defiantly, and Katrina lightened the moment by giving her a teasing brush on the chin.

"Good for you, Ellie."

"That's when he hit me. I started to run away then, but he called me ugly names and . . ." Ellie trailed to a stop.

"And?"

She finished in a rush. "And he said he'd be maakin' your acquaaintance soon." Ellie's usually muted accent was strong, clueing Katrina to how much this news distressed her. Not for the world would Katrina reveal how her own heart thudded at the thought.

"Don't worry about me, Ellie. I can hold my own. I have with more powerful men than Jack Hennessy. Now, what will we tell your father?"

"That I walked into a tree?"

"He'll see through that in a trice. How about we tell him you tripped over the furze and fell as you came from the barn after checking on the lamb?" Katrina rose and drew Ellie away from the river into the moonlight. "The finger marks are fading. I don't think he'll be able to tell what struck you."

"That's a good idea." Impulsively Ellie hugged Katrina. "I'm so glad you came to us."

"Thank you, Ellie. I'm glad, too," Katrina responded huskily.

Ellie whirled and led the way to the house, but as they opened the door Katrina saw how fixed and shiny her eyes were. So she spun a merry tale about the lamb's antics as they entered the kitchen. Rachel smeared Ellie's cheek with home-made herbal liniment without comment, but John's eyes were suspicious.

When Ellie had escaped upstairs, John caught Katrina's arm as she was about to follow. "Just a moment."

Katrina turned slowly. "Yes, John?"

"How es et that you dedn't catch my lass when she fell ef you was weth her?"

"Er, I tried, but missed her arm in the darkness."

"I see. Well, I'll have you know, lettle laady, that I doesn't mess much concernin' my bairns. Ef a certain brawny young man comes near my lass again, he'll have me to deal weth. Tell Ellie that from me."

"I don't think you need to worry about Ellie anymore, John. But I'll tell her." Katrina climbed a step, then turned her head. "And thank you, too, for your care for one who is not one of your bairns. Will told me what you said to your men."

John flicked a big, callused hand in the air. "'Tweren't notheng. Good night, Katrina."

"Good night, John." Upstairs, Katrina let Ellie talk until her throat was raw, but her eyes, thankfully, were dry. Just as she drifted off to sleep Katrina reflected that despite the challenges she'd found somewhere she really belonged. She liked every-one in this family, even Jimmy. She was slowly becoming as well liked in return, she believed. Love and belonging would surely follow. That aching, empty spot in her heart that not even Devon had been able to fill began to shrink.

Not since her father died had she felt this kinship with anyone. Even the good moments with Devon had been rife with emotion. This sense of homecoming was like a bedrock—safe, secure, a foundation upon which to build.

For the first time in years Katrina looked forward to the future.

Part Two

"And when I feigned an angry look,
Alas! I loved you best."

—JOHN SHEFFIELD, Duke of
   Buckingham and Normandy,
"The Reconcilement"

Chapter Six

1789; two years later

THE AIR IN White's most exclusive card room was stuffier than usual. The scents of smoke, stale cologne, and strong cheese mingled, but the miasma of greed overpowered all. A young fop with gold-embroidered waistcoat, purple satin jacket, and clock-decorated stockings sat opposite a lean man attired in ministerial black. The glint in the elder man's eyes was not benign, however. The other men at the table had thrown in their hands and waited, expressing varying degrees of curiosity, to see the outcome of this do-or-die rubber for the young fop.

With a trembling hand the lad pulled a slim sheath of papers from his jacket and set it atop the pile of chips. "The deed to Farnsworth Hall, Wendover," he said. His posture, leaning forward, fists bunched atop the table, was defiant, but his voice quavered.

The onlookers gasped and turned as one to Wendover.

After examining the deed, Wendover carelessly threw it back down. "Accepted."

In a nearby but isolated corner long, powerful legs shifted restlessly beneath a square of newspaper. One foot tapped, then came a muffled curse. Devon tossed his paper aside and angled his chair to watch the game.

He'd always despised the Marquess of Wendover, especially after learning he was a charter member of the Satyr Society. Any man who took pleasure in inflicting pain was corrupt to his soul. His cardplaying habits were no more palatable. The marquess lived comfortably on the fortune his estates and Cornish mines made him, yet he enjoyed fleecing the young pups who came in legions to London. Like Wendover's other victims, young Farnsworth was about to discover the hard way that town bronze, when acquired too lavishly, decayed a fellow's prospects rather than enhanced them.

Devon fought the urge to join the game. He'd always suspected that Wendover cheated, but had never been interested enough to try to prove it. If men were so dim-witted as to barter all they had on Lady Luck's whims, then they deserved to lose all, had been his philosophy. Curse it, the lad's downfall was already a fait accompli, and it was none of his affair. Yet something drew him to his feet. Sutterfield had been one of Wendover's sycophants, and the sight of the man who had acted as the owl on that night almost two years ago revived upsetting memories.

The pain Katrina's desertion could still arouse made him want to strike out; here was a perfect target. But as he sauntered to the table Devon told himself that curiosity alone drew him. Still, an odd little pang gripped him when young Farnsworth paled to a sickly hue as the hand progressed. Compassion, however, was as new to Devon as uncertainty, and he scowled. "Idiotish young jackanapes," he muttered beneath his breath. The hand ended as he had known it would.

Farnsworth clutched the edge of the green baize-covered table so hard his fingers scored the felt. He gritted his teeth, but the words seemed forced out of him. "Cheat! 'Twould be impossible for you to predict the cards so well any other way." He reeled to his feet.

Wendover thrust back his chair and lifted his hand to strike, but a cool, deep voice interrupted.

"You'll find me more of a challenge than this young pup." Devon shot Farnsworth a dismissive look. "I've so much more to fleece." Devon pulled out a chair opposite Wendover and sat down.

"Fie on you, sir! I'll gladly meet Wendover's challenge, and yes, yours too!" Farnsworth cried, turning on this apparent new enemy.

Devon threw him a bored glance, then lifted an eyebrow at Wendover.

Several young men caught Farnsworth's shoulders and dragged him away before he could make another outburst. One of them whispered loudly, "Put a damper on it, man, and leave while you still can."

None of the remaining bystanders even watched them leave. Instead their gazes shifted between Devon's negligent posture and Wendover's brooding one. With a last glare at the closing door Wendover sat back down in his place and began stacking his gargantuan pile of chips into neat rows.

"We've seen precious little of you these past two years, Cavanaugh. Have you lost your taste for life's finer pleasures, or did the chit geld you?"

Several men goggled in shock. They swung toward the Demon.

Devon paused in the act of writing a draft on his bank to purchase chips. His quill tip scored the paper before he finished his signature rather sloppily, but his reply was quiet. "So you have been in touch with Sutterfield. I wondered if you were so impressed by his toadeating as to send him funds. After tonight you'll no longer have the ready to do so, I assure you."

Devon handed the check and a tip to one of White's legion of polite servants. "And bring a fresh deck, if you please," he added. The man moved to obey, but Wendover caught his arm and drew him down to whisper something. He tipped him also, then the fellow melted away. Devon beckoned to another servant and muttered a request. With a peculiar look at him the man hurried off, returning soon after with a bottle and a glass.

"Do I take that as an insult to my honesty?" Wendover growled, turning back to Devon.

"You can take it however you please. But I always begin a game with a new deck." Devon poured himself a glass of wine and took a leisurely sip.

"That's true, Wendover," said Harley, an old acquaintance of Devon's.

When the pack was brought, Devon slit open the seal, then handed it to Harley. "Will you deal, please?"

Devon watched closely as the servant set a bottle and a glass at Wendover's elbow, but if he slipped Wendover another deck, Devon couldn't see it. Besides, with faro, where one card was turned up at a time, Wendover couldn't palm a card while another man dealt.

The game commenced. Devon was a bit rusty, since he

hadn't played much in the last two years, but the old facility for keeping an account of the cards in his head soon returned. Faro had always been one of his favorite games for that reason; luckily it was Wendover's game of choice, too.

Devon lost the first few hands, but deliberately conceded the fourth. When he was down by several thousand pounds, he made a bold bid. "My luck is about to turn, I opine, so shall we double the stakes?" He flung chips equaling three thousand more pounds into the center of the table. Wendover matched him.

When Wendover predicted the order of the next two cards, Devon winced as the marquess dragged in the pot of over ten thousand pounds. "Damme, but that's put a tidy hole in my income for the quarter." Devon tossed back his fifth glass of burgundy, but he was careful to keep his goblet away from the candlelight so Wendover couldn't see that the liquid it held was a paler red than usual. Devon wondered what old White would have done at seeing an earl request watered wine. Have a spasm, probably.

Devon's smile was lopsided as he unsteadily set his glass down. He glanced at Harley's frowning face, then quickly away. If his old school chum wasn't careful, he'd queer the game for him by ruining his charade. Unlike Wendover, Harley well knew that Devon had never mixed cards and drink.

Only ten cards were left. Devon had been counting, and all the face cards, aces, deuces, treys, and sixes had shown. He couldn't remember if he'd seen two fives and fours, or three, but he knew he'd only seen one eight and no tens. So that meant seven of the remaining cards were either eights or tens. Of course, they could be in any order, but he'd gone with the odds before and won. The next hand would probably offer even less of a chance.

"What say we really shweeten the deal, Wendover?"

Wendover quite playing with his chips to arrow a superior sneer at Devon. After a scornful glance at Devon's almost empty glass Wendover took a tiny sip of the same drink he'd been working on all night. "How so?"

"I've a tiny lil . . . lit-dle eshtate in the Cotswolshs, er, Cotschwolds, er, well, you know what I mean. Worth over twenty thousand, on last accountin'. I'll shtake it against F-Farnshworsh's property.''

Several gasps sounded from the onlookers. Harley stiffened, but this time he kept his gaze on the card bank before him.

Wendover frowned. ''That's not equitable. His acres are well run indeed by his manager, I hear.'' He waved away Devon's interruption. ''But I've lands in Cornwall that include a copper mine you may be interested in.''

Devon groaned inwardly, but it would be out of character for him to dismiss the offer out of hand. ''C-copper?''

''The yield was very profitable these last few years. With the land and house it should easily be worth that sum.''

Devon noticed that Wendover didn't boast about the yield *this* year, but his act would be spoiled if he commented on the omission. ''B-blasht the fellow, you know who I mean. I'd rather have his lands. Young pup inshulted me.''

Wendover shook his head. ''That's my offer.'' When Devon didn't respond immediately, he said, ''Well?''

Damme, it seemed they'd have to play another game. Wondering what he'd do with a copper mine, Devon said, ''Very well. I bet my landsh againsht your mine that the nexsht three cards will show an eight and two tens.''

''In that order?'' Wendover's smile was just short of open contempt at the risky bet.

Devon lowered his eyes over a mean glare. What the hell. He'd have to be daring to draw Wendover in. If God really did mind fools, then He'd be on Farnsworth's side, Devon thought. And his own as well. He nodded vigorously.

''Done.'' Wendover didn't even trouble to hide his rapacious smile.

Both players and onlookers held their breath as Harley slowly turned up the cards. Eight, ten, ten.

This time Devon's lopsided grin wasn't feigned. The rest of the game was anticlimactic, and when the deck was dealt, Devon picked up the scraps of paper he and Wendover had written their IOUs on. He pocketed them, making as if to rise.

Wendover snapped, ''Not so fast, Cavanaugh. As a gentleman you must give me a chance to recoup. Shall we say Farnsworth's estates against yours in the Cotswolds and the mine?''

When Devon blinked at him, Wendover slammed one palm against the table. "And you can cease the drunken act. No sot could have known the odds on eights and tens remaining."

Devon exchanged a rueful grin with Harley, then gave an elegant shrug. "Had you suckered for a while, anyway, Wendover."

Wendover bit back a curse. "Well?"

"Very well, Wendover. One more game it will be." Devon settled back in his chair.

As Harley moved to gather up the scattered cards Wendover reached for his bottle. His forearm knocked it over. Wine flooded the table and the cards.

"Satan's backside!" he exclaimed. "I'm sorry. Let's move venue. I'll call for a fresh deck." After they'd seated themselves at a new table, Wendover held up two fingers. The same man who'd served him before brought a new pack.

Devon thought Wendover's tip seemed a bit generous for the simple service, and he watched narrowly as Harley slit the seal and inspected the new deck. They were lovely cards, with a peacock in full feather centered on the royal-blue background.

Devon looked at them closely, but could see no flaw. As before, they started the game with small wagers, sweetening each bet as they worked up to the big stakes that consisted, at the moment, of scraps of paper. As he played Devon had no inkling of the impact that one small piece of paper would have on his life. He thought of nothing but the cards, and besting Wendover.

When Wendover lost several of the smaller hands, Devon's nerves tensed. Something in Wendover's manner bothered him. He was a bit too controlled, too sure of himself. He showed no emotion, whether he lost or won a hand, unlike the last game, when his mouth tightened at every defeat.

Devon stared so hard at the peacock that his vision doubled. His eyes widened slightly, then narrowed on the cleverest marking imaginable. The peacock had exactly thirteen eyes on its tail feathers—one for every card from deuce to ace. One of those feathers had a deeper blue in its center, Devon now saw. He counted from left to right. If he was right, the next card should be a jack, matching Wendover's bet.

Harley slowly turned the card over. A jack of diamonds.

Devon looked down to hide the gleam in his eyes. It was his turn. This one should be a trey. He watched calmly as the three of clubs was turned over. He and Wendover continued in this fashion, predicting accurately what each successive card would be. When they were halfway through the deck, Wendover began to go a bit green under Devon's cool stare.

One old fellow who watched from a nearby table trumpeted, "Damnedest streak of luck I've ever seen."

Given that both men could read the cards, the game was even when, near the bottom of the deck, Devon decided to make his move. He shoved all his chips as well as his slips of paper into the center of the table. Wendover hesitated, then reluctantly matched him.

All but one of the kings had shown. "This one will be the king of spades. Appropriate, isn't it, Wendover?"

"One card's not good enough for such a stake, Cavanaugh. You must guess the following two, also."

"Agreed, Wendover. On the condition that I be allowed to look at the backs of the cards, first."

"Deuced irregular," the same old man was heard to mutter.

"I quite agree," Devon said. "But if the cards aren't marked, what difference will it make?" On the words, the servant who had brought the deck tried to slink out the door, but Devon commanded, "Apprehend that lackey!" Two of the onlookers pounced on him. "Inform the manager that the man is susceptible to a bribe."

Devon's inscrutable gaze returned to Wendover. All eyes followed.

Wendover blustered, "Do you imply that I cheat, Cavanaugh?"

"No, I say it quite plainly." When Wendover leaped to his feet, Devon said wearily, "Oh, spare me the histrionics. I can prove it. Harley, let me see the backs of the next two cards."

After Harley had set them out, Devon tapped the fourth eye on one and the tenth on the other. "See this eye? If you look at it closely, it's a darker blue than the others. Counting over, the first card is a four, the next a ten."

Harley flipped each card. The king of spades. A four. A ten.

A collective gasp went through the room, then chatter burst

out as the observers stared aghast at Wendover. Wendover's mouth worked in fury, but his hands stayed at his sides.

Devon smiled sardonically. It was one of the few times his reputation had worked in his favor. It would be tiresome to have to duel Wendover, not to mention ridiculous. Not a man in the ton would act as Wendover's second under the circumstances.

Devon held out his hand. "Farnsworth's deed, if you please."

"But I won it fairly!"

"Whether the cards were marked or not, you took advantage of the lad." Devon turned an inquiring look on the others. "Don't you chaps agree?"

"Assuredly."

"By Jove he did."

"Besides, according to the rules by which you played, I won it. The last hand was to me, was it not?"

Wendover snatched the deed from his pocket and flung it at Devon's head. Devon caught it neatly. "Have a pleasant evening, Wendover," he purred as the marquess whirled and stomped off. Devon saw the manager of White's pull him aside and knew that Wendover would probably be barred. He fervently hoped that the Cornwall mine had made a large part of the marquess's income, though he doubted it.

Harley clapped him on the shoulder. "Capital show! I've always suspected Wendover cheated, and I'd grown tired of seeing him prey on every green sprig who came to White's. You put him to the roundabout handily, Devon."

Harley's eyes were warmer than Devon had ever seen them. Since their Oxford days, they'd circled society in different sets. Harley had always frowned on Devon's antics and, since his marriage three years ago, had become even stodgier. So why, Devon wondered, did he suddenly feel envious of this heavy-set, ordinary-looking man he'd only tolerated in the past?

"How is Ann, Harley?"

Harley beamed. "Right as rain. She's in confinement now at my estate. Our second, you know. Probably another handsome little boy, according to the midwife."

Devon almost winced at Harley's obvious happiness. Some of his own glow at besting Wendover faded. "Wish you both a healthy heir.'' He waved carelessly before walking off to call for his carriage.

He entered his town house just as the sun burst over the horizon. He yawned and stretched his aching neck. He must be getting old. Gaming the night through had never tired him so in his salad days. A voice arrested his weary climb up the stairs.

''Devvie lad, I've got the newest report, if ye want to see it.'' Billy came out of the study with a paper in his hand.

Devon turned eagerly and leaped down the three steps in a bound. ''Yes? Have they found her?''

Billy raised a hand, palm outward. ''Whoa there, lad. I said naught o' that. In truth the news is not good. But ye said ye wanted to always see the monthly reports soon as they come in. . . .'' Billy trailed off as Devon, his energy evaporating as quickly as it had formed, took the paper.

His arm brushed against his jacket, and a rustling made him pause. He drew Farnsworth's deed from his pocket and handed it to Billy. ''Send this along to young Farnsworth, but hire a messenger. I don't want my livery seen. No message goes with it.'' Then he trudged into the study.

Ten minutes later he crumpled the paper and tossed it aside. Resting his head against the chair back, he closed his eyes. Two years. Nothing in two years of looking. He and Billy had searched, at first. They must have questioned every hansom-cab driver in London.

None recalled a fare such as they described. A doctor? Where would a doctor take an ill girl? They'd questioned other physicians, visited asylums. Finally, no other choice remaining, they'd turned their attention to bawdy houses. Perhaps this ''doctor'' was no more than a quack who'd kidnapped Katrina to sell her to a higher bidder.

Some of the sights they'd seen still made Devon's stomach churn. If Katrina were imprisoned in one of those asylums where patients were treated like dogs, or one of the meaner bawdy houses where youth was soon made old, then the Katrina he'd known was probably already lost to him. She couldn't survive two years of hell and emerge intact.

The thought that he'd himself sporadically visited such places made him sick. He'd always assumed the whores had chosen the gay life. Thorough knowledge of houses of ill repute, the people who ran them, and how they operated had since disabused him of that comfort. Thank God the Satyr Society had disbanded under the public outcry. If it hadn't, he would have somehow put a stop to it. He owed Katrina that much.

As to what had happened to her at Madame Lusette's . . . His thoughts shied away. Sutterfield, apparently, had not gotten much satisfaction from her, so perhaps none other had either. If she became ill shortly after her arrival . . . But that way lay madness, too. What if she contracted the pox and was still ill when she left instead of well as the madam believed? Devon ground his teeth together in denial.

She wasn't dead. Somewhere she was healthy and cared for. He had to believe that. Something deep in the soul he too often denied knew he would see her one day. But how was he to bear these interminable, dreary hours until that day arrived?

Katrina. Kat. Without a glimpse of her for two years, or a whiff of her fresh scent, she was more appealing to him than the women who now sought his favor. At first, in his hurt fury, he'd availed himself of their charms even as he'd tried to drown his sorrow in wine. Both tactics had been self-defeating. Neither women nor wine could solace him. Katrina had touched more than his body. He'd not been able to face that knowledge before she left, but losing her had brought the truth brutally home to him: She was the only woman who could satisfy this need. Whether it was love, lust, or looniness, he couldn't say. But only finding her could free him of these cursed memories.

He remembered her laughing when besting him at chess, he remembered her crying as she told him of her fears, he remembered her reluctant but ardent responses to his embraces. He moaned and rubbed his burning eye sockets. "Damn you," he gritted aloud. As had been more and more the case of late, his feelings seesawed between anguish and anger. He was beginning to suspect she wasn't in London at all. And if he had the breadth of England to search, he'd probably never find her.

He had friends in the Foreign Office who were used to investigating and spying. They'd given him the names of retired officers who were, at a price, available to seek missing persons. Unable to find Katrina on his own, Devon had, six months ago, turned to two of them for help. However, they'd been no more successful. They'd expanded the search to the posting houses outside London and had thus far covered the eastern and northern roads. They still had the western inns to question, but Devon was not optimistic.

Surely, with all the hours and money spent looking, they should have found some trace of her by now. Besides, foolish it might be, but he felt that some gut instinct would warn him if she were dead or truly in danger. The conclusion was unavoidable: She didn't want to be found.

The pain that gripped him at the thought made him clutch his stomach as if he'd been punched. God, how could she do this to him? Perhaps he'd been hard on her, but surely even her puritan instincts should not sentence him to two years of hell in penance for one month of stolen pleasure. How much longer could he go on this way? None of his old habits appealed to him. Today was the first time he'd truly enjoyed himself in months. Perhaps he should consider buying his colors. . . .

In his misery he didn't hear Billy knock and then enter. "This just come for ye, lad." Billy dropped a document into Devon's lap and flung himself into the chair opposite.

Devon spread the papers open. His bleary eyes cleared a bit as he read. When he was finished, he tapped the sheaf thoughtfully against one knee. Finally he looked at Billy.

"What do you say to a visit to Cornwall, Billy?"

"Cornwall? I thought ye were hell-bent and determined to find the lass?"

Devon's lip curled. "She's probably safe as some man's mistress, gladly giving him nightly what I had to fight for."

"Ye don't really believe that, lad."

"I don't know what I believe any longer, Billy." Devon flung the papers on his desk and sprang to his feet. "But this I know: I've had enough of London for a while. I've always wanted to visit Cornwall, and since I've just won lands and a mine there, what better time? I've also got an old friend there whom I haven't seen since my Oxford days who's been urging me to visit. I'll have the reports sent on to me." Devon turned, saying over his shoulder, "Pack for a lengthy stay." And he was even heard to whistle as he climbed the stairs two at a time.

* * *

Two weeks later Katrina cast uneasy glances over her shoulder as she hurried her steps. She'd always enjoyed storms in Kent, thinking whimsically that they were manifestations of nature's temper. Here, on the moors, with no trees to shield the peninsula from the violent channel winds, she had discovered that Kent's storms were mere outbursts compared with Cornwall's maniacal rages. She had no desire to play rag doll to nature's tantrums.

Early that morning Rachel had warned her against going all the way to Gwennap. "There's a storm comen', and you'd not want to be caught en et."

"But with Will busy at the mine after the cave-in, who else is there to go? Birthing a baby is not so hard. I've assisted Will before."

"Et's Moll's fourth bairn, and her eldest girl can help."

"No, I'd never forgive myself if something happened." Katrina looked away from Rachel's puzzled eyes, drew her shawl over her shoulders, and hurried out. She couldn't explain to Rachel how compelled she felt to assist Moll. Had her own circumstances been different, she hoped someone would have been there when her time came. What if mother or child died because she'd been too afraid to risk a storm? She'd lost one innocent life out of cowardice and selfishness, and though she could never recompense either God or her own conscience for that shame, she could vicariously experience the miracle of life.

Now, ten hours later, Katrina was relieved that she'd gone despite the storm. The birthing had indeed been difficult, and Moll's daughter had panicked at her mother's pain. With Katrina's steady encouragement, however, Moll had found the last strength she needed to push the lusty baby boy, face wrong side up, out. Moll's maternal pride at holding her first son had brought tears to Katrina's eyes.

After she'd cleaned and diapered the small scrap of humanity, Katrina had planted a kiss on the downy little head and held him close. Then she'd swallowed her tears and given him to Moll to feed. When Moll drifted off to sleep after her own sponge bath and the baby was safe in his cradle, Katrina began the long walk home.

Rain had battered the cozy cottage during Moll's labor, and she'd hoped that the storm had spent itself. However, while she was still a mile from home, a gale began to blow. Katrina tied her shawl under her chin and bent her head into the wind. It seemed she progressed by inches rather than steps, and her legs began to feel like lead. Dusk was upon her, and unless she hurried, she'd have to grope in the darkness for the turnoff to the cottage.

Windblown bits of grass and earth stung her face as she at last spied the turnoff. She sighed her relief and pulled her shawl down over her face to shield it. She needed only to follow her feet on the track to the cottage. Thus she was unprepared for the rough grip that hauled her to a stop.

She bit back a scream and twisted at her arm, flinging her shawl back. At first she saw only a shadow towering above her, but then lightning flashed. She beheld bold, craggy features, handsome in a rough way, capped by thick black hair. She quit pulling at her arm and went still.

"What do you want, Hennessy?" she asked. Her heart rate slowed, but not by much. On her town outings, and at fairs and social events, she'd not been able to avoid the young men of the area. However, most of them accepted her gentle, but firm rebuffs. Not so Jack Hennessy. Katrina had always wondered if he pestered her because he knew she'd advised Ellie to give him up.

For whatever reason, his looks and innuendos were depressingly familiar and precisely what she'd come to Cornwall to avoid. She was tired, hungry, and a little scared, but her demeanor was calm. For one other thing she knew of Jack Hennessy: He was like a wild animal; if he scented blood, he went for the jugular.

"Only a word wi' ye, lass." But he leered down at her dress, where the wind and fine mist had made it cling to her legs. "Ye've done a pretty job o' avoidin' me, but now I'll say ma piece."

"Yes?" Her face didn't show her revulsion as his big, rough hand began to caress her bare forearm.

"I wants ye ta step out wi' me. P'raps we can even go inta Truro and dine at an inn." His chest puffed out as if he were proud of himself for being so generous.

"That's very kind of you, Jack, but I could never hurt Ellie so."

"Ellie, bosh! She ain't got no hold on me. She sent me off, remember?"

"Yes, I know, but it would still be upsetting for her to see me with you. So, though I thank you kindly, I have to be getting home." She tried to tug her arm away, but his grip tightened.

"Home, is it? Don't make me laugh. Ye'll niver be welcome here so long as ye have these hoity-toity airs. 'Thank ye kindly, Jack,'" he mimicked in a falsetto. He stuck his angry face into hers. "'Tis not yer thanks I wants, missy."

Katrina wrenched her arm away. "Well, that's all you'll get." She turned and began to walk up the path. The rain chose that moment to quit playing with them and began to fall in earnest.

He kept pace with her. "We'll see about that. Do ya think we be stupid jist 'cause we ain't from London? Well, I ain't slow as these Cornishmen. I'm from Manchester, and I know a choice bit o' muslin when I see one. Ye're jist holdin' out for a lord. . . ."

Katrina froze in her tracks, so furious that she didn't consider the consequences of her action. When Hennessy stopped, too, Katrina drew back her arm and struck him full in the face. "Don't you *ever* speak so to me again," she said through her teeth.

Lightning flashed three times, garishly revealing how his white shock changed to fury. He clenched a big fist and began to raise it, but Katrina was already several steps up the path. She'd trod it many more times than Hennessy, and she leaped over the rough patch of holes and stones.

Hennessy apparently stumbled behind her on the rain-slick stones, for she heard a curse and a thumping noise as he fell. Fear chased her tiredness away, and she ran as if her life depended on it; as it might have.

Hennessy seemed to think better of pursuing her, for she was almost to the cottage. However, he roared like a wounded bear, "This ain't the last o' this, bitch. Ye'll see me agin." Then she heard him no more.

She didn't quit running, however, until she reached the gate.

She sagged against it. Never had those warm lights been more welcoming. When her heartbeat slowed, she pushed the gate open and went to the door.

She found the family around the table. All except Jimmy. They saw little of him these days. Katrina still tried to teach him, but he balked at every turn. Even John seemed resigned to his rebellion.

The last time they'd discussed Jimmy, John had shaken his head wearily. "He won't lesten to sense. He's sixteen and almost a man now, so I can't strap hem as I used to. Never ded any good, anyway. He'll have to find hes own way, sence he won't take no guidance."

Katrina hoped now that his words would not be prophetic. She cast a wavery smile at the ring of concerned faces. "I'm fine, just a little wet. Gwennap numbers a fine healthy boy among its people now. Moll is recovering nicely."

"Good, good. I'm glad you made et back safe," Rachel said, rising to give Katrina a towel. "Here, I heated thes for you by the fire. I've saved you some broth. Get ento dry clothes and come on down."

After Katrina had changed and had her broth and pasty, she went to the bench where John smoked and stared moodily into the flames. Ellie and Rachel sat with him, chatting about tomorrow's chores.

Warming her hands at the blaze they needed this eve to chase the chill, misty winds away, Katrina asked, "And how are things at the bal, John? Have they gotten all the men out yet?"

"We got the last of them out today. Only one man was bad hurt, and Will thenks he'll recover." But John didn't seem relieved. He took a deep draw on his pipe, and expelled it in an angry gust. "But thes won't be the last caave-en lest we get the new tember and pump I've asked for."

"And Lord Carrington won't agree?"

"Nay."

Katrina sighed and sat down before Ellie, leaning her back companionably against her friend's knees. When Ellie stroked through the drying strands of Katrina's loose hair, Katrina's voice became a little slurred with tiredness. "Would you like me to talk with him?"

Katrina had met Lord Carrington, a tall, handsome widower, in Truro when she was with John to purchase supplies. He'd picked up the parcel she'd dropped and introduced himself. He'd even deigned to call on her at the cottage a time or two, but when she'd not encouraged his attentions, he'd quit coming.

"I don't want to drag you ento thes, lass. He might, er, expect you to be, er, obliging." John harrumphed and clamped his teeth about his pipe, refusing to meet her eyes.

Katrina turned her head to look up at him. "But I *want* to help, John. Lord Carrington is a gentleman and will ask no more of me than I'm willing to give." When he only gnawed harder at his pipe stem, she covered his big hand with her own. "Please, let me do this. I can never repay the kindness you and yours have shown me, but this, at least, is something meaningful I can do."

When John looked at her, his eyes still reluctant, she added, "Besides, many lives may be saved if we can convince Lord Carrington to help."

"All right, lass. But you're not to go to the manor alone. You'll waait until after lunch, when I can go weth you."

"Agreed." That settled, Katrina rose and sent a warm smile to the others. They had, as usual, silently listened to the debates between John and Katrina. "Since tomorrow is wash day, I'd best get to bed. Good night, all."

But once in bed, for the first time in some while she couldn't sleep. Even after Ellie and the boys retired, she tossed and turned. The winds calmed. Several stars winked at her through the small window, and finally she obeyed their lure and rose to kneel before the open casement. Breathing deeply of the rainwashed air, she repeated to herself some of the prayers she'd learned as a child, but even her communion with God offered no solace this night.

For months now she'd kept unhappiness at bay, but holding the beautiful babe had made her realize that she'd only bandaged over open wounds. She'd literally toiled to put the past behind her. Nothing was more restorative to melancholia than work, and eventually she'd managed equanimity, if not happiness. However, these days she wasn't busy enough. Her teaching duties had lessened of late because Bryan was now estate manager for a nearby landholder, Ellie had learned all she was willing to, and Jimmy wouldn't learn. That left only little Robert for her to tutor. She hated being inactive, so she'd cajoled Will into letting her assist him from time to time. She'd found her nursing chores to be the most fulfilling of all her duties.

Except for the birthings . . . During the joyful events themselves she was happy and moved. But later, when the glow faded, she was left with only the ashes of her own defeat. Specters she'd tried to banish rose up to haunt her yet again. Katrina rubbed her burning eyes, but finally she gave up the battle. Burying her head on her folded arms, she wept. For herself. For the babe she still mourned. And, yes, for Devon.

"Devon," she whispered. The sound of his name on her lips was so familiar, so bittersweet. So hurtful still. How many times had she dreamed of him, only to awaken in tears? How many times had she contained her misery only by telling herself she hated him? But no matter how badly he'd hurt her, it was always the tender, laughing Devon she remembered.

It was he she mourned. Two years they'd been apart, yet the image she carried in her head was as vivid as ever. No hate, no grief, no resolve had been strong enough to subdue it. What future did she have until she could put the past behind her?

Since Hennessy had become persistent, Will had renewed his own suit. For her protection, he said, but she recognized the hunger in his eyes. Not even for Will, however, could she pretend. He'd not be happy, in the end, with what she had to give. So she'd gently but firmly refused his tentative kisses and shy invitations. During the few social events she couldn't avoid she stayed with the family. Consequently, Will had become cool to her of late. She could hardly bear the hurt resentment in his eyes, but she couldn't, for his own sake, give him what he thought he wanted.

Yet she owed so much to Will Farrow. He was kind, handsome, and apparently well-off from his inheritance. Most of the unattached girls in the area were infatuated with him. But every time he took her into his arms, she stiffened. His arms were not strong enough, his chest was too slim, his hair was too light. Though she hated herself for the comparisons, as long as she found him lacking, more between them was impossible.

Wearily, Katrina rose. She wiped her eyes on her gown and went back to bed, but the darkness was evocative. Finally she pulled the sheet up over her head. She drifted off then, only to dream of smoother sheets and the warm, hard body that shared them with her.

The next day, when Katrina and John sighted Carrington House, its crenellated roof towering above the trees lining the drive, they stopped. Katrina wiped her sweaty palms on her best dress, the gray one she'd brought from London, though it was a sight by now. John gave her a piercing look.

"'Tes not too late to go home, lassie."

"No, John, I'll be fine. It's just . . ." How could she explain the foreboding that filled her at sight of the mansion, its white walls sparkling in the afternoon sunshine? She took a deep breath and traversed the drive to the formal portico's steps. John followed.

The butler who answered their knock gave a nod of recognition to John.

"We wesh to see hes lordship," John said. They followed the butler into the great hall that was filled with paintings and statues, then were led into the parlor on the left side.

"His lordship has a luncheon guest currently, but I shall tell him you wish to see him, my man." The butler stalked off. John lifted his nose into the air and brushed it with his forefinger, but not even his mimicry could ease Katrina's nervousness.

She looked uneasily about at the wainscoted parlor, the plasterwork ceiling, and the marble fireplace. This room bespoke the wealth and power she'd fled; she tried to tell herself that was the only reason for her nervousness. It was easier to keep her balance at the cottage, for John's house wasn't just Land's End from Devon—it was a world away. She did not have that comfort here, for she could easily picture Devon lounging on that wine velvet settee. She grew more and more jittery at every passing footstep. By the time, an hour later, the door finally opened, she and John almost jumped off their damask-covered chairs.

Warily Katrina looked behind Lord Carrington, but he was alone. Quit being such a fool, she scolded herself inwardly. Devon is miles away in London. She rose and smiled the smile she'd always been told could melt the coldest heart. Lord Carrington, dressed in formal day clothes, entered, leaving the door behind him open. He gave her a warm, surprised smile in return.

"Good afternoon, Lord Carrington. Please forgive this intrusion, but I have something of import I wish to discuss with you," Katrina said.

Carrington bowed. "I'm delighted by your visit, Miss Lawson. Holmes didn't tell me you'd accompanied John. May I offer you some refreshment?"

"Yes, please, the day is growing warm."

She accepted the glass of cool juice he poured her from a sideboard. After he'd given John one also, he invited her to sit. When she shook her head, he sat down on a chair. Katrina took a fortifying sip and began. "Lord Carrington, please don't think me interfering, but I've assisted Will Farrow and know what damage rotting timbers can do to a man."

Carrington's pleasant expression hardened, and Katrina faltered. At that moment she heard a footstep behind her.

A deep, courteous voice said, "Forgive my intrusion, Phillip, but I really must press on to my own . . ." The voice trailed off.

Katrina felt eyes boring into her back. She nibbled at her lip, staring unseeingly into Carrington's curious eyes. Telling herself her nervousness had made her imagine that she recognized that voice, she slowly turned.

The glass in her hand fell to the polished marble floor and shattered into bits. Juice and glass fragments flew, spattering her skirts and the trousers of the man standing only five paces behind her, rooted in the doorway.

"Oh God," she whispered, one hand going to her forehead. She wanted to run to him, she wanted to run from him, she wanted to scream with pain and joy. Was he a spirit called up by her longing?

If so, he displayed a very human shock. Those perfect features paled; she saw him sway on his feet as he sucked in his breath. He rubbed his eyes and looked again. Then, his face beautiful with joy, he took a great stride forward.

"Katrina!" he exulted, and reached for her.

If he touched her, she'd be lost. Somehow, deep inside, she'd known she'd see him again, but she was still not prepared. She could never have anticipated this emotional maelstrom. Knowing she'd lose all she'd worked for if he touched her, she shrank backward, her hands flying up to ward him off.

He went still. His face slowly changed again, and the beauty that had been soft with joy grew hard with anger. She saw in his eyes that he was remembering, as she was. Apparently his memories were no more pleasant than her own. For eternal moments they stayed frozen, her hands out to keep him away, his hands ready to grab.

And this time the look on his face was the one that had earned him the name Demon. . . .

Chapter Seven

To FIND HER SO unexpectedly, when he'd almost despaired . . .
Devon's hands fell and clenched into fists. He gritted his teeth
as he tried to control the conflicting needs to either kiss her
senseless or beat her. Relief, joy, and yearning to hold her close
mixed with fury, resentment, and jealousy into a volatile
combination. He felt as if the top of his head would blow off
if he didn't vent some of his emotions.

He glanced behind Katrina to the stocky man in homespun
with the dirty, rough hands of a laborer. He'd risen and started
toward them, concern upon his ugly face. Devon looked back
at Katrina. She still stood, her hands held out to keep him
away. She was fine, as he'd always suspected. If she'd suffered
in her brief time in the brothel, she bore no evidence of it. She
was slimmer, but *he'd* never inspired that healthy bloom in her
cheeks. Had this . . . peasant given her the happiness she'd
not accepted from him? He tried to tell himself no, but his
emotions were too overwrought for him to think calmly. He'd
found her in the company of another man. How could any male
with blood in his veins resist her?

With a guttural snarl he spanned the gap between them and
caught her shoulders to lift her to her toes. "Aren't you going
to pretend to be glad to see me, Katrina mina?" Devon bent a
scathing look upon the Cornishman who would have pulled
him away, so he missed Katrina's quick sideways glance that
warned John off. Tonkin stopped.

"No, Devon, I can pretend to no more joy than can you,
apparently." Katrina threw back her head and finally met
Devon's eyes. "We'd both be much better off had we never
seen one another again."

Devon's hands tightened reflexively on her shoulders as he

fought down the searing pain of her words. Why should this reaction hurt him so? She'd done all she could to escape him and leave no trace for him to track. His hands gentled even as his eyes blazed their need to inflict a like pain on her. His smile was insolent. "Better for you, perhaps. But I've missed those little cries you used to make in my bed." His smirk deepened when she flushed. He glanced over her head past Carrington's shocked face to John's worried one.

"You don't seem surprised, fellow. Is it because you know how loose her morals are?"

This time, when Katrina couldn't stifle a sound of distress, John ignored her frantic little shake of the head and strode up to pull Devon away.

"I knew she'd left England 'cause some devel wouldn't leave her be. 'Tes no pleasure to meet you en the flesh," John returned coolly, sheltering Katrina under one arm. "And et's plaain to see that you've plaaced blaame upon a good girl for your own sens."

Only the lifetime of etiquette instilled in Devon kept him from pounding the man's ugly face into an even more hideous mess. Carrington's salon was no place for a brawl. His glare at that brawny arm was keen enough to slice it off. "What has she told you of our affairs?"

John shook his head and gently led a dazed-looking Katrina to the door. "You've no claaims upon her now. Leave her be and let the past lie."

Devon planted his feet and crossed his arms over his chest, blocking their path. "She'll not leave here until I've had my say."

"You've said more than enou'," was the curt reply. "Can't you see the lassie is . . . destraught?"

Good, Devon thought savagely. It's little enough payment for the purgatory she's put me through. But when he saw the way her mouth quivered and her eyes watered, he wanted to relent. To take her in his arms and comfort her. To beg her never to leave him again. He felt his own shoulders begin to shake with the force of the emotions that seemed ready to tear him apart. He had to get out of here or embarrass himself. Never would he let her know how much she'd hurt him. . . .

He wrenched his body around, muttering, "Later, Phillip.

Must be getting on.'' Three steps out the door, he paused and cast a glittering look over his shoulder at Katrina. "As for you . . . Run if you like, but hell itself will not keep me from you. There will be an accounting 'tween us. Soon."

The sounds of his steps faded away. The front door slammed. Then a loud silence descended. Katrina covered her ears, unable to bear the echoing of past recriminations or the whispers of more to come.

When John ushered her to the door, she followed blindly. She didn't hear Carrington's, "This has been a most . . . illuminating visit. Please come again, Miss Lawson." His gaze raked her from top to toe.

John leveled a warning look upon the man who held such control over his life. "The lass es like a daughter to me. And I'll protect her as such." He held Carrington's angry glare for a moment, then led Katrina out the door, down the steps, into the sunshine.

Afterward Katrina remembered nothing of the short walk to the cottage. Despite the bright warmth she felt cold. Icy fear clogged her veins, making her sluggish. She stumbled often and would have fallen had John not caught her.

Oh God, how many times had she dreamed of him? How many times had she awakened with his name on her lips, believing, in her heart of hearts, that someday she'd see him again? Someday they'd quit hurting one another and have the tender reunion they deserved. Despite their ugly past she was still vulnerable to him, as her dreams proved.

And his first reaction upon seeing her had fulfilled those sweet dreams. Until she'd held her hands out, more to stop her own yearning to fling herself into his arms than to keep him away. How his face had changed then. She still labored under the dark hatred that had settled over her like a shroud.

And he would come again. . . .

When they reached the cottage, she stumbled upstairs and began to pack her belongings. He wanted to humiliate her, to make her suffer. Well, she'd had enough of suffering. For two years he'd haunted the chambers of her heart like an evil spirit. No longer. She'd banish him if she had to flee to the ends of the earth.

The tears fell hot and fast. When they dripped down on her

shaking hands, common sense finally prevailed. Running had not helped her forget him the first time. He was lodged in her bones like marrow. Wherever she went, he went. Unless . . . unless she refused to run. She fell to her knees beside her bed and silently prayed.

Dear God, show me what to do. Help me in this hour of need. The answer came to her, as clear as if illuminated by divine light. Running would accomplish nothing. She had to face him down, know him for the profligate he was. He'd been on his best behavior before in his attempt to win her eager submission. Now he didn't control her. Now he hated her. She'd not waste the rest of her life in devotion to a shade. The man she persisted in loving did not really exist. His fury would strip his false charm away, and with it, his sway over her emotions.

She lifted her head, wiped her tears on her sleeve, and rose to unpack her things. When she heard soft applause, she turned.

John, Ellie, and Rachel stood just within the loft, pride in her plain upon their faces. John spoke for them all, as usual. "You're as brave as I knew you would be. You've maade the right choice, lass."

"I hope so, John. I hope so."

"I must be gettin' back to the bal." He tipped his hat to her and hurried down the stairs. Rachel bestowed a warm smile upon Katrina and returned to her chores.

Ellie, however, came into the room and pulled Katrina into her arms. For the first time it was she who offered solace, Katrina who accepted. Ellie rocked her, making comforting noises. A few minutes later, feeling somewhat better, Katrina drew away and accepted Ellie's handkerchief.

She blew her nose fiercely, then offered Ellie a watery smile. "Thank you, Ellie, for understanding my foolishness."

"Et's not foolesh, Katrina," Ellie said, her accent more pronounced than usual, "to cry when you're hurt at a man's callousness."

"Your father told you, then?"

"Aye. But I suspected as much. If there's aught I can do to help—"

"I appreciate that, Ellie, but I'm afraid this time I have to depend upon myself. Devon will never leave me be until I convince him I don't care.''

Ellie whispered, "And can you convence yourself, Katrina?''

"I don't know, Ellie.'' Katrina turned to look out the window. "But with God's help I can try.''

They'd finished supper that night when an imperative knock sounded at the door. Katrina started; all eyes went to her. John began to rise, but she waved him back down on the bench.

"I'm certain it's for me.'' Her footsteps were measured as she went to the door, but her hand shook as she reached out to open it.

She drew a breath of relief when she saw only Billy. "Hello, Billy.''

"Greetin's, lassie. May I come in? I'd like a word wi' ye.''

Katrina held the door wide in answer. When Billy stepped in, his eyes went past her. They widened and made a slow, interested up-and-down sweep. Katrina turned to see Ellie returning the appraisal under lowered lashes.

"Come into the parlor, Billy. This is Ellie, the daughter of the house.''

Billy tipped his hat and bowed. "Pleasured, I'm sure.''

"Welcome, sir,'' Ellie replied, curtsying slightly.

"We'd like a word in private, Ellie. I'll be fine.'' Ellie nodded and turned to leave, but she cast Billy a final look over her shoulder before she did so. Billy returned it, with interest.

Katrina frowned as she led the way into the parlor. Ellie had eschewed entanglements since her disastrous ending with Hennessy, but Billy was not much better. He was probably like Devon; flighty as the wind.

"What do you want, Billy?'' Katrina asked crisply, seating herself on one of the rickety chairs and waving Billy onto the opposite settee.

"It's glad I am to see ye, too.'' He removed his hat and threw it down beside him. "Aren't ye glad to find me breathin'?''

Katrina flushed, but her chin stayed high. "I knew I didn't kill you, Billy. I checked your pulse before I left.''

"Generous o' ye.''

Katrina leaned forward. "What would you have done in the same circumstances? Stayed with a man who despised you and used you for his own pleasure?"

"And yours."

Katrina's mouth firmed. "And mine, admittedly. But I hated us both for it. That's why I left. That's why I want naught to do with him now. Demon Devon has nothing to offer that I want. Jewels and furs are poor substitutes for the true values of life: love, compassion, understanding. He wants only a light-skirt, but he'll no longer treat me as one."

Billy tapped his hand nervously against his knee, then burst out, "And what if I told ye he wants more o' ye? That no woman before or since has meant so much to him?"

"Are you telling me he *loves* me?" Katrina's voice rose with incredulity on the last two words.

"That I cannot answer. But he feels somethin' for ye. Somethin' that made him look for ye for two years. Do ye have any idea how much money he's spent tryin' to find ye?"

Katrina's lip curled. "He can afford it. And spare me the implication that he did so out of any emotion other than outraged pride. He's used to doing the leaving." She hesitated, but she had to know. "And how many more women has he kept in that house since I left?"

Billy opened his mouth, then snapped it shut. A few seconds later he growled, "That's none o' yer business. I can see I've come on a useless errand." He rose, crushing his hat down on his head.

"Why *did* you come?"

"I came to try to help you understand. And, mayhap, forgive. But both missions are doomed, 'tis plain." He turned to leave.

Oh God, how she wanted to believe him. But the man who'd reviled her this afternoon had no regard, much less affection, for her. Her own pain made her words harder than she'd intended, but at that moment she meant them. "Let him beg for mercy before God, for I'll have no more for him than he gave to me." Katrina's composure didn't waver as she escorted Billy to the door. Hatred was a poor defense, but it was the only one she had against feelings she could never give in to again.

On the steps Billy turned. "Do ye hate him enough to wound him even more?"

"I don't know what you're talking about."

For the first time Billy's voice gentled. "I know what happened to ye in the brothel, lass. And why ye almost died."

Katrina took a shocked step back. "And Devon? Does he know?"

"No. And if ye're as God-fearin' as ye claim, then ye won't tell him. 'Twould hurt him to no purpose."

Katrina laughed harshly. "We couldn't have that, could we?" When he stayed silent, grimly waiting for an answer, Katrina rubbed her throbbing temples and shook her head. "He'll not hear the sordid tale from me, Billy. I, too, you see, have pride." She stepped back and slammed the door in his face.

Billy sighed heavily and turned to leave, but a curtain twitched above him, catching his attention. He squinted up, glimpsing a winsome face framed by lush, shining dark hair.

He winked and blew the pretty Cornish lass a kiss. The curtain hastily lowered. Billy strode off.

For three days Katrina started at every tap on the door. She stayed near the cottage, not accompanying Will on his rounds as in the past. For the first time in weeks she helped Rachel in the pantry. She was dismayed to find their stores so low. Usually the shelves almost groaned under the weight of fresh and canned fruits and vegetables, and salted fish. They were half-empty now.

"Rachel, why is the pantry so bare? I know you've been sending baskets to some of the ill miners, but usually we have plenty to spare."

Rachel was busy sorting grain and seemed not to hear. When she'd finished the small pile, Katrina covered her hand with her own. "What's wrong, Rachel? Am I not a member of this family, too?"

Rachel set her bowl aside. "Aye, lass. I just dedn't want to worry you when you have so much else to thenk upon." Rachel drew a deep breath, then rushed on, "Our supplies are dwendlen' 'cause John es paid based on production, and the ores they can reach es almost gone. And weth the cave-en . . . Besides, weth what corn costs 'cause of those rascally millers and farmers, we can't buy much on what John maakes.''

Due to poor crops and heavy taxation the price of corn had risen sharply in the past two years, Katrina knew. But she'd not realized straits were so dire. "But what of the share from Carrington's land? Isn't Jimmy still helping him farm?"

"Jimmy quit helpen' hem some weeks ago. He doesn't want to do anytheng but carouse weth that worthless Hennessy—by daay.''

Rachel looked away, but Katrina, too, knew what Jimmy did by night. Unlike many families in the area, the Tonkins disapproved of smuggling. John and Jimmy had had many arguments on the subject, but Jimmy, stubborn hothead that he was, refused to quit his nocturnal activities. Katrina made a mental note to speak with him. He probably had no idea how bare the larder was. And whether his gains were ill-gotten or not, they would still keep starvation at bay. Her own meager hoard left from her employment had long since been spent on necessities.

"Don't worry, Rachel." Katrina patted Rachel's hand. "We'll manage." A knocking came at the door on the words. Katrina almost jumped out of her skin. Her eyes met Rachel's.

"I'll go. You staay here."

But Katrina rose. "No, I'll go with you."

Rachel opened the door; Katrina's held breath escaped slowly through her lips. So the day of reckoning had come. At least she need no longer dread it. She stepped forward when Rachel would have slammed the door in Devon's face.

"No, Rachel. I'll see him."

Reluctantly, Rachel stood back, but Katrina noted that her eyes widened when Devon stepped into the cottage. Even dressed in simple riding breeches, he had an overpowering presence. Never had the cottage seemed smaller or more rustic. Rachel worried with the edge of her apron, her eyes glued to Devon's handsome face with what Katrina could only wryly describe as awe.

"Go on with what you were doing, Rachel. I'll call if I need anything. Come into the parlor, my lord." Katrina preceded Devon into the small room and sat down on a chair.

He seated himself on the settee and stared at her for so long that she had to control the urge to flee those roving, hungry eyes. Where was the anger, the hatred that had blasted her three days ago? This Devon was much harder to deny. This Devon was the one who haunted her, waking and sleeping. But never, ever, would she let him know that.

When he smiled invitingly and patted the spot next to him, she shook her head. "I'm fine here, thank you. What may I help you with?"

His smile slipped. "Don't you think this formality is a bit ridiculous under the circumstances?"

"No. We're strangers to one another, my lord. We only ever had one thing in common, and have not even that any longer." Katrina looked away to control her misting eyes. Actually they'd had two things in common, but he'd not hear of the babe's loss from her.

"Why so sad, my dear? We could have that, and much more, if you weren't so blasted stubborn." His teeth snapped together as if he regretted the harshness. He leaned forward and took her hand. "Katrina, I've come to apologize for my . . . behavior a few days ago. The shock of seeing you, when I'd searched so hard, was too much for my composure."

Katrina's eyes jerked up from her lap to meet his. She'd expected acrimony, not apology. The old Devon would have demanded a hearing instead of pleading for one. Was this change genuine, or yet another of his chameleon mood switches designed to charm her? Those mellow, gold-flecked brown eyes made her feel as if he bathed her in warm brandy.

The analogy fortunately recalled a memory of a night long ago, when a demon in man's flesh stole her very will. "Apology accepted. Now, if you'll excuse me, I've chores to tend to." She made to rise, but he jerked on her hand and pulled her back onto her seat.

"That's all you have to say to me? After two years? After leaving me without even a missive to reassure me that you were well?"

"Actions speak louder than words, sir." She tried to pull her hand away, but he tightened his grip until her fingers ached.

"Meaning that you cared not a whit for my worry, or my pain, I collect. Cared not how many nightmares I had over what could have happened to you in that cursed brothel."

His voice had gone dangerously soft. Instead of quailing as in the past, however, she flung back her head and boldly met his eyes. Those gold sparks were flashing like frustrated fireflies seeking an outlet.

"No more than you cared for my pride, or my shame. As for what happened to me, that's none of your affair. An . . . illness I soon recovered from."

This time his anger was overt when he snapped, "Damn you, I have a right to know!" When she raised an imperious eyebrow, he changed his tactics. "Very well, you can tell me later. But one thing you must admit."

He dropped her hand to lean forward and tightly grip his knees. "Confess, Katrina. It's your pride that suffered far more than your morals. That's why you left, and that's why you treat me to these sullens now."

"And that, my lord, is why we parted, and why we can never mean aught to one another again. To wit, if you really believe that pride drove me away from you, then you understand me not at all. I, however, understand you all too well."

"I question that, but you dislike what little you know, obviously."

She didn't deny it. "So you see, we have no foundation on which to build. Now please, leave me be. . . ." She stood on the words, but ended on an oof of surprise when he snatched her hand and pulled her onto his lap.

They groaned simultaneously as her soft hips met his hard thighs. Devon clasped his arms about her waist and turned her so that one of her breasts crushed against his chest.

He said huskily, "Tell me truly now, Katrina mina, that we've no foundation to build on." He tipped her chin up with one hand, but she closed her eyes so she didn't have to see that hungry look that made all her feminine instincts feel ripe for the picking.

Morality and sensuality warred as Katrina savored, despite herself, the feel of him. So hard he was, so reassuring, so masterful. How very easy it would be to give in and play the harlot. Just once more. But he was like an opiate; once would never be enough. . . .

Only picturing her father's serene face gave her the courage to say evenly, "We've nothing, Devon. No mutual respect, no shared values, not even personal liking.'' He went so still that she finally had to open her eyes. His cheek twitched as his thick black lashes lowered. She sensed that she'd hurt him.

She wanted to call the words back, but she'd paid dearly for the distance two years of separation had gained her. Nevertheless, when he set her carefully on her feet, she stayed rooted, her eyes locked on his pale face. She didn't dare tell him that she respected many of his qualities—his breeding, his strength of will, his intelligence, his humor, his loyalty to his name and to Billy.

Their moral codes, however, were continents apart. As to whether she liked him . . . no, the feelings he stirred in her were much too powerful to bear such a mediocre name. How could hatred and love wear the same face? It was not hatred that led her to open her mouth for a retraction. However, in that instant, he looked at her, and she forgot the need to comfort in the primitive urge to flee. Did he really despise her so?

He rumbled hoarsely, ''Then since I'm so lost to virtue, I've naught to lose in allowing my instincts free rein, have I?'' He took a stride toward her, but she hastily backed away. He stopped, his hands clenching and unclenching at his sides. ''Leave me. We shall continue this conversation later.'' The words seemed torn from him.

Katrina needed no second urging. She began to edge toward the door, eyeing him as she would a salivating wolf.

''You've not seen the last of me, my virtuous little hypocrite. You'll have many opportunities to prove how steadfast your morals are. Do you find the prospect appealing?''

Her heart pounded too hard in her throat for an answer. Devon stalked her retreat, and they were both in the hall when the front door abruptly opened. Katrina looked over Devon's shoulder and slumped in relief.

Will froze at the sight of Devon, then carefully shut the door behind him. ''Do you need my help, Katrina?''

Devon whirled at the sound of his voice. Katrina couldn't see Devon's face, but from Will's expression dislike was being exchanged in full measure.

''So, here is the good doctor,'' Devon purred, nodding toward the leather satchel Will carried. ''How delighted I am to meet you at last. Tell me, did Katrina make a good patient?''

At Will's flicker of surprise Devon added, "Oh, you were described to me well enough, Will Farrow. Your name will be forever emblazoned upon my memory as the man who stole my woman. And took considerable trouble to cover his tracks."

Will set his satchel down on the small table next to the door. "Not well enough, apparently." He leaned against the closed door, raking Devon up and down with a disdainful blue gaze. "As to the rest of your little homily, the type of patient my betrothed has made is none of your concern."

Katrina shut her eyes at Devon's shocked intake of breath. Then she opened them to send a frantic plea to Will, but his gaze was locked on Devon. "Lesser men, I'm afraid, rarely understand the nobility of medicine. Particularly men of such dubious character that they earn the name Demon."

Katrina saw Devon collecting himself for a lunge. She did then the only thing she could, even knowing that her actions would ultimately inflame Devon further. She leaped forward, pushed him aside, and stood beside Will to take his arm.

"Hello, Will. What an unexpected pleasure. We didn't expect you before supper." She gave him a flirtatious glance.

Katrina felt Will control a start of surprise, but his smile was warm and unaffected. "The injuries from the cave-in are healing nicely, I'm happy to report." He sliced a glance at Devon. "Besides, I learned of the new arrival and thought you might need my company."

My protection. He didn't say the words, but all three heard them reverberate.

Devon asked hoarsely, "Is this true, Katrina? Are you really betrothed to this . . . this . . ."

Katrina's head lifted proudly. "Wonderful man? That's none of your affair, Devon. What difference does it make? I am, in any case, lost to you."

Devon took a half step back. His teeth gritted together for a moment, then the tormented expression left his face. "Doubtless you are correct, madam. Your affairs"—he emphasized the word—"are no longer my concern. You are, in any case, beneath me." He strode toward the door with the majestic strides he'd learned in knee breeches. When they moved aside, he carefully opened the door and snicked it shut behind him.

The sounds of his retreating footsteps faded. Firm, controlled—definite.

Katrina swayed, almost faint. But not with relief. Dear God, why couldn't she feel vindicated at least? This was really the end. He was gone for good this time. Devon, come back, her heart cried, even as her mind knew this ending had been inevitable. She began to slump as her lungs labored for air.

Will shook her arm. "Katrina, what's wrong?"

I've sent away the only man I can ever love. The knowledge was clear to her in that moment as never before. There was no other explanation for this pain that made her feel her back would break because it had not been able to bend.

Will's touch was suddenly repugnant. She flung his arm away and fled down the hall toward the kitchen, swallowing sobs.

"Wait, Katrina!" Will strode after her, but stopped when she whirled and flung him a glare made more poignant by the glittering tears.

"Don't you *ever* interfere so in my life again. I owe you my respect and gratitude. And nothing else!" She spun back around to continue her headlong flight to the haven of her room. Every step seemed to pound the words deeper into her brain: *beneath me . . . beneath me . . .*

A short distance away Devon drew his winded, lathered stallion in. He stared blindly at his cozy little manor, wondering vaguely how he'd arrived so soon. He recalled nothing of the headlong ride, or even that he'd almost lost his seat when his stallion caught his hoof and stumbled.

Lost to you, lost to you . . . He couldn't bear the echo of those words any longer. He dropped the reins to cup his hands over his ears, but he still couldn't block them out. Pressure built in his head until he wanted to scream. How could she call another man wonderful, promise him the lifetime he'd yearned for? Deceitful bitch. Even as he thought the words he knew them untrue, but that only increased his anguish.

"Damn you!" he yelled. The cliffs behind the red brick, Georgian-style manor caught the words and flung them mockingly back to him.

The burst of fury faded as, for the first time in his life, he did feel damned. He'd lost the only woman who'd ever been more to him than a vessel. As to why . . . well, he couldn't come to grips with that yet. Aye, he had much to condemn in himself, but acrimony was so bestial only when gorged upon hatred. What had he done to make her detest him so?

He dismounted and tied his horse to the front gate. He stumbled up the paved walkway, blind to the pretty spring flowers and carefully trimmed hedge. Only when he was almost upon him did he see Billy standing in the doorway eyeing him, concern etched upon his face.

"Did ye see her?"

"Aye." Devon shouldered past him and shuffled into the tiny study, where a sideboard held crystal decanters sparkling in the late-afternoon sunlight.

Billy watched Devon pour a hefty draft of the best French brandy so readily, if stealthily, available in Cornwall. Devon held the glass to the light and circled it from side to side. He brought the snifter to his lips, then paused.

With the feral snarl of a trapped animal he flung the snifter away. It shattered against the hardwood floor with a satisfying crash. "Hell's teeth, I'll forget you without benefit of soporific." Devon bent his head, his shoulders quivering with his effort to master himself. A few moments later he turned to Billy, only the hectic color burning in his cheeks evidencing his distress. "Billy, what say you to a night in Truro? Surely even in this godforsaken county they've some comely whores."

"Whatever you want, Devvie lad. But do ye really think women and wine will help ye forget? Ye've already tried that once."

"What else would you have me do? Your advice to wait a few days only firmed her resolve against me. I tried apologizing, charming, then threatening—"

"Did ye try asking?"

Devon's open mouth snapped closed. He shrugged. "A man doesn't ask with a woman like Katrina Lawson. She's too strong-willed to respect a milksop."

Billy shook his head. "Did it occur to ye that she respects *your* strength but wants a mite in return for *hers*?"

Devon bent his head in consideration. The concept of a

woman demanding respect was alien to him. In his experience women demanded admiration. Upon receiving it, they meekly accepted their inferior position to men in English society. He didn't think Katrina was much different. Not really.

Yet . . . he'd used every wile he knew on her, in the past and today. Still she refused him. If she had really become affianced to a doctor, certainly avarice didn't motivate her choice. Then what did? If that tiny little gold circle made such a difference to her feelings, why? Could it really be respect she craved?

Wearily, he said, "A mere man can never figure out the labyrinthine thought processes of a woman. And truth to tell, Billy, I no longer give a damn. She's engaged to the good doctor, apparently." When Billy frowned, Devon added savagely, "I wish them pure misery together!" Devon brushed back his loosened hair and flung Billy a reckless smile. "Are you coming with me to Truro or not?"

"I'll follow ye to hell, and ye know it, Devvie lad."

"Good intentions were taking me there rapidly, anyway, Billy. I might as well enjoy every step of the way." Devon took Billy's arm and marched with him to the door.

By the time Katrina came down for supper that night, only her red eyes betrayed hours of crying. The storm had passed, but now she felt becalmed. Numb. Had she not wanted to talk to Jimmy, she would have stayed in her room. But Jimmy was rarely home these days, and she'd seen him return a few minutes ago. Besides, she'd not upset Rachel any more. She must pretend to an acceptance she didn't feel.

The minute she entered the kitchen, all eyes riveted on her, and she knew the entire family had heard of Devon's visit. She nodded. "Good evening." She took her usual seat next to Ellie, across from Jimmy.

"Broth again. How lovely." The strong scent of the fish-head soup made her upset stomach churn, but she accepted a ladleful with a smile.

"And how are you this fine day?" John asked heartily.

"I will be fine, John. What happened today was for the best." And that was all she intended to say on the subject. She looked around the table. "Where is Will? I thought he was coming for supper?"

"He . . . had an unexpected call to make," Rachel answered. She took a sip of broth so quickly that she coughed.

Katrina looked down dully at her own soup. She hadn't meant to hurt Will, but if he hadn't interfered . . . What? Would she this moment be lying in Devon's arms? Her head swam with longing, then fury at her own weakness. She should have thanked Will rather than reviled him. She dropped her spoon in her soup, not even feeling the hot spatter as several droplets struck her sleeve.

A gentle hand wiped at the stain. She forced a smile and turned her head. "Thank you, Ellie. I'm . . . feeling clumsy today." She picked up her spoon and took a sip of soup. Robert was animatedly telling Jimmy about the chick he'd watched hatch. Jimmy nodded and sent his little brother an indulgent smile.

Katrina had often remarked the close relationship between the pair. Jimmy was relaxed and cheerful around Robert, as he was not around the other family members. If Robert came down with a sniffle, it was Jimmy who visited him most often, taking him clever toys he'd whittled. No young man who loved his brother so much was totally lost to decency, as John feared.

When both brothers turned their attention to their soup, Katrina said, "It's good to see you, Jimmy."

Dark eyes sliced a glance up at her, then back down. Jimmy didn't reply.

"And it's good to see you, too, Katrina," Katrina mocked in a deep voice. This time those dark eyes lingered, but Katrina would rather have a glare than the indifference Jimmy usually treated her to. "We haven't had a lesson in some time. How about tonight—"

"Nay. I've plans."

"I see. Well, maybe tomorrow, then." When no response came, Katrina's tone grew sharp. "Jimmy, are you going to be happy spending the rest of your life roistering about or do you intend to make something of yourself?" She bit her lip after her outburst, throwing an apologetic look to John. Such talk, after all, was his right, not hers.

He sent her a wry shrug. "'Ee'll get no desagreement from me, lass. Many's the time I've said as much to hem."

"And it's sick I am of hearin' it!" Jimmy pushed back his empty bowl and leaped to his feet. "And I don't know why I come home, since this pap is all I get to eat." He turned toward the door, but John leaned across and grasped Jimmy's shirt.

Slowly, he stood, his face taking on the mottled hue of rage. "'Ee'll not talk to your ma that waay. Nor your teacher, neither."

"Teacher, huh! She's nothin' but a lord's whore who thinks herself too good for us common folk."

John's grip slackened, as if he couldn't believe his ears. Rachel gasped and Ellie moaned in distress.

John broke the tension by stepping around the table to haul Jimmy to his toes. He clenched his fist and began to raise it, but Katrina leaped up and reached over the table to put her hand on his arm.

"No, John, don't. He is, after all, right." John hesitated, looking from his son's white face to Katrina's paler one. The women, too, stared.

Katrina was afraid to see their expressions, so she watched the play of emotions on Jimmy's face. Shock, satisfaction, then lust, out in the open for all to see.

She wanted to slink off to her room and hide, but she quelled the instinct. The truth was out at last. Maybe it was for the best. She lifted her chin and looked Jimmy squarely in the eye. "Yes, I was a . . . kept woman. For one month. If not against my will, against my judgment and my beliefs. And I've since paid dearly for every stolen hour."

When John let his son go, Katrina walked around the table to grasp Jimmy's shoulder. He smirked down at her. She gritted her teeth, but said calmly, "I'm determined not to repeat my past mistakes, however. I've done my best to make amends these past two years. Can you say the same, Jimmy Tonkin? What have you learned from this?" Lightly Katrina fingered a nasty bruise on his cheek, doubtless a legacy from his most recent taproom brawl.

He caught her hand and squeezed it. "I've learned much I'd like to show you." John growled and took a step forward, but Rachel caught his arm.

"Let her put hem en hes place. She's earned that right."

Katrina heard her whispered aside, and Rachel's faith bolstered the spirit that was weary of men's lusts, though hungry for their respect. "Have you, Jimmy? Would you know which fork to use for meat, which for dessert, at a lord's table? Do you know where Cathay is? Or what the Magna Carta says, or can you recite any of Shakespeare's sonnets?" When Jimmy scowled, Katrina shook her head in a manner that she intentionally made condescending. "Then you've little to offer me. You can ask your sister if women are drawn for very long to men who know little besides smuggling, drinking, and fighting."

Jimmy brushed her hands away. "What makes you think I want more than a toss in the hay with you, woman?"

"I pray to God you don't want even that, Jimmy. I offer you my friendship, and to share my knowledge. I've nothing else. For any man. But you are an attractive young fellow, and there are others who will find you so, if you change your wild ways."

"There's plenty who like me as I am!" Jimmy flung back, his proud young face outraged.

"Then seek them out. And see how long they satisfy you."

With a distempered growl, Jimmy turned away. Katrina finally looked at Rachel and Ellie. The understanding in their eyes brought tears to her own. John patted her shoulder.

"Thanks for tryen', lass. 'Ee maade a gallant effort, but I fear Jimmy's beyond help." His features tightened as he met his wife's eyes. She put out a supplicating hand, but John bit off his next words, as if he found them as revolting as she did. "We've got no choice, Rachel. He don't contribute none to thes household, so why should he be allowed to staay? He thenks hemself a man. Let hem act as one."

Katrina shook her head wildly. "No, John. Not on my account."

"Et would have come anywaay, lass. 'Ee only maade et happen sooner. Maayhaps ef he has to support hemself, he'll learn the importance of family." John strode toward the door. Little Robert, who'd seemed confused by the interchange between Katrina and Jimmy, understood well enough where his father was going, apparently, for he jumped up, his round face crumpling.

"No, Da, don't send him away!" he cried, running on his short legs to catch his father's hand.

"Robert, 'ee don't understand. Et's for the best, lad." John pulled gently away when Robert tried to cling to him.

Katrina couldn't bear being the source of such conflict. She clasped John's arm. "No, please, let me talk to him once more."

"Et'll do no good—"

"Let me try."

John hesitated, then he indicated that she precede him. They caught up with Jimmy on the road to Truro. He whirled when his father called him.

Scowling, he snapped, "What did you bring her for?"

"We've both a mite to say to 'ee. She can go first."

"I'd like to speak to him alone, John." John looked confused, but he went several paces back toward the cottage.

Katrina's voice was low and urgent. "Do you know how little food there is in the cottage?"

"Stores is always low this time of year, 'fore the crops come in—"

"And where will the Tonkin share come from since you don't help farm Carrington's lands any longer?"

Jimmy was silent at that. "That was only a mite. We buys most of our meat and grain—"

"And do you know how little money your father's making? With the condition of the mine and the lack of good ores, your father's share is not likely to rise."

"And what would you have me do, fancy woman?" He looked her up and down. "You could earn more money in a night than I do in a quarter."

Katrina's breath hissed through her teeth. By an extreme effort of will she kept herself from slapping him. "What of your share from smuggling?"

Jimmy's hobnail boot sent a pebble flying. "'Tis a pittance, since I only help them bring it ashore. Hasn't been many runs lately, anyway. My share's all spent."

Katrina's eyes closed in despair. What would they do?

"Do you still want to belong to this family?"

"O' course. You got no right to ask that."

"Then you must contribute to it. Go back to Carrington and ask to help in the fields again."

Jimmy groaned. "No, I hate it."

Katrina made as if to turn away. "Then don't be sad as you watch Robert starve."

Jimmy reached out to grab her arm. When she pulled away, he gave a resigned shrug. "Durin' the day, I guess. I'll talk to J- er, the leader, and see if he'll let me go across on the next run. I'd make a goodly sum in one night, then."

Katrina sighed in relief, and when John impatiently strode up to see what was keeping them so long, she sent him a brilliant smile made even prettier in the radiant sunset. "Jimmy is going back to work for Lord Carrington, John. We'll soon have his share of vegetables again."

Katrina caught John's tiny sigh of relief, even though he made a good job of disguising it with a scowl. "Ais, well, that's somethen'. As long 'ee see the value of work, there's hope for 'ee." He stabbed his son's shoulder with a stubby finger. "But ef 'ee ever talk to this *lady* again as 'ee ded today, 'ee'll have to leve where such language es appreciated. Does 'ee understand?"

Jimmy looked a little shocked, but at his father's stern look he snapped his mouth shut. He nodded. He looked between the cottage and Truro uncertainly.

"Come along home, Jemmy. Let's tell tales as we haven't en an age. 'Ee know how much Robert loves to have 'ee home," John urged.

"Please do, Jimmy. I love those wild Cornish stories. I imagine you, with your flair for drama, can tell a grand one." Katrina held her breath as she awaited Jimmy's response.

He looked regretfully toward Truro once more, then he wheeled toward the cottage. John sent her a grateful wink, then strode to catch up with his son. Katrina's glow of satisfaction grew warmer when they entered the house. Rachel and Ellie shed some relieved tears, but it was Robert's cries of joy that misted Katrina's eyes.

Rachel served up the last of her hoard of preserved pears for everyone while the others settled about the table. John had already started in about the knackers. "I've never seen them myself, but oh, the taales I've heard. Such wee lettle spirets they be. Some of the old ones saay they're no begger than a sixpenny doll, yet look and dress like hearty old tinners. Good luck they can bring, since they's nearly always seen near a new lode. And bad, if 'ee don't leave them a crust.'' John smiled down at Robert's enchanted face, but he sent Katrina a sly wink.

She realized John was too devout a Methodist to believe in goblins, but he obviously still enjoyed the tales. "Have you any good ghost stories to tell?''

"Ais, there's more than a months' nights o' callin' I could relate.''

Jimmy took up the tale. He took a puff from his pipe, and through the mysterious blue wreath he intoned, "Like the one about Reverend Dodge of Talland who was good at exorcisin' spirits. When the parson of Lanreath was pursued by a black coach and headless driver and horses, Dodge stepped in their way. The ghostly coachman shouted, 'Dodge is come! I must be gone!' and disappeared forthwith.''

Despite herself Katrina felt a chill creep up her spine at Jimmy's sepulchral tone. "It's a pity we can't exorcise the evils in men so easily,'' she couldn't resist saying.

"You mean it's a blessin'. You women would take all pleasure out of life for a man if you could,'' Jimmy retorted.

John chuckled. Rachel, too, glared at her son. "Ais, but thenk of the pleasures denied us without the trials of women.'' John cleared his throat when Rachel's glare was turned on him. "And what of the one about the pellar of Towan? Ah, a fine witch was she, the seventh daughter of a seventh son—'' And the tales went on, there in the cozy kitchen, with the wild Cornish winds blowing across the bare landscape.

Part Three

"To every action there is always opposed an
equal reaction: or, the mutual actions of two
bodies upon each other are always equal, and
directed to contrary parts."

—SIR ISAAC NEWTON,
Laws of Motion, III

Chapter Eight

THE NEXT TIME Katrina saw Will, several days later, she drew him into the parlor. His icy stare warmed as she said haltingly, "I . . . want to apologize for my harsh words the other day, Will. My only excuse is that I was . . . upset."

"I quite understand, Katrina. Perhaps I shouldn't have interfered. But I couldn't help it. When I heard he was here, I knew he'd be after you, and then to see him stalking you that way, well, my instinct was to protect you. I know you haven't given me leave, but I feel . . . responsible for you."

She had to look away from his pleading look, for she couldn't give him what he really wanted. Even now. Especially now, with Devon so near. "I know, Will. And I'm flattered that you care. Shall we put the incident behind us?" They both rose.

"I can, Katrina, but can you?"

"I intend to, Will," she muttered, turning to the door.

"Wait."

He stepped up to her until she had to tilt her chin back to look at him. "He'll not leave you be, you know," he said gently. "If you truly want to put the past behind you, you must free yourself of him. What better way to do that than to form an attachment to another man? Our supposed engagement sent him on his way, didn't it?"

Katrina stared at Will's fine linen stock to avoid those searching blue eyes. He always dressed in the height of fashion. As in the past, she wondered what kind of inheritance had left him so well-to-do. He could certainly not dress so on the salary Carrington paid him.

He was waiting for an answer, but she could only manage a nod. Indeed, Devon had left her easily enough. She was still grappling with her despair, still telling herself that she was better off. Even work had been no solace these last few days, but she was determined that no one would know how miserable she'd been. Not even Will.

"I don't think we need prevaricate further, Will. He'll not be back."

Will's gaze traveled from the top of her burnished head to the tips of her slippered feet. "If you truly believe that, Katrina, you're an innocent still, no matter what you did in the past."

Katrina blushed. That masculine, encompassing look was not one she liked to associate with Will. With a weak smile she turned and fled to help Rachel, unaware of the hungry, determined stare that followed her.

Worries built upon worries in the ensuing days. The thrice-daily meals dwindled to two, and those were sparse. Robert took to fishing in the river, but there was so much sediment from the mine upstream that he seldom caught anything. Daily, Jimmy stomped off at dawn to Carrington's fields. Katrina saw how he hated the backbreaking, sweaty work, but her respect for him rose when this time he persevered.

She'd watched him go into the larder one morning to see for himself the extent of their stores. From his pale expression on emerging she knew he hadn't realized money was so tight. Jimmy was paid in both a crop share and in a small stipend, which was not due to him until the end of the quarter. Since the grain was not ready to harvest or the vegetables ripe, Jimmy's toil had thus far gained them nothing.

Rachel and Ellie tried to take in sewing, but the affluent preferred the modiste in Truro, and the poor could not pay. Ellie wanted to go to work as a barmaid in Truro, but John forbade it.

"Soon as we get this rubble cleared, we can start brenging up copper again. We'll manage tell then," he told them all more than once. But his face grew haggard with worry.

Nevertheless, they still had food, unlike many in the area. Rachel insisted on giving what little they could spare to neighboring miners. Many of John's workers had larger families and a smaller profit share to support them, so their straits were even more dire.

Katrina saw the poverty the miners were suffering when she accompanied Will on his rounds. One housewife, her formerly round, healthy face growing pale and wan, was grubbing around on her knees on the ground when they arrived. She lifted her head when she heard them and waved at Will, but then she bent intently over the ground again.

Katrina paused to ask her what she was doing, but Will hurried her along. "Leave the poor woman her pride."

"What do you mean, Will?"

"She's gathering snails to make broth. Probably that's the only source of meat they've had for weeks. The last cave-in blocked off the only producing lode left in Carrington's mine. There's been little profit from it for months, anyway. He'll probably close it soon."

Katrina had feared as much from John's increasingly grim aspect, but her heart lurched in dismay. She pinned a cheerful smile on her face, however, when they entered the tiny cottage to tend to Big Tom Corrigan. Two little girls were cleaning the spotless single room in a listless manner. They gave a wan smile before going back to their dusting and sweeping.

Tom had six girls ranging in age from one to ten, Katrina knew. With no sons to help bring in a working wage, the family was dependent upon his income.

His flesh hung loosely on his big frame when he struggled up to a sitting position to greet them. "Good day to 'ee, doc. And to 'ee, Miss Katrina." His black eyes seemed unnaturally bright in the dimness. After returning his greeting, Will put a hand to Tom's forehead. He frowned.

"How long have you had this fever? Why didn't you send for me?"

"Et only started yesterday."

Will pressed his ear to Tom's chest. "Take a deep breath and hold it."

Katrina saw from Will's face that he was concerned. While Will drew back the sheet to examine Tom's broken, bandaged ribs and fractured hip, Katrina mixed the herbal paste Will had showed her how to make. She could tell by the whistling in Tom's lungs that congestion had settled in. She prayed that one of Tom's ribs had not punctured a lung. Katrina knew that miners were susceptible to lung problems because they'd spent so many years breathing fine ore dust. She slathered the fish-oil-based paste on Tom's wide chest while Will mixed up some medicine.

Tom's grin was weak but playful. "Et's a good theng my missus esn't here. She'd let me have a broken nose to match my rebs for lyin' here enjoyin' the touch of such a pretty lass."

Katrina smiled perkily back. "Let that be a warning to you. If you want peace in your household, you must get well so I'll not have to smear this witch's concoction on you." She brought her hand close to his nose.

He gagged and turned his head away. "Whoosh! That smells like my missus's soup."

"I heard that, Tom Corrigan," his wife said, stepping into the cottage and setting the crockery pot down on the small cupboard that served as her kitchen workboard. She shook a finger at him. "And does 'ee thenk 'ee can tell a pigsty from a rose bower weth that broken nose?"

Tom rubbed his big, crooked nose with a fingertip. "Et's proud I am of thes snout, as 'ee should be, Mina, knowin' how et got busted."

Mina's mock-stern expression softened. As Katrina drew the sheet up over Tom's freshly bandaged chest, Mina said, "I well remember, Tom, your idea of courtin'." She rolled her eyes at Will, who chuckled.

"And I remember what the other fellow looked like. It was watching the old doc put him back together that made me want to be a physician," Will said reflectively. He gave Tom a spoonful of the brown liquid he'd left in a small vial beside the bed. "This should help clear his lungs, Mina. Give it to him every six hours. If his fever doesn't break by dawn, you're to send for me."

Her cheerful smile didn't slip. "Yes, Will." But her voice shook when she said, "Es he goin' to be all right?"

"I expect so." Will shook his head, anticipating her next question. "And no, he cannot go back to work for some time. If you'd only let me help—"

"That's enough, doc," Tom broke in tersely. "Sence 'ee won't even let us pay for the medicine, we can't take no more from you." But there was a tension in Tom's voice that puzzled Katrina. Something more than pride seemed at play here. She looked from Tom's adamant expression to Will's stiff one.

"But as a miner you're my responsibility," Will reminded him. "I've told you before, you owe me nothing—"

"Go on weth 'ee and let me get some rest." Tom drew the sheet up to his obstinate chin and folded his hands over his chest.

Mina followed them to the door. Katrina handed her the small basket she'd set on the step. "This isn't much, but it may supply a couple of meals. Rachel sent it."

"Thank you, Miss Katrina." She sent an abashed look at Will. "I'm sorry—"

Will sighed. "That's quite all right. Tom's a proud man, and I suspect he doesn't know how bad things are. You save the best food for him, don't you?"

Mina nodded. "But we thank 'ee for the offer."

They waved and began the long walk back to the Tonkin cottage, where they parted, for Will to go on to his own cottage close to the mine. The memory of those hollow-eyed little girls haunted Katrina all that afternoon as she helped Rachel about the house. Would Robert soon look the same?

Katrina snapped down the pot she'd just dried, hung up her towel, and turned away. "I'm going out, Rachel. It may be late when I get back, so don't worry."

Katrina paused at the parlor mirror to pin her hair up more neatly. Her hands froze about her head. Her best dress had long since faded from its dove gray to an indistinguishable dun color. The patches at her elbows were fraying. What good family would hire her, looking as she did, to tutor their children?

She took the fine lamb's-wool shawl Rachel had made her and draped it about her shoulders. The pale blue color brought out her eyes and made the dress look slightly better. Sighing, Katrina turned away. She hadn't thought about her appearance in almost two years, except to assure herself that she was neat and clean. She looked like a beggar maid.

As she began the long walk she was tempted, briefly, to go to Devon's manor and ask for help. He owed her, for she'd never taken a penny from him in payment for the services she'd so richly rendered. Her lip curled. But if she did so now, doubtless he'd see it as a sign that she was offering to sell herself again. And never would she do so. Even if every one of them starved.

The wind was not quite as wild today, and Katrina enjoyed the walk over the heath. Wildflowers, pink, white, and yellow, bloomed in the rock clefts and in wet patches on the rolling moor. A kestrel keened as it circled above, looking for prey. The sun winked in and out of clouds, keeping rain at bay for the moment.

As the road descended into Truro Katrina had to step aside for the occasional cart, laden with goods being taken to market. The quay must be busy today, she thought. Truro had an estuary to Falmouth harbor that was deep enough to bear ships of a hundred tons and served as a channel outlet for the inhabitants from miles around.

Katrina paused on the rise overlooking the city to enjoy its pretty aspect. Truro stood on a vale at the confluence of two rivers, and was somewhat triangular in shape. It had commodious streets lined with shops and neat houses. A stream ran in the middle. Here and there lay great blocks of tin awaiting coinage. Katrina looked at them, wondering how many other Britons were as ill informed as she had been about the ancient system, unique in the isles.

John had explained to Katrina that since 1337, when the Duchy of Cornwall was created and gifted to the Prince of Wales, regulation of the tin mines had been conducted by the prince's council. The duchy was divided into mining areas called stannaries, and the duke took the place of the king in regulating tin-mining affairs. The stannaries had their own courts that settled mining disputes. In the past, at least, such courts were not subject to common law.

In return, representatives of the prince assayed and stamped each tin block with his arms. For every hundredweight so marked, the prince received four shillings, supposedly largely to fund the stannary system. Thus far, copper was not so regulated. John was fervently glad of that, yet, from his explanation, the cost-book system that governed most copper mines seemed almost as unwieldy and unfair. Katrina had been appalled to discover that most Cornish copper mines were primarily in the hands of investors outside Cornwall.

John's mine, or bal, as he called it, was a rare exception since it lay on Carrington's lands, and due to his rich estates in other counties, Carrington had capital enough to be the primary investor. He held over half an interest. Yet close as he was to the day-to-day working of the mine, he seemed no more sympathetic to his workers' lots than the remote Prince of Wales.

How much, Katrina wondered, had the mines earned the prince and Carrington's family over the years? Yet neither nobleman nor future monarch apparently cared that the miners who earned them the vast sums were on the verge of starvation. A brooding frown on her face, Katrina descended the road into Truro and turned into the first shop she came to, a millinery.

The proprietress looked her up and down as she haltingly asked for a position. "Go on weth 'ee," the small, sharp-faced, sharp-tongued woman snapped. "I've got no work for such as 'ee."

Katrina got the same response from every shop she entered, even the apothecary's. He, at least, was kind.

"I've scarce enough work to keep me and my family busy, lass. I'm sorry. Why don't you try the Cock and Hind Tavern? It's two streets over, and I hear they're looking for a barmaid."

Katrina gave him a wan smile and trudged out. Times were hard here, too. Indeed, why should anyone hire her, when they all had families of their own who needed employment?

Telling herself she was only going to stroll about before returning home, Katrina wandered from shop to shop until the sun lowered in the sky. Yet somehow she found herself near the wharf, on a rougher street. A peeling sign portrayed a garish cock crowing atop the back of a handsome stag. Katrina stood across the street, hesitating. Her belly rumbled at that strategic moment, reminding her that she'd not eaten since breakfast.

Goaded, she crossed the street. Merely to look in the window, she told herself. The bow windowpanes were sooty and she saw only the dim glow of candles. Taking a deep breath, she entered the tavern. The heavy door closed behind her with an ominous thunk that made her start. Could she go through with it? She sighed. Did she have a choice? She lifted her chin, wrapped her shawl tightly about her shoulders, and stepped confidently into the taproom.

A quick glance showed her several tables where games of chance were being played, and others where men clanked together frothy mugs of ale. But it was the sight of a barmaid rubbing herself against a seated customer in a manner Katrina could only call indecent that made her halt barely two steps into the room. She was too busy staring to notice the attention she was drawing.

One tippler's eyes widened. Slowly, he set his mug down and nudged his tablemate, spilling the fellow's ale down his shirt. He scowled and turned on his friend, then saw what he was staring at. He set down his own mug.

The buzz of conversation died as she became the cynosure of all eyes. Out of her corner vision Katrina saw the flash of two shapely, bare legs swinging from their position upon the lap of a gamester. Katrina cringed inside. If the barmaids were expected to entertain patrons in *that* fashion, she couldn't work here. But the player's uncommonly long, powerful thighs clothed in expensive satin knee breeches seemed somehow familiar. Katrina realized two things simultaneously: She had to leave, but first, she wanted to see what kind of local roisterer could afford such clothing. Before she could look, however, a brawny arm caught her by the waist.

She gasped and tried to squirm away, but Jack Hennessy's voice, rich with satisfaction, said, "Faith, I knew ye'd change yer mind. But ye didn't have to come all the way into Truro, darlin'. I'd have met ye wherever ye pleased."

Katrina forced a polite smile to her lips. Guilelessly she met Jack's lustful eyes. "It's good to see you, Jack, but I'm afraid I came in search of employment. Do you know where I might find the proprietor?" Gently she tried to pull away as if to seek the owner out, but Jack's arm tightened.

His wide chest rumbled with laughter. "And glad he'd be to have ye here, for ye'd draw the lads like flies to a honey pot. But I've other plans for ye, darlin'." He began to pull her to the door.

Katrina planted her feet and struggled harder, casting desperate glances about the room. "No, Jack. I don't want to go—" Instinctively, she looked toward the well-dressed man.

She gasped. Awareness of the whispering patrons, even of Jack's insolent touch, escaped her as her world narrowed to one man.

There, his long white hand intimately high on the barmaid's thigh, sat Devon. Stubble dotted his face, and his hair hung partway down his shoulders, having long since, apparently, escaped its queue. A bottle and a half-empty glass sat at his elbow. Their eyes held for a timeless moment. She saw his shock change to anger as he looked at Hennessy's encroaching arm. Her mouth curled, and she controlled her panic by pure iron will. Not this time, my fine rake, she thought. I'll show you I don't need your help. Jack abetted her intent by pausing in trying to drag her out. She deduced that he, too, was staring at Devon.

She nodded regally toward the corner. "How nice to see you again, my lord. In your natural habitat, as it were."

He flung down the cards he'd been holding and dumped the barmaid off his lap. She screeched, but he merely stepped around her. As he approached he gave an elaborate sigh.

"And somehow you seem just as out of place despite the fact that you look so much the part." He encompassed her patched gown, peasant shoes, and simple shawl with one scornful glance. "But I, as ever, shall be magnanimous and save you from this lout." He continued his advance.

Vaguely Katrina noticed that his steps were steady, but his eyes glittered. With drink? For the first time in her life she wished for a dram herself—anything to make her senseless so she didn't have to suffer this humiliation. He'd "saved" her before; she'd no wish to experience again his brand of mercy. Certainly, he might spare her a ravishing in the bushes, only to subject her to a seduction on a bed. In her heart Katrina knew there was a difference; in the mind that still resented him there was little.

"You've a real facility for attracting ruthless suitors, my dear," Devon drawled, stopping several feet away. His eyes, brown, fathomless as a Cornish bog, looked only at Hennessy. Jack's grip about her waist loosened as his attention focused on Devon. Katrina felt Hennessy stiffen alertly.

Damn them both, she thought. I'll have neither their "help" nor their "admiration." Katrina inched away enough for leverage. "Indeed, my lord, you should know." Devon's gaze slipped from Hennessy to her. She smiled sweetly and brought her heavy clog down on Jack's foot, simultaneously ramming an elbow into his gut. With an oof of pain he released her. Mentally she thanked John for showing her the maneuver after she'd taken to walking the moors alone.

She swiveled free and shot a triumphant look at Devon. She turned to the door, tossing over her shoulder, "And I'm also learning how to deal with them." Before she could exit, Hennessy straightened painfully and grabbed her arm.

"Ye bitch! Ye ain't too good for Jack—"

"Scum? Or is that your middle name?" a soft voice asked.

Jack turned to shoot a glare at the man who rocked casually on the balls of his feet. The rakes who had sparred with the earl would have recognized that stance as anything but indolent, but Hennessy was not so fortunate.

"Ye stay out o' this, if ye don't want that pretty face smashed," Hennessy snarled, jerking Katrina's arm to turn her so they could leave. He was too busy dodging her kicks to notice when one of Devon's forward rocks propelled him into a lunge. Hennessy found himself pinned against the sturdy tavern door by a patrician hand at his throat.

Since Jack still held Katrina's arm, she was jerked alongside them, feeling like part of one of the Earl of Sandwich's new snacks. She didn't envy Jack his part as the meat, however.

"Let her go, else find your *ugly* face smashed," Devon warned cordially. When Hennessy sputtered a denial and brought up his free hand to shove Devon away, Devon caught his wrist and twisted it. His long, fragile-looking hand tightened its grip about Hennessy's throat. Hennessy let go of Katrina to try to pry Devon's fingers away, but he was already winded, and Devon slammed his body against Hennessy's to trap his other struggling arm.

"On second thought," Devon purred, "I'd rather see you turn purple." Devon cocked his head to one side as Hennessy gurgled and went red. "That's close, but not quite right. You Cornish barbarians painted yourselves blue not so long ago, so purple shouldn't be too hard for you." His grip tightened again.

Devon, his face curiously remote yet intent, apparently

didn't hear the grumbles from the other patrons growing to roars at his words, but Katrina did.

"Hey there! Let the lad go. 'Ee've made your point," one man called.

From other quarters came shouts of "Aye!"

A slim but powerful-looking man Katrina had often seen in Jack's company shoved his chair back and jumped to his feet. "'Ee ain't in London now, your bloody lordship. If 'ee's aimin' to see how *barbaric* Cornishmen be, then come to me and find out."

Devon didn't even give the fellow a glance.

The door was blocked, Katrina told herself. She couldn't leave. But she shot the patrons an uneasy glance, wondering what to do. Only then did she spy Billy, sitting at a table adjacent to Devon's.

He spread his hands at her pleading look, and she had the feeling he half hoped Devon would indeed get his pretty face smashed. She agreed that Devon richly needed the thrashing he'd never gotten as a lad, but his arrogance couldn't hold a baker's dozen of muscular Cornishmen at bay. Wondering why the thought of Devon being hurt caused her pain, Katrina marched to the nearest table and snatched a full mug from a surprised miner.

She went back to Devon and flung the strong ale into his face. He blinked in shock and let Jack go. Coughing, Jack stumbled away and flopped into a chair one of his friends shoved behind him. His face was one shade away from purple.

Devon didn't notice. He jerked the mug out of Katrina's hand and flung it against the wall, then caught her waist and hauled her against his muscular frame. "Vixen! You really enjoy putting a damper upon a man's fun. Literally, in this case." His face relaxed into that whimsical, charming smile that usually went straight to her heart. This time it missed its mark, for she was casting worried glances over her shoulder.

"If you don't get out of here, *now*," she muttered, "you'll learn an insulted Cornishman's idea of fun."

Devon quirked an eyebrow and looked over her head to see several more men coming to their feet and balling angry fists. "I see what you mean." He released her, then strolled forward into the room to inspect Jack, who still cradled his throat. He ignored the angry glares blasting him from every quarter.

The door was free now. Katrina cast it a look, but somehow she was compelled forward instead of back. She had little influence here, but at least she'd been marginally accepted. She knew enough, now, of how these men thought to realize that they considered Devon an interloper. John had told her the tales circulating about Devon's arrival in Redruth.

He was considered a rich outsider who had won one of the oldest mines in the district on the turn of a card. A spoiled aristocrat who'd been reared to think himself above other men, especially Cornishmen, who were often considered inferior by other Britons. He'd probably bilk the mine of every shilling, then close it and leave them with hungry families and no way to feed them. Too many outsiders had done the same. And now this profligate had insulted them as Cornishmen. . . .

Katrina read these thoughts and others on their swarthy, angry faces. She knew they didn't fear Devon, despite his display of toughness. To men who battled daily with the indefatigable earth and sea, Devon was not a formidable enemy. Lord or no, he needed a lesson.

Fear for Devon, not concern for Jack, led her to block the way of the tall, slim man who strode forward to examine his friend. "Here, let me, since I'm partly to blame for his state." Katrina snatched the kerchief out of his hand and dipped it in a pitcher of water on the bar. She hurried back to wrap it about Jack's throat. She straightened and smiled brightly. "There. It's just a bruise, I think. He'll be fine. Now, if you'll excuse me, I must be going." Casually, she took Devon's hand to tug him to the door.

He cast her a surprised look, then gently pulled away. "You should know I'm not a man to flee conflict, Kat." He propped his hands on his hips and said to the slim man who was coming around the table to meet him, "Here I am, fellow. I'm all yours—if you can take me."

Katrina groaned, but she hastily stepped between the two men before they came nose to nose. She turned her back on Devon to meet the other man's eyes. "Now, er, it's Davie, isn't it?" Those midnight-black eyes didn't waver from Devon's face, though he nodded.

"I'm more sorry than I can say for the trouble I've caused," Katrina continued. "But really, haven't I the right to refuse to leave with Jack? He would have dragged me out had not this man intervened."

"Maybe," Davie replied. "But thes blighter took a wee bet too much joy en chokin' the life out of my friend. And then he ensulted us—"

"He was angry and has obviously been drinking. Please, let us be on our way without further incident." Katrina ignored Devon's gentle push and hissed command to quit protecting him.

Davie tossed his head of unruly black curls at the door. "Be on weth 'ee, then. Et's hem"—he stabbed a finger beside Katrina's head into Devon's collarbone—"I've a longin' to have . . . words weth."

"I only hope you're better at pugilism than elocution, my man," Devon drawled.

Davie's handsome, reckless face flushed. "Let's see how fancy ye be weth my fest en your mouth." He shoved Katrina aside. She stumbled and almost fell. Devon's eyes narrowed at the action, and when Davie swung a wild punch at his chin, he ducked and returned with a blow to Davie's jaw.

The crack echoed in the tense silence. Davie stumbled back, but caught himself and charged forward, his head low on his shoulders. His arms latched about Devon's waist. The two men crashed against the bar in a tumble of pummeling fists and kicking legs.

Katrina ran to Billy and caught his arm. "Billy, do something! Davie may hurt him."

"Aye, lass, he may. And mayhaps it'll knock a nonce o' sense in him," Billy answered, never taking his eyes from the action near the bar. Katrina winced at a pained groan, but she forced herself to turn and look.

Devon already had a cut swelling above his eye and a bruise on his cheek. Davie was in even worse shape. His mouth was puffy and bleeding, and one eye would probably be a lovely purple by tomorrow. But his wounds didn't seem to hamper him. As she watched, Davie landed a punch square in Devon's middle. The earl gave an oof of pain and clutched his stomach, but he managed to dodge Davie's follow-up blow that would doubtless have broken his glorious nose.

With a ferocious grin that Katrina would have sworn was gleeful, he caught Davie's extended arm and pulled it up behind his back. Davie's grunt of pain only made him twist harder.

"Cry quarter, Cornishman," Devon growled.

Davie's reply was a sharp elbow into Devon's tender abdomen. Devon winced but gave such a furious tug on Davie's arm that the man fell to his knees with a cry of pain. Katrina closed her eyes, expecting to hear cracking bone. When the sound didn't come, she looked again. She slumped with relief to see Devon releasing Davie. Davie cradled his strained shoulder and stayed on his knees, his face red with exertion and, doubtless, Katrina realized, humiliation.

Devon stepped away from him and cast a challenging look about the room. "Does anyone else want to test a nobleman's mettle?" His disdainful half smile was refined by ten generations of blue bloods. Katrina wanted to slap it off his face, so she knew exactly how the others would react.

When two muscular miners stepped forward, she couldn't bear it. She ran behind the bar and snatched up a bottle of whiskey, then ran back around to where Devon stood.

He sent her a surprised but warning glance. "Thanks, Kat, but I don't need your help. Now step aside, like a good girl." He reached out to push her out of danger.

She slapped his hand away and muttered, "Well, you're getting my help, anyway. Sorry, Devon." And she brought the bottle down, hard, on the back of his head. The glass shattered, spraying them both with whiskey.

His disbelieving eyes closed. He slumped. She caught him in her arms but couldn't bear his weight and began to fall backward. "Billy," she cried.

Billy was there in an instant to heft Devon over his shoulders. "I've got him, lass. He'll not thank you when he wakes, you know, despite the fact that you doubtless spared him worse pain."

"I know." Katrina sent an apologetic shrug to the watching Cornishmen. She saw several admiring grins, but more disappointed scowls. "Sorry to cheat you of your entertainment, boys, but women will be women, too, you know."

"Aye," Jack growled hoarsely. "Interferin' busybodies. Ye didn't care when he was about to choke *me*." He rubbed at his raw throat.

Katrina responded coolly. "I suggest you remember that, Jack. I think I've made my opinion of your . . . attentions clear." She held the door for Billy to carry Devon out. She closed it behind them with a sigh of relief. She looked about. "Where's your carriage?"

"Over there." Billy pointed to where a boy guarded the restive grays hooked to a curricle.

Katrina helped arrange Devon in the seat, but he kept falling and Billy couldn't hold him and drive. She shared a wry glance with Billy, lifted her skirts, and climbed in beside Devon to hold him in her arms.

With the toss of a coin to the boy and a click of his tongue, Billy got them under way. They'd not gone far up the road leading to Redruth before Devon groaned and stirred against Katrina's bosom. Immediately she stopped her surreptitious stroking of his hair and tried to help him sit up.

His eyes opened and blinked at her. With a loud groan he subsided back into her arms. "If I hadn't awakened so pleasantly, I swear I'd beat you, Kat," he muttered into her right breast. His arms came up to clasp her tightly about the waist.

She tried to pry him away, but he was fully conscious, and fully determined to take advantage of their position. "I'd have thought you'd had enough of beating for one day. Neither Jack nor Davie make pretty sights."

Devon gingerly touched the cut above his eye. "Nor do I, doubtless." He tilted his head back on her shoulder and cast her a winsome smile. "Do you want to kiss it and make it better?"

"No, but I might consider giving you a matched set," she answered sweetly.

He rubbed the back of his head. "Somehow I don't doubt you." But his tone was more wry than angry, and Katrina couldn't smother a smile.

"You deserved it. And you really should thank me, you

know. Had you stayed much longer, you'd have broken bones instead of a sore head.''

''And you can't bear to see my manly countenance ruined?'' he asked, with so much the air of a hopeful little boy that this time she couldn't smother a giggle.

''Maybe I don't want to see your manly countenance, period,'' she said, striving for dignity.

He tweaked her lofty nose with a finger. ''That's fine with me. The manly part I really want to show you has nothing to do with my face.'' He rubbed at her rosy cheeks with his fingertip. ''Ah, Kat, I'm so happy to be with you again that I don't even care my head's aching like the very devil.''

He groaned and rubbed his forehead back and forth on her shoulder. Instantly her embarrassment changed to concern. She felt his brow. He seemed a bit warm.

''Take Miss Lawson home first, Billy.'' When Katrina protested, Devon said, ''I'll not have you walk alone so late. It will be dark soon.''

When Billy jerked to a stop before John's gate twenty minutes later, Devon roused enough to slump against Billy's shoulder. He waved a listless hand. ''Bye, heartless girl. Billy can treat my wounds as well as you, doubtless.''

Katrina stepped down and forced herself to turn away. Then she spun back around and snapped, ''Oh, very well. Come down. Since I caused one of your wounds, it's the least I can do.''

A quick, triumphant flash of teeth warned her his words were a sham, but when he stepped gingerly down and groaned in pain, she still went to help support him. As Billy sniffed the air she sighed.

''You too, Billy. I'll see if Rachel has enough.'' One meal, as low as their stores were, would probably make little difference, she reasoned. Besides, it would do Devon good to see how the majority of the English lived. She cast both men, who towered above her, a chiding glance as she led the way into the cottage. ''But don't think you fool me for a minute.''

She hid a smile as they both tried to look angelic. Katrina hurried into the kitchen, where Ellie and Rachel bustled about, setting out crockery.

"Good even' to you both," Katrina said. "Rachel, may we have two guests for dinner?"

Rachel turned from stirring the kettle. Her eyes widened when she saw Devon and Billy peeking into the kitchen behind Katrina. She paused, then smiled into Katrina's pleading gaze.

"Sure, lass. Et's a good time, for we've fresh pilchards to sup on. John brought them home. One of hes men repaaid hem for a loan." She commanded the two newcomers, "Set 'ee down. We'll be ready soon."

Devon sat near the middle of the bench, where Katrina indicated. Billy sat one space down. He stared at Ellie so intently that she blushed and fidgeted with her cap. Katrina looked into the kettle bubbling over the hearth. She sighed in relief. Turnip-and-potato soup. At least it wasn't fish-head broth. She tried to picture Devon eating what had become one of their staples, but her mind boggled.

Katrina walked to the pantry and fetched an old, clean rag. She wet it in the water Rachel had drawn from the well and went to Devon. He lifted his face to her ministrations with an expectant smile, but Katrina was brisk. She was careful not to show her own mixed emotions at the touch of his warm skin as she swabbed at his various cuts until the bleeding stopped.

He winced at a particularly brusque touch. "Maybe I should have let Billy doctor me, after all."

"Maybe you should have," Katrina agreed.

Both of the Tonkin women peered at Devon, but Katrina knew they were too polite to ask what had happened. She rinsed the cloth and spread it over the line hanging in the dairy, then returned to the kitchen to set the table.

Taking two extra plates from the cupboard, Katrina asked, "Where are John and Jimmy?"

Ellie, who was dipping broth into a large crock, answered. "They're fixing Nanny's pen." She exchanged a serious look with Katrina.

Katrina nodded. She didn't need to be told how important that task was. Since John had sold the cow, Nanny the goat was the only source of milk they had. Ellie turned, holding the hot container of broth by its handles.

Billy stood. "Here, lass. That's too heavy for a mite like ye." Billy admired Ellie's slim figure, then carefully took the crock from her to set it on the table. Their hands brushed together. Their eyes met for a long moment before Ellie reluctantly turned away to help her mother chop the onion to mix with the sliced pilchards.

Katrina watched the pair, frowning. She didn't think John would approve of Billy's suit. He wanted an educated, affluent man for his daughter, preferably a Cornishman. Devon, too, watched them, a smile playing about his lips. When he saw Katrina's concern, he lifted an eyebrow at her as if to say, So what? She turned away and went to the back door to call Jimmy and John.

The strong scent of the fish wafted over the table as Rachel proudly set the pilchards before Devon. Katrina sat down on the bench in time to see Devon's nostrils quiver. She sent him a warning look. If he turned up his lordly nose to a single bite, she'd never forgive him.

John and Jimmy tromped into the room. They both stopped dead at sight of the visitors. John's eyes narrowed in dislike, but when he met Katrina's pleading look, he sighed and, without a word, went to wash his hands. Jimmy's scowl, however, only deepened as he saw Devon sitting in his usual place.

John nudged him. "Wash up, boy." Jimmy complied, but after he'd dried his hands, he swaggered to the table and stood over Devon.

"You're in my spot," he said.

Devon rose immediately. "I'm sorry. Where shall I sit?"

Jimmy's "You can ride to town on my knife, for all I care," was fortunately muffled by Rachel's loud comment.

"You staay there, my lord. Jimmy, you set next to Robert and let Katrina set by hes lordshep."

Obediently, Devon sat back down. But from the puzzled look he sent Jimmy, Katrina figured that he, too, had heard Jimmy's aside. Jimmy hesitated.

Robert bounced up and down on his seat. "Jimmy, I found the biggest frog today! After supper I'll show it to you." Jimmy's hostile face relaxed a bit as he went to sit beside his little brother, opposite Devon and Katrina.

John sat at one end of the bench, on Devon's other side. Rachel sat on the adjacent bench, next to Ellie. Billy sat opposite her, next to Katrina.

"Would you like to lead the blessing, my lord?" John asked.

Katrina felt Devon shuffle his feet, but he replied politely, "Certainly, if you wish." He bowed his sun-streaked head. His hair was neat again, for he'd tied it back before entering the cottage. "Lord, for what we are about to receive, make us truly thankful. Teach us to be as generous with one another as you are with us. Amen." John nodded approvingly and began to ladle out soup.

Devon raised his head and smiled into Katrina's suspicious eyes. She sniffed, conveying her opinion of him invoking the Lord to further his own selfish ends.

"That's an appropriate prayer, Devon. It will surely take divine intervention to teach you generosity," she hissed into his ear.

"You misjudge me yet again," he whispered back. "I've always wanted to be generous to you, but you've never let me."

When Jimmy turned his head toward them as if straining to hear, Katrina bit her lip over another retort and took a sip of soup. She watched as Devon took a dollop. He held the strong-tasting turnip soup in his mouth for a second, a strange look on his face, then swallowed quickly. Katrina wondered if the Earl of Brookstone had ever tasted a turnip in his life.

He sent Rachel a warm smile. "Delicious." He took another bigger sip and swallowed it even faster. She noticed that he barely chewed the chopped turnips and potatoes, and knew he found every bite repugnant.

Admiration for his courtesy nudged some of Katrina's resentment aside. One could say many things about Devon Cavanaugh, but he was always a gentleman, even to those he considered far beneath his station. Still, she couldn't resist teasing him.

"Have you heard the saying, my lord, that the devil never comes into Cornwall for fear of being made into a pie?" Katrina took a composed sip of her own broth, smiling inwardly when Devon choked on a bite of turnip.

He coughed discreetly into his napkin, then cleared his throat. "I hope you've no pastry handy. I've already been tenderized today; I'd as soon not be roasted as well." He emphasized the *roasted,* but his arch look make it plain he didn't mind her teasing.

Katrina couldn't smother a giggle. Billy snorted into his soup. When the others looked confused at the joke, Katrina explained, ''My lord is known in some quarters as Demon Devon.'' This drew a smile from John, Rachel, and Ellie, but Jimmy nodded sourly.

''That don't surprise me,'' he muttered.

Devon sent him another puzzled look, obviously wondering what he'd done to stir the lad's resentment. Katrina went on quickly, ''In easier times, if we still had flour, we'd be eating pilchard pie. We call it starry-gazy pie because we cook the fish whole in pastry, with its head poking through the crust. We'd have put it in pride of place before you, my lord. Wouldn't it have whetted your appetite to have it stare at you as you cut into it?''

Tilting her bowl to scoop up the last drop of soup, Katrina pretended not to see Rachel's surprise. She felt Devon's needle-sharp stare poking her.

''Oh, indubitably,'' was all he said, however. He, too, swallowed his last drop of soup, but he couldn't disguise a tiny sigh of relief as he was able to push his empty bowl away. Rachel immediately put a large helping of pilchards upon his plate, then served Billy and everyone else.

Katrina saw his nose quiver at the scent. His palate was probably used to caviar and Dover sole. Pilchards were considered a delicacy by Cornwall's poor, but it was obvious Devon didn't agree. It would be interesting indeed to see if he could get half the serving down. ''Pies are infinite in their varieties, you know. We make them out of meat as well as fish. One of my favorites is muggety pie.'' She waited until he'd taken a cautious bite. His throat worked, and she could see he was trying not to gag. ''It's made from sheep entrails flavored with spices and cream.''

He chewed once, then gulped. ''How . . . delectable.'' He seemed a bit pale, but he scooped up another bite with his spoon. He sent her a pleading glance. Katrina allowed herself a small smile, but desisted.

Jimmy had been glancing between the pair. He wolfed down a couple of bites of pilchards, then said reflectively, ''I think my favorite pie of all, Ma, was that one you made with my find on the beach that time when I was ten.''

Rachel smiled. ''Ais, that was a good one. Some think eel don't maake a good paasty, but I thenk they do.''

''Eel?'' Katrina repeated. She took a dainty bite of her own fish. She'd long since learned to like the heavy flavor, but the smell sometimes bothered her still. ''I've not heard this story.''

''I found a big conger eel on the beach and brought it home to Ma,'' Jimmy explained. Katrina noticed that John shook his head and made a hushing sound, but Jimmy concluded, ''I never did tell you why it was so bloated. There'd been a shipwreck, you see. And the fellow had been so greedy that he couldn't slither away when I caught him. Never did find all the pieces to those bodies.'' He savored his last bite of fish, looking around innocently when everyone at the table, except John, gagged.

Katrina went a bit green and put down her spoon. She shared a look with Devon that called up memories of Yorkshire pudding and roast round of beef. For the first time in ages she felt homesick for England east of the Tamar. They did have some things in common, she thought with a jolt. He saw that knowledge in her eyes, she knew. She hastily averted her gaze and moved her hand when he tried to clasp it.

Rachel said in disgust, ''I'd not have cooked et had I known that.''

''You promised not to tell, boy,'' John growled at his son. ''Now you've put us all off our food.''

''Good. That leaves more for me.'' Jimmy reached for the serving spoon, but John slapped his hand away. ''Not until we've offered more to our guests.'' He glanced inquiringly at Billy, who shook his head, then at Devon.

''No, thank you, Mr. Tonkin,'' Devon said. ''This is plenty. Might I have a dram to wash it down with?''

''Of course.'' John rose to go to the pantry. He brought back a jug of home-brewed ale, which, since he was a strict Methodist, was the only brew he'd partake of. Katrina knew how he'd been hoarding this last bottle. But he took down one of Rachel's good china cups from its peg above the cupboard and poured a hefty draft, then did the same in two more cups.

"Me too, Da," Jimmy said, licking his lips. John hesitated, then he poured half a cup for his son.

Ellie rose to help him bring the cups to the table. She gave Billy his cup and blushed when he whispered something to her. John paused in midstride on his way back to the table. Only when Ellie had taken her seat again did he come forward. He sent a glare at Billy as he sat down.

After Devon had taken a careful sip, John asked, "What do 'ee thenk? I maade et myself."

"It's quite good," Devon said in a way Katrina knew was sincere.

John raised an eyebrow at Devon's half-full plate. Devon sighed slightly and picked up his spoon. John glanced at his wife. "Where's your manners, Ma? Give his lordship a bet to bread his basen weth." Katrina froze and lifted her head.

Rachel hesitated, then stood and went to the cupboard. She unwrapped and brought to the table two small barley cakes. They were insignificant-looking things, but Katrina's mouth watered. They were their last, she knew. Rachel had been saving them for the Sunday meal.

"Thank you kindly," Devon said, taking one cake and passing the other to Billy. Both men began to crumble the cakes into their plates.

An odd silence descended as they realized they were being stared at. Devon looked about. Everyone hastily averted their eyes to their plates. Everyone except little Robert, who was too young for subterfuge. He stared hungrily at Devon's half-crumbled cake, and even licked his lips.

An appalled expression settled over Devon. Then, like the lord he was, he tactfully handled an awkward situation. "Here, lad, share this with me. I'm full, anyway." Devon leaned across the table to put the rest of the cake upon Robert's plate.

Robert sent his mother an inquiring look. When she nodded, he gobbled up the cake in one bite. Billy, without a word, put the rest of his cake on Ellie's plate.

Katrina couldn't resist it; she leaned forward to see past Devon. John was staring thoughtfully at his guest. When he met her eyes, he smiled as if to say, He's not a bad sort, after all. Katrina's heart felt lighter than it had in many a moon as she ate the last of her fish.

She felt Devon's look and slowly lifted her head to meet it. She couldn't stop the soft smile she sent him; for once she didn't try. Even when his eyes began to dance with those gold sparks, she couldn't look away. She felt bathed in light rather than singed, and every feeling she'd worked two years to subdue rose eagerly to revel in that warmth. . . .

Chapter Nine

AFTER DINNER, KATRINA rose to help Rachel with the dishes, as usual. However, to her amazement, Devon took the plates from her and carried them to the sideboard. She was still staring at him when he returned to the table to pick up the empty serving dishes. He gently closed her mouth with the tip of his finger.

"Earls are not incompetent, you know," he teased, stacking the soup crock on top of the platter.

"I wonder if your servants would agree," Katrina responded dryly, joining Rachel at the sideboard to help wash the dishes. But she gave Devon a grateful glance when he set the crockery beside her.

Meanwhile, Ellie wiped off the table, but when she came to Billy's end, her smooth movements became jerky as she leaned across to clean his place. They each reached at once to move his mug of ale, but Billy's eyes were fixed on her full bosom, and hers were steadfast on the rag in her hand. Their grips clashed and knocked the cup over, spilling the dregs of the ale into Billy's lap.

He made a strangled sound and half rose, catching everyone's attention. Ellie gasped and automatically reached out to swipe up the stain, then froze and went beet red. Devon, from his position next to Katrina, made a funny noise that sounded remarkably like a stifled laugh. Katrina shook her head at him and moved forward to hand Billy the towel she was using to wipe the dishes with.

He took it with a grateful smile. After he'd wiped up the front of his breeches, he murmured to Ellie, "There, lass, there's no need to be embarrassed. It's just as much my fault. I was, er, distracted." His wink left no doubt as to how attractive that distraction had been. His mobile mouth curved into a smile that gave his irregular features a stunning magnetism.

When Ellie smiled back at him, her pretty face alight with pleasure at the compliment, John called sharply from his position by the fire, "Come here, Ellie, and light my pipe."

Ellie glared at her father, but she tossed her cloth down and obeyed, then sat next to him. Billy levered his long legs over the bench and moved to join them, but Katrina took one look at John's set face and elbowed Devon in the ribs.

"Go sit next to Ellie," she hissed.

"You might as well try to stop the tide as to keep Billy from pursuing a women he wants," he whispered back, staying put.

"Like master like servant, I see."

"No, like two friends who have known each other since they were in short coats together," he flung back. He strode aggressively to the bench and sat down on John's other side, directly next to the fire. Billy had already sat next to Ellie and begun to converse with her in a low, intimate tone.

Devon addressed John. "Mr. Tonkin, I understand you're a mine captain. . . ." Courtesy forced John to turn to his guest. Billy took full advantage of Devon's diversion and leaned closer to whisper in Ellie's ear.

"My own mine captain tells me that our profits aren't likely to improve as long as we have to smelt our ores abroad," Devon said, tilting an inquiring brow at John. "Do you agree?"

John sighed. "'Tes partly true. Those rascally smelters in Bristol and Waales have done all they can to monopolize and offer mine adventurers whatever price they agree upon—leaven' them weth a profit ten times what we maake. But weth the price of coal, and consederen' how far we have to transport it, starten' our own smelter here esn't a practecal idea. The Hayle works barely survived, and 'twas dangerous for workers there. Besides, most miners hereabouts prefer to work on agreement and get paid based on profets. We'll have no werking man slavery here in Redruth." John looked grimly determined about that. He glanced at his daughter, who was smiling at Billy, but Devon interrupted again.

"And what do you think of the Anglesey mines? Is their ore quality as poor as rumored?"

"Ais, our entire endustry es sufferen' 'cause of the greed of

Thomas Williams of Anglesey. He wants to ruin Cornish copper-mining enterests and es en a fair way of doen' so by dumpin' so much ore on the market.'' John crossed his arms over his chest and said hardily, ''But I tell 'ee thes: He's already overproducen' and the veins he can exploit by the open-cast method, whech es cheap, well be exhausted soon. No, I fear the real threat to our endustry es the cost of fuel and the expense of engines powerful enough to pump at the deeper and deeper levels we need to work.'' John looked as if he might be about to say something, but he snapped his mouth closed.

Katrina, who had been listening as she helped Rachel with the dishes, had no such loyalty to Carrington. Drying a plate, she turned to look at Devon. He was, after all, apparently good friends with Carrington. . . . ''A concern John has expressed many times to Lord Carrington, but he won't approach the other shareholders about purchasing a new engine system. Too expensive, he says. Production doesn't warrant it since the mine is so old and no new veins have been discovered in so long.'' She turned to stack the plate on top of the others, leaving Devon looking thoughtful.

''And I know the ores are there, rich enough to be viable, even so low.'' John smacked one frustrated fist against the other. ''I've worked the mines all my life, but all the adits we've dug have done all they can to aid weth drainage. Only one of the new engines by Watt will help us find new veins.''

''Which are extremely expensive, of course,'' Devon inserted.

''Aye, but weth his separate condenser engine, the saven' en fuel more than makes up for his high premiums.''

''I see,'' Devon said. He opened his mouth to ask another question, but John went first.

''Now, that's enough of work. 'Ee should talk to your own mine captain.'' John peered around Billy's bulk at his daughter. ''Ellie, why don't 'ee taake your brother upstairs and put hem to bed?''

Ellie, it seemed, didn't hear. Or if she did, she ignored her father. Robert was playing happily in the corner with the toy soldiers Jimmy had carved for him, in any case. Katrina glanced over her shoulder at Billy. The look in his eyes was one she'd often seen in Devon's. When she looked at Ellie, unfortunately, she also recognized her expression. She bit her lip over a sharp comment to back up John, dried the last plate, and stacked it on top of the others with a clatter that earned her a pained glance from Rachel. Katrina gave her an apologetic look, took the plates, and stood on her tiptoes to set them in their place in the top of the cupboard. Why was Devon abetting Billy's flirtation? Didn't he realize that Ellie would never be happy anywhere but in Cornwall? If not, she'd have to set him right, quickly, before John did so less diplomatically.

She was unaware that as she strained upward Devon's gaze wandered from John's face, fastening on the slim ankles peeking beneath Katrina's dress. Katrina caught his glance when she turned. His eyes lifted to hers. Katrina unconsciously licked her lips; she had no idea how much she resembled a cat looking at a bowlful of cream.

John did. His eyes sharpened. He looked from Devon, to Billy, who was still whispering to Ellie. She gurgled a soft laugh.

"We've foxes loose in the henhouse, Ma," he rumbled.

Rachel dried her hands on a rag, peering from Ellie to Katrina and back again. She slapped the rag down on the sideboard so hard that she caught Devon and Billy's attention.

"And what do you suggest we do about it, Da?" Both of her guests shifted nervously under her stern blue eyes.

"We could try bolten' the door, but the hens seem to like the smell of the fox. Or should I say foxes?" John folded his arms over his chest with a challenging air.

"Ellie, I think we've both just been called hen-witted," Katrina said, her mouth curled in rueful amusement. She sent a last wistful look at Devon, then went to take her friend's arm. "We'd best retire, since tomorrow is wash day."

"The fox would like a word with the hen before she ruffles her feathers too much." Devon's smile deliberately showed too many teeth, and Katrina knew he was goading John.

"That's all right, John." Katrina patted his arm when he made to rise. "After your timely reminder my wits are firmly about me again." She cocked her head to one side as she studied Devon. "He does have a red cast to his fur, er, hair, doesn't he?"

Devon rolled his eyes. "You've likened me to a cat, a demon, and now a fox." He stood, ignoring John's scowl as he clasped her arms. "Why can't you see me as what I am? Just a man. Or is that even more frightening to you?"

"A man, my lord? You, who wear your rank like a crown?" Katrina shrugged off his touch. "You've already proved earlier today, in Truro, that you consider yourself above the common man's touch. Well, I make no pretense that I'm more than I am. Do you still wish to talk with me?"

"Yes," he bit off, wheeling toward the door. "On the bench outside." But he paused a couple of steps later, turned back around, and strode over to Rachel. He kissed her hand. "Thank you for the meal, Mrs. Tonkin. It . . . was an experience I shall long remember fondly." He smiled warmly at Ellie and at Robert, who had glared at him all evening, imitating, as usual, his big brother.

Devon's nod at John was less warm, but still cordial. "Thank you for your hospitality. I should like to invite you to sup with me at my own home—"

"When hell freezes over," Jimmy inserted, sotto voce.

"Within the next few weeks," Devon went on, as if he hadn't heard, though from his cool look at Jimmy he obviously had. "I shall send an invitation 'round. Katrina?" He offered his hand, but she'd already turned to lead the way out of the kitchen. "Join me when you're ready, Billy."

Billy nodded and turned to ask John more questions about the mine. Ellie grimaced when her father jerked his head toward the stairs, but she obeyed—after a last flirtatious smile at Billy over her shoulder, which was warmly returned.

When they reached the bench, Katrina moved to sit down, but when she saw Devon stretch his arm casually about the top slat, she straightened. "I'll stand. What did you wish to discuss with me?"

He looked at her so long and silently that it required all her nerve to meet that brooding stare. The brilliant moonlight reflected on his wind-ruffled hair, sheening him in a romantic aura. Only by reminding herself that the gloss hid a multitude of sins was she able to stifle her longing to fling herself into his arms.

"Well, if you've nothing to say, I'll go in." But he caught her skirt when she tried to turn.

"Why did you lie to me?"

"Lie to you? I don't know what you're talking about," she answered honestly.

"Why did you let me believe that you were betrothed to Farrow? You must have realized I'd discover, soon enough, that it wasn't true. I wasn't in Truro above a day before I heard your name on a dozen masculine lips." His smile was both melancholy and relieved. "It reminded me of how the bloods in London used to describe you—ripe for the picking but hard to reach."

"Yet you managed, didn't you?" Katrina ground her teeth together and forced the bitterness out of her tone. "I neither denied nor affirmed his claim, if you recall. As usual you jumped to conclusions about me."

"As usual you abetted those conclusions. It seems you prefer that I consider you shameless." He tugged on her skirt to make her sit beside him, but she jerked the material away so hard the worn fabric ripped.

"Shameless?" Her voice was high with incredulity. "At least Will wants to make me an honorable offer, whereas you—"

"Whereas I want only to cherish you and make you happy." His caressing tone was matched by the hand that stroked her hip through the thin dress. "You should be dressed like a queen, yet you seem content to wear rags." This time he pulled her down beside him with a strength that would not be denied. "Do you really think your provincial doctor can give you what I can?"

"I've told you before that I don't want jewels and furs—"

"What makes you think I'm speaking of tangible things?" His voice had gone mellow. He tilted her chin up and bent to whisper into her face, his breath brushing her cheeks. "I saw in your eyes earlier today that you remember, and long for, the same things I do. Even in the presence of others you can't stifle your hunger for me." He bent closer still, but before his lips took hers, she turned her head sharply away.

"And I'm a fool. I have more reason to despise you than you

know.'' She bit her lip and tried to stand, but he wrapped his arms about her waist to keep her still.

''What do you mean?''

''Nothing.'' She pulled away and sat straight as a board.

His eyes narrowed as she twisted nervously at her apron. Her hands went still when he wheedled, ''Please, Katrina, don't torment me any longer. Tell me what happened to you in that awful place, and why you left England to come here.'' When she still wouldn't look at him, his tone grew hard. ''One way or another I'll find out. I'll not let my past sins ruin my present.''

With a high, unnatural laugh she said harshly, ''What meaning does a present without a future have?''

When Devon tried to shape her face with his hands, she flung her head away so desperately that he looked hurt.

She closed her eyes to the sight of his dear, familiar face. ''Please, Devon, grant me the right to live as I please and leave me be.'' She slumped back against the bench, too weary to resist when he again embraced her.

''I can't, Katrina. I've tried, believe me, but I think about you day and night. No other woman interests me—''

''Oh yes? I suppose you accidentally put your hand on that barmaid's thigh, thinking you were clasping a post.''

Devon's lips relaxed into a pleased smile. ''You noticed, did you? I'm glad.'' He bent his head to nuzzle her ear as he murmured into her skin, ''That's as far as it went, I assure you.''

Katrina had already regretted her tart comment. Her peace of mind, what little she had left, depended upon keeping him at a distance. So she said steadily, ''Then you had best seek her out again, Devon. For you'll get naught from me.'' This time, when he wouldn't let her go, she poked him in the ribs with her elbow and twisted out of his arms.

He rose to face her, his jaw flexing, but his tone was even. ''You've made that abundantly clear, Katrina. But has it occurred to you that you can get much from me?'' When she looked puzzled, he waved an angry arm at their simple surroundings, then sent a derogatory appraisal over her dress. ''I'm neither blind nor stupid. Phillip has already told me that he and his shareholders are considering closing his mine because of its poor production. It's obvious this family you've adopted is barely subsisting. Let me help.''

When she didn't immediately reply, he went on passionately, ''You don't know how it pains me to see you living so. How can you bear to survive on such food, and cultivate such common company?''

Katrina had been touched and tempted by his offer, but at his words the softening about her mouth hardened to iron. ''I might have known you'd judge my family by appearance rather than worth.'' When he looked taken aback at her fury, she shouted, ''Yes, my family!'' She began to stride up and down, so agitated that she couldn't keep still. ''The Tonkins are each worth ten of your fancy friends.'' She stopped in front of him and stabbed her finger into his chest with each word. ''True worth is measured not by material things but by spirit and heart.''

She stepped back, so sad, suddenly, that her eyes misted. ''And your inability to understand this basic truth is the main reason why we have nothing to offer one another except a passion that shames me. It is you, sir, who are poor.'' She whirled to leave, then spun back around. ''And keep your money. I think John would rather starve than accept a farthing from you.''

''Aye,'' a harsh voice added, arresting Katrina as she began to walk away. She and Devon both turned to look at the angry young man who stepped out of the shadowy cottage doorway. Jimmy slammed the gate back against the fence and strode forward.

''We don't need your help, your *lordship*.'' Jimmy spat the title as if it were an epithet. ''And you'd best leave while you still can.''

Devon crossed one ankle over the other and drawled, ''Oh yes? And you, I perceive, enjoy my company so much that you want me to stay.''

Jimmy's hands balled into fists, but when he tensed to leap forward, Katrina ran to him and caught his arm. ''No, Jimmy, he's leaving. Aren't you, my lord?'' Her challenging look was returned full measure.

''Am I? I thought you more astute than that.'' Devon unfolded his ankles and marched toward them. ''I'll leave when I'm ready, and that won't be until I know why this young pup dislikes me so.'' He stopped two steps away, his eyes deeper and more impenetrable than ever in the bright moonlight.

''I hate everything about you and your kind,'' Jimmy spat. ''Gentry! You who live like kings on the profit of our blood and tears. And to come here, lifting your lordly nose at our food, telling Katrina she should leave—we'll not tolerate your arrogance no more. There's many who feel as I do, your bloody lordship.'' Jimmy's voice softened with menace. ''As you may find soon enough if you don't leave us be. Her too.'' He jerked his head toward Katrina and put a proprietary arm about her shoulders.

Normally Katrina would have shrugged off his touch, but she smelled the fury hovering in the air like a damp, smothering mist. She did then the only thing she could, despite the pain it caused her. Her loyalties had been decided two years ago; indeed, Devon had pushed her into the choice.

Thus, when Devon narrowed glittering eyes on Jimmy's arm and snarled, ''Methinks 'tis *you* who presume too much, you insolent boy. This woman is far above your touch,'' Katrina pushed Jimmy toward the house before he could lift his fist to strike.

''Jimmy's only trying to protect me. I honor him for it.'' Katrina's voice shook a bit, but she forced the words out anyway. ''More than I can ever honor you. Go, Devon. And don't come back.'' She turned, caught Jimmy's hand, and pulled him with her inside the gate. Tears blurred her eyes, and she almost blundered into Billy, who was standing, back propped against the cottage wall, listening to every word. She couldn't bear the sympathy in his eyes, but it was Devon's gentle promise that made her freeze, one hand clasping Jimmy's, the other the cottage doorknob.

Strangely, Devon didn't sound angry. ''As you will, Kat. For now. But I will be back. Why? Because you want me. No matter what went between us, or what will come, you long for me even as I long for you. You've proved that today, in protecting me, and in the hunger in your eyes for the joy we tasted so briefly. And by all the saints, my darling, we will taste it again." He beckoned Billy, then whirled and strode toward his carriage.

Katrina flung Jimmy's hand away and rushed inside, up the stairs to her room, deaf to Rachel's, "Lass, staay and have a cuppa," and John's sharp, "Be 'ee well, my girl?"

Katrina flung herself down on her cot and hugged her hard straw pillow to her breast. This ache was more of the heart than of the flesh, for she knew that despite Devon's promise only sorrow awaited them. He weakened her; she brought out all his worst instincts. They were a sickness to one another. Pleasurable though that fever was, they could give in to it at their peril or scorn one another like the plague. Katrina had learned the hard way which it must be; if she spurned Devon every time she saw him, he, too, would learn. Sensible though she knew she was, she buried her face in her pillow and blessed it with her tears.

The next day was as dreary as Katrina's spirits. She helped with the washing, scrubbing each garment vigorously, but she still could not banish thoughts of Devon. By the time Will stopped by, she was eager for any diversion—until she saw his face. She turned from hanging the last item over the line to spy him five feet behind her, a look in his eyes she'd never seen before. She took a step back, then pushed one of Ellie's chemises out of her face when it wrapped about her head. When she looked again, Will's expression was mild.

His voice, too, was even. "Jimmy tells me your old, er, suitor was here last night. And I've already heard of the ruckus in town. Have you lost your mind, Katrina? Associate with such as him and you'll earn the very name you've worked two years to eradicate."

Anger spurted hotly, but she told herself he interfered out of concern. "Perhaps, Will. But from the reception I get from Hennessy and others, that's already the way I'm regarded."

Will put out a pleading hand. "It doesn't have to be that way, Katrina. If only you'd marry me—"

Katrina shook her head wearily. "Don't, Will." His hand dropped in defeat and he began to turn away. She hurried forward and caught his arm. "Please, try to understand. I've no intention of involving myself with the Earl of Brookstone—*or anyone else*. I'm . . . just not ready.''

Will caught her in his arms and hugged her. "I do understand, Katrina. I, better than anyone else, know what you went through. But seeing the man who caused you such mental and physical agony doing all he can to worm his way into your affections again—well, it's more than I can bear, caring about you as I do."

That was as close to a declaration as he'd come; she didn't dare let him go further. She inserted lightly, "Have no fear. My wits went woolgathering yesterday, but I don't think the price of fleece is worth the toil. Do you?"

He returned her whimsical look with a grim stare. "No." He hesitated, then murmured, "I'm glad you feel that way, Katrina, because there's something you should know. Something I've forborne to tell you because you'd been hurt enough, and until now it didn't seem to matter."

Katrina eased out of his arms, sensing she needed to hear this news while firmly planted on her own two feet. "Yes?"

After an agitated stride away, then another back, Will stopped directly in front of her. "Even if the earl were willing to marry you, you couldn't wed him now."

"What?" Katrina took a deep breath and moderated her voice. "Whatever do you mean?"

"Have your menses been regular since the, er, happening?" When Katrina shook her head, he nodded. "I feared so." He paused, then said rapidly, as if eager to get the words over with, "The infection damaged your reproductive system. You . . . can't have children."

Katrina went ashen and took a step back. "No, it can't be true."

"I wish it were not, but I fear it is. And I needn't tell you how important heirs are to a man like Cavanaugh."

Katrina swayed on her feet, then turned blindly toward the house. Will supported her arm, but she barely felt his touch. She was seeing and feeling instead the babies she'd delivered. Even more enervating were the images of children with dark gold hair and brown eyes she'd dreamed of. As with all her other dreams they would never come true. . . .

When they reached the house, Will helped Katrina up to her

room and seated her gently on her bed. She sat as woodenly as a carving, even when he knelt before her and circled his palms over her knees. "Katrina, I'd not have told you except that now Cavanaugh is here, you needed to know."

There was still no answer. Will cupped her cheeks and said deeply, "But I don't care about heirs. My children are my patients. Give me a chance, please. You deserve happiness and I want so desperately to help you find it."

Katrina shuddered at the plea and finally looked at him. There were tears in his celestial-blue eyes, and she knew he was sorry for hurting her. Moisture came to her own eyes. Oh, the waste, the terrible waste. Four lives had been shattered on that night more than two years ago: her babe's, her own, Devon's, though he didn't yet know it, and Will's. Katrina leaned forward, bent her head against Will's slight but strong shoulder, and sobbed. Will embraced her and patted her back awkwardly until, with a hiccup, she subsided.

She accepted his kerchief with a watery smile. "You should let me do your laundry, since I have such a propensity for soiling it." She blew her nose fiercely. Twisting the fine linen about her fingers, she murmured, "Will, I owe so much to you. If you truly want me, then you have my leave to court me." Katrina's icy doubts about her decision dissolved under the beatific warmth of his smile.

Catching her hands, he hauled her to her feet and began to whirl her about the room. "Katrina, Katrina, you've made me so happy! And I, in return, will do the same for you." He stopped, brought both her hands to his mouth, bent his shining golden head, and kissed them.

Thus he didn't see the tears misting Katrina's eyes again. "I hope so, Will." But to herself she thought, One of us, at least, deserves to be happy. And you, Will, are the most worthy one.

But after Will had departed to return to his rounds, Katrina stood looking out the small window at the rain-swept moors. She hoped Rachel had brought the laundry in, she thought vaguely. The mundane thought released the floodgates again as she realized that such would probably be her lot in life from now onward. A clean house, cooking for her loving husband, perhaps a dog and cat.

But passion? Love? Thrilling, heart and body, to a voice, a

touch? Those were dead. May they rest in peace, even as she would. She'd been fooling herself before, she knew now. Some spark of hope had lingered within her that someday Devon would change and accept her as she was, love her as she was. But now, if such a miracle occurred, she could never wed him.

Will was right about Devon; heirs were very important to him. His heritage, his duty to his name had sustained him even as her faith had sustained her. Should he ever love her, be willing to sacrifice those for her, now she couldn't let him. The spark of hope died, leaving the chambers of her heart dark, empty, and lonely.

Katrina turned away from the window, resolutely wiping her tears away. "Good-bye, Devon," she murmured. Then she turned, descended the stairs, and sought out Rachel to help her with the chores.

That night, when John didn't return from the mine at his usual time, Rachel and Katrina didn't at first worry. But when he still hadn't arrived even after the meager supper dishes were cleared, they began to start at every sound. Rachel was drawing her shawl about her shoulders to go to the mine herself when there was a commotion at the door.

Katrina ran to it and pulled it open, holding the lantern high. "Oh God," she whispered. John was being carried by two brawny miners, Will at his side taking his pulse. And even in the uncertain lantern light Katrina could see blood. Blood everywhere. It seemed to coat John from top to toe. Rachel, who had come up behind her, screamed.

Katrina flung the door wide and caught Rachel's stiff arm to pull her out of the way. The men carried John into his room and set him on top of the quilt Rachel had spent so many nights making. If she cared about the blood soaking every fiber, she gave no sign. She knelt beside her husband and stroked his brow with a shaking hand.

"John. John, do 'ee hear me?" When no response came, she looked at Will, who had turned up the wick of the lantern that stood beside the bed. Tears glittered in her eyes like fallen stars. In that moment Rachel looked her age, for tragedy had come to her too many times for her to be very hopeful now.

Outside, Ellie drew a crying Robert away to the stairs.

Jimmy, who was home that night, clutched the door frame with white-knuckled fingers as he, too, awaited the verdict.

"I'm not sure yet, Rachel," Will said gently, drawing her to her feet and ushering her to the door. "I think I've stopped most of his bleeding, but I need to look at his wounds more closely. I'll call you when I know more." With a meaningful look at Katrina he shut the door.

"Come, Rachel, I'll fix you a cuppa." Katrina led a dazed Rachel to the kitchen and seated her before the hearth while she hung their iron kettle over the fire to heat the water. Ellie came back down from tucking Robert in and sat beside her mother.

Both women sobbed quietly, clutching at each other, while Katrina brewed the tea. Jimmy stood at the entrance to the kitchen, staring toward his parents' room. Katrina served Rachel and Ellie first, then took Jimmy a cup. With a great effort she kept her own tears at bay. She loved John like a wise older brother, but only by being strong could she help the Tonkins now.

She almost had to force his stiff fingers about the handle. "Jimmy, your father is the strongest man I've ever known, in body and heart. He'll be fine." Jimmy flung his cup away and convulsively hugged Katrina.

"Oh God, what if he dies?" he muttered into her hair. "That mean-spirited bastard. If he dies, I swear I'll kill him."

Katrina drew away to look at him. "Who are you talking about?"

"Carrington. If he'd funded a new pumping system, this would not have happened." He bit off several more foul names, but Katrina interrupted.

"You don't know that's what happened, Jimmy."

"Et's true, mess." One of the waiting miners spoke up. He'd twirled his battered hat in callused hands as he awaited news of his captain; more, Katrina had deduced, his friend. The anger in his tone was almost as great as Jimmy's. "John 'us tryen' to fex one of the pump arms extendin' down ento the mine when et broke loose. The wall fell on hem, tembers an' all."

"And if John were in poor health, the accident would have been the end of him." Everyone in the kitchen leaped up at the sound of Will's voice.

He smiled soothingly into the many anxious eyes. "His heart rate has stabilized, and the bleeding has stopped. He'll be sore, and he may not have total use of his left arm, but he should survive."

Rachel fell limply back down onto the bench, then surged to her feet, pushed past Will, and hurried into her chamber. Ellie soon followed.

Katrina closed her eyes and said a silent prayer of gratitude, then she smiled at Jimmy. "Thank God murder won't be necessary."

Jimmy did not return the smile. His expression had lightened, but Katrina didn't like the brooding set to his mouth.

"No, but violence may be."

Katrina looked aghast at Will. "Will, not you too!"

"I abhor violence, Katrina. I've seen the results of it too many times. But I'm so tired of this senseless waste of human life. Many's the time John has pleaded for help from Carrington. Did you know Carrington and his investors have even begun scrimping on vital supplies such as candles and rope? Have you any idea what it's like to be fathoms deep below the ground and run out of light?"

"Hear, hear," said one miner. From the other: "Truer words 'ee could not saay."

"No, I can't imagine it, nor would I presume to try," Katrina said steadily. "But I also know that two wrongs don't make a right. Besides, what good will violence do? It's surely only more likely to make Carrington close the mine altogether, especially as it's not producing well."

"I'm the practecal miner," said the other miner, scars on both sides of his face. "And I'm as certain as I've ever been that there be a rich lode there. But we'll never find it wethout the new pumpen' equipment that lets us go deep." He drummed his fingers angrily on the table, then turned to go, throwing over his shoulder, "But sence asken' hasn't helped, mayhap we should try tellen'." He slammed out the door, followed quickly by his mate.

Katrina looked at Will. "Surely you don't agree."

Will was washing his hands over a bowl on the counter. He lifted one pinkened hand to emphasize his words. "I don't know what to think any longer, Katrina. But I've seen enough of this color from one class of men. Maybe if Carrington and his ilk realize their blood is just as red, we'll make progress. It's sure we've made none by asking.'' Will dried his hands, then returned to his patient, leaving Katrina alone in the kitchen.

They were speaking out of anger, she tried to reassure herself. They'd never harm Carrington—or anyone else. The thought that Devon, too, could be in danger from his own men tormented her. She shouldn't care what happened to him, but it seemed that neither grief nor anger nor even hopelessness could stop her from caring. Being Katrina, she decided to do something to alleviate the tension. Slightly comforted, she waited until Ellie reported that John was sleeping soundly, then retired. She had much to do tomorrow.

Katrina's heart lurched when Carrington's manor came in view. How well she remembered the last time she'd been here. But surely she'd not be unlucky enough to see Devon yet again. She scanned the empty drive and sighed in relief.

The butler answered her knock. Katrina had borrowed Ellie's best church dress, but the pins couldn't disguise the fact that Ellie was taller and more voluptuous. "Please tell Lord Carrington that Katrina Lawson would have a word with him.''

The butler looked down his long nose at her. "My lord is at luncheon, but I shall inform him you're here.'' Reluctantly he cracked open the door, but he didn't even offer her a chair. He left her standing just inside the hall.

Katrina stuck out her tongue at his retreating back, wondering what tales he'd heard of her. More filth spread by Hennessy, doubtless. Of course, she only perpetuated the gossip by coming here alone, but she didn't have a choice. There were more important things than her reputation.

Carrington exited from a door far down the hall, still wiping his mouth. He tossed his napkin to his butler and hurried forward. "Well, hello, Miss Lawson. How pleased I am to see you." He scanned her from burnished, severely dressed hair to clogged feet.

Katrina didn't like the appreciative glint in his eyes, but she accepted his offered arm and followed him into his drawing room. He seated her courteously on the settee.

"May I offer you some refreshment?''

"No, thank you. My lord—"

"Please, call me Phillip." He seated himself beside her and put a casual arm along the settee back.

"Phillip, did you know that John was injured yesterday?"

"Yes, one of the men came to tell me. I've already sent my condolences along to Mrs. Tonkin and promised to pay any medical expenses over and above what Farrow supplies."

When Katrina looked at him expectantly, he frowned. "I don't know what else you want me to do. 'Tis more than many of my friends will pay for. Mining is a dangerous profession, and each and every worker knows the inherent risks. John most of all."

"Yes, he, most of all. Especially since he's already lost two sons to your mine. He may not ever have full use of his arm again."

Carrington shrugged. "That should not cause him any great hardship since most of his work is of a supervisory nature."

"Then you do intend to keep the mine open?" Katrina asked baldly.

"That is none of your concern." Carrington snapped his mouth shut, then said more mildly, "I hold fifty-one percent of the shares, and the other investors have only agreed to keep the mine open as long as we have for that reason, and because the mine is on my land."

He was being evasive, but she didn't like his hint. "Please, I must know. Will you close the mine?"

"Blast it! Yes!" When she paled, he explained in a rational tone, "It hasn't been a paying concern for months now. I've only kept it open as long as I have because so many are dependent on its income. But for those on the cost-book system, like John, since we haven't been producing much, they won't earn much. They'll have to seek other work, anyway."

Katrina swiveled on the settee to look him pleadingly in the eye. "But your practical miner believes there are rich ores present, deeper in the shafts. He says one of the new pumping systems would help you recover them."

Carrington sighed impatiently and explained slowly, as he would to a half-wit, "So he's told me. But the capital investment required is simply not justified when what we're making now isn't even paying expenses. No, my girl, I've little choice. I'll wait until John is back on his feet, but then I'll have to close it." He patted her knee in a way that made her skin crawl, but she forced herself not to move away.

She could see he was growing impatient with the subject, but she had knowledge he lacked. "For your own safety you should know that the men are . . . restive." Grim satisfaction shone in her eyes when he stiffened and snatched his hand away. "If you close the mine, I'm not sure what they'll do."

"Do you dare to threaten me?" Carrington snarled.

"Not I. In fact I have argued your side." When he relaxed, she added, "But I've little influence over your men. John, of course, will do what he can, but since he's hurt . . ." Katrina watched him absorb the significance of that. "If you'd share your grain with them, they'd look more kindly upon your largesse."

"I'll not bribe them! Besides, I don't have enough on hand to supply all my men." Carrington patted her knee again, and this time his touch lingered. "Enough of this unpleasant subject. I'm sure whatever you heard was spoken in anger. Why, for three generations Carringtons have worked smoothly with good Cornish folk. If I'm forced to close the mine, I'm certain my men will remember their loyalties."

Loyalty is the luxury of a full belly, Katrina longed to say, but she knew when she was defeated. Sighing, she tried to rise, but Carrington's fingers tightened about her knee.

"Don't go. I have something I'd like to speak with you about."

"Yes?" Katrina asked warily, shifting so Carrington's fingers fell away.

"I've long thought you were too beautiful a woman to waste yourself here. But not until I realized you knew Devon, er, intimately, did I dare to hope you might accept an offer of protection from me." Carrington's eyes were appraising the trim figure even the ill-fitting dress couldn't disguise, so he missed Katrina's revolted look. "I'd be delighted to lease a house for you in Truro. We've assemblies, theaters, and gay life aplenty. Nothing to compare to London, of course, but we could even journey there together, when my business warrants it."

When Katrina didn't reply, he looked at her. He apparently

took her white-faced disgust for coyness, for he took her shoulders in his hands and began to draw her to his chest. ''I shall be generous, my dear. . . .''

Katrina swatted his hands away and leaped up. ''I'm not fool enough to believe that. If you show your loyalty to the men who have spilled blood for you by closing down their source of livelihood, what reason have I to believe you'd be generous to a kept woman?'' She turned toward the door, but strong, angry hands caught her about the waist and whirled her back around.

''Your disdain sits ill upon you, wench. Common you may be, but your passion for life glows from you like a chandelier. Devon is not an easy man to please, yet he still wanted you even after you left him.'' He moderated his tone. His hands gentled and began to stroke her back. ''Come, let me take you away from this penury and give you the setting where you can shine like the jewel you are.''

''Release me,'' Katrina said through her teeth.

Slowly his hands slid away. ''I take it you're refusing my offer.'' Phillip's gaze shifted behind her, to the opening door, but Katrina was too angry to notice.

''How astute of you.'' Katrina sneered. ''Perhaps your men are right after all. You and your kind are parasites, each and every one. You feed on the misery and pain of others.'' She gave him a curtsy that was rife with mockery despite its grace. ''This commoner taikes great pleasure in tellin' 'is nibs to take 'is h'offer and eat h'it. I 'opes ye chokes.'' Soft applause behind her made her whirl.

''Marvelous acting, Kat. I've seldom heard a cockney accent done better.'' Devon closed the drawing-room door and advanced silently across the carpet. ''I warned you, Phillip,'' he said, his tone hardening, ''that she'd not accept you even if you ignored my wishes and tendered her an offer.'' He paused three feet away from Carrington.

His erstwhile school chum shifted under the brown glare. ''You can't blame a fellow for trying. She came to me. I didn't seek her out.''

''Indeed?'' That stare shifted to Katrina.

Icy blue eyes gave as good as they got. ''Indeed. As to why, that's none of your concern.'' She marched out the door.

"We'll discuss this later, Phillip." Devon hurried after Katrina.

When he held the front door for her, she exited, her head held high. He said, "You should have known better than to come here alone. Billy was returning from town when he saw you arrive, so I came to aid you."

"To guard what you consider your property, you mean." Katrina shunned the arm that would have ushered her to his curricle and turned up the drive.

"Now, see here, you've no call to berate me for trying to protect you." A stiff back was his only answer. He bit off a curse, caught her arm, and spun her to face him. "Why did you come? Surely you knew Phillip would take advantage of your visit." Her hostile silence was matched by a glare. He shook her arm. "Answer me, damn you!"

"I owe you no explanation." She wrenched her arm away.

"Please, Katrina." The soft entreaty froze her in her tracks as the demand had not. "Something must be very wrong to bring you here alone. I only want to help."

Katrina slowly swung about. The pain in her breast extended to her fingers and toes at the sight of him. He was so tall, so true, every line bespeaking grace and strength. She longed to lean her head against his shoulder and beg his aid. Maybe Phillip would listen to him. Yet Will's revelation was a nettle, spurring her on to fight. With no future they had no choice but to forget the past and deny the present.

"Leave me be, Devon. For both our sakes." Despite her best efforts, her voice quavered. For one instant longing was bare in her eyes, but then her gaze dropped. She resolutely turned away and began the walk home.

She didn't see his own troubled look, or that he took a great stride after her before he caught himself. He looked between her, and Phillip's house, then back at her retreating figure. "Go for now, little coward. Run to your bolt hole. But when I find out what the devil is going on, you'll be seeing me again." When she didn't respond to his vow by so much as a turned head, he angrily stomped back to Carrington House and ascended the steps.

Chapter Ten

DURING THE NEXT three days, Will showed Rachel how to bathe John and keep his wounds clean. Still, John grew delirious with infection. His fever rose along with Will's concern. Will and Rachel rarely left the bedside, refusing Katrina and Ellie's offers of help. Rachel's usually merry blue eyes grew dull and red-rimmed from lack of sleep and the tears she tried to hide.

Finally, on the fourth day, John's fever broke. They all had a brief prayer meeting that day to give thanks. Will left rather abruptly before the meeting, Katrina assumed to attend to other patients. He'd been preoccupied of late. Since she had more than her own share of worries, however, she dismissed his odd behavior.

Yet again she went to the larder to search every cranny, hoping they'd missed something. But no, they only had food enough for a few more meals, and those would be spare. Katrina closed her eyes and sagged against the wall, but when she heard steps, she pinned a smile on her face and exited.

She shook her head at Ellie's hopeful glint. "No, Ellie, we've missed nothing." Katrina couldn't bear it when Ellie's spine slumped. She braced Ellie's shoulders with her arm. "With John sick and the crops still not ripe, it's up to us to feed this household. And we shall, somehow. Perhaps we can find something to barter. Something of value that we could still do without."

Ellie shrugged, but agreed. "Perhaps." They searched the house for over an hour. Aside from their clothing and furniture the only things valuable enough to trade were a few dishes Rachel had inherited from her mother.

"Ma would rather starve than sell those," Ellie said flatly. She set the delicate bowl carefully back in the parlor cupboard and closed the door. "I'll start lunch," she mumbled, and fled, but not before Katrina caught the shine of tears.

Katrina brought a fist to her mouth to smother a cry of despair. Oh God, and to think pride had made her dismiss the king's ransom Devon had bestowed on her. Bestowed? She swallowed bitter gall. Paid for services rendered. Go to him, he owes you, part of her said. I'll never be indebted to him again, the stronger part said.

I could go to Will, she thought, yet she dismissed the idea immediately. He'd already sneaked them food against John's wishes. Katrina didn't wish to upset John, but even more she felt a deep, driving need to be the bulwark of the family until John was better. She didn't want to depend on anyone's help outside the family. Not Will. Not Devon. Yet starvation made pride a luxury they could not afford. . . . Feeling as if contrary feelings would tear her apart, Katrina forced her heavy steps into the kitchen.

Together she and Ellie chopped the last of their salted fish, making a soup to stretch it as far as possible. She and Ellie ate sparingly, then Ellie prepared a tray for her parents. They gave Robert their last dried apples.

He gobbled them up in two bites and asked for another bowl of broth. Ellie hesitated, then filled his basin again. He drank it just as quickly. "Where's the pasty, Ellie?" he asked his big sister.

"There's naught, Robbie. Go on back to your chores now." Robert looked at the sideboard bare of its customary summer fruit bowl. Young as he was, he understood. He nodded gravely and exited to collect more faggots for the hearth.

His bravery almost undid Katrina, but she choked back her tears and rose to help clear the table.

When they were finished, Ellie whispered, "Katrina, what are we to do?"

Katrina shook her head, afraid to trust her voice, but her eyes met Ellie's. The fears there mirrored her own. Katrina snatched up her shawl and ran from the cottage, heedless of Ellie's call to wait.

She paced up and down by the stream. She couldn't be strong any longer. She was afraid, and not just for herself.

What would happen to these people she so loved if she didn't quell her stubborn pride and go to Devon?

She closed her eyes and visualized his dear face. He'd help her in a minute, she knew, and probably ask for naught in return. But she remained sane only by holding him and the things he made her feel at bay; being indebted to him would not help her in either endeavor. Once he'd given her money for food, he'd surprise her with clothes. She was so weary of looking like a hag and she wanted so desperately to depend on him. Would she be able to resist his gifts? If not, she'd feel indebted, more prey than ever to the ravening love that would consume her in one bite—if she let it.

Whether God or the devil heard her, Katrina couldn't say, but at that moment carriage wheels thumped on the uneven path. The sun broke through clouds to bathe the driver in light. He lifted a gloved hand and waved.

Katrina stood transfixed, afraid to retreat, more afraid to advance. Was Devon right? Were they linked in some peculiar way? Perhaps so, for never had she needed him more than now. Her emotions so overwhelmed her that she had to strain to listen as he drew closer.

"I heard about John," Devon said, pulling to a stop beside her. "A servant told me today. I've brought blankets, brandy, and food." He jumped down from the curricle and went to her. "Silly girl, what am I to do with you? You should have told me—"

He broke off with an oof. Katrina's heart had led her where her head would not—straight into Devon's arms.

Burrowing her nose into his chest, she sobbed, "I'm so glad to see you. I've wanted to come to you, but I—I was afraid."

"Afraid? Of *me*?" Incredulity warred with tenderness in his voice. His hand shook a bit as he stroked her hair. "Katrina mina, I'd never hurt you. . . ." He tried to lift her chin to make her look at him.

Now was not the time for more recriminations, so Katrina bit back a counter. She took a deep breath, wiped her eyes with her hand, and pulled back to give him a bright smile. "Thank you for coming. Let me help carry everything in."

The carriage held a treasure trove to her starved eyes. It took them several trips to bring in the baskets of vegetables, grains, and meats. Wonder of wonders, he'd even brought them a ham! Katrina's mouth watered just from looking at it.

Ellie seemed stunned as they brought the goods into the kitchen. She peered from the basket in Devon's hands to his face. Her mouth worked, then her face crumpled. She threw herself at him so quickly that his basket went flying. Squash, potatoes, and carrots rolled about the kitchen floor.

Ellie hugged Devon's neck then moved back abruptly, going red at her own daring. "Thank 'ee, your lordshep," she trilled. She bobbed a curtsy that Devon returned with a grave bow.

Smiling, Katrina retrieved the vegetables, wondering who was more discomfited.

Ellie made them tea from the leaves Devon had brought, and they were soon seated at the table chatting like old friends.

"How is your father doing?" Devon asked Ellie.

"At least his fever finally broke. The doc says he'll live, but how well he'll be able to work—" Ellie shook her head.

"I've brought brandy and laudanum for him. If you want him to see a doctor in London, I can arrange that."

Katrina groaned. She didn't have to look at Ellie to know her smile had disappeared. Even hinting at English superiority to a Cornishman, or woman, was like poking at a rabid beast.

"He'll do just fine here—your lordship." Ellie rose, nodded with dignity, then left the room.

Devon looked bewildered. "What did I say?"

"The Cornish are proud folk, Devon. They don't like feeling inadequate. Indeed, who does?" Katrina watched him, hoping, praying, he'd have some understanding, but his handsome face still looked mystified. She glumly swirled her tea. Why should he understand? What did this English lord know of deprivation, or of yearning for things he could never have?

Had she read his thoughts at that moment, Katrina would have realized Devon knew more of the latter than she supposed. While she stared at her tea he stared at her, yearning bare in his eyes. That awful gown. How he longed to rip it from her, love her, then clothe her in the silks she deserved. He smothered a sigh. Even that unlikely pleasure would not be enough. Any woman could give him sex; only Katrina could grant him happiness. One step at a time. After all, she'd voluntarily embraced him. In gratitude, aye, but it was a start. He'd ask nothing in return. If she wanted to give? Ah, that was another matter.

"May I see John?" Devon asked.

"Now is not a good time. Rachel scarcely lets *us* in the room. He's sleeping now, anyway. Which is just as well." Katrina shook her head wryly.

"Why is that?"

"If he knew what you'd brought, he'd be furious."

"Poppycock! It's little enough to do for a neighbor." Or for the woman one . . . wants, he said to himself.

"Oh yes? Have property boundaries suddenly changed? The last time I looked, this house sat on Carrington land."

He made a dismissive gesture. "I was speaking figuratively. Damme, you've become as stubborn as these folk you've taken so to heart."

"I'm glad to hear you understand that at least. Are your miners giving you trouble?"

He snorted. "That's a mild description. They're kicking and screaming as I try to pull them into the modern age. They're even arguing about the type of pump I want to buy. I don't know why they won't accept a reasonable wage. It's a much more reliable way to feed their families than this outmoded cost-book system."

"Perhaps because they fear what your idea of a 'reasonable wage' is. Those who already work for wages are paid a pittance. At least those who share in the success or failure of the mine have a stake in its future. Can you not see the difference? Especially to men of pride?"

"Of course. But so many of the copper mines hereabouts have become so expensive to operate that it's hardly any wonder some of the miners are living in such penury." Devon glanced around the kitchen. Odd. He'd remembered vegetables hanging from the rafters the last time he was here about a week ago. He opened his mouth, but Katrina hurried into speech.

"You need to be careful, Devon. I've . . . heard rumors that some of the miners are so discontent that they're talking about . . . violence."

He knew she was trying to distract him from looking about the kitchen. Why? He humored her, more out of amusement than concern. "Really?" he drawled. "I daresay you think my face could stand some rearranging." He lifted a taunting eyebrow. She didn't disappoint him.

"Oh no! I like your face just the way it is." She blushed and sent him a shaming look when he burst into laughter.

"And that, my dear, is the most honesty I've had from you in many a day. Shall we try for a little more?" He put his palms flat on the table and levered himself to his feet. God, she was adorable when she blushed. He longed to pounce on her and kiss her senseless.

Apparently she recognized his expression, for she leaped up and tried to leave the kitchen. He blocked her easily, so she swung in the other direction.

He followed, coaxing, "Come, let me show you how much I admire you, too. We've danced about one another long enough. It's time for the climax of the performance." He let his voice go deep and low, matching her retreating steps with advancing ones.

He was satisfied when she went from pink to vermilion. Her eyes dropped, and he was glad of his long coat. She shook her head and turned blindly away into the door behind her. He followed. He knew she wasn't ready to come to him again, but it was so delicious to tease and pretend. He'd learned as the veriest lad that a woman who feels wanted, wants more readily in return. He'd not take her crudely here, even if she lost her head, but dear Lord, he longed for her lips. Five minutes could give him the fifty years he yearned for. . . .

She froze two steps into the small, dim room, and he bumped into her. He caught her shoulders to turn her into his arms, but something in her tension gave him pause. The stiffness in her muscles owed naught to passion. For the first time he glanced around. Nothing but bare shelves. Except . . . he reached out a long arm.

Inside a small jar sat three forlorn dried pears. The larder, as he now realized this was, held nothing else. He slammed the jar back down, dropped his other hand from her shoulder as if burned, and staggered out of the tiny room. Once outside, he took deep breaths, and the fury that had made him light-headed settled to a nauseated lump in his stomach.

When she came out and looked at him warily, he crossed his

arms over his chest and said evenly, "So, you prefer starvation to me. If ever a fellow had a clearer send-off, I've yet to hear of it. Keep your virtue, madam. What's left of it." He spun on his heel and hurried to the door, his eyes burning with hurt tears he refused to shed.

He was three steps out the front exit before she caught up with him.

"Wait, Devon!"

He turned his head haughtily. The tears streaming down her face eased his resentment some. She was hurting, too.

"Why do you torment us this way?" he burst out. He longed to snatch her close, but didn't dare. She had her own arms clasped about herself as if she'd fly apart without their support.

She shook her head, muttering over and over, "Don't you see? Don't you see?"

"See what?" he shouted. He closed his eyes, then looked at her and went on, "I see a beautiful woman who reciprocates the passion of the man who wants her desperately. I see a man who wants to clothe her as she deserves, feed her until she's fat as a sow if she so wishes, gift her with jewels enough to delight a princess. And this woman, who obviously wants this man and all that comes with him, treats him as if he's got the plague."

She composed herself at his words. Her arms dropped. "And do you know what I see?" she countered, wiping her eyes with a steady hand.

"I apprehend you intend to tell me."

She continued as if he'd not interrupted, "I see a man who knows much of women, but little of me. I see a man I . . . desire." She held up a staying hand when he took a stride forward. He stopped. "A man who's bad for me, because he steals my wits, seduces my body, and leaves me with naught but self-hatred. This is a man any woman of sound mind would avoid."

"Or a man any woman of sound mind would cleave close to." He hesitated, but if fear of being hurt again kept her from him, he had only one way to convince her to take that chance. Never had he put his pride at such risk, but never had he known anyone more worth the gamble.

He spanned the small gap between them and caught her hand to bring it to his chest. He put his own hand gently over her left breast. "Anger parted us, two years separated us, counties divided us, but still we found one another again. Here we stand, our hearts throbbing as one. Were I a peasant, you a queen, I believe we would feel the same. Why can't you see that our differing positions in life matter not a whit? In the end we'll crumble to the same dust and stand before the same God. Let me share with you our small measure of time before that day."

A tiny, telltale gasp escaped her. She stepped back, forcing his hand to drop, and he sensed that she had to distance herself or leap into his arms. By an effort of will he stayed put, leaving the next move up to her.

"Do you . . . mean what I think you do?"

A glimmer of a smile lit his mordant eyes. "As declarations go it's the best I've ever made." When her face fell, he clarified. "In truth the only I've ever made. I'll go down on my knees if you like."

She nibbled at her lip, then stammered, "D-do you offer marriage?"

He closed his eyes in fury at himself. Damme, he should have couched his words more carefully. Must they always replay the past's mistakes? He took a step toward her, longing to lead her into a better future, but she backed away, her hands lifting to ward him off. He hated it when she did that; hated it when her color paled to match his linen.

The harsh sound that escaped her was neither laugh nor groan, but a combination of both. "I see from your face that you don't. Then your fine words mean nothing, do they? A devotion so shallow would scarce last a year, much less a lifetime."

He slammed a fist into his palm and bit off, "Equating the measure of devotion with a gold band is as superficial as equating a woman's soul with her body. I quit doing that with you long ago. Why can you not do the same?"

She lifted her head. He stared, for she might have been the princess he longed to make her as she said quietly, "Because to me, body and soul are not separate entities. I cannot give the one without giving the other. Do you know how it would hurt me to be your kept woman and see you wed another, beget heirs on another?"

It was his turn to pale. Somehow, in all his deliberations

about her, he'd never considered that. Had he been willfully blind?

"If you ponder how it would hurt you to see me wed another, with another man's children"—her voice broke before she steadied it and went on—"sitting in my lap, you'll have some idea of why I've kept you away, why I was even willing to starve rather than be indebted to you. Indeed, did you not prove just minutes ago that when you give, you want to receive?"

He winced. He deserved that. But truly, concern for her and those she loved had brought him here. Could he help it that once he came, he couldn't restrain his own longing? "I only wanted a kiss, Katrina. Not in payment for what I brought, but given freely in the spirit of what we were to one another, and could be again." His breath caught as her expression softened. Had her eyes ever been so blue, her smile so sad?

Her silken voice whispered gently over him. "That's easily enough supplied. Perhaps then you'll understand what I'm trying to say to you." While he was still gaping in shock she lifted graceful arms about his neck and brought his head down to her level.

Soft lips covered his. Passion was a weak word for the feelings she communicated with her gently sucking mouth. He stayed still, for the first time in his life knowing how it felt to be loved by a woman other than his mother. Warmth filled him, and he was afraid to move lest she cast him out again. Yet . . . as the kiss deepened, he began to understand.

Would that he could say his wits went begging, for then he could enjoy the pull of her luscious mouth without the concomitant tug on his heartstrings. The depth of her emotion vibrated from her, to him, and back again. Who was maestro, who was violin? He couldn't say. He only knew the music they made together was both the sweetest he'd ever known, and the saddest, for it had no climax. It echoed gently to a stop, the poignant notes dying midrefrain. He knew he had only to look in the mirror to see the author of the cruel destruction.

When she pulled away, he could no more hide the sheen of his tears than she could. "You really love me, don't you?" he whispered huskily.

"Did you feel a bottom to my love?" Her own voice was choked with emotion.

"No, only an end. One forced upon you."

"Then you understand." With the gentle pride that was so much a part of her, she lowered her lashes and turned away.

"Kat . . . Katrina, wait." He cleared his aching throat, but his madly beating heart seemed permanently lodged there. What could he say? The only words that could make her stay seemed stuck somewhere between the heart that encouraged and the mind that kept him silent.

She stopped, but said without looking at him, "Please, Devon. You know now why I don't dare let you close. Not because I care too little, but because I care too much."

"And what if I tell you I feel the same?"

She turned her head at that. "Then I would tell you to go home. You're swayed by the emotion of the moment and will come to your senses soon enough. Besides, even if . . . you were willing to wed me, it's too late."

"What do you mean?" Alarm stabbed through him. There it was again. That hint of some disaster that had befallen her that had forever changed her. Why wouldn't she tell him what it was? He caught her arm and pinned her gaze with his. He read only sadness through the hazy tears.

"Nothing. Please, just let me go. . . ." Her voice broke. She seemed fragile, and he'd never enjoyed smashing beautiful things, especially those he cherished. He released her.

"Go, Katrina. But I want you to think as well. Love is too scarce in this world to throw away out of pride. Yours or mine. In the meantime I want to send you food. Please. Relieve me of that worry at least?"

She shrugged. "I have no objection, but John won't feel the same. Let me speak with him when he's better. You've been generous. We have enough for several weeks. Soon after that the Carrington crops will be ripe." She didn't admit that she feared being indebted to him, but Devon understood.

He'd change her mind about that, too. He knew a capital way to begin, but he only said, "That reminds me, Katrina. Stay away from Phillip Carrington." Her drooping spine stiffened as she sent him a glare. He hid a smile and added, "It was foolish of you to go alone to his house. He's a rake who will not hesitate to take advantage of you.''

"That must be why you're such close friends," she said.

"Birds of a feather flock together?" He rolled his eyes drolly.

"No, rakes of a mind sleep in kind."

He pretended to be horrified. "Katrina! You of all people know better."

A weary smile, but a smile nonetheless, stretched her face. "Warning taken, Devon. I hope you'll take mine as well. Don't go about alone and offer angry men more of a challenge than you already have."

"Very well, my dear. Take care of yourself for me." He turned to his curricle.

"The same to you, Devon." Katrina hurried toward the cottage.

"You've only to send word if you need anything!" he called after her.

She nodded as she closed the door. Devon clicked to his restive team. He felt limp with spent emotion, yet stronger than ever before. Katrina loved him! A love so strong as hers could not stand much longer before the onslaught of their mutual need. He'd make her feel so cherished that she'd understand that in wedlock, or out of it, he would adore her and keep her safe.

If a niggling doubt still persisted, he squashed it. They'd found one another again. He'd not waste this chance God had given him, perhaps his only chance to win a worthy woman. If proving the measure of his regard in the many ways he'd planned was still not enough, then . . . He left the words unspoken, even in his mind, but the image of Katrina, garbed in white with a long, flowing veil, haunted him as he made his way home.

After the hearty evening meal in which even Rachel partook, Katrina strolled outside. A full belly only made her mind more active. Now the basics of life were supplied, she could not stifle her longing for the intangible. She'd been too busy surviving these past years to think much about whether she was happy. Her most recent encounter with Devon had settled that question.

She could never be happy without him. She knew that now. Spending her life in good works, even sharing her sickness and health with a kind man like Will, could not compensate her for the pure joy Devon's simple presence gave her. Sickness or no, when she was with him, delirium seemed an enviable state of mind.

Somehow, now that she'd admitted her love to him, she felt as if a weight had been lifted from her shoulders. She was glad he knew the truth. That lie was between them no longer, forsooth. At least she had the solace of knowing she'd reached for happiness with both hands.

Nevertheless, she knew they had no future. Even if he came to her, hat in hand, and begged for her troth, she could not wed him. His countess must be one thing above all: healthy, able to supply him the many heirs he both wanted and needed. Pain jolted her as she thought once again of the child they'd both lost, but the usual, searing anger toward Devon did not come. Yes, his overweening pride had driven her away, but her own pride had exacerbated her fate. Had she not been so sexually weak that night, or had she accepted his gifts, she never would have gone to that quiet little inn where Sutterfield had so effortlessly stolen her. She was not blameless, either.

A deep sigh escaped her. It was lost on the clean, summer breeze to become one with the earth it passed; in sympathy Gaea bestowed on Katrina a measure of her own serenity.

No, she could not wed him, but she could still be his love.

So simply pass the morals of a lifetime, Katrina thought fleetingly. She pictured her father's beloved face, but somehow he was smiling. She knew his advice: It would be a graver sin to say those immortal vows to Will and mean them in her heart to another.

If she shared her thoughts, her dreams, and aye, her body, with Devon, but accepted only the same in return, did she really have reason to hate herself? Many would name her whore, but if he didn't pay her earthly coin, then in her heart she would feel clean. That was all that really mattered. She needn't worry any longer about the consequences. No innocent life would suffer the sins of the mother. If wrong it was to let a love so deep and true guide her, then for the first time in her life she would gladly embrace sin.

Katrina hugged herself, so happy that she took two steps toward Truro and the road to Devon's manor before she caught herself. Of course, if she couldn't allow Devon to help them any longer, then she had to find some kind of employment. When she had a working wage, *then* she could go to Devon.

Rubbing her elbows with her palms, Katrina stopped and looked up at the full moon. It was bright and clean as a preacher on Sunday. But clouds gathered in the west, and she smelled the scent of rain. A visit to Truro would have to wait until morning.

Katrina turned to leave the riverbank and go back to the cottage, but she froze. A stealthy figure exited the rear. As the man made his way to the front and turned south, Katrina recognized his silhouette and the way he walked. Jimmy. Judging from his direction, southeast toward the channel, he was leaving for a smuggling run. She wasn't even aware he'd returned, but he'd apparently sneaked upstairs for his slicker after she left the cottage. Ellie was probably with her parents and hadn't noticed.

Katrina started to call to him, but changed her mind. She stared after him thoughtfully, took one hesitant step to follow, and another, firmer one. Then, with a determined flick of her shawl across her shoulder, she hurried after him.

Katrina had heard stories about free traders for as long as she could remember. Those of Cornish smugglers were the most lurid of all. One West Country smuggler king was said to have cut off the heads of his enemies—usually excisemen—to drink their blood. Law-abiding Englishmen feared to visit a place where the land itself—all crags, muddied inlets, hidden caves, and rugged bays—abetted the dastardly intents of the wreckers and smugglers who therein plied their trades.

Having lived in Cornwall for over two years, Katrina discounted most of the stories. Smugglers were ordinary miners and fishermen, taking what chances they found to ease their desperate poverty. And if in so doing they could thumb their noses at English authorities, why, so much the better. After all, English law perpetuated their trade by setting unreasonable duties on goods every Englishman should be able to afford.

Katrina smiled to herself as she stayed just close enough to Jimmy to keep him in sight. She *had* changed in the past two years, many would say not for the better. In the space of one day she'd decided to consort with a man out of wedlock and to cheerfully break the law she'd always respected. If she would be allowed to.

The skies chose that moment to visit their wrath upon her; she hoped it was not a portent of the night to come. None of the smugglers would be happy to see her, Jimmy least of all. How on earth could she convince them to let her join them? Katrina was still debating when, at last, she saw lights beaming up ahead from the rocky point Jimmy had led her to.

This area of the coast, between Lizard Point on the south and Deadman's Point on the north, by its desolation, made Katrina feel the same. She'd passed the last trees some distance back and knew not even the hardy Cornish variety could survive on the gale-swept peninsula. Lightning flashed, and she spied a rough, rocky path leading down the cliffs to the beach. This, then, must be the landing. She wondered how many tiny harbors and sheltered bays the smugglers took advantage of, as had their ancestors before them. She'd never have known where to seek them out if she hadn't followed Jimmy.

When Katrina turned her head again, Jimmy was far ahead. She ran after him, knowing he'd never hear her steps in the gale. She faltered when she saw where he was headed. The surreal light made a melodramatic backdrop for the cockeyed steeple perched atop a rotting pile of slats. This woebegone wreck, Katrina realized, had once been an Anglican church, apparently abandoned since Wesley brought Methodism to Cornwall.

She blinked in bemusement. Trust Jack Hennessy to choose this place to conduct his lawless business. As Jimmy opened the sagging door she ran the last few steps to catch the door before it could close behind him.

When Jimmy entered the church, the buzz of conversation halted briefly, then began again. Up front, Hennessy was arguing with a slight man wearing an expensive greatcoat and boots. They were too far away for Jimmy to understand what was being said, so he walked further up the aisle, unaware of the flash of gray serge behind him that disappeared beneath a row of benches.

Jimmy took off his slicker and shook off the rain, then he flung the coat over his arm and swaggered toward the cluster of men. His strut was spoiled, however, when his toe caught a loosened flagstone. He stumbled, bumping into the broad shoulders of the man in front of him. The man turned and glowered, then looked resigned as he steadied Jimmy.

"Evenen', lad. Ded 'ee hear the news?"

"What news, Davie?"

"Our usual contact es poorly, and he sent hes brother to tell us where to land—'cept he can only speak that heathen French. Et's not near Brest, at the usual place, es all we can figgur."

"Why can't he just guide us?" Jimmy had to smile as Jack moved toe to toe with the Frenchman and shouted into his ear, as if volume could penetrate where good English could not. The Frenchman sputtered back in a language equally incomprehensible to Hennessy.

Davie sighed. "That's been goin' on for the past hour. Ef we understand hes gesturen', he esn't goin' back. He's taaken on a job at one of the manors en Devon. We thenk he's a cook." Davie spat in disgust. "Stuped frogs. Senden' a *cook* to do a man's job."

"Why not make him draw a map?" Jimmy suggested.

Davie looked thunderstruck, then he slapped Jimmy so hard on the back that he stumbled. "We'll maake a smuggler out of 'ee yet. Ho there! Jack! Lesten to Jimmy here."

Looking harassed, Jack ran a hand through his coarse hair and turned away from the red-faced Frenchman. "What?" he growled.

"Ah, why don't you get him to draw a map?" Jimmy asked nervously.

Fingers rubbing thoughtfully at his scalp, Jack turned to the men closest to him. "Any of 'ee got paper?"

"Pshaw, Jack, what would we breng paper for?" asked a burly, red-capped fair trader. He guffawed. Others joined in at the ludicrous request. Most of them couldn't even write.

Jack's hand came down and bunched into a fist. He whirled on Jimmy. "Mister smart-mouth, does ye have paper?"

"Me?" Jimmy fumbled in his pockets, then shrugged. "No, but we could get him to draw in the dirt."

"Might work. Damn Junot anyway for changin' the landin' and bein' so havey-cavey about it." Jack bent such a glare on the Frenchman that the little man's red face paled. He cast uneasy looks about at the unfriendly ring of tough faces.

"Does 'ee thenk et's a trap, Jack? Maybe Junot told the revenuers," one man said quietly, stating everyone's fears.

"Naw, Paulie. Junot stands to lose too much if we're caught."

"There's others, " Paulie said stubbornly. "Them at Gull Rock es just waiten' for us to make a mestake so they can take over our run."

After a long pause Jack muttered, "There's only one way to find out. I've been wantin' to get me a piece o' frog for a spell." He cracked his knuckles and turned toward the Frenchman.

The Frenchman had watched the byplay intently, and when Jack grabbed his arm, he protested, *"Non! Je ne—"*

"Oh, shut up!" Jack snarled, shoving the man so hard that he stumbled. The other smugglers moved back to give Jack room.

Jimmy said, "If they was settin' a trap, Jack, they'd use someone who could speak English. Just get him to draw the map and let him go."

"No, Paulie's right. We got to be sure. If he's part o' a trap, he's comin' with us." Jack caught the Frenchman's collar and dragged him around. Face-to-face, Jack snarled, "Frenchie, this be your last chance. If ye really understand, ye'd best admit it and tell us why yer brother changed the landin'."

The Frenchman cast a pleading look over Jack's shoulder, but only Jimmy's face was sympathetic, and he made no move to help. *"S'il vous plaît, attendez-moi—"*

"Have it yer way, Frenchie." Jack drew back his fist to strike.

A soft voice spoke from the aisle behind them. Everyone turned in shock.

"Bon soir, m'sieu. Je parle français."

Jack glared; Jimmy groaned in recognition.

"What'd ye bring her for, Jimmy?" Jack demanded. His fist dropped to an aggressively outthrust hip.

"I didn't know she followed me." Jimmy started toward Katrina. "Are you crazy, woman? This is no place for you."

As she came into the glare of the lanterns Katrina drew her sopping shawl closer. She was drenched from the rain, and her clinging dress revealed much to many interested appraisals. The shawl bolstered her courage more than her modesty. "To the contrary I'm invaluable to you at the moment." Turning to the Frenchman, she questioned him.

After a relieved sigh he blasted her with a hail of French, gesturing with his hands.

She nodded, saying *"oui"* at strategic intervals and inserting terse questions at others.

When he was done, he sagged with almost palpable exhaustion. *"Merci beaucoup."*

Jack demanded, "Well? What did he say?"

She folded her arms over her bosom. "Much that was interesting. He told me where you're to land, what and how much you're to take on, and when."

"Come on, come on, tell us." Jack held his hand up and waggled his fingers impatiently.

"This could be dangerous for me. Aiding smugglers is a crime against the Crown. Of course, if I had something to gain . . ." She trailed off, letting the insinuation speak for itself.

Jimmy watched her, frowning, but Jack raged, "Blast it, woman, ye ain't got no right to come here and interfere. Either tell us what ye know or get out."

Without another word Katrina flung her shawl over her shoulder and turned away.

Giving Jack a quelling look, Davie caught her arm. "What does 'ee want, lass?"

"The same thing you all want. To feed your families." Katrina came forward into the light again and looked at each face in turn, even Jack's. "You all know John was injured a few days ago. We've little food in the house and no hope for more unless one of us finds steady work. I've already tried in Truro. Jimmy doesn't bring in enough from his share."

Jimmy looked down and shifted his feet. They all knew his

share would help, if he didn't fritter it away, but no one said anything.

Katrina took a deep breath. "I want to go on your runs with you. Starting tonight." For the first and last time she witnessed unanimity among the free traders.

With a collective voice they shouted, "No!" Jimmy was loudest of all.

Katrina waited until the furor died, then said reasonably, "I admit I wasn't sure what I had to offer—until I arrived. How often has it been a problem that none of you speaks French?"

All eyes went to Jack. That braggart's silence was enough proof for Katrina. "You need me, especially tonight, since Junot won't be there. Henri"—Katrina nodded toward the Frenchman—"says the man who's delivering the goods doesn't speak English, either."

"So? Once we know where to land, all we have to do is pick up the stuff." Jack shook his head. "Ye ain't goin' nowheres."

"And what if you have to haggle over price?" Katrina asked. "Henri says the load is larger than usual. You'll need two boats. And the cargo is different."

Jack looked torn between dismay and greed. Their price had always been agreed upon in advance, but this changed things.

Paulie, a small man wizened by too many battles with the sea, growled, "Et's bad luck, taaken' a woman on a crossen'."

Some of the men nodded their agreement; others looked doubtful.

Davie spoke up. "I says the lassie has as much right to feed her family as we do."

"Aye," a couple of the younger men inserted.

Jimmy, gnawing at his lip, said nothing.

"Let's geve the lassie one chance. Ef she's trouble, she don't go again." Davie's suggestion seemed a reasonable compromise, to most. After considerable discussion all but Jack and Paulie agreed.

"Now, woman, tell us what ye knows," Jack growled, obviously unhappy at being outvoted.

Katrina sniffed, but said, "You're to land at Cherbourg."

"Cherbourg! The hell we will. That's almost half again as far."

"Junot unexpectedly got not only a big shipment of tea, but silk and lace as well. His supplier is coming from inland and won't sail up the coast. It's Cherbourg or nothing."

After a moment of grim contemplation Jack looked at his men. "Lads?"

"Ef et's worth the haul, mebbe we should try et," Paulie said grudgingly. "But I still thenks the frog should come."

Others nodded their agreement. Jack turned on the Frenchman again. The little man scooted behind Katrina and peered over his shoulder at the door. She saw his yearning for flight, so she put a cautionary hand on his arm. He'd not make it out the door before they were upon him.

"He's still sick from coming over and could get seriously ill if he's forced to cross and come back so soon." Katrina matched Jack's glare.

"So much the better. One less frog to stink up the channel," Jack threw back and advanced on the cowering Frenchman.

Katrina's next words stopped him cold. "Somehow I don't think Junot would agree with you. Making his brother ill is no way to keep good relations with your contact." She studied her nails. "There's an easy compromise. Have him held here and guarded. If things go wrong, we'll have him to bargain with."

Davie chuckled at Jack's startled expression and clapped his friend on the shoulder. "'Ee'd best be careful lest the lassie taake over." He sent an admiring look at Katrina. "That un's got a good head on her shoulders, right enough."

The others chuckled, but Jack's hostility never wavered. "On yer heads be it, " he finally growled. "Make ready both boats. Jimmy, ye can guard this frog until we gets back."

Looking pleased, Jimmy hustled the woeful cook to a bench and used the man's own scarf to tie him to it. Katrina followed the other smugglers outside, curious to get a look at their boats.

Jack and Davie were left alone in the front of the church.

"The man won't like this," Jack muttered. "Ye knows he wants the lass himself."

Davie shrugged. "Won't be the ferst time he's disapproved. But he don't own us. Long as he keeps hes lily hands white and just handles the destrebution, he can't whine at how we get the stuff here."

"If ye be so sure, *you* tell him."

Davie's eyes widened, then narrowed. "Who says he has to know?"

"Aw, he'll find out somehow."

"Then we'll tell hem when we have to. Besides, maybe the lassie well be trouble." But Davie didn't appear to think so, for his eyes held more admiration than doubt as he watched Katrina enter again, chatting animatedly with the free traders. They'd come back to fetch the pile of barrels they'd hidden in the church. She pushed helping hands aside and lifted a heavy cask herself, staggering under its weight but managing to get it outside.

"No mebbes about it. But sometimes trouble adds a bit o' spice to life." Jack's tongue rimmed his upper lip as he stared after Katrina.

Davie laughed at the joke. Jack didn't. Even in the dim church, his eyes glittered. . . .

Part Four

"Hope, like the gleaming taper's light,
    Adorns and cheers our way;
And still, as darker grows the night,
    Emits a brighter ray."

—OLIVER GOLDSMITH,
    The Captivity, an Oratorio

Chapter Eleven

THAT NIGHT, KATRINA learned the true reality of smuggling: it wasn't romantic, but bone-chilling, backbreaking work. True, prosperity literally rested upon the backs of the men, but it was hard won. Trip after trip they made through the shallows to the anchored luggers, carting tub upon tub of brandy and bolt upon bolt of oilskin-wrapped silk and lace. They seemed tireless to Katrina, who was already exhausted from the rough crossing and the long, bitter price negotiations.

Nevertheless, she persisted in loading the silk until a gentle but firm Davie led her to the beach and pushed her down on the sand.

"Staay, my girl. 'Ee've done enough for one night." Davie glared at the source of Katrina's tiredness, a cadaverous Frenchman who stood, skinny buttocks resting against his huge wagon, and watched the laboring Englishmen.

As he reached into the wagon for another load Davie brushed against the man, knocking some of the coins from the Frenchman's counting fingers. A challenging grunt was offered and returned. Davie dropped the bolts and straightened martially.

Katrina leaped to her feet and took Davie's stiff arm. "Please, don't spoil all my diplomacy. Sullen though he is, we may need this frog again in future. Remember how fine the silk is. . . ."

"Jack's kind of negotiaten' seems more producteve weth hes kind." After a final hard glare Davie hefted a pile of bolts.

Katrina hid an agreeing grimace by bending to rescue the Frenchman's coins. She, too, found the fellow distasteful. She almost regretted that she'd not translated for Jack the many insults the Frenchman had bestowed on them. When the

Frenchman snatched the coins out of her hand, she nodded regally.

"*A votre service,*" she said pointedly when he didn't thank her.

He shrugged and dropped the coins into his pouch. Katrina turned a haughty shoulder to his lewd appraisal and returned to helping the men. She was not eager for the long crossing, but she was eager to see Cornwall again. She cast uneasy looks about the deserted beach.

Neither side bothered with adieus when the wagon was finally empty. As the two luggers swiftly left French shores relieved sighs drifted away on the stiff sea breeze. Betrayal came in many forms, and none of the Cornishmen had cause to trust the bellicose Frenchman.

"What a bugger," Jack said flatly. "Hope we don't have to deal with him agin." He patted one of the brandy tubs. "Though I can't fault the quality o' his goods." He raised his voice. "Hurry on it, me hearties, else we'll catch the dawn."

Katrina knew they'd not allow her to help with the sails, so she watched as the lugger's canvas fluttered to the mast tops and grew pregnant with the wind. When they were under full sail, Davie sat beside her. He frowned when she shivered and offered her his heavy slicker. She shook her head, but he put it about her shoulders anyway.

Jack snorted. "How gallant he is. But he only wants one thing from ye, lassie. The same thing we all wants."

Covert glances grew overt as Jack put all their thoughts into words. Katrina shoved her arms into the oversized slicker and drew it over her drenched gown, using the movement to disguise the tremors she hoped they'd attribute to the cold. She knew better than to show her fear, so she stared down each man in turn, coming last to Jack.

"Then you're all fools. You can get that from any woman; do you know another who can aid you as I have tonight? You'd have clubbed the man rather than haggle with him, Jack, and brought down upon you the wrath of every supplier on the French coast. Do you deny it?"

The silence spoke for itself. Katrina sniffed. "Then I suggest you appreciate my qualities—in a business way only."

Jack's mouth worked in rage. Surprisingly it was Paulie,

who'd been most adamant that Katrina not come, who inserted quickly, "The girl speaks true. Besides, who'd suspect her of helpen' us? Stifle it, Jack." For now.

He didn't verbalize the aside, but all heard it nonetheless. Katrina knew that if her usefulness ended, she'd find herself in peril of her virtue, and perhaps her life, if they saw her as a threat. She'd just see that she stayed useful, she resolved to herself. But her shivering didn't stop even as her body warmed. . . .

Weary hours later Katrina sat beside Davie in his cart. Dawn began dancing on the water as they lurched away from the church. Hidden in the back of the wagon beneath a load of hay were reams of silk and lace. Jimmy lay atop the pile, the very picture of a snoozing farm boy, but Katrina knew his sleep wasn't feigned. Had she been less weary, her mind less active, she'd have joined him.

Katrina hadn't asked where they were taking the contraband, and Davie didn't offer. She'd noticed that some of the brandy kegs were lugged inside the church, others loaded on wagons for transport.

As he followed her stare after a cart rattling off in another direction, Davie grumbled, "Trust a woman to want to know all. 'Twon't harm to satesfy that womanly nose. We hides the goods hether and yon—caaves, haaymows, barns. Leaves less of a traail for the revenuers, and maakes destrebution easier."

"Who handles that?"

Davie's smile faded. "Best 'ee don't know that. Only me an' Jack know who he es." He patted her knee. "Don't worry. 'Ee'll get your share—equal to all who crossed—soon. I'll breng et myself."

She longed to retort that she'd earned a greater share since violence would have transpired had she not been present, but she bit her tongue. As for who distributed the contraband, she was probably safer not knowing. However, something else troubled her. On this, at least, she'd have an answer.

"Davie, I didn't notice anyone keeping a record of all we brought back. I'd be glad to keep the accounts, if none of you wishes to." She suspected most couldn't cipher or write well enough to do so, but she could hardly say so.

Davie's head veered sharply toward her. The rising sun shone directly in his eyes, yet she saw no limit to their impenetrable blackness. "Just see that 'ee keeps to your plaace, melaady. We've managed for years thes waay and can manage longer." Davie slapped the leads against his pony's back.

Katrina swallowed her hurt. What had she said to deserve the cutting remark? Surely it would be advantageous for all to have a strict record kept. Why would Davie resent the suggestion unless . . . unless he had much to lose? She peered at him from the corner of her eye. He was such a likable sort, yet what did she really know of him? He was a smuggler, after all. Yes, and so was she, after last night. Mentally, she reviewed the approximate number of tubs and bolts that had been carried into each lugger. Perhaps she'd start a record anyway. The risk to life and limb was too great to be less than meticulous with the spoils. This time she couldn't be exact, but next time . . .

Only when they reached the Tonkin cottage did Davie break his grim-lipped silence. His manner was surly as he helped her down, and the minute her feet touched earth he let her go.

Arms crossed over his broad chest, he growled, "'Ee knows not to speak of thes." She nodded. He went on, "And 'ee'd best keep to enterpreten' and let Jack and me decide what else es emportant."

He apparently observed her mutinous mouth, for he took her arm roughly. "Asken' too many questions es a good waay to get hurt. We don't like outsiders comen' here to order us about, whether they be uppity earls or pretty laadies. The West Country has a waay of teachen' outsiders our waays—easy or hard. Understand?"

This time his eyes were not impenetrable. Katrina read pure menace in them. She croaked, "Yes."

Without another word he swiveled, went to the back of the wagon, and shook Jimmy awake.

Jimmy stumbled out of the wagon and came to Katrina's side, watching as Davie urged his laboring pony away. "What bee's in his bonnet?" he asked.

Katrina barely heard him. Davie hadn't directly threatened Devon, but even the hint frightened her. What had she done in involving herself with such men? Yet now she was committed.

She rubbed her elbows until her shivers eased. Gamely, she told herself that if the miners were indeed plotting against the gentry, then being part of their smuggling was a good way to discover details.

Thus, when Jimmy repeated his question, she shrugged. "He's just tired, I guess." She yawned as she dragged herself into the house. "I'm going to get cleaned up, then I'm for a nap."

Hours later Katrina was roused from sleep by a gentle hand. "Katrina, you've a guest below. A gentleman caller." Rachel beamed her a warm, approving smile, then hurried back down to the kitchen.

Katrina stifled the urge to throw on her clothes and dressed slowly. Devon! Though she'd seen him only yesterday, it seemed an age ago. She brushed her freshly washed hair, but as she reached for her pins her fingers stopped of their own accord. Smiling to herself, she left her hair loose, enjoying the sensual slide against her neck and arms as she descended the stairs.

As she entered the parlor her welcoming smile froze on her face. Phillip Carrington rose to greet her, setting a wrapped package beside him on the settee. He came forward to kiss her hand.

"How charming you look. I'm flattered that you were in such a hurry to see me that you didn't even take time to coif your hair." He sent an admiring glance over the plush hair that was as shiny and thick as golden sable.

Katrina pushed her hair back over her shoulders, trying to hide both it and her dismay as she sat down on a straight-backed chair. "Good day, Lord Carrington. What may I help you with?" Kindly leave, taking your roving eyes and eager hands with you, she longed to add.

"Rather should you ask what I may help *you* with." Theatrically, Carrington held out the parcel. Katrina didn't take it. He cajoled, "Please don't view this as aught but what it is: an apology. I quite misunderstood your, er, relationship with Devon. He and I have had a long talk this morning, and I fear I insulted you to no purpose. Please accept this small token of my regret."

She'd have been less than gracious to refuse again, but Katrina unwrapped the package gingerly. Shiny turquoise silk and crisp white lace spilled into her lap. Her hands luxuriated in the fabrics.

Carrington said, "It's obvious you're both pleased and surprised. I'm gratified, but even silk so fine is a poor match for your beauty."

Katrina didn't even hear the fulsome compliment. She was afraid to look at Carrington lest he see the arrested expression in her eyes. Her mind buzzed with questions. Where did he get the silk? How so quickly? And what motivated him to give this precise present to her? Did he know of her involvement? Had Davie gone to him? The facts led to one conclusion: Carrington must be the mysterious disperser of their contraband. Was this his way of warning her to mind her own affairs?

"This is most kind of you, sir, but I cannot accept so rich a gift." She wrapped the bolts and tried to give them back.

He rested his hands on his knees. "Refuse them if you must, but I'll burn them rather than see another in them. That color was meant for you."

Katrina wondered if there were another, hidden meaning in his words. She searched his eyes, but saw only the usual feeling she aroused in men. She looked back down at the silk, longing to feel it against her skin. Perhaps she could pay him out of her share.

"Very well, I'll keep the material, but only if you let me repay you."

His pleased smile switched to a stubborn scowl. "No."

She held the bolts out as her wordless response. When he still wouldn't take them, she rose to drop them in his lap.

"Oh, very well." He named a ridiculously low sum.

Mentally she made a note to pay him twice that. Her share should still leave enough to purchase a month's supply of food, if she was given what Davie had promised. Holding the bolts to her breast, she began inching toward the door.

"Thank you, Lord Carrington. Now, if you'll excuse me . . ."

"But I thought we could talk. I'd like to invite you to be my guest at the festival."

''I always attend with the family. Now really, I've much to do.''

With a stiff bow he left her, banging the front door behind him. Katrina slumped against the wall. Dear Lord, who would have thought it? How ably Carrington lived his double life: country peer and head of a smuggling ring. Yet, as she took her precious burden to her room, her brow crinkled. Something still didn't fit. Carrington's wealth was too old to owe all to smuggling. And Carrington was a pompous man, conscious of the differences between the classes. Would he actively pursue a calling that would require him to have close contact with men he considered beneath him? Yet, if he was not involved, how had he gotten the silk so quickly?

Katrina set the bolts on her bed and went to the drawer where Rachel kept her sewing supplies. As her fingers flew, sketching a design for a simple but elegant gown, her thoughts remained on other subjects. An hour later she had a completed sketch and a firm decision to show for her toil. Which design would end the neater was a moot point now; her mind was made up to pursue each. Both were daring, perhaps, but if she were to risk liberty and virtue, she'd do so in style.

When Rachel told her, after lunch, that John had asked to see her, Katrina gladly set aside the pattern she was making. Rachel had strictly regulated family visits, and Katrina had only seen John for brief moments.

''He's better then?''

Rachel flushed. ''Ais, 'tes selfesh I've been, not to let you see hem more.''

Katrina patted Rachel's shoulder. ''That's all right. I know you only wanted him to rest. I'm just relieved to hear he's on the mend.'' She hurried into John's room.

His once brown face looked pale, but his broad, welcoming smile sparkled as much as ever. He patted the quilt beside him. ''Set, lassie. How have 'ee been?''

''I'm well, John,'' Katrina answered huskily, touched by his concern. Most men would have thought only of themselves in the circumstances. She sat beside him and took his outstretched hand.

''I know thes has been hard on 'ee. My messus was no help,

as feared for me as she were. Yet 'ee found food, and plenty of et, from what Rachel has been brengen' me. Where, lassie?''

Katrina had been ready with a vague excuse, but under those direct brown eyes she couldn't lie. ''His lordship.''

John looked stunned. ''Carrington?''

''No, no, Devon Cavanaugh.''

''Ahhh.'' John drew out the single syllable.

Katrina blushed. ''I was in no position to refuse. I gave him nothing in return save my thanks, I assure you.''

''Nothing, my girl?'' John teased.

Katrina remembered that passionate kiss and went even rosier. ''I've already told him we'll not accept more. And I . . . think I've found employment, so we'll not need to.''

''Yes? What 'employment'?'' John's eyes narrowed when Katrina shifted her feet.

''I'd rather not say, John.'' Feeling guilty, Katrina pulled her hand out of his slack grip.

John leaned his head back and closed his eyes. ''Not 'ee also, lass. Two smugglers en the famely es two too many. Esn't there another waay?'' He opened his eyes and glared at her.

Katrina didn't know how to banish the frustration she saw there. She understood he felt helpless, adrift now he could no longer be the family's primary support. She bowed her head, searching for comforting words.

Before she found them, he said grimly, ''I'd rather 'ee went to Cavanaugh. At least he'd not endaanger 'ee.''

Her head reared up, and for the first time anger kindled in her eyes. ''I never thought to hear you say that, John. You know why I can't be indebted to Devon.'' She cleared her throat and said more softly, ''You just concentrate on getting better. When you're well again, I'll stop. I promise.''

John's grunt proved what he thought of that, but he obliged her by changing the subject. They discussed the various family members, but he seemed concerned most about Ellie. ''Has she seen that Englesh rascal?''

In truth Katrina had been too worried to heed Ellie's activities, but Billy had visited twice since John had been hurt. ''A couple of times.''

''Send Ellie to me,'' John said. When Katrina reached the door, he added, ''And please, lass, be careful. Though many of them be my friends, the free traaders can be a ruthless lot, 'specially them who deals weth the placen' of the goods.''

"I'll be careful, John," Katrina said without turning her head. As she went in search of Ellie she decided it was a good thing John didn't know she planned to discover as much about the smugglers' activities as she could. Men bold enough to defy the law would be the ones who threatened the gentry. The risk to her own safety was less important than feeding the family and protecting Devon.

The next few days were peaceful. Katrina wasn't bothered by male visitors. Even Will was absent, aside from one harried examination of John's healing leg and ribs. Katrina started at every knock on the door, but the visitor she hoped for didn't appear. She was glad, she told herself, yet the fear grew that Devon had finally taken her at her word. If that wasn't just like him—after she'd finally decided to throw her scruples to the wind, he left her dangling in it. With feminine perverseness Katrina decided she'd soon change his mind.

Her frown softened into a smile as she caressed the billowing skirts in her lap. He'd take notice right royally if this dress turned out as she hoped. She turned to Ellie to gauge her progress. By making the skirts less full than fashion demanded, they'd saved enough silk to stitch Ellie a gown, too. Ellie had the skirt finished and was tacking on the bodice insert. Katrina nodded in satisfaction. If they were diligent, they should each have a new dress for the summer festival, which was one of the county's most anticipated events.

"Do you attend the fair with anyone, Ellie?" Katrina asked in apparent idleness. Inwardly she tensed as she awaited the answer. The day John summoned Ellie, Katrina had heard their raised voices.

Ellie sighed. "Billy has invited me, but Da doesn't want me to go with him. What do you think I should do, Katrina?"

Having her suspicions verified didn't please Katrina. Here was just one more problem she'd brought into this family, indirectly or not. Katrina shared John's worries about Billy's intentions, but how could she warn Ellie against outsiders when she herself planned to consort with one?

"I can't make the choice for you, Ellie. I understand how

you feel, but only you can decide which is more important to you: your father's peace of mind or Billy's company.'' Katrina nipped off her thread and smiled sympathetically into Ellie's anxious eyes.

As she measured another length of lace Katrina thought wryly that this year's fair should be more eventful than those in the past. . . .

The cottage's grim atmosphere lightened when that late June day finally arrived. Even John became eager for the celebrations. His loyal men had presented him with a sturdy litter, and four of them would come at dusk to carry him to the hill where the festival would begin. Rachel scurried hither and yon, preparing her finest pasties and using some of the precious sugar Devon had given them to make tiny cream-and-currant cakes. Ellie and Katrina worked frantically to finish their gowns so they could help Rachel with preparations.

Robert jabbered from dawn to dusk. ''Can I carry a torch this time, Jimmy, please?'' The affirmative reply didn't satisfy him long. ''Will you wrestle this year? I can't wait until I can.'' When Jimmy escaped to help carry furze for the bonfire, Robert badgered Ellie and Katrina until they hurried into the loft to try on their finery.

Hopping with excitement, Robert turned to his harried mother. ''Can I jump through the fire this year, Ma? Please?''

''We'll see, Robbie. Maaybe Jimmy well help 'ee.''

When he tugged on her skirts with another question, Rachel slammed her fingers down on the dough she was kneading. ''Land's End, son, go talk to Da.''

Robbie scampered away, leaving her in peace. She'd just finished the cakes and put them in her Dutch oven over the hearth when she heard a rustling. She turned. She brought one floury hand to her mouth to cover a gasp.

Ellie came first into the kitchen, biting her lip nervously. ''What does 'ee thenk, Ma?'' She turned slowly before her mother.

The gown she'd fashioned was a sleek fall of silk that emphasized her willowy figure. The tight waist was low and pointed, emphasized by a pleated inset of cream linen. The same pleated linen made a narrow band about the hem and trimmed the elbow-length sleeves. A fichu of the same linen framed Ellie's pretty shoulders. The linen looked expensive because it was; it had been Rachel's best tablecloth until she pressed it upon a reluctant Ellie. They'd not had enough lace for both gowns.

Katrina glided down the stairs next. Rachel blinked in astonishment. She'd always known Katrina was lovely, but properly gowned, Katrina seemed too exquisite to be real. Katrina had embellished her best petticoat with silver-embroidered stars and lace, then turned the silk skirts back away from it in scalloped tiers. Stars decorated the peak of each scallop and made a decorative band about her elbows above the fall of exquisite lace. The deep, square bodice was trimmed with an upstanding ruffle that moved with Katrina's breaths. Rachel well knew what effect that ruffle would have on every male present. She suspected Katrina knew also. What was the girl up to?

"I've ne'er seen two prettier ladies." Rachel finally sighed. "But surely 'ee won't wear such finery tonight to the bonfire."

"I can't wait, Ma. I'll not be leaping the fire this time."

"Nor I," Katrina added.

"'Tes lovely 'ee both are, as 'ee both know. But 'ee'd best sneak out of the house wethout seein' John. He'll not let 'ee out ef he sees 'ee."

Katrina winked at Ellie. "'Tes yourself 'ee should be lookin' to, Rachel Tonkin," she teased. "Go and see what lies on my bed."

"In a moment." Rachel looked only mildly interested as she checked her cakes. Then, after washing her hands, she preceded the girls up to the loft.

Her eyes widened as the setting sun lingered on the soft white dimity. She picked up the dress, held it to herself, then scurried over to the tiny mirror. Katrina and Ellie leaned against one another, watching. When tears came to Rachel's eyes, they each blinked rapidly.

"It wasn't fair that you couldn't get a new gown as well," Katrina said simply. "So we refashioned your wedding gown. Do you like it?"

Rachel nodded and smoothed out the dress with trembling fingers. Katrina had patched together the last pieces of silk, then smocked them to hide the seams. She used the trim to make a wide ribbon for the waist and narrower bands at high, ruffled neck and wrist-length sleeves. Using material they'd scrounged from the too long hem, they'd let out the waist to accommodate Rachel's more matronly figure, then attached the ribbon to cover the mending.

When she could speak again, Rachel said huskily, "But I was saaven' thes for Ellie's wedden'."

"Who knows when that will be?" Ellie asked, hugging her mother. "You've sacrificed enough for your bairns, Ma. You needed a dress, too."

"Thank 'ee, daughter." Rachel kissed her daughter's cheek, then beckoned Katrina and pulled her into her other arm. "And thank 'ee—daughter. Ef not of blood, surely of heart."

Katrina swallowed and buried her head in Rachel's yeast-scented shoulder. She would not cry, she told herself. Her own mother had died when she was a babe. Was this how it felt to know a mother's steadfast love? What luxury. In truth Rachel had been as much a mother to her as any daughter could have wished for. Katrina pushed away the thought that she'd never know this joyous give-and-take with her own children.

She lifted her head and smiled tremulously at the two dear faces. "What I've given has been but a mite of the measure I've received. Now, before we all turn to watering pots, we've preparations to make!" Katrina whirled and led the way downstairs.

When they were finally ready for departure, Katrina and Ellie held their shawls close to keep from upsetting John. However, his eyes seemed glued to his wife, who blushed like the bride he was obviously recalling. As his men carried him she walked next to him, holding his hand.

Katrina and Ellie each held hoops of flowers interwoven with herbs. Jimmy carried a blazing torch, lighting their way to the highest tor in the district, where the bonfire had been set up. Robert held a smaller torch, rotating it above his head, imitating his brother. The arcing motion lent a mysterious, flickering quality to the faces that were turned eagerly toward the tor.

Traditions like this had sustained generations of Cornish. It was hardly any wonder, Katrina decided, that the people of

Cornwall so fiercely held to their independence. It was bred into them from the cradle with rituals such as these.

"I wonder if our ancestors looked the same as they lifted their torches at midsummer to defy the increasing night," Katrina murmured to Ellie.

"And if they made hoops like these, and threw them on the fire to ward off evil spirits—or to invoke good ones," Ellie added, her eyes searching the thickening crowd.

"Ye've no need of witchcraft, Ellie," a deep voice said from behind her. Ellie froze. "For the sight of ye in that dress is magic enough."

Slowly Ellie turned to meet Billy's eyes. He bowed and kissed her hand.

Katrina smiled to herself. She should have known Billy wouldn't leave Ellie a choice. John turned his head. He frowned, but when his daughter's pleading face turned in his direction, he sighed. He waved her away. Her eyes reflecting the torches, Ellie took Billy's arm and disappeared into the crowd.

John and Rachel exchanged a smile. Rachel bent to kiss her husband's cheek, but he turned his head and took her mouth instead. Discreetly, Katrina looked away.

Only years of shared toil and plenty imbued a couple with that wordless understanding of one another. If she became Devon's . . . bedmate, then she would never know that comfort. She didn't delude herself that she could hold his affections indefinitely. He'd grow weary of Cornwall and leave her. Would she be enriched or impoverished when that day came? She couldn't answer that question. Yearningly, she searched the crowd for that one face, trying to quiet the forebodings chanting again in the back of her mind.

When she couldn't spy Devon, Katrina told herself she was glad. She needed to speak to Will first, anyway. He'd made no effort to court her as he'd vowed to, so she hoped he'd not be upset at her decision. Honor required that she release herself from obligation to one suitor before encouraging another. She would have told him before now, but had lacked the opportunity. She wondered yet again what had kept him so busy this past fortnight.

Katrina was too occupied searching the crowd to realize the

stir she caused as her shawl slipped away from her shoulders. Farm boys, millers, townsmen alike stared as the blazing torches reflected off her burnished hair and tinged her fair skin to rose. The breeze caught her bodice ruffle, making it flutter just enough to entice, but not reveal.

Katrina didn't see Jack stiffen in the act of bringing a jug to his mouth, or notice as Davie let go of a dairymaid's hand to peer after her. Carrington whirled from conversing with one of his tenants to follow her progress with hungry eyes.

There he was! "Will," Katrina called, weaving her way toward him. She didn't see the richly dressed man veer toward her at the sound of her voice. He followed her as she reached Will and put a hand on his arm.

"I've wanted to speak with you for days." Katrina forced a smile under the sweep of his eyes. She pulled her shawl back over her shoulders and added, "May we talk privately?"

Possessively, he put her hand through the crook of his arm. "Certainly, my dear. I've missed you, but I've not been deliberately delinquent in my attentions." He led her out of the crush to a cluster of huge boulders standing just past the curve of the hill. He seated her atop one, his hands lingering at her waist. The many torches and brilliant moon revealed his face.

"Have you been so busy, then?" Katrina didn't move as his hands slipped about her waist. A snapping twig caught her attention, but Will's comment distracted her before she looked behind him.

"Dull business that wouldn't interest you, but I'm done for a time. I would have called, except I knew I'd see you here. I'm so glad you watched for me, but I'd have found you in a much larger crowd than this." Will's lips inched forward. Katrina turned her head, and his mouth drifted across her cheek.

Katrina was too intent on carefully framing her words to notice the low growl that issued from behind Will. "Will, when we spoke the other day, you caught me at a sad moment. I've since . . . reconsidered. I don't want to hurt you, but I . . . can't let you court me when my affections are given to another."

A short distance away broad shoulders heaved a relieved sigh as Katrina went on. "Please, try to understand. I'd be doing you as much a disservice—nay, more—to encourage you falsely." She couldn't bear Will's stricken features, so she turned her head away and finished quietly, "Forgive me. I literally owe you my life, but my love, it seems, is not mine to give as I would." She kissed his cold cheek, scooted down from the rock, and hurried back up the hill, dashing away her incipient tears.

Will stood where she left him, his hands braced on the boulder, his fair head bent.

Katrina almost ran into the wide chest of the man who turned to block her path. Her shawl slipped. "Hello, Kat," Devon said quietly.

The picture of Will's face, locked in a rictus of pain, ruined the joy Katrina had expected to feel at sight of him. She nodded coolly. "How gracious of you to associate with the lower classes, my lord."

That old, bold smile flickered to life as he scanned her trim figure from stem to stern, lingering at her bodice. He cleared his throat and said huskily, "You're in error. From the look of you I'd say it's you who are slumming with the rabble, myself included." He took off his hat to sweep her a deep bow. "Never have you looked more like an angel, my very dear lady. You've still got stardust clinging to you."

"A very fallen one, sir, as you well know," Katrina said, then bit her lip in regret at the tart comment.

He slipped neatly into the opening she'd left him. "Indeed. It is my fondest wish that you let me catch you once again." When she tried to push past him, he caught her arm. His voice grew serious. "I cry quarter, Kat. Tonight even such repartee does not satisfy me. I want only to be your escort among these people you've taken to your heart, and try to understand both them and you."

Anger failed her under his earnest intensity. She'd made this dress for him; she'd hurt Will for him; she'd endangered her own safety for love of him. She'd be foolish to spoil this moment. Past recriminations would not ruin all her hopes for the future. She took his proffered arm.

"Thank you, Devon," she said gravely. "I shall be delighted." They strolled to the top of the hill to watch the lighting of the bonfire, oblivious to the resentful eyes that followed them.

One of the tar barrels ignited. Flames trickled like liquid gold over the pile of stumps and sticks, catching another strategically placed barrel, then another. The bonfire roared into life. As more and more wood caught, the flames climbed toward heaven.

The Cornish broke into a cheer and began to dance wildly about the fire. Devon pulled Katrina away from the stomping feet and stared as several young men, whooping in glee, leaped through the lowest edge of the bonfire.

"Are they mad?" he asked Katrina. Several young women followed suit.

"Perhaps. On the joy of midsummer. You're watching an ancient tradition, Devon. Your own ancestors no doubt practiced it. They believe that leaping through the flames helps protect them against evil. It purifies them." She slanted him a sidelong look. "I'll wait a day or two if you want to follow suit."

He lifted her chin and said softly, "Wipe that smirk off your face, my girl, or I shall kiss it away." When her smile faded, he added, "If you still fear for my soul, Katrina, there's a more effective way for you to save me."

She was suspicious of the gleam in his eye, but she asked anyway, "How so?"

He came closer still until his breath stirred the hair at her temples. "Why, by the love of a good woman. Won't you redeem me, Katrina mina?"

The curious stares, the roaring fire receded. Katrina's world was filled with gold-brown eyes. Brandy seemed to flow through her veins, intoxicating her. She melted against him, but then a dancing couple jostled her. With a drowning gasp she backed away from Devon.

"Must throw this in the fire," she muttered. She stumbled around the dancing couples to fetch her discarded hoop and throw it into the flames. She watched the flowers cringe, crumple, then blacken. Quaint custom or not, she closed her eyes and said a brief prayer. She knew God heard, and if a few heathen spirits were listening as well, she'd not eschew their help.

Strong hands caught her waist. "Come, dance with me, earthly angel."

Devon held her close and began to move to the rhythm of the fifes, drums, and flutes playing a slow tune. Katrina gave up all thoughts of propriety and rested her cheek against his broad chest. When her shawl slipped, he lifted it to cover her lovely shoulders from staring eyes.

The last, haunting remnants of the past dissolved under the heat of the flames. The whispers that warned of future retribution were muffled by the beating of the heart Katrina lay against, and the one that answered. For once she'd heed only the bliss of the present. If, for a fleeting moment, she remembered what had happened the last time she lived the moment, she pushed the thought away.

"Don't you want to know why I haven't been to see you?" he asked, his voice muffled against the top of her head. He breathed deeply of her rosewater-scented hair.

"I suspect I know why," she answered. She lifted her head and fingered the top button of his waistcoat.

He caught her hand as she traced the path of buttons to his waist. "Be still, wench, lest I embarrass us both. Tell me why, then."

" 'Absence makes the heart grow fonder.' "

He chuckled huskily and pushed her head back against his shoulder. "You do know me. But you can hardly complain. I only obeyed your own request to leave you be." When she stayed silent under the provoking remark, he demanded, "Well, don't keep me in suspense! Did it work?"

She peeped up at him with languid eyes and smiled when she felt his heart—and something else—surge against her. "Perhaps. Maybe I can tell you. Later." He stumbled, his hands growing slack about her.

She laughed joyously at his shocked expression and caught his hand to drag him away from the dancers. "Come, visit with John. I know he wants to thank you for the food."

She felt his eager eyes as they walked, but this time she made no effort to shield the fluttering ruffle. He could hardly mistake her signals, but she was past shame. This bold seducer of women should sample his own tormenting brand of flirtation.

As they wended their way through the families picnicking on blankets, Katrina stopped here and there to greet people. In each case she introduced Devon; in each case they responded curtly.

Devon's smile grew fixed as a mother pulled her daughter out of his path. "Do they think I'll mow her down?" he muttered to Katrina.

In answer she tugged harder on his hand. John was respected in the community. Mayhap when the others saw how cordially the Tonkins treated him, they'd come around.

Katrina waved when she spied John's litter. Rachel paused in cutting a slice of ham for Robert to nod in welcome. Robert, who sat next to his mother, squirmed with his usual excitement.

After greeting John, Katrina sat next to him on the quilt and drew Devon down beside her. She kissed the top of Robert's head. "And has the fair been to the master's liking?"

Robert pouted. "Ais, it's been fun, but Ma won't let me leap through the flames."

"Now, Robbie, 'ee knows 'ee can't do et alone, and Jimmy has gone off weth those . . . friends of hes." Rachel slammed the slice of ham down on a thick chunk of bread and handed it to her son. She looked inquiringly at Katrina. Katrina nodded, so Rachel made two more sandwiches.

"Thank 'ee for the ham, and the other thengs," John said gruffly to Devon.

Devon accepted the sandwich Rachel thrust at him. "It was my pleasure. If I can help again in any way, please just let me know."

"We'll manage well enough, weth the lassie's help." John took a draw on his pipe and seemed not to hear Katrina's hissed, "Shhh!"

Devon paused in taking a big bite and lowered the sandwich. "What does he mean, Katrina? Have you found employment?"

"Er . . . yes." She tried to avert more questions by setting aside her own barely touched food and drawing Robbie into her lap. "Mayhap I can swing you through the flames, Robbie."

"You're not strong enough, lass," Rachel said.

Devon let the diversion work, for now. As he nibbled he looked thoughtfully at the bonfire. It had begun to burn down, and now many fathers were swinging their offspring over the more feeble flames. "I can take him, if you like, Mr. Tonkin."

"Call me John, my lord. 'Tes up to the lad."

"Please, my given name is Devon." Devon rose and held out his hand to Robbie.

Robbie looked from Devon's hand, to the bonfire, back to Devon. Katrina could feel his tension. Would the dislike of Devon Jimmy had taught him win against his longing to experience one of the most anticipated rites of a Cornish childhood? She wasn't surprised when he virtually leaped off her lap.

Shyly he took Devon's hand. Devon smiled down at him; Robbie smiled back.

As they walked toward the fire Katrina reflected that even small boys were not proof against Devon's charm. When they reached the fire, she watched as Devon securely caught Robbie's hands and swung him high above the flames. Robbie laughed in glee as Devon stepped back and began to whirl him in a circle. One second Robbie's face was alight, the next dark as he swung away from the fire. Devon set him down, but Robbie caught his arm and turned a pleading face up to him. Devon went down on his haunches to talk to him, catching Robbie's shoulders in his strong hands.

"He'll maake a good father one daay," Rachel .said, enunciating Katrina's secret thought. When Katrina closed her eyes in pain, Rachel clapped her hand over her mouth.

John caught Katrina's hand and pulled her closer to him. "'Ee love hem, do 'ee not?"

Unable to speak through the lump in her throat, Katrina nodded.

"Then go to hem, lass. Taake what happiness 'ee can." John looked toward Devon thoughtfully. "'Ee maay be surprised at what response 'ee gets."

Katrina threw her arms about John and hugged him, hard. "You're like my father, come to life again, John. I can almost be happy at the sorry turn of events that led me to you."

John patted her back. "'Ee've had enough grief, lass. Go on now. Follow your heart."

When Devon came back, Robbie skipping happily beside him, he didn't notice that those he passed seemed more polite than before, but Katrina did. His hair mussed, grass clinging to his satin coat, he seemed less intimidating, reminding the others that he was a man first, a peer second. He'd not scorned their customs, either, which Katrina knew had not gone unnoticed.

She smiled at him brilliantly when he sat down beside her.

The flames seemed caught in his eyes as he smiled back. His gaze dropped to her bodice. She took a deep, shaky breath, making her ruffle bounce. He swallowed, staring at her cleavage, but the moment was spoiled when a cultured drawl interrupted them.

"She is pretty as a picture, old chap, but you've had her long enough." Carrington caught Katrina's arm and pulled her to her feet. "Come dance with me."

Katrina smelled the liquor on his breath. She turned her head, but tried to keep her reply polite. "I'm tired, but thank you for asking."

"Let her go," Devon ground out through his teeth, standing slowly.

"You've no hold on her, as you told me yourself," Carrington said without looking at him. "I'm glad to see you took such beautiful advantage of my gift, pretty lady."

Devon's advance stopped. "What are you talking about?"

Insolently, Carrington fingered Katrina's bodice ruffle. "Where do you think she got such fine material?"

Even in the dying glow of the flames Katrina saw Devon pale. "What does he mean, Kat?"

"Not what his filthy tone implies. I bought the material from him, Devon." She wrenched away from Carrington.

"Oh yesss?" Carrington drawled. "I've yet to see a shilling." He looked Katrina up and down. "But I can think of a better way for you to pay me—"

Growling, Devon leaped on him. Katrina bit her knuckles as the two men rolled over and over in the grass, trading punches as they went. Even sober, Carrington wouldn't have been a match for Devon. Drunk, he was hopelessly outmanned.

The Cornish watched as the two lords tussled in the dirt like farmhands. Some of the men who'd sniffed in disdain at Devon's passage looked grudingly impressed at Devon's prowess.

Devon straddled Carrington and drew back his fist. His punishing uppercut caught Carrington's chin, echoing in the night air. Carrington went limp. Heaving more with rage than exertion, Devon rose. He held his hand out to Katrina.

"Come," he said imperiously.

Only the pop and hiss of the bonfire disturbed the tense silence as all watched for Katrina's response. If she accepted his hand and let him lead her away, every soul present save the youngest children knew how they would end the night's revelry.

Katrina glanced nervously around. She'd intended to go to him, yes, but not so publicly. She looked back at Devon.

Devon's imperious chin lowered a notch. "Come, Katrina mina," he whispered for her ears alone.

The longing in his voice struck a chord within her, for she, too, vibrated with that need. She rose and was reaching for his hand when she caught movement behind him.

"Look out, Devon!" she screamed.

He whirled, and the cudgel bounced off his shoulder instead of his head. He caught the stick and jerked it from Jack's hands. He flung it into the dark and began, "I've no quarrel with you, man—" He broke off with an oof as Jack caught him about the waist and threw him to the ground.

"But we've all a score to settle with ye, me fine little lordling," Jack growled. He drew back his boot to kick Devon in the ribs, but Devon caught his foot and pushed. Jack grunted as he fell backward. He looked dazed for a moment, and that was all the time Devon needed. He straddled Jack and drew back his fist.

Davie charged out of the dark and pounced on Devon. Devon flexed his shoulders and tried to throw him off, but then Jack, shaking his head to clear it, sat up and added his strength to Davie's. Paulie joined the melee, helping pin Devon's struggling arms to the ground. Jack began raining blows on Devon's face.

Katrina gave an anguished moan and ran after the cudgel Devon had thrown away. She was dragging it back when a pistol shot exploded into the air. She blinked at the bright flash of powder, then sagged to her knees in relief when Jack turned in shock.

John threw aside the pistol he'd snatched from Paulie's belt. "I'd expect such from 'ee, Jack, but 'ee, Davie, and 'ee,

Paulie''—he looked sternly at each man in turn—''should have more respect of your naames as Cornishmen than to gang up on a man so.''

Agreeing grunts came from several quarters. As Jack turned back to Devon Paulie reluctantly let Devon's arm go. He picked up his pistol and stumbled off. With one arm free Devon was able to pry Davie's slack grip away and push Jack off. He rose and levelly met Jack's mean glare. Jack also lumbered to his feet.

Violence lingered in the air as strongly as the powder's acrid stench. Realizing she was partly the source of the discord, Katrina smothered her instinct to go to Devon. John could handle this far better than she.

''Go on now, Davie. 'Ee've had too much to drenk and well be sorry come mornen'.''

Davie looked about the staring crowd, then reluctantly turned away. But the look he sent at Devon over his shoulder promised a different end to their next meeting.

Carrington, who had recovered consciousness but was cradling his head in his hands, lifted his head as Davie passed. Davie's eyes met his briefly, but then he hurried off.

Jack stood firm as a sturdy oak, then he rolled up his sleeves. ''I don't need their help. I'll be right glad to stomp ye into the ground me ownself.''

''Hush, Jack,'' John said with a weary shake of his head. ''Can't 'ee see the lassie's spoken for? Et's her choice after all.''

Katrina followed John's gesturing hand and went to Devon. She wet her kerchief in the water Rachel had brought and tenderly bathed the bruise on his jaw. He caught her hand and held it tightly to his cheek. Their eyes met.

In that moment the rumors were substantiated. Some of the women shook their heads in condemnation. No banns had been read, yet there was possession offered and accepted in that simple exchange between lord and girl. Others of a more moderate bent sighed, longing, perhaps, for their own golden days when love had seemed strong enough to bridge all.

Many of the men present looked at Devon with new eyes. He'd done well tonight. They could relate to a lord who was willing to take on three at once, if necessary, to protect his lady. More than one man sighed as he looked at Katrina. Who could blame him?

Some distance away Ellie shed a few happy tears into Billy's shoulder. He smiled and saluted the pair who seemed oblivious to the stares. "It's past time," he said to himself. Then he hugged Ellie close.

With a frustrated snarl Jack turned away. "Ye've not seen the last of me, ye sorry excuse for a man. Ye'll not always have this little slip to protect ye. And ye, girlie, ain't seen the last o' me, either." He stomped off.

Katrina didn't even hear his threat. Her eyes, luminous with tears, locked with Devon's. "Are you all right?"

His shoulders lifted with his deep sigh. "I've never felt better in my life. Come, my love." He took her hand, but paused to look down at John. "Thank you, sir. I'll have a care for her, don't worry."

"And so 'ee better, young man," John answered. He waved them away. "Go on weth 'ee. Ee maakes me feel like bones molderen' en my graave." But as he watched them walk away his face reflected that, aches and pains or not, he felt young and gay. He took his wife's hand.

Katrina rested her head against Devon's shoulder as he led her to his tethered curricle.

Many stared after them, whispering. But Will, standing off to himself gazing in contemplation at the stars, didn't even turn his head. He maintained his lonely vigil as the others drifted off. The glowing embers of the bonfire died slowly. Soon, even his slim, solitary figure could not be distinguished against the night.

Chapter Twelve

ON THAT RIDE to Devon's manor, life hummed joyously all about Katrina. The hoarse croak of mating frogs provided bass accompaniment to a cooing dove soprano. Tenor was supplied by chirruping, gamboling squirrels, and alto sounded from a bellowing, rutting bull.

Yet the mating sounds were but background to the primitive syncopation of two human hearts. With her head against Devon's shoulder, his arm about her, Katrina knew life's true bounty. Why had she struggled so long against this fate? Here, in this man's arms, she belonged. Though it was neither sanctified by God nor man, somehow Katrina knew this night was meant to be. And no matter what the future brought, she'd have this memory to linger over like a warm toddy.

That certainty obviated the shyness Katrina might have felt. Thus, when Devon leaped down and threw his reins to a sleepy, waiting stable boy, it was his hands that shook as he reached up for her; his eyes that searched hers uncertainly. Some imp of mischief made Katrina shield her own eagerness with long, fluttering lashes.

At a less emotive time Devon might have wondered why her hands were rock steady on his shoulders as he lifted her down. Scrutinize her as he did in the bright moonlight, he couldn't read her thoughts. Though his virility throbbed in painful protest, the conscience Katrina had activated was more insistent.

Holding her close, her toes dangling above the ground, he growled into her ear, "If you've changed your mind, now's the time to say so."

At that Katrina's lashes lifted. She allowed him a brief, heady glimpse of her thoughts. The moon smiled in unison as she teased, "You have changed, my darling demon. The man I knew two years ago would never have allowed me a choice." She pushed at his shoulders and he reluctantly set her down.

"The woman I knew two years ago would have damned me for even asking." He watched her suspiciously as she skipped up the front steps to his carved mahogany door. "And if you think it's escaped me that you didn't answer me, you're much mistaken." He bit back even more heated words as the manservant he'd inherited with the house opened the door.

His surprise at seeing Katrina was quickly masked. "Your lordship, I've set a cold collation out for you in your rooms."

"Thank you, Simpson. That will be all." Simpson retreated to his quarters at the back of the house.

Katrina barely glanced at the spacious, marble-tiled hall illuminated by a small but exquisite chandelier. Instead she looked up the red-carpeted stairs. She went to the foot of them to run a caressing hand over the smooth oak banister.

Devon muttered around the pulse beating in his throat, "Katrina, answer my question. This time I must have your verbal and willing consent. I'll not make the same mistakes that tore us apart in the past."

If Katrina heard, she didn't answer. She began to ascend the stairs, her hand trailing sensuously over the banister. When she was almost at the top, her response finally drifted back to him. "Come along, Devon. All that dancing made me hungry."

Devon gritted his teeth. Damn the girl, didn't she know what she was doing to him? Good intentions could triumph over violent desire only so long. If she carried this teasing game into the bedchamber, he couldn't answer for his reaction.

Feeling like a puppet on a string, Devon stalked after Katrina.

Katrina peeked in doors until she found the tray of food, then entered a luxurious chamber bedecked in blue and gold. She glided about, fingering this vase, touching that inlaid escritoire, seeming not to notice her effect on him. For sanity's sake Devon left the door half-open behind them and stood barely within the room.

What was the girl about? Invading his sanctum, touching his things in a way that made him ache. The candlelight formed a nimbus about her. In the blue silk, her skin and hair luminous, she did in truth *look* angelic. She *acted* quite the opposite.

She let her shawl drape past one shoulder, then trail behind her on the floor. Pausing at the small table beside the bed, she picked up a scone from the array of delights his man had left. She took a tiny nibble, chewed slowly, then set the scone back down, licking her lips, to wander about the room again.

"You're welcome," he snapped.

"Oh, excuse me." She picked up the tray and brought it over to him. "Do you see anything you like?" When his only answer was a stifled groan and a hungry glance at her fluttering ruffle, she leaned over to set the tray down on a nearby table, apparently unconcerned at the way her breasts pushed insistently at her tight bodice. She selected a sweetmeat. She took one bite, then popped the rest of the candied pear in his mouth.

Enigmatic blue eyes held his as they chewed. She finished first. "I've worked up *such* an appetite. What about you?" As if to emphasize her point, she delicately licked her sticky fingers one by one.

He gulped too quickly and coughed, his throat now aching as much as the rest of him. She reached out to beat his back, but he shied away from her like a fractious stallion.

"Touch me at your peril," he finally choked out, shooting her a watery glare. It was wasted as she shrugged and turned away—toward the bed.

His breath stopped. She sat down gingerly on the edge of the bed, smoothing the blue satin coverlet with one hand, then both. She tried an experimental bounce, then sighed luxuriously.

"It's been such an age since I felt a real mattress," she said, flopping on her back.

Her skirts tumbled wantonly about her, revealing too much slim ankle and shapely calf for Devon's comfort. Indeed, Devon was long past comfort—or reason, or shame. Two long years of dearth made him feel nigh dead from sexual deprivation. Here, in his own room, in his bed by her own will, lay plenty. Breath rushed back into his lungs as, snarling, he slammed and locked the door and lunged.

Yet when she propped her head on one hand and smiled at

him, she stayed his mad rush as effectively as a bullet. He
halted beside the bed, teetering on his feet.

The words were torn out of him. "Oh God, Katrina, either
yea or nay, but put me out of my misery." He closed his eyes
briefly, then looked at her again.

The teasing glimmer died. Her eyes darkened as she looked
up at him. Her lips trembled, then she smiled again. This time
the smile was different. This time Devon's resentment melted
away, for with this simple movement of her lips she touched
his soul.

So this is what it meant to look upon the face of Love,
Devon thought vaguely. Yes, she was beautiful, but that
glowing serenity came from her spirit, not her person. She
seemed Woman incarnate; not Eve, the tempter, nor even
Venus, the lover. He searched her eyes, looking for the elusive
memory. It came to him with a force that humbled him.

Here lay Penelope, steadfast, loving Penelope, true to him
despite her many ardent suitors, and the isolation his absence
had thrust upon her. He, errant Ulysses, was being welcomed
back with open arms, despite his arrogance and unfaithfulness.
Devon looked down at his hands, then rubbed them against his
breeches. He'd soiled them with other women, while
this . . . love of his life had been true to him even when she
thought she'd never see him again. Devon closed his eyes in
pain and, for the first time in many years, begged his Lord's
forgiveness. He didn't deserve this woman, but if he didn't win
her, nothing in life would matter to him anymore. Least of all
his name, for he'd have no one to share it with.

Compelled, he opened his eyes again. Head on one side, he
tried to picture what their children would look like. If a tiny
flicker of doubt still troubled him, he'd not admit it to her. He'd
sire a parade of idiots if that's the only way he could take this
woman to wife for life. Yet his own fears shamed him.

When she held her arms out to him, it was too much. He
swallowed harshly as he saw himself clearly for the first time
in his life. He was a coward. He'd used ancestral pride as an
excuse not to make commitments because he was afraid of
being hurt. And his own shortsightedness had cost him dear,
would cost him this . . . pearl beyond price if he didn't
overcome his own past, the way she'd obviously overcome

hers. He stayed where he was, unable to retreat from his sole hope of happiness, but unable to grasp it, either, with his former selfishness.

When he didn't accept her embrace, Katrina sat up. A small, pained frown shadowed that lovely smile. "Devon . . . do you not want me?"

The moan that escaped him was so low, so deep with pain, that Katrina gasped. "Not want you? I'll die without you, but surely I'd rather perdition claimed me than take you against your will again." He put one knee on the mattress and tenderly brushed away the truant locks of hair on her cheek.

He gritted his teeth and jerked his hand away. "Tell me to go, and I'll never trouble you again. Tell me to stay, and I'll do all within my power to be worthy of you."

His words rang with a surety that acted on Katrina like an aphrodisiac. The last fetters of the past sprang free, releasing her to follow her instincts. She loved this man; she wanted to give her heart and, aye, her body to him. If he truly understood now, as his eyes seemed to proclaim, nothing held them apart any longer.

She sprang to her knees and flung her arms about his waist. "Stay, my love." She felt his hands tremble as he stroked her hair. Her voice shook with the same emotion when she quavered, "I—I was wrong two years ago. Love is enough to mend even the cruelest wound. Many's the time I tried to cut you from my heart, but I couldn't. I know now I never shall. And right or wrong, I won't try any longer. . . ." Her voice drifted away as she felt wetness on her temple. "Devon?"

He drew back so she could see his tears. "And you were right. I was poor in all my luxury. Only now do I know what true wealth is. I, for one, will never be miserly again." Wed me, be my love in the world's eyes, too, he started to say, but she drew him down on the bed and kissed him.

With the first touch of her lips the sublime became practical. Only one way remained to them to cement their emotional bond, and recklessly, joyously, they took it.

They lay full length upon the bed, their mouths twining as urgently as their limbs. Hands wandered, legs rubbed together, but they were balked by clothing. Devon reached for the tiny buttons on the back of Katrina's gown, but his shaking fingers were clumsy. He didn't want to spoil her creation, so he stifled his yearning to tear every shred away.

While he labored, his face beginning to perspire with frustration, Katrina managed to push his coat off his shoulders and open his waistcoat. She made swift work of his shirt, then slipped all three garments off his shoulders. A vast golden meadow was revealed, all lushly thatched hollows and open spaces. Katrina sighed her pleasure and prepared to gambol.

She ran her hands over him admiringly, then nuzzled his neck with nose and tongue. Devon gasped, his hands clenching behind her. "I can't undo you, wench, if you don't cooperate."

Katrina merely smiled wickedly against his nipple, then stabbed it with her tongue. "I'm honored, demon mine. If I've managed to sew a gown that a rake of your stamp can't remove, then I must market it as a chastity belt." She drew back and dimpled at him, then moved aside to work on his breeches.

His chest heaved, but he managed to gasp out, "Then you'd best look to your design, for you've a flaw." Gentle fingers tunneled through her crumpled skirts and found her.

It was Katrina's turn to groan, Devon's turn to sigh with pleasure. She was already wet and ready for him. He lifted his head to try to see, and she took advantage of the movement to twitch her hips aside.

Growling like a hungry kitten, she pulled so hard on his last button that it popped. She gasped when his flesh sprang free, agile and eager as an acrobat. He kicked the breeches aside, leaving himself bare before her. She'd forgotten. . . . She fingered him tentatively, then flushed when he muttered something incoherent and arched his hips toward her. She obeyed by giving him the longer, more thorough touch he wanted.

A last time he pulled at her bodice, but he gave up when she lay beside him, one hand possessively holding him prisoner, and took his mouth with hers. By the way she languorously played chase with his tongue, Devon sensed her delight at this reversal of their old role. Now it was he who lay naked and vulnerable, she who was clothed and in control. The piquancy of the situation whetted his own starved appetites until he thought he'd explode . . . but he didn't. He owed her this. And more.

Katrina trailed the very tip of her tongue teasingly from one corner of his mouth to the other, and started when his manhood leaped in her hand. She lifted her head and smiled down at him, her eyes soft with sensuality and the deeper emotion that inspired it. Then she turned her head to watch what her hands were doing to him.

Katrina fingered the swelling she'd aroused, sighing her pleasure at the touch of him. So round, so hard, so velvety smooth. How had she ever been afraid of such a magnificent work of art? Thought gave birth to an action that seemed so appropriate that she obeyed her instincts without hesitation. While he was staring at her with dilated eyes she lowered her mouth to give homage to his beauty. Her hair bathed his tense thighs like a warm golden pool. The twin touches of soft mouth and silky hair made him stiffen against the bed.

His fingers clenched in her hair. "Oh God, stop!"

She felt him hardening in her mouth and knew what that portended. Reluctantly, she gave him a last kiss and rested her cheek against his flat belly.

He panted for several moments, then sighed. "Your turn, my love." He tried to push her flat, but she straddled him and twitched her voluminous skirts aside.

"My turn? Then this is what I want, before it's too late." While he stared in shock, his eyes glazed with passion, she cupped him in her fingers, lifted slightly, and sat on the hungry tip of him. "Waste not, want not," she teased huskily.

When he didn't smile, her eyes dropped to what held his rapt attention. She looked down. The sight of her moist opening being cleaved so cleanly and so well was too much for her. The leisurely slide she'd intended somehow became a famished lunge. As they watched, the whole throbbing length of him disappeared between her legs. Their eyes closed in unison; they groaned in concert.

Two years was a long time, but Katrina barely noticed the pain. So deeply he inhabited her . . . Though her visitor was large, Katrina welcomed his ingress and wanted only to acquaint him with every hidden passage. She flexed her muscles about him, needing to take him deeper. Her belly was full of him, yet it wasn't enough. She lifted her hips, then drove down, sighing in delight as he slipped further into her.

She was too intent on her own actions to notice how his hands clutched desperately at the sheets. He gnawed so savagely at his lip that he drew blood. But somehow he stayed the tide and resisted his own urge to play the conquering male. It was right that she take her pleasure upon him.

Her skirts had fallen forward at the frantic activity, shielding their joining from his eyes, but somehow that made their intimate union all the more erotic. "Oh God," he groaned as she took him deep again until he thought he could feel the tip of her womb.

Katrina flung her head back, moving wantonly now, up and violently down. Her breasts, still cruelly contained in the bodice, felt full to bursting. She clutched at her stays and muttered, "Off." She pulled weakly at the ruffle, then gave up when another deep insertion distracted her.

Devon smiled up at her tenderly, barely holding his own needs at bay. He cupped her breasts through the material. When she moaned, caught his hands, and tried to force them down her bodice, he acted on instinct. With a savage grunt he caught the bodice and ripped it downward.

Days of work were ruined, but she seemed not to care. As her breasts tumbled forward to blessed freedom she arched herself into the divine touch of his hands. He cupped each flushed globe gently, then ran his fingers around their fullness.

She paused, holding his pulsing urgency prisoner within her body, and luxuriated in all the incredible sensations she'd never thought to know again. When he tugged on each breast, she obediently lowered her torso. He took dainty licks at first, but when she gasped and squirmed upon him, he muttered hoarsely against her skin, squeezed her breasts closely together, and feasted. He suckled first one nipple, then the other, and when she was pebble hard, he raked her with his teeth.

The sensual touch shivered throughout her body, lodging deep in her womb where she held him. She felt her pulsing growing, growing, and panting, she sat up and leaned backward, the more to take of him.

He knew what she wanted. Propping himself up on one elbow, he rose enough to give her better leverage. She was so tight, so sweet, so warm. He'd wait on her, truly he would. But when she splayed her legs even wider and began to heave up and down, he went so deep his ears began to roar with the passion he could no longer contain.

"Kat, please!" he cried. He bowed against the bed and felt blindly for her own turgid arousal. The single, gentle touch was enough. She screamed. Her head reared back on her shoulders so far that her hair flowed over his thighs.

The clenching release on every oversensitized inch gave him joyful ease. With a triumphant cry he pushed as deep as nature would allow and showered her belly with the seeds of life. He caught her hips in his hands and stayed her writhing, spending himself within her, stamping her. At last, she was his again. His mate.

Her eyes opened wide as she felt that pulsing warmth. She watched his face, shiny with sweat. Exultation filled her with every drop. Never had he been so primitively male, so gorgeous in his arrogance. He'd let her play with him as she willed; this moment was his. She stayed still, submissive upon him, until the potent splashes finally died.

He went limp, pulling her down atop him. She lay inert, listening to his slowing heartbeat, and enjoyed every moment of the happiness she'd earned. Lethargy washed over her. She slept.

Her awakening was slow, blissful, and scandalous. Her clothes were gone, her limbs were arranged to suit his pleasure, and masculine hands were exploring every inch of her. Still half-asleep, she stretched under that skillful touch. A husky laugh made her eyes pop open.

"How appropriately you're named, my darling Kat. Purr for me louder." Lips followed hands.

Only then did she hear the sounds she was making. Devon gave her no time for embarrassment, however. Never had he kissed her so, or caressed her so, gently, possessively, seeing to her pleasure rather than his own. This was the Devon she'd always dreamed of: one guided by love rather than lust.

He pushed her legs further apart and bent his head. She gasped and tried to move away, but he muttered, "Be still," and held her so. "Let me show you how you make me feel." He did so, wordlessly, in the most intimate way possible.

Tenderness, pride, devotion, protectiveness; all were communicated by his mouth and hands. Tears came to Katrina's eyes as he virtually worshiped her. And when her pleasure had come and gone under the tender ministration, she pulled him atop her when he would have let her rest.

"Come, we've two years to make up for," she told him, still panting.

"But I don't want to make you sore—" His protest ended on a groan as she grasped him and put him where she willed.

She smiled against his mouth when his masculine instincts responded to her invitation. The smile faded to a long, delicious sigh as slowly, drawing out every exquisite movement, he used his body to heighten her pleasure again. Only then, many long, long moments later, did he take his own.

When she awoke the second time, dawn bathed the man sitting beside the bed in a ruby glow. Devon wore only a scarlet dressing gown and a sensual smile. She couldn't help it; she blushed under that knowing gaze.

"What a wanton you are," he teased. When she flinched, his voice went soft. "What a lucky man I am." He lifted her into his arms.

He wouldn't let her hide her face against his shoulder. "None of that. This time you've nothing to be ashamed of. As my instructors at Oxford would tell you, I learn quickly." He picked up a glass from beside the bed and held it out to her.

"Drink with me, my love. To the past that brought us together, and the future that will keep us secure." He drank deeply of the champagne, never taking his eyes from her face.

She sipped, vaguely aware of a tinkle in her glass, but too depressed to care. The night was over; reality came with the dawn. She'd have to dress and sneak home, watching others pretend they didn't know where she'd been, or what she'd been doing. She had to force herself to listen as he went on.

"I went through two years of misery without you, Katrina, but now I realize that had you stayed with me then, happiness would never have been ours. You would have left me for another, for only in losing you did I know what you meant to me." Devon put his glass down and picked up her hand to nuzzle it. "Your generosity tonight tore the blinders from my eyes for good and all. I can never be completely worthy of you, but with God's help I intend to try.'' He cupped her hand to his cheek and smiled at her.

Katrina's stirring resentment died. Inexperienced she might be, but she knew love when she saw it. It glowed from Devon's eyes, rang in his voice, and throbbed in his touch. She'd be a fool to reject it, no matter its guise.

She lifted her head proudly. ''I, too, have learned, my darling. Nothing is ever simple 'tween us. Least of all my feelings for you, or yours for me, as you told me years ago. I'd stay if I could. . . .''

Devon touched her trembling lips with his finger. ''Shhh. Shower no more gifts upon me, my dearest. Allow me some pride. I, too, want to be generous with the woman I love.'' He lifted her glass to her lips. ''Drink deeply, and know the full measure of my devotion.''

Her eyes locked with his, Katrina drank to the last drop. When something cold and hard touched her lips, she looked down into her glass. She clasped Devon's wrist to pull the glass away. Gingerly she picked up the ring. The sapphire was small but perfect, surrounded by diamonds. It was not as ostentatious as his gifts of old. At a calmer time she might have wondered why.

Instead she flung it back into the glass and set both down with a snap on the bedside table. ''I will be your lover, Devon, but not your kept woman. Don't insult me with gifts again.'' She tried to turn an offended shoulder to him, but he caught her arm and pulled her back around.

Her tight mouth dropped open when she saw his expression. Laughter? At such a moment?

Indeed, his voice was rich with mirth. ''I can't blame you, my love, for misreading my intent, as I have unwittingly misled you in the past. But this time you err in the wrong direction. Right is firmly on my side at last.'' So saying, he rescued the ring and forced open her clenched hand. ''Let me show you where to wear it.'' He slipped the ring on the fourth finger of her left hand.

When hesitant blue eyes flickered from his face, to the ring, then back, he nodded gravely, all mirth gone. ''Yes, my love. I beg the honor of your hand in marriage.'' He swallowed

harshly as those eyes deepened from turquoise to indigo and
began to fill with tears.

He hauled her into his arms and muttered into her hair,
"Forgive me for my tardiness, my love. But I want you by my
side night and day, in church and out, before man and God."
When she still hid against his shoulder, he lifted her chin with
one finger. "Most of all I want your love without reservation,
as mine is for you. The past is dead, Katrina; walk with me into
the future."

Devon rose and extended his hand.

Katrina stared blindly at that fine hand. Exaltation filled her,
but it had a mournful tone. She'd won—two years too late.

Her own hands burrowed into the covers to keep from
clutching that hand and all it offered. Her eyes closed on the
temptation. Dear God, why do you torment me? No matter how
much he loved her, Devon desperately wanted, and needed,
heirs. No matter how they longed to put the past behind them,
its scars condemned her to a future as his lover instead of as his
wife.

Irony weighed heavily in her tone when she answered
wearily, "You don't know what you ask, Devon. Please, don't
speak to me of marriage again." She threw the covers back and
began to rise, but he was on her in a flash.

He pushed her flat on the bed. "If you want to punish me a
little, I grant you the right, but please, select another way."

Unshed tears glittered in her eyes. "How about this? You
offer me marriage because that's your best chance to hold me.
You still have reservations about my background; you just
can't help yourself."

His jaw flexed, then became rock hard. "This time, you do
me an injustice. I'm honored at your love, Katrina. I'll shout
my joy at our union from the church steeple at noon, if you'll
let me."

Each word hammered at Katrina. She'd resigned herself to
having only part of him. Now he offered all, unaware that she
no longer had power to accept. Oh God, if he only knew that
his own past mistakes kept him now from his heart's desire.
Some might see a rough justice in the situation, but Katrina
was too miserable to feel vindicated. But even to make him
understand, she could not be so vile as to tell him the truth. She

felt sobs building in her chest and knew she had to get away.

One answer, however, he owed her. He had changed, yes. But how much?

The words came of their own accord. "Very well, then answer me truly: Do you as gladly embrace the thought of siring your only heirs on me?" When his hands faltered, she sneered. "I thought not. How horrid if my peasant blood should dilute your blue and produce idiot offspring." She tried to rise, but he held her shoulders down, his grip strong and certain again.

"The lessons of a lifetime take long to overcome, Katrina. *You* tell *me* true: Do you really feel no guilt for what we did an hour past?" When her gaze flickered away, he sighed. "I thought not. Yet the remedy for your uncertainty is within your grasp. Sanctify our bedding with a wedding."

When she shook her head violently and cried, "I cannot! Don't ask me again!" his grip tightened enough to hurt.

His breath whistled through his teeth, then his hands gentled. "Katrina mina, don't do this to us. We've suffered too much to cast each other away now out of cowardice. I have fears I cannot calm despite myself, I admit, but I yearn to marry you anyway. Doesn't that tell you how much you mean to me?" When she still wouldn't look at him, his touch wandered. He stroked her nakedness from shoulder to ankle, then settled one big hand over her abdomen.

"You, too, have one irrefutable way to put me in my place: Prove me wrong." He stroked her quivering stomach. "We may have conceived my heir this very night. How royally you shall mock me on the day you bring him forth, lusty and true as you are yourself."

She gave a tortured sob and flung his hands away. He sat back on his heels and shook his dazed head. This could not be. Kat wasn't teasing him now. She was in deadly earnest, and so eager to get away from him that she hadn't even noticed he'd had her bodice mended. He clutched the bedcover so hard that the satin tore, but he could master neither his surging pain, nor his anger. He uncoiled his long length from the bed, feeling like a whip poised to strike.

When she was fully dressed, she ran for the door—and froze, for he blocked her path. He knew his grim purpose was bare for her to read, but he couldn't let her leave. Not now. Not ever. Still, his gut twisted at the fear in her face. He longed to see only happiness in her eyes, but if she cast it away so rashly, this time she had only herself to blame.

The bitter irony of the situation was not lost on him. Had he made this offer two years ago, she'd have accepted gladly. Now, when he was ready, even eager, and a better man for it, she refused him. What had happened in the interim to change her mind? Something drastic. Something she'd hinted at before. This time he couldn't allow her reticence, for the stakes were too high: their future.

He took a deep, calming breath. "Katrina, you've no reason to be afraid of me. I'll let you leave, for now, but first I want some answers. Why will you not wed me?"

She stared at the wall and didn't answer.

His level tone grew rough. "Damn you, you'll not leave my house until I know why." When she only bent her head and rubbed her elbows, he leaped across the small gap between them and took her shoulders in his hands. "Something happened to you two years ago to set you against me. Something . . . awful."

Her head reared back. "How do you know? Did Billy—" She bit her lip.

His eyes narrowed. "No, Billy didn't. But he will, if you won't. Wouldn't you rather I heard it from you?"

"Heard what? I assure you I've nothing to hide—"

"Too late, my dear. You're not a good liar." When her mouth tightened stubbornly, he let her go in disgust. Had she been playing with him all along, to get her vengeance on him? If so, he'd not let her see the bang-up job she'd done. He felt as if she'd ripped his heart out to tromp on it.

Tonelessly, he said, "Very well. Be mysterious. I hope your secrets whisper to you sweetly in your bed at night." He unlocked the door and held it open for her. "Leave me."

As she started for the door inspiration struck. "You shouldn't be privy to my little chat with Billy. He wouldn't want you to witness his beating."

She stopped dead. "You wouldn't!"

"You think not?" He raised a quizzical eyebrow. "You know my sobriquet, Kat. You've used it often enough." He turned as if to exit.

She rushed forward and grabbed his arm. "No, Devon, he kept his peace for your own good!"

That did it. He rounded on her and shoved her back against the wall, pushing her flat with his own body. "For *my* good? It's for *my* good that the only woman I've ever cared about won't accept my hand? It was for *my* good that my servant— no, my friend—kept secret information so vital to my future? If he's known what happened to you for two years, he should have told me. Perhaps I could have helped you. . . ." His tirade trailed away at her ugly little gurgle.

It was a combination of a whimper and a laugh, and the desolation in it sent a shiver up his spine. He braced himself.

"Helped me? Dear God, that's rich. It's because of you that I almost died." She shoved him away and stood straight. "You want to know what happened to me, Devon? Very well. Why should you not share the burden, especially as your own past actions have condemned our future."

Hectic color burned in her cheeks. She wanted to slap that blank look off his face. He'd no right to arouse the painful memories she'd labored so hard to forget. "The night I left you I was taken to a brothel. You know that, I suspect. Billy told me you tried to find me." He nodded. "It's as well you didn't. You'd not have arrived in time, and I . . . wouldn't have wanted you to see me that way. At that moment I think I truly hated you."

He shook his head in denial, croaking, "No, please, you weren't . . . I know Sutterfield didn't . . . Who?"

Her laugh was bitter. "No, it wasn't that. None has had me save you." When his broad shoulders slumped in relief, her mouth twisted. "But there are worse things. Like—"

Her words were cut off by the shattering of glass. Shards splattered inward from the broken window, barely missing them. A deep voice Katrina recognized called from outside, "Come out, yer bloody worship. Yer neighbors wish to make yer acquaintance." Loud, drunken laughter greeted this sally.

Devon stared dumbly at the rock that had flown into the room. Katrina blinked. Her transition from fury to fear was slow, but she'd barely put thought to action before she'd grabbed her shawl and flown out the door. She had to stop them!

Briefly, Devon teetered in shock, then he bolted after her. Billy was at the door before them. Through the front windows they caught the glimmer of torches against the brightening sky.

When Katrina reached for the door handle, Billy grabbed her arm. "They've been drinkin', lass. It's not safe for ye now. . . ." He trailed off, but his look at Devon spoke loud enough.

"A fallen woman I may be, but some of these men are my friends. And they'll listen to me before they will to you or Devon." Katrina shook him off and opened the door.

Devon erupted into the foyer, crying, "Stop her, Billy!" Billy grabbed for her, but Katrina was already out the door.

The laughter stopped. Silence descended, then one voice shouted, "Whore!" and another, "Allus knew 'ee was nothen' but a fancy woman!"

Katrina's face didn't show her pain. She drew her shawl close and stood tall, there on the doorstep, the rising sun illuminating the dishabille of a woman who had been loved long and well.

She stopped another comment cold with a disdainful, "Whore I may be, but at least I don't threaten the innocent with violence." Her gaze slipped over the crowd. Jack, as usual, was the ringleader, backed up by Davie and Paulie. But she also saw the miners who'd carried John's litter, and others she knew. Her gaze slipped over a silent figure in the back, then paused. Dear God, even Will had come. She couldn't see his face clearly, but even at this distance she felt his silent scorn.

Jack snorted. "Innocent? Ha, that's a laugh. If his lordship's so bloody pure, why's he closin' down the mine until he can bring in foreigners from Anglesey?"

"What are you talking about? Carrington owns the mine—"

"Not no more he don't. Told me hisself he sold it to yer fancy earl." Angry mutters rippled through the men. Several brandished torches and clubs as Devon exited to stand behind Katrina.

"Get back, Devon," Katrina warned over her shoulder.

"Shut up, you foolish woman," he hissed back, "and let me handle this. You're so much in a pother that you can't even please yourself."

Stung, Katrina snapped her head back around. Very well. Let the idiot get his head bashed in, or worse. Perhaps it would do him good.

"As you're all aware, my onetime friend Phillip Carrington would say anything to get his revenge on me for our, er, contretemps earlier." Devon pushed Katrina aside and stood casually, one hand propped on his hip, apparently not one whit disturbed that he faced a mob in a dressing gown.

"Fancy words don't change the facts," Davie growled. "Now, thes es your last chance—"

"And it may be yours as well." Devon scanned the crowd, letting them wonder at what he meant. When they were muttering again, he added, "Why in Hades do you think I'd buy a mine only to close it down? Or go to the expense of importing workers when I have such experienced help close at hand?"

There was a general shrugging at this. "Gentry don't have the sense God give a goose," Jack finally threw back.

"Brilliant deduction, Hennessy—if you substitute the word *woman* for *gentry*." Devon's gaze slipped to the woman at his side. His witticism surprised a few appreciative chuckles from the men, but Katrina bridled. Devon clasped the back of her neck when she opened her mouth. Her lips snapped shut and tightened.

"In a sense, however, your information is partly correct. I do intend to close the mine."

"See? I told ye all," Jack crowed. He came forward, a club clutched in his hand, but stopped dead at Devon's next loud comment.

"I'll close the mine only long enough to install a new pumping system. I've already sent for one of Watt's best engineers." Devon leaned casually back against the door frame and looked over the stunned faces.

"But . . . why?" one of the miners asked.

"Why, for the profit of us all. Your own practical miners have convinced me that there are rich ores lying in wait for us, if we only go deeper. When it's installed, I'll call you all back. You'll have interim wages until then."

Profit. That, at least, made sense. "Thank the Lord," one man was heard to mutter. And from another, respectfully this time, "Thank 'ee, your lordshep." Relief settled over other tough faces. One man threw his club aside, then another. They began to drift away, until soon only Jack, Davie, Paulie, and Will were left.

"Ye may have fooled these slowtops," Jack growled, "but I don't trust ye. Not one bit. Ye've got another reason."

"Of course he does." Will spoke for the first time. He nodded at Katrina. But his gaze was not admiring, or even grateful.

It required all of Katrina's willpower not to bow her head, but somehow she met Will's cold blue eyes. She flinched when Devon's arm dropped about her shoulders.

"She's partly the reason," Devon agreed. He lifted her left hand and turned it so the sun struck off the ring. "You can be the first to wish us happy, gentlemen. A mine makes a lavish wedding gift, wouldn't you say?"

Katrina started to deny it, but Will said rapidly, "Congratulations, Katrina." And, with erect dignity, he turned and walked away.

"Will, wait!" Katrina called, but he ignored her. She threw Devon's arm off her shoulders. "You had no right! You know I refused you." She bit back more when she realized they had an avid audience.

"We'll settle our little quarrel later, pet," Devon said mildly, trying to hustle her back inside.

Nothing changed, it seemed. Katrina was too raw, too hurt, to ponder his motivation in buying the mine. Had he truly intended it as a wedding gift? Pain washed through her anew. She rubbed at her temples, but clear thought was beyond her. Rage dulled the ache, so she deliberately told herself the mine was only another extravagant attempt at bribery. Even now, when he claimed to love her, he made her feel like bartered goods before these men she had to work with.

She gave him a look that would have made Medusa envious. Her answer was wordless but explicit. She ripped the ring off her finger and threw it at his broad chest. It bounced and clattered against the drive.

She walked down the steps, passed Davie, Paulie, and Jack, and started for home. Jack, with a mocking look at Devon, followed her and engaged her in conversation. The other two scurried after them.

Devon caught, "I always knew ye was a sensible lass. We're off tonight. Meet at the usual place at eleven. . . ." Then he could hear no more, but he'd heard enough to be suspicious. He'd be outside the Tonkin cottage at ten, by George. If he had to strip Katrina bare, literally and figuratively, to find out all her secrets, he would do so.

Fists clenched at his sides, Devon watched Katrina walk away. *Flee, my darling, while you may. I'll have you in my house, where you belong, soon enough. Once you're in my bed, pregnant with my child, you'll not be able to deny me, or yourself, any longer.* He picked up the ring, wheeled, and stalked back into the house.

Billy had sensibly made himself scarce, but he also knew better then to ignore that angry bellow.

"Billy, get your ass down here. Now!" Billy made a wry face, buttoned his shirt, stamped on his boots, and joined Devon in the study.

A snifter of brandy sloshed in one hand as Devon prowled up and down. Billy knew that look, and he paused warily inside the door.

Devon turned on him. "I want to know what the hell happened to Katrina in that brothel and why in bloody blazes you haven't told me long before now." Devon took a big gulp of brandy. His eyes, steady on Billy's face, caught the sunlight.

A captured lion's eyes he'd seen at a London freak show had glowed in just that savage way, Billy reflected. The big cat had been so frustrated at his imprisonment that he'd lashed out at anything unwary enough to get in his path. Billy stifled the urge to run a finger about his tight collar. The easiest thing to do, of course, would be to give Devon what he wanted. But how would the girl feel about that? Billy knew how persuasive Devon could be. If she still hadn't told him the truth, then Katrina was adamant that he not know. Billy couldn't betray that trust, not when Katrina's happiness was entwined with Devon's. He didn't say a word, though he took the precaution of putting a couch between him and his friend.

Devon flung the glass of brandy at him. "Answer me, you traitorous dog!"

Billy ducked, but the glass shattered on the wall behind him and showered his clean clothes with brandy. His slower temper began to simmer. "Aye, and so have ye treated me—pat me on the head when ye're happy, kick me when ye're mad." Billy propped his fists on his hips. "Well, ye got no one to blame for the mess ye're in save yer own self, Devon Cavanaugh."

With a garbled "Aagh!" Devon launched himself over the couch. Billy caught him in a bear hug and squeezed, but Devon jammed him in the ribs with an elbow. Billy dropped him. He barely dodged Devon's fist, and he smiled grimly when Devon hit the wall instead.

Cursing, Devon cradled his bruised knuckles in his other hand. When he looked at Billy again, Billy braced himself.

Then, strangely, Devon collapsed like a burned soufflé. His legs buckled. He slid down the wall to rest his elbows on his knees, his head in his hands. His voice muffled, he said, "Forgive me, Billy. I know you'd never betray me. It . . . just hurts so bad. She won't wed me, Billy. And she won't even tell me why. If you won't tell me either, what in hell am I to do?"

So that was it. Billy slumped next to his friend. He asked cautiously, "What exactly did she say?"

"She said some crazy nonsense about my past condemning our future. That she almost died because of me." When Billy didn't answer, Devon lifted his head. There was grim understanding in Billy's face instead of mystification. He clutched Billy's arm.

"If you understand what she meant, in the name of God tell me!"

"Poor wee lass," Billy whispered, shaking his head. The sorrowful sympathy in his voice made Devon flinch.

"If she meant what I think, Devon, she probably will never marry ye now," he murmured. When Devon shook his head in violent denial, Billy said even more quietly, "And if she ever does decide to tell ye what happened, lad, ye may wish ye'd never asked." He patted his shoulder, rose, and exited.

Devon stayed where he was, Billy's warning ringing in his ears. He had found Billy to be right in his predictions more often than not, but this time, he vowed, Billy was wrong. But uncertainty, all the more troubling for its rarity, haunted him as he ascended the stairs to dress warmly for the eventful night.

Unbidden, but somehow natural, a prayer came to his lips. The words were a bit rusty and garbled, but heartfelt. If the Bible were true, then God was always overjoyed to welcome a sinner back to the fold. Then surely He wouldn't be so cruel as to take from him the woman who had led him there. . . .

Chapter Thirteen

THE CLIFF TOWERED above her, a dark challenge that would have intimidated her had she been less tired. As she carefully matched her steps to Davie's Katrina reflected that an aching body helped soothe an aching heart. The crossing this time had been shorter because their landing on French soil had been closer, but lack of sleep and low spirits had left her exhausted. Too tired to brood over her bitter parting from Devon. He'd be back, she knew, when no flying rock would deliver her from explaining. Next time, however, she'd not be so vulnerable. He had her refusal now, and she'd not let herself get so emotional again. Stolen passion would have to be enough. For both of them.

Desolation at the thought made her clumsy. Her foot slipped on the crumbling ledge. One hand lost its grip. The sea crashed into the rocks far below, yawning black and hungry at her feet. For an instant she teetered literally on the edge of disaster, but then Davie grabbed her skirts, steadying her long enough for her to plant both feet again. She leaned her cheek against the cold, wet cliff face, almost dizzy with relief. Her harsh breathing disguised the muffled curse on the path a short distance behind her.

When she was composed, she said, "Thank you, Davie. I'm fine now. Though why you and Jack insist that I come along—"

"Jack says the letter he wants 'ee to translate es en the caave."

Why hadn't Jack brought the letter with him on the crossing? Katrina wondered irritably, following Davie again. In fact she didn't understand why Jack had wanted her along on this trip. Her interpretation skills had not been needed, for they'd used their usual contact and agreed on the rate in advance. Maybe Jack had feared complications would arise.

Had she been less tired, the explanation wouldn't have satisfied her, but now all she wanted was her bed. The sooner the better. Glowing light and warmth split the sheer wall, and gladly Katrina followed Davie inside the cave. Jack awaited, his hands held out over a blazing fire. He turned to meet them, his body backlit, his features indistinct against the brightness.

Katrina sat down on a rocky shelf to catch her breath. She saw a lone brandy tub and several bolts of cloth, plus some burlap sacks that she assumed held tea. She frowned. If this was one of their safest hideaways, as Davie had told her, where was all the contraband?

Her share from the last run had been considerably smaller than Davie had estimated, as had Jimmy's. With two runs so close together this cave should be filled with contraband. Of course transporting fragile goods here would not be practical, but surely this would be a good place to store brandy and cloth.

Her instincts had been right, she feared. She put her hand in her cloak pocket, patting the tiny, reassuring crackle of paper. While the others had loaded the goods, she'd listed each item: five crates of rare French champagne and four crates of Limoges ware. If someone was stashing part of their haul for his own use, then she'd know soon enough. This time she was armed with numbers.

As Davie had kept a lookout on the French shore while the others loaded, Katrina had approached him and asked casually, "Why did we make a run so soon for such a small load?"

He'd shrugged, as if uncertain himself, then answered, "We rarely gets a chance at champaagne. Et fetches a dear price, as do the china."

"How much?" When Davie gave her a hard look in answer, Katrina pointed out, "I only ask because your last estimate of my share was too high. I'd like a reasonable guess as to what I'll make this time."

Davie sent a glance at Jack, then answered rapidly, "We usually gets about five pounds a crate for the wine, and twelve for each set of dishes." And he'd hurried back to help his friends, as if regretting his loose tongue. Only Davie, Jack,

Paulie, and two others had participated tonight because the trade had been so small.

Now, while she rested, Katrina made some rapid calculations. Davie had told her that the man who distributed their haul usually took about half of the profit for him and his men. That meant that she and the others stood to make less than six pounds each.

Why risk a crossing with so little return? So soon after the last one? Katrina lifted her head to ask Jack, but something in his posture gave her pause. Instead she cleared her throat. "I'm waiting, Jack. Give me the letter and I'll read it to you. Who is it from?"

"I'll satisfy ye soon enough," Jack rumbled. He jerked his head at Davie. "This be a private matter, man. Go on with ye. I'll see the lassie home."

Katrina's peculiar unease deepened. She noticed a pile of blankets spread by the fire, and suddenly Jack's odd behavior made sense. She sent a desperate look at Davie. The Cornishman was already eyeing his friend suspiciously.

Hoping she was wrong, she suggested, "If it's so private, I'll tell you its contents quietly." She rose, but stopped at Jack's bark of laughter.

" 'Tis just as I would have it, girl—ye whisperin' sweetly in me ear." Jack came forward until the torches at the cave entrance lit his features.

"Oh God, not again," Katrina muttered wearily. She backed away and looked about for a weapon, uncertain of where Davie's allegiance lay.

Perhaps Davie wondered that himself, for he looked from Jack's sharp, hungry features to Katrina's pale ones. He hesitated, then moved to block Jack's path.

"No, Jack, leave her be. Ee can't tell me *he* wanted ee to try this." Davie caught his friend's muscular arm.

"Ah, he don't scare me none. I'm only taken' what he wants, what she gives to her fancy swell. Ye can share, after." Jack shook him off and strode toward Katrina.

Katrina ran for the entrance, but a strong arm caught her dress and hauled her up short. She whirled, her hands bunched into fists, but found she didn't have to use them. Davie, looking pained but resigned, tapped his friend on the head with a piece of firewood. Jack blinked and shook his head, then released Katrina.

Davie backed a pace. "That's just a warning, man. Don't maake me do more."

"Since when did ye become her protector, Davie? Or has she give ye what I wants?" Jack stalked after his onetime friend, his features set with a different kind of lust.

Another long arm snaked around Katrina out of the darkness as she inched toward the entrance. She drew breath to scream, but a familiar voice whispered fiercely, "Come along, you foolish chit, while you still can." She sent a last look at Davie's sweating face, then let Devon push her in front of him up the path.

They'd gone a bare ten feet when an angry bellow echoed from the cave. "Stop this nonsense, man, she's gettin' away!"

"Let her go—" A crack cut Davie's words off, then heavy boots pounded after them.

They hurried, but too much haste was dangerous in the thickening fog. Apparently Jack could see them. His feet sure from long practice, he quickly closed the gap.

Devon glanced over his shoulder, then bit off, "Go on. I'm going to hold him here. Run!" And he braced himself on the narrow ledge.

The fog had grown too thick for Devon to see what lay far beneath their feet, but Katrina knew. Sharp rocks and gravity were indifferent to good and evil. The picture of Devon lying broken like a porcelain knight was too vivid. She had to do something! She looked desperately around. Her gaze landed on the ledge they'd just passed. It was crumbling slightly at the spot where she'd slipped on the climb up.

Katrina gestured just past Devon's feet. "Look! Stomp your feet!" Devon spared her a furious look for disobeying him, but he held tightly to the cliff, lifted one strong leg, and slammed down with all his might on the ledge. It loosened, rock flakes drifting downward.

"Go on, dammit!" he ordered, his boot pounding rhythmically. More sediment floated away, then one chunk of rock broke loose, and another. With a crunching sound that echoed oddly in the muffling fog, the ledge gave way just as Hennessy rounded the corner.

Simultaneously, Devon's right foot lost its purchase. His arms flailed. He grabbed at the cliff, missed. Her heart leaping in terror, Katrina reached for him. God, he was heavy. For an instant his weight pulled her sideways. Then, bracing her legs, she swiveled from the hips and heaved on his left arm, pulling him back to safety.

She rested her cheek against his damp jacket, weak with relief. Then, her wits returning, she released him to hurry onward. After a glare at Hennessy he followed.

"Ye lily-livered coward. Why don't ye stay and fight like a man?" Jack railed. He eyed the three-foot gap in the ledge. The distance wasn't far, but the path was slippery in the fog, and the ledge was narrow at that point. . . .

"Come on, Jack. Prove your own bravery," Devon jeered. "I'll gladly fight you like a man when we reach solid ground."

Jack hesitated, then shook his fist at them. "That time's comin', fancy pants." He turned and sidestepped back to the cavern.

"Probably to get a rope," Katrina said, her voice quivering with laughter. Her jubilance died when Devon sent her a look of unadulterated fury.

They made the rest of the descent in silence. When they reached terra firma again, Katrina turned toward the cottage, but Devon hauled her up short.

"Not so fast. You've some explaining to do." He dragged her, protesting, to the closed carriage that was hidden some distance past the beach in a clump of tall gorse.

"You were there all along?" Katrina squeaked.

"I saw the whole sorry spectacle. I followed you from the cottage, then went and fetched my coachman while you were crossing in case we needed to get away quickly."

Frowningly, she digested this. Love didn't make her an imbecile who needed minding. Or did it? His next words took some of the sting away.

"Take me to the Tonkin cottage, Henry," Devon ordered, vaulting lightly into the coach after lifting Katrina inside.

He lit the interior lantern, then jerked the curtains across the windows. Her relieved sigh only seemed to make him angrier. He flung a warm lap robe about her shoulders and drew it tight. He muttered through his teeth, "Don't be too premature, my girl. If I don't get the answers I want, I may still kidnap you again and take you back to my house, where you belong.'' His hands dropped away, but he stayed poised on the seat edge so he could watch her face.

Sullenly Katrina settled into her cocoon. She stared over his shoulder, determined not to say a word.

''I'll tolerate no more secrets 'tween us. Tell me why in the bloody hell you've taken it into your beetle brain to become a smuggler.'' When he didn't get a flicker of an eyelash in response, he added languidly, ''It's a crime in England, m'dear.'' He patted her head.

That deliberate condescension did the trick. She threw his hands off and exploded. ''*You* dare to lecture *me*? That's a fine turn of events. Demon Devon moralizing. I'd laugh if I didn't want to slap you senseless so badly.''

His handsome face lowered. ''Go ahead, if it will make you listen to reason.'' All his fears for her were bare in his pleading eyes.

Her anger collapsed, leaving her as lifeless as a broken fan. ''You don't understand, Devon. Never can, really, I suppose, through no fault of your own. Laws are made by men like you who know nothing of hunger. Only those like the Tonkins suffer for it. Yet if you check your own cellars, you'll doubtless find a bottle of brandy or two.''

He made an impatient gesture. ''You and the Tonkins won't starve. I won't allow it—''

Anger stirred again. She sat upright. ''How generous of you!'' She bobbed her head. ''Thank ye, me lud. Such alms ye give to us poor folk—''

He caught her arms and hauled her to his chest. Neither of them noticed as the carriage jolted to a stop. ''Yes, I want to be generous to you. Is offering you all my worldly goods, legally and morally, not enough?''

''No, it isn't enough!'' Katrina shouted. When he flinched and let her go, she sighed and caught his strong face between her hands. ''Please, try to understand. I don't want your largess, I want your love; I don't want your refuge, I want your respect. And if I let you keep me, I'll have neither.''

Devon hauled her close again and groaned, ''Ah Kat, I do

respect you, and you know I love you. Why, why won't you marry me?''

A soft finger covered his lips. ''Shhh. Let's not argue anymore. It serves no purpose, because I have no choice. Smuggling is the only work I could find.''

''You could have been raped tonight.''

There, it was out in the open.

She shivered. ''I know. But Davie would have saved me, even if you hadn't come along. I have friends among the smugglers, as well as foes.''

''Someday he may not be there. What do you plan to do about it?'' He eyed her hopefully, but instead of giving him the words he obviously wanted, she gently pushed him away.

''Why, I'm going to learn to shoot.'' She threw off the robes and reached for the carriage door.

His mouth gaped, then he sputtered, ''Y-you twitter-witted . . . female!'' He caught her hand. ''What do you think that bastard will do if you pull a gun on him?''

''Leave me be, or learn how a sieve feels.'' She pulled her hand away, shoved open the carriage door, and jumped down.

The bravado only seemed to make him angrier. He leaped down after her and uttered coldly, ''Very well, do as you must, as shall I. The next time I see Hennessy, I'll get him to tell me how a sieve feels.'' When her eyes leaped to his face, he smiled nastily. ''To satisfy your curiosity, of course. Anything to please a lady.''

This time *she* hurried after *him,* catching his arm as he reached for the carriage door. ''Devon, you mustn't. Jack has some prominence in the parish. If you kill him, others will resent you even more than they do now.''

''And do you think they'll hail you if you plug him full of holes?''

''No, perhaps not, but they'll grant me the right to protect myself.''

''And they'll grant me the right to protect my woman.'' He pulled his hand free to brush her straggling hair out of her eyes. ''Deny that publicly all you want, Katrina mina. The only person who matters knows the truth. *You* know you're mine.'' He shoved her cloak aside to plant his hand over her heart. When that contrary organ leaped against his palm, he smiled.

Slowly, sensually, he whispered, "Sleep. Dream of me. I'll be back in the morning. I want you to accompany me when I visit some of the miners."

After a quick kiss he leaped into his carriage with that supple grace he used to such effect in lovemaking. "Take us home, Henry."

Katrina snapped smartly about, ignoring his wave, and marched up to the attic, her cheeks burning. "Who does he think he is to order me about? I should be thankful I can't wed him. What a martinet he'd make as a husband." She barely suppressed the urge to slam the door behind her, even angrier at the knowledge that she was prevaricating to appease her own longings. She threw off her damp clothes, put on her most virginal nightgown—fat lot of good that did her, she thought tartly—and drew the covers up to her chin.

Humor came to her rescue when Ellie turned over and mumbled, "Billy." She subsided with a sigh, cradling her cheek against her palm as if recalling the big hand that had lately rested there.

Katrina smothered a giggle. Featherbrained peahens, they were, the both of them, dazzled by two strutting males who were better at preening than they were at nest making. With a wistful sigh she drifted off to sleep. In her dreams, however, when Devon came to her as he'd promised, he wore a lush, shiny white coat and sported a long, whorled horn. She rode his broad back, her hands tangled in his thick mane, as he guided her through a gloomy thicket of thorns into a fertile valley where children gamboled. . . .

The next morning Katrina felt more rested than she had in years. She stretched, still smiling at her lovely dream.

Ellie sank to the cot beside her. "Oh Katrina, I'm so glad you're awake. I need to talk to you."

Katrina sat up and brushed away the tear staining Ellie's cheek. "What's amiss?"

Worrying at her gown, Ellie blurted, "Billy wants me to wed him."

"That's wonderful! But . . . why are you crying, then? You love him, don't you?"

A miserable nod answered her, then Ellie took Katrina's hands and squeezed so hard that Katrina winced.

"Oh, sorry." Ellie dropped her hands and rose to pace the tiny space between the cots. She paused to stare out the window. "I . . . don't want to leave Cornwall, you see."

Katrina did see, at last. Angry at her own obtuseness, she leaped out of bed and clasped her arm about her friend's trembling shoulders. "Have you asked him to stay?"

"Of course. He says he goes wherever his lordship goes." Ellie whirled to meet her friend's eyes. She said more softly, "Billy thinks if you wed the earl that he'll stay in Cornwall."

Katrina flushed and turned away. How could she be responsible for Ellie's future, too? Katrina had never been one to rail at an unkind fate, but she was tempted to lift her fists to the sky and curse. If she wed Devon now, she'd secure Ellie's happiness but sacrifice theirs. She could not wed Devon under false pretenses; he'd never forgive her.

Yet if she somehow found the courage to tell him the truth, he'd probably withdraw his proposal. He had more than his own desires to think of. He might be willing to accept her background. If, by some miracle, he didn't care that she was . . . barren, then it was up to her to do the right thing. Devon would have beautiful children.

By someone else.

Clasping her arms about her aching stomach, Katrina turned to face Ellie. "I can't wed him, Ellie. Even for you. I'm . . . sorry." She dressed and fled down the stairs, her eyes burning almost as much as her heart.

She took a deep, composing breath when Will rose from his position at the table to greet her.

"Hello, Katrina," he said gravely.

"Hello, Will. It's good to see you." She smiled in genuine pleasure. "Where have you been?"

"It's good to see you, too. I've been . . . about. Just very busy."

"Has there been another accident?" Katrina sat down next to John and picked up her fork. She wondered at the grim set of his mouth as he watched the conversation. What was wrong?

"No, no. Nothing like that. In fact I shouldn't be here now. I just wanted to see you."

Katrina's throat tightened at the huskiness in his voice. Before she could compose a reply, Will sighed heavily and rose.

"Duty calls. Thanks for the meal, John."

John nodded curtly. "Duty, eh?"

Will wheeled smartly about and rapped over his shoulder, "Yes, duty. Good day to you both." He stalked out, slamming the door.

Slowly, Katrina set down her fork. "Why are you angry with Will, John? Is that why he's been by so seldom of late?"

John answered noncommittally, "I fear he has been frightfully busy."

Katrina was still pondering the reply when Devon strode into the kitchen.

She glanced up at him, then hastily down, hoping he wouldn't see her red eyes. He quirked an eyebrow at John, who sat, one foot propped before him on a stool. John shrugged.

"Good morning, love." Heartily Devon bussed her cheek. She didn't even look up.

"John, I want to visit some of the miners today." Devon dropped next to Katrina, apparently unaware of her ill humor.

"That's a right good theng to do, lad." While Rachel fixed Devon two eggs John suggested which men would welcome a visit.

"I've brought baskets of victuals with me. Do you think they'll be insulted if I offer them?" Devon asked.

"Mayhaps they would have been before 'ee bought the mine, but now I thenk they'll taake et, and gladly," John answered.

"Good." Devon smiled his thanks at Rachel when she set his plate before him.

"Do you mean to tell me that John knew you'd bought the mine?" Katrina slammed her fork down on her plate.

"Why, yes. He and his practical miners are the ones who convinced me good ores lie undiscovered." Devon took a bite of egg.

Jimmy came in at that moment, yawning. He stopped when he saw Devon, then smiled hesitantly.

Devon nodded at him cordially. "Good morning, Jimmy. How are you this fine morning? I want to thank you for those wrestling holds you showed me. Wrestling is as much an art as pugilism, wouldn't you agree?'' He sat back and wiped his mouth. ''Thank you, Rachel, that was delicious.''

''That it 'tis. I hope I can one day be as good with my fives as you be.'' Jimmy sat down next to his father and grabbed an oatcake from the serving platter.

''Practice, my lad, practice. We'll have another bout again soon.''

Katrina followed this exchange sourly. Apparently Devon had seen members of the family during her absence, charming them with his usual ease. He seemed quite at home, and even Jimmy welcomed him. So easily had Devon won Jimmy's liking when it had taken her two years to earn more than surly looks from the boy. Boxing indeed! Somehow it had never occurred to her to challenge Jimmy to a fight, though in truth some of their arguments bordered on such. It only remained for Robert to skip into the room with his usual energy and hug his new friend.

When Robert did exactly that, Katrina ground her teeth in frustration. Casually, Devon discussed the weather, the bonfire and the fair that followed it, and even the latest news from the former colonies. With every word Katrina's sense of betrayal grew. This was her family. She'd labored hard to become part of it. What right had Devon to come along and in a few short weeks gain such esteem? Once he held the Tonkins' regard, it would be even more difficult for her to refuse him. Temptation was a sore enough trial without this.

Pain made a dyspeptic breakfast partner. Katrina shoved back her plate and snapped, ''If we're to visit many homes today, we'd best be off.'' She rose and stomped toward the front door.

She didn't hear Devon's comment, but apparently the Tonkins thought him witty. Their laughter only made her isolation more acute. Katrina grabbed her shawl and hurried outside.

The coachman was helping her into the carriage when Devon caught up with her. ''Here, Henry, I'll do that.''

Devon lifted her by the waist into the carriage, then vaulted up beside her. Immediately she swiveled and sat on the opposite seat. Devon sighed. "Out with it, Kat. What are you mad about now?"

Her mouth quivered, then tightened. "Nothing. Where do we go first?"

"John suggested the Peterses' cottage. Would you give Henry directions?"

After she'd done so, she whisked the curtain aside and stared out.

"It's about the mine, isn't it? You think I should have told you."

"Well, shouldn't you? Do you think I like being treated like an investment? Maybe you should reconsider, Devon. Perhaps you're throwing good money after bad." Katrina clasped her hands tightly in her lap, but she was glad the words were out.

Devon leaned forward and covered her hands with one of his. "Katrina, I admit I decided to buy the mine partly in hopes of softening you toward me, but now I truly want to make a go of it for my own reasons. I've been down into both my mines; I've seen the conditions in which the men work. Poor lighting, inadequate ventilation, clammy moisture that must be hard on their lungs—it's hardly any wonder so many miners die young. There's a purely practical side in that healthy, safe workers will be more productive, but believe it or not, I want to relieve some of their burden. Can't you grant me enough humanity to believe that?"

Slowly Katrina lifted her eyes to his. That swirling amber pattern of brown mixed with gold never failed to move her. Aye, she believed him. Love swelled her heart, pushing anger out. This man was still Demon Devon, hot-tempered, autocratic, and selfish. The past two years had changed him, too. He'd also become a true peer of the realm: setting a responsible, generous example as a leader of English society. Her throat was too thick for a response.

When she didn't answer, Devon moved next to her and drew her into his arms. "Ah, Katrina mina, tell me what's amiss." Tenderly he tilted her head back against his shoulder.

The love in his eyes hurt too much. She turned her cheek into his coat and sniffed his familiar, comforting aroma of fine linen, brandy, and man. How much easier it would be to reject the old Devon. In one way, however, he was still the man who'd driven her away. She tried to whip up bolstering ire by recalling their fight of two nights ago. He still wanted perfect heirs. He'd admitted as much. Only because he loved her was he willing to accept her as the mother of his children. She should be grateful, really, that she was barren. Otherwise she would marry him—and feel like a brood mare expected to deliver a champion. Would they shoot her if she didn't?

Abruptly she pulled away just as the carriage jerked to a stop. "Now's not the time to discuss this, Devon."

"Very well. When?"

Katrina pretended not to hear as she shoved the door open and jumped to the ground. She pinned on a bright smile, accepted a basket from Henry, and knocked on the Peterses' door. The upper half of the door swung outward, and she had to hasten back, bumping into Devon. He steadied her with his hands on her shoulders.

Jem Peters himself stood there, blinking at the bright sunlight. "Good mornen'." He looked from Katrina to Devon and back. "And what brengs 'ee here?"

Katrina suspected the picture they made: lord and lady visiting the poor. The image was as distasteful to her as it must be to Jem. "Why, I want to see your lovely wife. Rachel sends a jar of her peach preserves." Katrina held up the basket, knowing that Rachel had contributed a jar for each parcel.

Jem opened the door and stood aside. "That's right neighborly of 'ee."

Sighing in relief, Katrina went into the two-room cottage that was divided into sleeping and living quarters by a partition. It was sparsely furnished with homemade furniture, and the Peterses had so many children that the left side seemed lined wall to wall with pallets.

Devon glanced at the pallets and looked around. Only one child was present, a toddler boy. Devon sat where Peters indicated, in a rickety wing chair with frayed upholstery. Devon shifted, looking ill at ease on what was obviously the Peterses' best piece of furniture.

While Katrina helped Mrs. Peters put the food away Devon said, "I need your help, Peters. John Tonkin tells me you handle supplies for the mine."

Peters nodded guardedly. "So it be true. 'Ee did buy the mine."

"Yes. Can you give me a list of the most urgent needs? I want to make an order right away so we are fully supplied once the new pumping system is installed."

"That's easy enough done." Peters unbent enough to smile dryly. "Order everythin' and 'ee not be far wrong. Rope, candles, tools, fuel, timbers—that be just a start."

"Somehow I'm not surprised. Phillip Carrington has certainly changed a lot since I knew him at Oxford." Devon continued to discuss the mine with Peters, apparently unaware of the sharp look Katrina sent him.

Did Devon suspect what else Carrington was involved in? Or was she jumping to conclusions at an innocent remark? Katrina resolved to question him. Surely few would know better than he if Phillip was capable of heading a smuggling ring.

At first, however, she had no opportunity. They left the cottage in a somber mood. Watching him, Katrina realized Devon was shocked at the poverty he'd witnessed. John, as headman, had a comfortable cottage compared with most.

"Where are all the children?" Devon asked bluntly as they lurched down the abominable road.

"Why, at work, of course."

"Of course," Devon echoed, wincing. "How old are they?"

"The youngest boy you saw, the eldest is ten. He usually works in dressing the ores, preparing them for stamping, but now that the mine is closed he's probably in the fields somewhere, as are the other children. Surviving here usually requires a family effort, Devon. The wages are low. Even in good times Jem probably only makes about thirty-five shillings a month."

Katrina watched Devon frown as he digested this. She wondered idly what he'd done as a ten-year-old. Probably studied and played.

Throughout that long day Katrina said little. She didn't need to. With every cottage they visited Devon became grimmer as he found that the Peterses lived in virtual luxury compared with some of the laborers. Many of the cottages were mere one-room huts with packed-dirt floors. Their owners were as proud as kings, however, and as often as not the huts were sparkling clean. Their hostesses, when not working, offered them refreshment varying from hoarded tea to water.

By the end of the day they were sloshing. As they left one tiny cottage Devon grimaced at her. "I'll float away if I have to drink another sip."

"They'd be insulted if we refused."

"I know. What do we have left?"

"We've only one basket left, and this one I packed myself. One of the women in the parish is recently widowed."

"What happened to her husband?"

"He died from lung consumption. She had a baby only a few months ago."

"How is she surviving?"

"She gets a widow's portion from the mining club, but it's not much."

They found Moll rocking her son before the fire. Her eldest girl let them in, nodding at them before returning to her chores. The baby cried, rooting at his mother's breast in frustration.

Moll looked up at Katrina, then blushed when she saw Devon. She hastily closed her gown.

Katrina hurried forward, the basket on one arm. "Don't be embarrassed, Moll. His lordship bought the bal and only wishes to see how you're doing."

Moll's big blue eyes filled with tears. "My melk dried up. What well I do?" She held out the bottle sitting beside her, which consisted of a jar and a soft hide nipple. "He won't drenk."

"Let me try. This is for you." Katrina traded the basket for the baby.

Moll shifted through the generous portions of meats, breads, and cheeses, sighing her relief. The warm smile she sent at Devon earned an uncertain smile in return. Devon shifted his feet.

Walking back and forth, Katrina cradled the dark-haired infant to her breast, humming a lullaby. Gradually, he quit crying and started nibbling on his tiny fist. "Have you a spoon?" Katrina whispered.

Moll gave her one. Katrina handed the bottle to Devon. "Take off the nipple." He did so, but his eyes never left the child, resting so quietly against Katrina's full bosom.

"Drizzle some of the milk into the spoon."

Again he obeyed.

"Now, hold it to his mouth." Katrina pulled the fist away, and when the tiny mouth opened to cry, Devon dribbled milk inside. The baby swallowed, then licked his lips.

"More," Katrina murmured.

Devon repeated the process several times. His face seemed unusually soft in the dim room. Was it a trick of the light? Katrina's humming tremored, then stopped as the inevitable comparison overwhelmed her. In another reality this might have been their child. She closed her eyes in pain, missing the arrested expression on Devon's face as he looked from her to the baby and back.

"She delivered hem, ded 'ee know?" Moll whispered over Devon's shoulder.

He turned in shock, taking away the spoon.

The infant began to cry, and Katrina rocked him in her arms, unable to hear the whispered exchange.

"Alone?" Devon asked.

"Aye, she came en a storm, and walked home en the dark. Ef she hadn't, I could have been dead." Moll nodded at Katrina's protective manner. "She vesets often. I thenks she almost weshes he be hers."

Katrina snatched the spoon away from Devon and wiggled it before his eyes. "Can't you hear him crying? Give him some more." She handed the spoon back.

When the baby calmed, Katrina relaxed. "Here, Moll, try the bottle again." Moll hurriedly attached the nipple and sat back down in her chair.

Before Katrina could give her the baby, Devon said, "Let me." Carefully he took the soft little bundle and held it as he'd seen Katrina do. He accepted the bottle from Moll and coaxed it into the rosebud mouth. With a greedy grunt the baby suckled. Moll got up and offered her chair, so Devon sat down.

"The milk must have been strange to him. He seems to like it well enough now," Devon murmured, his free hand stroking the downy head.

Katrina could see Devon's face clearly in the light from the window. She cupped her hand to her mouth, whirled, and ran.

Devon looked up at the anguished sound. He called her

name, but she ignored him. "He's a beautiful child," Devon told Moll, rising and handing the infant over. He started after Katrina, then paused.

"I've need of a cook, if you're interested. You could bring the children with you and keep them in the kitchen." Devon barely heard Moll's ecstatic acceptance as he hurried after Katrina.

He found her huddled in the carriage, sobbing her heart out. "My dear one, what's wrong? The child will be fine. Moll told me how you care for him since you delivered him." He tried to cradle her in his arms, but she pushed him away. He rapped on the carriage roof, and Henry urged the horses forward.

Crossing his arms over his chest, Devon forced himself to wait. But when they were almost at the Tonkin cottage and Katrina's tears didn't abate, he dropped his arms and leaned forward. "Katrina, please don't cry any longer, unless you want me to turn into a watering pot, too."

A distracted shake of her head was her only reply. She huddled deeper into her corner.

With a frustrated groan Devon hauled her, struggling, into his arms. "Enough!" He gave her a hard squeeze. "I can't make you tell me what's wrong, but I'd remind you that secrets do not make for wedded harmony. Let's get everything right and tight now."

They'd pulled to a stop at the cottage when Katrina finally gave a watery sniffle into her kerchief and propped her head back on Devon's shoulder. "You enjoyed holding the baby, didn't you?" Her voice was still thick with tears.

"Very much. But I enjoyed more watching you hold him." Devon rained gentle kisses on her brow and forehead. "You'll make a wonderful mother, Katrina mina." Katrina buried her face in his jacket and burst into tears again.

Blast it, what had he said? Devon wondered. He cradled her closer. "Katrina, stop this foolishness. If you're still worried that I don't want children on you, you're wrong. If I get such joy seeing you hold someone else's child, how do you think I'll feel when it's mine? Marry me soon so we can begin work in earnest on our heir."

The tears didn't seem to relieve her anguish, so Katrina bit her knuckles and literally forced them back. She took several shuddering breaths, then calmed. After rubbing her tears away with the heels of her hands, she looked up at him.

The mingled frustration, concern, and love in his eyes almost set her off again, but she gritted her teeth and asked steadily, "Are heirs so important to you then?"

"Of course. My title is one of the oldest in the land. It's my duty to my parents and to all those before them to see that it endures." When she couldn't hide a flinch, he frowned and trailed a fingertip around her cheekbones to wipe away the last of the tears. "If I die without issue, the title goes to a very remote cousin. The man's a sapskull and a wastrel. I shudder to think what he'd do to my lands." Devon did just that.

Now she knew. Despair almost overwhelmed Katrina. Tell him. Tell him now, and end this torment. Her mouth opened, but the words wouldn't come. She couldn't. Not yet. Dear God, forgive me, she prayed, but I can't lose him yet. Give me this summer, at least, to sustain me in all the lonely years ahead.

Her smile was as bright and false as a plug penny. "Well, you needn't worry about that. I'm sure you'll have many fine sons." She scooted off his lap and exited the carriage.

Devon followed more slowly, wondering at her pronoun selection, but she caught his hand and distracted him.

Her eyes were bright, her cheeks flushed. "Please, will you teach me to shoot? You teach *soo* well."

Devon sighed in relief and swatted her sassy rear. "It will be my pleasure, madam. Let's hope you learn as quickly here as you do in other, er, matters." He dropped a sly wink, then returned to the coach, lifted a cushion, and retrieved something from a hidden compartment.

He returned with a small pistol, powder, and shot. "Are there any other cottages close about?"

"No."

"Then we can practice wherever you like."

"Behind the house, into the woodpile, would be a good place."

"Lead on."

Devon picked up a piece of charcoal from the ashes discarded from the house and drew several graduated circles on the end of a log projecting from the pile. He threw the charcoal down, wiped his hands on her kerchief, and returned.

"This is a German-made, double-barreled weapon of extreme accuracy, but only at short distances because of its size. You can load two shots at once. Like so."

Katrina watched carefully as Devon loaded one side of the gun, and when he handed it to her, she followed the same procedure with the other.

"Very good. Now, when you shoot, steady your right hand with the heel of your left. No, not like that." He stood behind her and wrapped his arms about her. "Like this."

The contrast between the lethal steel in her hands and the warm life at her back was unsettling. Could she really kill a man? Actually holding this weapon made her realize that self-protection would not be without cost: injury, and possibly death, to a fellow human. Her finger grew lax on the tiny trigger. She lowered the pistol.

"I can't, Devon. Even to avoid rape I couldn't shoot a man."

Devon slipped the gun in his belt and turned her into the circle of his arms. His smile was tender, and she realized with a jolt that he wasn't surprised.

"Bravo, my love! I wondered when you'd realize it."

Katrina rubbed her nose into his jacket. "I'm a coward."

He tipped her chin up. "No, my dear, never that. You're a care giver; such hatred is simply not in you. That's no flaw, Katrina. God knows we need more women of your stamp." He grimaced wryly. "Tell nary a soul I said this, but mayhaps we could use a few more men of your stamp as well."

"Are you telling me you're going to become a pacifist?" Katrina blinked her long lashes at him.

He tweaked her chin. "Minx. You know better. But I'm not in government, and I don't have the inclination to start wars. I become aggressive only when provoked. Such as having my woman threatened . . ."

He let the words trail away, the implication chilling Katrina. "You're not to challenge Jack, do you hear?" His eyes became impenetrable. She caught his lapels. "Jack has too many friends who live by aggression."

"Then cease your smuggling."

Katrina stepped away. "It seems men of your stamp don't quail at blackmail, either."

"I'd not call it such, but the end will be the same. Your safety. And I'll have it despite you, if necessary." When her jaw became a miniature Rock of Gibraltar, he sighed. "How about a compromise? Inform me when you cross so I can lie in wait to protect you if necessary, or I challenge Hennessy. The choice is yours."

Neither was palatable, but she took the lesser of the two evils. "I'll inform you. But if you're discovered, I can't answer for how they'll react."

"Leave that to me. Since many of the smugglers are doubtless workers in one of my mines, I don't think they'd risk killing me."

Some of Katrina's worry eased. She hadn't considered that. Luckily he hadn't realized what could happen during the crossing. Still, as long as Davie was present, she'd be relatively safe.

That brought to mind something else. Katrina glared at the lowering sun. "We must hurry in. Rachel is expecting us for supper." Her smiled glowed with mischief. "She's making her favorite fish-head pasty for you."

Devon groaned. "Perhaps I can pretend to an ailment."

"It's actually quite good, if you can ignore the eyes staring at you." Katrina's smile faded. "Devon, do you think Phillip Carrington is daring enough to handle the distribution of the goods we bring back from France?"

"What the deuce . . . Where'd you get a crackbrained notion like that?"

Succinctly Katrina explained the basis of her suspicions: the silk, the peculiar respect Jack seemed to show Carrington, Carrington's affluence even when his primary source of income—the mine—showed little profit.

Devon frowned as he listened. After she finished, he said slowly, "Phillip's always been a toplofty sort. I can't see him fraternizing with smugglers, but it's true his family fortune was never large. And the haste with which he obtained the silk *is* peculiar. Do you want me to question him?"

"Of course not. He'd really have cause to hate you then. I just want your opinion because, well, because I'm afraid someone is keeping part of the contraband for himself. And the person who handles the distribution seems the most logical suspect.''

''And what if you're right? What can you do to stop it?''

''Tell the others. When and if I have proof.'' Katrina started to tell Devon of the records she was keeping, but when she spied the anger kindling in his eyes, she thought better of it. ''At the very least they'll get someone else to handle the dispersal.''

''And what of the danger you're courting, you little fool? Do you think Phillip or whoever will just let you be if he discovers what you're doing?'' Devon caught her arms and pulled her to her toes.

''He won't. No one else suspects, I'm certain of that, and you're the only one I've told.''

His tense grip relaxed. Her feet touched the ground again as he clasped her tightly in his arms. ''Woman, if anything happens to you—''

''Yes? What will you do? Haul me out of my grave for a scolding?''

''That's not funny,'' he said gruffly. ''If you'd marry me, this havey-cavey business wouldn't be necessary.''

With a false laugh Katrina evaded his arms and his statement. ''Come along. Rachel should be serving up any minute.''

''Let's hope it's tastier than the guff you've been feeding me.'' Devon stalked after her. ''And if you think this conversation's at an end, my dear, you've forgotten how persistent I can be.''

That, she thought as she entered the fragrant house, she was unlikely to ever forget. A shiver trailed up her spine, but somehow her sigh was wistful rather than frustrated. She had a presentiment she'd see many examples of his persistence over the coming weeks. Right or wrong, she'd enjoy them to their fullest. While she could . . .

Part Five

"Wise wretch! with pleasures too refined to please;
With too much spirit to be e'er at ease;
With too much quickness ever to be taught;
With too much thinking to have common thought.
You purchase pain with all that joy can give,
And die of nothing but a rage to live."

—Alexander Pope,
Moral Essays, "Epistle II"

Chapter Fourteen

ONE HALCYON SUMMER day dreamed into the next. Katrina spent most of her time with Devon. On the frequent rainy days, they lazed before a fire, either at the manor or at the cottage, the Tonkins growing fonder of Devon apace. Katrina scarce had time to consider their feelings, however; she was too busy quelling her own.

Sexual intimacy had made emotional distance impossible. She'd been naive to think otherwise—or willfully blind. With every coupling Katrina felt closer to Devon, her eventual rejection harder to contemplate. His uncanny ability to choose her weakest moments to press his suit made her control ever more perilous.

On a late July day, as they returned from visiting the miners, Devon ordered Henry to stop. The sun made its first appearance in a week, peeking like a sulky child around its mother's billowy skirts.

"Why are we stopping?" Katrina asked, looking out the window at the ancient circle of boulders. She'd passed this cairn numerous times and had often wanted to investigate.

Devon's only answer was a mysterious smile. He jumped out and offered his hand.

With a little grumble she took it. "No one ever tells me anything." She smiled as Henry opened the door for her.

"Perhaps that's because you don't heed good advice," Devon answered dryly. "Fetch us in a couple of hours, Henry."

The coachman nodded and climbed the steps to his perch.

The carriage rattled away, revealing the basket and blanket Henry had set on the opposite side of the road. Katrina knelt.

327

She found wine, cheese, bread, pastries, and fruit. Her indignation began to wane under appetite's sway.

"Did Moll pack this for you?"

"That she did. She's hurt, you know, that you don't visit her in the kitchen more often."

"I see her sometimes when you're not there." Only when you're not there—Katrina sighed to herself—can I bear to hold the lad. Seeing Devon and the child together was too painful a reminder of what might have been.

"It was fortuitous that you took me there that day. Moll makes the best scones and pastries I've ever tasted."

"And she's grateful for the work. You were generous to employ her, Devon."

He shrugged. "She earns every shilling."

Katrina looked about for a likely place to set out the impromptu supper.

"Over there, milady." Devon swept his arm outward in a ceremonious bow.

Obediently Katrina went in the indicated direction, within the encircling stones. The central part of the monument consisted of three huge slabs of granite, two on end, one horizontal, set up to resemble an archway into another world.

Indeed, as Katrina walked beneath the arch, shade absorbed the sun's warmth. Standing here, she could see only a world of gray behemoths, relics of another time. She couldn't shake the feeling that when they exited this sacred circle, they'd find themselves in a time of witchcraft and warfare. She shivered as the old trapped feeling almost overwhelmed her. "Is it safe?"

"It's stood for centuries, my love. I don't believe even the force we generate together will be enough to shake it loose." Devon smiled when she blushed. He knelt to spread out the blanket. "I thought you'd be as charmed by this legacy as I. Somewhere in the past we probably have the same blood flowing through our veins, Katrina. We've explored our differences enough, my love. Can't we at last celebrate our common bond?" Devon rose to take her hands.

A harder woman than Katrina would have been touched at his romanticism. Her stifling closeness eased. The sky above stretched to heaven; the world below had narrowed to the limitless horizon of his eyes. When he pulled her down to the blanket, she went without a second thought.

He served her plate, then his own. He leaned back on one elbow and watched her eat. Nervously she licked her lips, but then his gaze settled on her mouth. Suddenly her dress felt too tight.

Her voice higher than normal, she asked, ''Have the engineers finished measuring yet?''

''Almost. They judge it will take a fortnight to get the equipment here to begin installation.''

''So the men should soon be back at work?'' Katrina set aside her half-full plate and folded her hands demurely in her lap, unable to meet that intense stare.

''When the work is done, the pump tested. Watt's men estimate it will take about a month to install, since the works are so spread out and they'll have to extend the system so deep. I know the men are getting restless.''

''The harvest should be in soon, and that will help, but many of the farmers export their grain because they can get a better price. There have been riots in the past. John worries that some of the men are agitating now.''

''I know. But the best way to help these men to prosperity is to give them decent jobs. I can't do anything about the price of corn.''

But will the mine be finished in time? Katrina wondered.

''Enough gloom and doom, Katrina. I didn't bring you here to discuss the price of corn.'' Devon scooted next to her and drew her head down on his shoulder.

Katrina smiled against him. ''Why *did* you bring me here?'' She rubbed her nose into his jacket.

''Wretch.'' He titled her chin back. ''That's not the only reason.'' He hesitated, then admitted, ''I want to talk to you. This waiting is devilish hard on a fellow. You must admit I've been patient.''

That she could not deny. Aside from several hints and wounded looks, he'd not referred to marriage again. Katrina drew away from him. She couldn't think clearly when he held her. And judging by the smile playing about his lips, the scoundrel knew it.

Bending her head, Katrina gave great attention to her new

skirt. She'd used her last smuggling share—which had indeed been less than expected—and bought herself and the rest of the family new clothes. On seeing her in the plain garments, he'd sighed, but hadn't urged her to accept clothes from him. He was, indeed, trying to understand her. How much easier were he not . . .

His head cocked, he appraised her neat figure. "You win, yet again. But only for the nonce." He lifted his wineglass. "To the day, and the most stubborn, irresistible woman God ever created."

The fine mixture of frustration and desire in his eyes made Katrina's neck prickle, but she lifted her goblet to his. "To the day."

As soon as she'd sipped, he took her glass and set it, and his, aside. "Do you know, Miss Prim and Proper, the neater you are, the more I want to muss you?" He caught her waist and lowered her to the blanket.

His lips and hands suited action to words. His hands unbuttoned her high-necked blouse and unlaced her chemise while his mouth disarranged her neat bun, then lowered to her neck and sucked. He drew back and appraised the tiny red mark. "Good, no one can doubt whom you belong to now."

Katrina's heavy eyelids fluttered open. "The whole county knows, from Land's End to Devonshire." She watched her fingers working at his shirt buttons, so she missed his pained expression.

With a sound halfway between a groan and a snarl, he jerked her chemise down beneath her breasts. But as soon as he touched her vulnerable skin, his hands gentled. He traced each globe with lush thoroughness, sighed deeply, and bent his head to sustain himself.

Katrina arched beneath the skillful lips and tongue. Never had his touch been so sweet. Her breasts felt tender, yearning, but she was too caught up in the moment to question their unusual sensitivity. She barely comprehended his frustrated mutterings into her heated flesh. "I hate the way men talk of you." He lapped at her erect nipples, then turned his cheek to rest his head against her. "I'm tired of sneaking around, pretending to foolish errands so we can be alone."

"Shh." Tenderly she stroked through the hair she'd loosened from his queue. "I don't care what they say. I knew they'd talk." She laced her fingers about the back of his head and lifted it. "I'd pay any price to know these moments with you." She scooted down to bring his lips to hers.

Puissance throbbed between them, incited as much by the pain in their hearts as the naked slide of skin against skin. Devon's touch grew desperate when her skirts wouldn't cooperate, but Katrina didn't notice because she was too busy jerking at his breeches. Buttons flew, material ripped, but finally they were able to merge.

Luxury! Each stayed still, the better to savor. He buried his nose in her neck; Katrina ran her hands over his tense back. Oddly, neither concentrated on the exquisite sheathing of man-flesh into woman. Instead they closed their eyes and reveled in the emotional intimacy. In that brief moment each forgot the past and ignored the future. Only this oneness mattered.

Katrina felt tears threatening. Deliberately, she flexed her muscles around him. Let passion serve where tenderness could not.

He gasped. "Stop that, woman. I want to last."

Again, longer. She dragged his mouth to hers and flicked her tongue inside.

The twin sensations were too much for him, but as Katrina had learned, passion was insatiable. Its satiety required two victims. Gladly she sacrificed her weighty morality. This she could accept from him, and give as richly in return.

Above and below he accepted her challenge, inserting himself tirelessly, skillfully, until thought was beyond her. Their bodies slapped together, tension building apace. When it snapped, they went with it. The very earth did seem to rumble beneath their bodies, the arch above them sway under the impact.

For a timeless moment their energies combined in a combustion that made them feeling rather than flesh, emotion rather than entity. Briefly, they felt invincible, one mystical being. But when the pulsing died, the power dissipated. They became a tangle of arms and legs, hair, heart, and bone. Two people who loved one another, but who knew, once more, that love sometimes couldn't conquer all. The past hovered over them again, a dark omen to their future.

Devon moved to her side and drew her head to his chest. "Ah, little love"—he sighed— "what a delicious torment you are." He settled her more closely against him, pulling at her as if he would climb inside her skin and keep her any way he could.

With the intimacy went the euphoria. It was ever thus, only each time the pain seemed worse. Katrina listened to his slowing heart rate, cursing her own stubborn tears.

"Had anyone told me a few months ago that I'd be in this position, I'd have laughed in their faces."

Katrina cleared her aching throat. "What position?"

"Stud service!"

A delighted smile stretched Katrina's mouth. She pushed the dark despair away with a laugh. "Now that, my very dear lord, you must admit is a wry turn of events." She rested her forearms on his chest to look down at him. She tried to kiss his sulky mouth, but he turned his head.

"No. You got what you wanted. I've a mind to charge you." He set her aside and rose to his knees to glare at her.

Katrina's appraisal was as slow and thorough as the many he'd subjected her to. "Be certain the price is dear." She ticked off on her fingers. "Shoulders, broad; arms, strong; legs, powerful." She leaned forward to pull down his sullen lower lip. "Teeth, good."

"Blast you, woman, do you think I look like a horse?"

She tapped one finger thoughtfully against her mouth. "Well, your mane is rather tangled at the moment, but it's thick, shiny, and healthy." When he snorted, she giggled and added without thinking, "And you've certain other attributes that put me in mind of one." Her eyes lowered.

This startled a smile to his face that turned into a laugh when she went as red as her impudent nipples. "A vicar's daughter, eh? Tsk, tsk. What do you know of such things?"

"You've made me intimately familiar with 'such things,'" Katrina had to say tartly, even in her embarrassment.

"Then let's utilize your skill. I exact payment now. In kind." He hauled her to her knees and crushed his mouth over hers.

She responded as desperately. She blinked in shock when he flung himself away with a frustrated snarl. "Enough. Accounts are even. Henry will be back soon. We'd best be ready."

Katrina swallowed her hurt and dressed. She helped him pack the supper away. She rose with dignity and moved to step out of the ring of stones.

He caught her arm. "Katrina, I'm sorry. You . . . hurt me, so I wanted to hurt you back. Forgive me?" He traced her trembling lips with an index finger.

"Of course," she mumbled, pulling away. Pain dogged her every step as she left the monument and weaved back into the present. Soon, if she didn't send him away, he'd begin to hate her out of sheer frustration. Dear God, how much longer did she have? How many more memories could she ferret aside before eternal winter descended?

They each leaned back against the stones, watching the sun drop below the horizon, taking light and laughter with it. When carriage wheels clattered in the distance, each drew a relieved sigh.

They walked to the path to meet Henry, but when the carriage rounded the corner, Katrina took an instinctive step back. Devon cursed and fumbled in the basket for his small pistol.

"Well, well. What a fortuitous encounter. I wouldn't, old boy." Carrington threw the reins to Hennessy and jumped down, holding Devon squarely in the sights of his big carriage pistol. "Take your hand out of the basket, slowly."

Devon obeyed, his jaw flexing with fury. "How the hell did you know we were here?" He casually hooked the basket over his arm.

"I didn't. Just out for a drive, you know."

A disdainful smile stretched Devon's mouth. He eyed the loaded wagon, its cargo covered by a tarp. "Certainly you are."

Katrina wondered what they were distributing. She knew better than to ask, however. Carrington needed little excuse to kill them. What did he plan to do? She edged closer to Devon.

"We've room for one more. My dear, can we escort you home?" Carrington's eyes never left his onetime friend as he spoke.

"We've a carriage coming any moment," Devon inserted before she could speak. "We'll bid you good day." He took Katrina's arm with his free hand.

"I think not. In the wagon, wench." When Katrina stayed put, Carrington cocked the pistol. "Now. Unless you want to see your lover with a new hole in his face."

Katrina paled and took a jerky step forward.

"No!" Devon pulled her back.

"Interesting. She must be quite a talented whore if you're willing to give up your life for her."

"You always were a coward, Phillip. No one touches her but me. Not while I live. And if you kill me, you'll have a deal of explaining to do."

"A duel, you know." Still, Carrington hesitated.

"Get on with it, man," Jack growled, shifting restively on the carriage seat.

Katrina's heart fluttered like a trapped bird. She dug her nails into Devon's arm. He glanced sideways at her. She mouthed, "Now," put a hand to her forehead, moaned, and pretended to faint.

Carrington started, his finger lax just long enough for Devon to throw the basket. The basket hit Carrington's arm, deflecting his aim. The pistol shot exploded harmlessly into the air.

Devon sprang at Carrington's throat.

Hennessy made a move to jump down, but carriage wheels sounded on the hard path. Cursing loudly, he whipped the horses up the trail in the opposite direction.

Carrington wasn't able to shout after him for the simple reason that Devon's hands were cutting off his air. Devon shook his old college chum. "You pox-carrying spawn of hell, I'll kill you!"

Katrina tried to pull Devon away, but he ignored her. "Henry, come help!"

Henry threw his reins aside and leaped down. Between the two of them they pulled Devon off just as Carrington's knees sagged.

Retching, he cradled his abused throat, wavering on his feet.

Devon watched him emotionlessly, then snarled out of the side of his mouth, "Tie him and throw him in the luggage compartment, Henry. Take Miss Lawson home first, then drive me to the constable's. I want this man arrested on suspicion of smuggling.'' Grabbing Katrina's arm, he hauled her after him to the carriage.

Somehow she managed to match his angry strides with three of her own, and she didn't protest when he tossed her inside. He followed quickly, sprawling on the opposite seat, his hands still flexing with anger.

The carriage lurched as Carrington was forced into the rear, jounced again as Henry climbed aboard, and then they were off. Katrina eyed Devon warily, deciding against telling him of the scheduled run that night. After this he'd be furious if he knew she still planned to go. Now that Carrington would be out of the way, she had to be at each transaction to see if the account was still short.

"You've your own stubbornness to thank for this,'' Devon burst out as if he couldn't contain himself longer.

Katrina's head swiveled around. "What?''

"If you'd wed me weeks ago, Hennessy and his ilk wouldn't consider you free game.'' He shifted his long legs. "Blast it, how am I to protect you when I can't always be with you?''

"You're not. We're each responsible for ourselves, Devon. I can take care of myself.''

A snort made short work of her pretension. "You'd be sprawled between the two of them right now if I hadn't been there.''

Somehow she doubted it. Carrington had attacked with an air of purpose that had little to do with lust. However, at Devon's crudity, all thoughts of discussing her suspicion flew out the window with her composure. She leaned forward to fix him with a snide smile. "Who's to say I might not have enjoyed it?''

Glittering brown eyes locked with blue, then Devon erupted in a fury of motion. She barely had time to shrink away before he had her pinned against the velvet squabs.

"If you're so insatiable, my dear, we might as well both benefit.''

Stormy darkness raged within the tiny carriage, challenging the peaceful night. Katrina beat her hands against his shoulders—at first. But soon her clothes hugged her waist and his mouth gentled from brutality to desperate passion. Her claws re-formed into fingers, exploring the sudden beauty anger had wrought.

With a tortured groan Devon shoved her away. "It's not enough. Part of you is not enough." He turned his head aside, his jaw set in granite.

When the carriage lurched to a stop, Katrina wondered if this was God's cue to end it. Wearily she straightened her clothes, intoning, "Two years ago I would have been ecstatic that you finally understood that. Now?" She shrugged. She buttoned her last button and reached for the door handle.

"Now it means naught, apparently." He grasped her arm so hard she knew she'd be bruised in the morning. "Tell me, has this all been some obscene plan to avenge yourself on me?"

She bit back an hysterical laugh. "Believe what you will. It's too late for us. It was too late that night I left you, those years ago." Shaking him off, she leaped down and ran into the cottage.

Devon covered his face with trembling hands, trying to master the dark despair. Why didn't he just leave her to her fate, as she'd left him to his? He'd tried every tactic he could think of, but Katrina, in her inimitable way, resisted him. Yet she claimed to love him. The two conclusions were at odds, and he wondered if even the key to what had happened in the brothel would solve the riddle she posed. What could have been so terrible to keep apart two people who loved one another? Together they could conquer anything. He truly believed that, but he no longer had heart to convince her. She was bleeding him dry. If he didn't leave, he'd be an empty caricature of the man she had helped form.

When they clattered onto the cobbled streets of Truro, Devon forced himself upright. Very well. Once more he'd try to wheedle the truth from her. He'd wine and dine her as if this were their last night, as it well could be. If she still denied them both, he'd seek her no longer. London would be a cold, dreary place after the strife and joy he'd known here, but there he'd have solitude to lick his wounds. Who knew? Maybe some of the old demon remained in him. What had morality and kindness bought him? The deepest despair he'd ever known. Even the shallow life of gaming and whoring offered better than that.

Yet, as the carriage rattled on toward the constable's, deep inside Devon knew he fooled himself. The demon was gone, too dead for him to mourn the loss. Katrina had dragged his better half into the light only to condemn him to darkness. If she forced him to leave her, he would ever after be a twilight denizen. Condemned to purgatory, fitting nowhere, unhappy everywhere.

And Katrina? Somehow he knew she would never wed. She'd spend her life in good works, spreading that unusual ability to love so deeply on many, rather than giving it to the one man God had sent her. If that were not so, why did He unite them and give them such a tantalizing taste of what they could share?

"Oh love, don't sentence us both to misery." Bowing his head, Devon prayed, his former lip service now fervent to the deity he'd once doubted.

Much later that night Katrina paced nervously as they awaited the Frenchman. Why was he so late? She glanced over her shoulder at Hennessy, then quickly away. Aside from a mean glare, he'd not looked at or spoken to her. Rumors of Carrington's captivity were already circulating in the district. The excisemen had searched Carrington's house and found enough contraband, apparently, to prefer charges against him.

Ostensibly they were left without a distributor. If so, why hadn't Hennessy canceled this run? Surely it was dangerous to store the goods for long. They'd been lucky so far partly because of the speed with which the cargo was dispersed. And Hennessy hadn't accused her of betrayal, as she'd half expected. Surely he would have done so if the smuggling leader had been captured partly through her interference?

Katrina frowned unseeingly into the night. Their appearance at the cairn had been too convenient. How had they known they'd be there unless they'd followed? Katrina flushed as she thought of the passion the pair might have interrupted, but the stones had concealed them. Still, why had they come? It would have been easier to kidnap her on a night like this than to openly challenge a powerful man like Devon. Had someone else sent them for a reason she didn't understand?

Who? Why?

Katrina had a chilling suspicion that she'd soon find out.

A stealthy footfall made them all start. They whirled, hands reaching for weapons. The cadaverous Frenchman scrambled down the beach, his hands before him in protest.

"C'est moi, mademoiselle." He relaxed when the men put their guns away.

"You're late," Katrina reprimanded him in French. "Where is your wagon?"

He jerked his head toward the rise.

"And what do you carry that was worth such a hasty run?"

"The finest brandy. It should fetch even more than usual. Silk and tea from China."

"We'll want to see every bolt and taste every tub."

"But of course." He looked about. *"Où est monsieur?* I was told he would come himself tonight. I arranged this meeting with him."

"Lord Carrington is . . . indisposed," Katrina replied, watching the man closely.

Jack stiffened when he heard Carrington's name and approached him.

"Carrington? Who is that?" the Frenchman asked.

Katrina wasn't surprised when Jack took her arm and said roughly, "Get on with it, gal."

She threw him a bland look. "Why? This is *such* an interesting topic."

"We've work to do, and I don't like the feel o' this." He nodded at two of his men, and they scattered to search the area.

"Who is this person you're expecting? I can tell you if he's here."

But the Frenchman was frowning suspiciously. "None of your affair. Come. I will show you the goods." He led them up the rise.

She and Jack both looked uneasily about, but all seemed calm. Katrina was brisk during the negotiations, and her unease heightened when the Frenchman lowered his price so easily.

He shrugged under her curious eyes. "I am not greedy. I grow weary."

Katrina barely stifled a skeptical sniff. She had little choice but to take him at his word, however. As the men began to load the luggers she sat on a rock some distance away, turned sideways, shielding her paper and pencil with her cloak.

Her fingers ached when the loading was finished. They should all make quite a nice profit this time, she thought. She also could make a fair estimate of what the goods should fetch since this was their typical cargo. The brandy *had* been unusually fine, so she'd increased the estimate slightly. She was so busy with her calculations that she didn't hear Hennessy approach.

He growled over her shoulder, "Come on with ye then if ye'd not wish to be left behind. . . ." His voice trailed away as she guiltily stuffed the paper in her cloak.

"Just writing a letter." She smiled brightly and rose. "I'm ready." She hastened up the beach and accepted Paulie's hand into the dinghy that would take them out to the lugger.

As he always did, Jack made his last walk about the beach to see that they'd left no evidence of their presence. They were all aboard the dinghies awaiting him when he gave a satisfied nod and turned to join them. Several men dressed in uniform scrambled over the hill.

The officer in the lead shouted in English, "Halt! You're under arrest!"

Jack turned and ran. The other dinghy shoved off, the smugglers too busy rowing to return fire. Paulie glared at the Frenchmen, gauged how far Jack had to come, and bit out of the side of his mouth, "Away with 'ee." To Jack he hollered, "Swem for et, man! We'll peck 'ee up."

A bullet knocked Jack's hat off. He gathered himself and made an athletic lunge for the water. He let the breakers carry him out, then began to swim in powerful strokes.

The Frenchmen knelt on the beach, steadying their muskets, but they could barely see Jack now. A few minutes later the first lugger sailed alongside to pick him up. Katrina saw Jack catch a line and cling as he was hauled up. The Frenchmen reloaded and fired again, but they could see only shadows in the night.

They reached their own lugger soon after. The darkness swallowed them as quickly.

"Phew! That was close. Jack was lucky," Paulie said.

"Hurry on it, men, in case they've ships waiting to give chase."

Never had the men hoisted sail so efficiently. A fair wind to England soon skimmed them across the channel to the God-fearing side. They sighted no boats, and the night was quiet when they hove to.

Jack, however, was almost foaming at the mouth with rage. "Who's the sneakin', traitorous bastard what set me up? Those men come for me!" He grabbed sleeves to glare into each face, but he apparently didn't see guilt. He whirled and stomped away to begin dragging cargo ashore.

"But I don't understand. Why weren't they after all of us?" Katrina asked. It *had* seemed as though they'd only pursued Jack.

Paulie answered, "Them wasn't revenuers. They was army. Jack kelled a French officer who was veseten' in London. He deserted rather than faace charges. That's why he come to Cornwall from England."

Ahh . . . This was apparently an open secret among the men. Any of them could have laid that trap. But why? They seemed content to let Jack lead them on the runs. Katrina stared into the distance, but a movement caught her eye. She looked up.

At the top of the cliff she saw a figure silhouetted against the fitful moonlight. A hat shielded the face; a cloak flapped in the breeze. She could distinguish little except that the form seemed tall. Something in its menacing stillness trumpeted anger, even at the distance. Katrina leaped to her feet and opened her mouth to give the alarm, but the figure turned. With a fluttering whirl of cape it disappeared.

Katrina sat back down, frowning. Something told her she'd just seen Jack's tormentor. If her suspicions proved correct, he was also the leader of the whole enterprise. Like a spider in his web he manipulated men at his will, even lords like Carrington. But why would he want Jack out of the way?

Who could it be? Who in the district besides Carrington possessed the crafty drive necessary to plan so many bold operations? Could it be Davie? His illness had certainly come at a convenient time. The memory of the way he'd threatened her still rankled.

The new puzzle occupied Katrina as Paulie drove her home, the back of his wagon loaded. She was bone weary when they finally reached the cottage, but she refused Paulie's offer to see her inside.

"Where is Davie?"

"Laaid up seck," Paulie answered. "''Ee should have your share en a few daays." He offered one of his rare smiles. "''Ee ded well, girlie. Most women would have faainted dead at bein' fired upon."

Katrina shrugged and covered a yawn. "I might have if I'd been a bit less tired." She returned his smile and entered the gate. The wagon rattled away.

Katrina was reaching for the door handle when a hand shot out of the darkness and grabbed her wrist. She drew breath to scream, but another hand covered her mouth. She was dragged, kicking, away from the cottage to the riverbanks, far enough from the house that she knew her screams wouldn't be heard.

"Make a peep and I'll knock ye senseless."

In other circumstances Katrina would have been terrified, but Jack's voice was edgy rather than husky with lust. She nodded.

Warily he let her go, but took the precaution of clasping her wrist. "Do ye know who tried to trap me tonight?"

"No." When his eyes narrowed in a mean glare, she added hastily, "Truly I don't. I did, however, see someone standing on the cliff watching us as we unloaded tonight. He was too far away for me to see clearly, but I sensed . . . anger. Frustration. He wanted you caught very badly, Jack. Despite the fact we haven't seen eye to eye, I'm glad you escaped."

The sympathy in her voice shined from her eyes. Jack let her go and shook his head ruefully. "I'd be a mean sort indeed to keep pursuin' ye after that. Ye can go, missy. I'll follow ye no more. Ye should know that we didn't plan to . . . take ye when we took ye today. The man wanted ye away from yer pretty lordling. He paid me to do it, and blackmailed Carrington by threatenen' to turn him in."

"I see. Thank you for telling me. That, at least, makes sense. But why does he care whom I see?"

"He wants ye, lass. Badly."

Katrina was stunned, and she barely heard Jack's next comment.

"I only come here tonight because I thought he might have told ye what he planned. Them notes ye was makin' seemed mighty . . . suspicious."

"You know who sent the men after you, then?"

"As sure as I'm standin' here. What I don't know is what to do about it." Jack paced restlessly, his foot scuffing a rock out of his way.

"Jack, I don't understand why you think this person would confide in me."

Stopping, he turned to peer at her. "Ye really don't know who leads us, do ye?"

"I've no idea. I thought it was Carrington for a while, but now . . ." She shrugged. "One thing I do know, however, is that he's a cheat."

Jack stiffened. "What do ye mean?"

After a brief hesitation Katrina admitted, "I've been keeping a record of our contraband. Three loads now, our shares have been short. I think whoever is heading the distribution is keeping some of the goods for himself."

Jack slammed a fist into his palm. "The sneaken' bastard! I suspected it me ownself. I just didn't want to believe it." He approached Katrina and took her shoulders in his hands. "Will ye stand by me, lass, if I go to the men? Have ye the papers to prove ye right?"

"Yes, Jack. On both counts." After he patted her shoulders she pulled away. "On one condition. I want to know who is responsible for all of this."

Jack sighed. "It'd be best for ye if ye didn't know. I suspect that's why he tried to get rid o' me."

Stroking her elbows to quell her own fears, Katrina said steadily, "But I must know. What if something happens to you?"

Jack stepped back from her, rubbing his chin. Finally he nodded. "Ye be right, lass. It's—" A flash ignited from the hedge to their left simultaneous to the shot. Jack didn't even have time to groan, or to clutch his shattered heart. He dropped soundlessly to the ground, his eyes still open.

Katrina screamed, and screamed again. She dropped to her

knees beside Jack, vaguely aware of running footsteps. Shakily she felt for Jack's pulse, and was not surprised when she found none. She bowed her head and covered her face with her hands, muttering, "It's my fault. If I hadn't insisted—" Then the tears came.

That was how Jimmy found her a few minutes later. Soon after, John hobbled up on his crutches. "Lass, what es et? We heard a shot and saw 'ee standen' here—" He broke off when he spied the figure on the ground.

"Jimmy, fetch the magistrate." John lifted Katrina to her feet and drew her to his good side. "There, lass, don't keep a saayen' that. How's it your fault?"

"Oh John, everything's such a mess." In a garbled rush the whole sorry story tumbled out. The missing goods, the fight with Devon, everything.

"There, there, girl, et's too laate to worry about et now. Come along. I'll maake 'ee a hot cuppa. En the mornen' we'll talk more."

When morning dawned after a few short hours of sleep for Katrina, however, she found no opportunity to talk to John. First Will visited, arriving just after Katrina sat down to breakfast.

"I heard the news, Katrina. Are you all right?" Will appraised her anxiously.

"I'm fine." But Katrina played with her food, not sampling a bite. She pushed her plate back and rested her elbows on the table, her head in her hands. "The mere scent of food makes me nauseous. I keep remembering—" She cupped her hands over her mouth and leaped up to run out the back.

Those still at table heard her retching.

"Why be 'ee here, Will?" John asked, an unwontedly hard note in his voice.

Will looked slightly offended. "I was but concerned for Katrina when I heard she watched a man killed." He frowned as he stared at the door where Katrina had disappeared.

"How ded 'ee hear that?"

"It's common news around Redruth. I imagine the magistrate told someone. I heard it on my first round this morning."

"Ded 'ee?" John tamped tobacco into his clay pipe. His

brown eyes were veiled by smoke as he lit the pipe and took a deep draw. "A mite early for rounds, esn't et?"

Slamming his palms down on the table, Will rose. "What the devil are you hinting at, John?"

Katrina stumbled back in before John could answer.

Will supported her to the table. When his arm brushed her breast, she winced. His steps faltered, then continued. When she was sitting, he asked, "How long have you been sick like this?"

"This is the first time. I think it's because of last night." She shuddered and collapsed onto the bench. "But I feel better now. In fact I'm starved." She rescued her abandoned plate and speared a large chunk of cooling egg.

Will's eyes never left her. Those blue depths no longer looked celestial, as Katrina would have noticed had she been watching.

John was. He raised an eyebrow when Will bolted to his feet.

"Must be off. A deal to do today." Will hurried out the door in such a rush that he forgot his hat. He didn't return Katrina's good-bye.

"Katrina," John began. A knock sounded at the door Will had just closed. John sighed as Rachel led the magistrate into the kitchen.

He questioned Katrina for well over an hour. She was little help, since she'd not seen the killer, and she was stymied by the fact that she had to hedge about the details of her last conversation with Jack.

When the magistrate became more insistent, John broke in. "She's told 'ee all she knows. Let the poor lass alone. How many have 'ee babbled thes to?"

Squashing his hat on his head, the magistrate rose. He nodded curtly. "I've told no one, yet. Just as well. You've given me precious little to pursue." He tromped out.

"Phist! 'Ee'd thenk 'ee'd done the deed, the waay he acted." John shook his head disapprovingly.

"I might as well have. I think the killer heard our conversation and knew Jack was about to reveal his identity." Katrina stared blindly at her empty plate.

"Have 'ee thought of who et es?"

"I've thought of little else. But for the life of me—"

"Who does 'ee know who's neither working class nor gentry, who knows everyone in the district and yet has contacts in London?"

Slowly Katrina raised her head. "Why no one. Except—" Her eyes widened. She gasped. "Not Will!"

"I fear so, lass. I dedn't want to believe et myself, but today he just proved et. How ded he know of the kellen' ef the magestrate dedn't tell of et?"

Katrina croaked, "Will's not capable of such violence." Yet she felt as if blinders had been ripped from her eyes. The many memories she'd pushed to the back of her mind paraded before her eyes. Will's statement that sometimes blood must be spilled when diplomacy couldn't serve; the distaste Jem had shown in refusing to accept charity from Will; his presence among the mob that had descended on Devon; his cruelty to his horses when he was in a rage; the unexplained prosperity he'd attributed to an inheritance. The clues had all been there, awaiting her. She'd refused to see them because she didn't want to believe the dear friend who'd saved her life had a darker side to his sunny nature.

Katrina covered her mouth, feeling nausea rising again. "Oh Will, how could you?" she whispered despairingly.

Patting her arm, John encouraged, "Et's good 'ee know the truth. I quit liken' Will when he tried to manipulaate 'ee."

"That's why he quit coming around, isn't it? You no longer made him welcome." Katrina's mouth tightened in self-disgust. "And I was so self-absorbed I never even considered why."

"'Ee had the right, lass. Don't be angry at yourself."

Anger *was* stirring in Katrina, but not at herself. Her nausea subsided. Her skin tingled with renewed life. She leaped to her feet. "Well, he's not going to get away with it any longer. I'm going into Truro to get the magistrate."

John rose, too. "I'm comen' weth 'ee. We'll tie the ox to the cart and both ride."

It wasn't until she'd run upstairs to freshen up and fetch her shawl that Katrina realized she had a far more important reason to see Will behind bars than to promote justice. Her fingers froze around the ends of her shawl. Devon! Will would go after Devon next. Somehow she knew it.

Katrina ran down the stairs, almost tripping in her haste. She was so busy visualizing the horror of what Will could do to Devon that she had no time to consider the physical changes in her body. When she had time for reflection, she'd wonder at the tenderness in her breasts, the illness followed by hunger. At the moment, however, she was too scared to consider that a man who stooped to murder wouldn't think twice about lying. . . .

Chapter Fifteen

AFTER MAKING HIS accusation against Carrington, Devon had waited while men searched Carrington's manor. Hours later the magistrate called him in to Truro again for more questions. However, the man was summarily interrupted when his servant entered.

"There's a lad here who says a murder's been committed."

The magistrate, a bluff, hearty man unused to crimes more severe than theft and drunken disorder, cursed.

"I regret the inconvenience, my lord, but I must request that you await in town until I return."

Devon grimaced and shifted wearily on his hard chair. "Very well. I'll put up at the Red Lion Inn."

The magistrate nodded and hurried from the room, straightening the clothes he'd thrown on for Devon's benefit.

As Devon rode to the inn his spirits were the lowest he could remember since finding Katrina. Had God reunited them against such odds only to split them apart? He almost doubled over at the pain incited by the thought. Once, not long ago, he would have stoically borne his own humors alone, good or bad. Now, however, he was not ashamed to admit the emotional need for someone to talk to. He thought of the one man who truly understood him, who'd been his best, indeed his only, friend, for more years than he cared to count.

"Fetch Billy to me, Henry," he told his coachman upon alighting.

When Billy arrived an hour later, he found Devon sitting in a Spartan chamber, brooding out the window. Billy stopped cold. "What's amiss?"

Devon replied without turning his head. "Everything. Katrina won't give up her smuggling, she uses me like a stud and accepts sexual favors but shuns my hand.'' He laughed shortly. ''A dubious honor, perhaps, but one she wanted badly. At one time. I wouldn't have her, then. Now she won't have me.'' He laughed louder.

Billy winced at the sound. ''Can ye not accept what she gives ye?''

''I thought I could. But it's not enough. I can't bear the way people talk of her, look at her.'' Devon propped his elbows on his knees and cupped his aching head in his hands. ''God, it's so ironic it's laughable. Two years ago I didn't even understand how I dishonored her; now I do, largely because she taught me, and she seeks her own ruin when I would offer her all I possess.'' He shook his head. ''Billy, what the hell am I to do?''

After a brief hesitation Billy strode to his friend and laid a big hand on his tense shoulder. He expected to be thrown off, as he had been so often in the past, but Devon only sighed and patted his hand in thanks. ''It's against me instincts, but if ye try once more to get the lassie to tell ye what happened, and she won't . . .''

Devon's head bobbed up.

''I will. Use all yer wiles on her, Devvie lad. It would be best if she told ye. But one way or another ye'll understand why she acts as she does.''

''Thank God. That's been the torment of it, Billy. Not understanding what's so awful to drive us apart when we love one another.'' Devon jumped up, buoyed by renewed hope. ''This time she'll not deny me.''

Billy turned away so Devon wouldn't see the doubt in his face.

The next morning, after a hasty, insipid breakfast, Devon and Billy exited to return to the magistrate's. They stopped when they spied the coach nearby, but they didn't see Henry.

Devon frowned. ''I told him to meet us at nine.'' He strode out into the street to look both ways. Some distance away a group of men congregated on the intersection of two of Truro's busiest districts. Shops of every description crowded the lanes.

They were too far away for Devon to understand their words, but several men were shaking their fists in anger, and

Devon could hear rage in the raised voices. His eyes narrowed on a familiar figure at the edge of the crowd. "Come along, Billy. Henry's up the street." Devon walked toward the men, unaware of the opening door behind him.

Two shops down, Will Farrow exited from the greengrocer's, his arms loaded with supplies. He stopped short when he saw Devon walk past. His blue eyes glazed with icy hatred. He looked toward the angry voices, then hurried to his carriage and threw the goods he'd purchased inside.

"Wait for me up the street, and be ready to depart quickly," he ordered his coachman. He set his hat at a confident angle, then, wearing his usual calm demeanor, he followed Devon.

Katrina bit her lip to deny the urge to lash the oxen. "I could have walked more quickly," she grumbled.

They'd come from Devon's manor and were now on their way to Truro. Some of Katrina's anxiety had eased when Devon's servant told them that he'd not come back from the magistrate's and had sent for Billy to join him.

Surely Will wouldn't try anything with so many potential witnesses. No, he'd wait until Devon was alone upon the moors. As he'd waited for Jack. Katrina pushed away the memory and clucked to the oxen.

"We'll be there any moment, lass. Calm down. Ef et 'tweren't for thes blasted leg—"

Katrina forced herself to take a calming breath. "You're lucky to still have it. I'm sorry to be so impatient." Hurry, please, she soundlessly begged the plodding beasts. The bright morning was an odd ambience for disaster, but Katrina felt it hovering over her head like a grim portent. . . .

Devon stopped when he heard what the men were saying.

"Blood suckers, one and all. They sell their corn outside just for a few pennies more, and don't care that their fellow Corneshmen staarve."

"Ais, et's more than a body can bear, to see hes cheldren cryen' from hunger." The man, who wore a miner's working clothes, added, "The bals have been my leven', and my da's and grandda's, too, and could be my son's ef et weren't for these blasted foreigners."

A grizzled, rough-hewn miner hawked and spat his agreement. "They put their money en many mines so as to spread their resk. What do they caare, up en London, when we die because they won't maake the bals saafe? Or ef we push ourselves to seckness tryen' to produce more and more so they won't close us down?"

A soft voice agreed from the back of the crowd, "'Tis true. I've seen more men than I care to remember die because of the likes of him!" Will pushed to the head of the crowd and whirled to point an accusing finger at Devon.

Everyone turned. Some recognized Devon. One man agreed, "He bought Carrington's bal. He *says* he's goen' to reopen et after he puts en a new pump. . . ." The words sank like stones into the heavy silence, each plunk proclaiming doubt.

Inwardly flinching, Devon reacted only by a raised eyebrow. He'd opened his mouth to retort when Farrow continued.

"More empty promises. I, for one, am tired of the gentry living like kings on our sweat and toil." Angry agreement was shouted from every quarter. Will raised his voice, warming to his subject. "They may own our source of livelihood, but they don't own our pride. Right, men? And if blood must be spilled to prove we'll not be taken advantage of any longer, then so be it!"

Will grabbed up one of the staves the men had torn from the sides of the miller's emporium they'd intended to attack. Others followed suit, but one of the men who'd been present during the confrontation at Devon's manor held out a staying hand.

"No, et ain't that waay. He's brought engeneers en to the bal, truly—"

If he was heard, the men ignored him. Fear had fed their frustration for months; here was meat for their fury. This man represented everything they hated. By striking a blow at him they'd rebel against all the injustices they'd suffered. And overhead, the skeletal specter of death hovered, slavering in appetite. . . .

"Holy hell, let's get out of here," Billy hissed, trying to pull Devon back from the surging tide of men.

Devon shrugged him off. He didn't notice when Billy ran to the carriage, for his eyes were fixed on Will Farrow. Devon had made many enemies in his lifetime, but never had he seen such twisted hatred on a human face. He'd listened to Farrow with almost the same sense of revelation as the men, for with every vile lie, understanding dawned.

Why hadn't they seen it before? Who had better contacts in the district than Will Farrow? Who else in the district besides Carrington knew people in London? He'd never been able to picture Phillip working closely with Jack Hennessy, but Farrow? That was another matter. Most telling of all Farrow had a prime motivation to embezzle the spoils: Katrina. He'd do whatever necessary to win the woman he craved. Stealing was only the first step; murdering the rival was next.

Be damned to him! Devon held out his hands and cried, "Wait!"

The men hesitated, then those in the back, who would not have to strike the first blow, pushed the leaders forward.

Devon swallowed, but he held his ground.

Billy pounded back to Devon's side, pointed the carriage pistol in the air, and fired.

The mob stopped cold.

Devon took quick advantage. "I understand your frustration, but killing an earl will buy you naught but more trouble."

"Who's to saay which of us kelled 'ee? They can't hang us all." The brave soul in back who'd spoken pushed at the men in front of him.

"Come on, men, don't be fooled by his lies," Will urged, taking a step forward.

A few matched him, but more hesitated. Devon couldn't have said anything better calculated to give them pause. Self-preservation was a powerful inducement to rationality.

"Lies, is it, Will Farrow? Mine? Or yours?" This time it was Devon who pointed an accusing finger in deliberate imitation of Will's drama.

Will nodded at Billy, who was hastily reloading. "It's just a diversion for his man. Don't give him time—"

"You scurvy bastard, why don't you meet me like a man on a field of honor instead of inciting a mob to do your dirty work?" Devon's own anger took hold. His hands clenched and unclenched.

Even those in front paused now. They couldn't see Will's

face, but they caught the tension in his stiff shoulders. And the fury that was reddening the lord's face seemed genuine. They waited, the staves sagging to the ground as they watched.

"You there." Devon nodded. "And you." He jerked his head in another direction. "You've worked in the free trade with my woman, Katrina Lawson. Did you know that the man who heads your raids is leading you now to doom?"

"He lies—" Will tried to say, but Devon cut him off ruthlessly.

"And did you know that he's been stealing from you for months? Why do you think your shares have been less than you expected?"

The smugglers gasped and stared at Will.

Will turned to face the men. Despite his apparent calm, sweat gathered on his brow. "He's lying to save himself." When the smugglers still stared at him, torn between doubt and fury, Will blurted, "Who will you believe? This . . . outsider, or one of your own?"

Silence descended over the crowd. The men looked from Will, to Devon, then back.

Devon watched their faces. He opened his mouth to feed their uncertainty, but a new voice interrupted.

"It's true," Katrina called, running from the wagon to Devon's side.

All eyes turned to her as, deliberately, she took Devon's hand. "I've got the proof at home. I've been keeping a record for some time—" Her words became garbled as Devon covered her mouth with his hand.

He nodded at the magistrate, who was puffing his way up the street. "What's going on here?" he demanded. He sent hard looks at several of the men. "I'll have none of your trouble-making this day. I've got a murder to solve. Get along home with you."

No one budged. One of the smugglers in the lead said stubbornly, "We got a right to be here ef we please." He turned on Will. "Well, Farrow? What have 'ee to saay?"

Will shrugged distastefully. "Of course *she'd* lie for him." He crossed his arms over his chest and said coolly, "Believe what you will. But there's hardly a man among you I haven't bandaged or stitched up."

At the truth of the comment the men shifted their feet guiltily.

John had hobbled on his cane into their midst in time to hear the last few statements. "Ais, and me too. I'd be en my graave without 'ee, Will Farrow." He drew a deep sigh. "And et's sorry I am to have to saay thes, but I cannot turn my head aside any longer. There's a vast defference 'tween smuggling and murder."

"Murder?" The word blasted through the crowd like a whirlwind, collecting impetus as it went from man to man.

"Now see here, Tonkin, this is my business—"

John barely spared the magistrate a glance as he continued, "Will came to me only thes mornen' to ask how Katrina was after Jack Hennessy's murder. She were there, last night, when Jack were shot in the heart."

"Jack? Dead?" Several of the men stepped back in shock. Even those who hadn't known him, knew of him. They shook their heads in regret.

"I dedn't thenk anyone knew yet. And ef he"—John jerked his head at the magistrate—"dedn't tell nobody, how ded Will know? And Jack was kelled just as he were about to tell Katrina who heads the, er, dispersal." He glanced at the magistrate, but that worthy stared at Will.

John was one of the most respected men in Cornwall. Many would have doubted Devon; John would never lie. The most telling proof, however, was Farrow's face. He glanced from side to side like a hunted animal, his legendary calm at last ruffled.

The magistrate stood with his mouth agape. His lips worked several times, then he gasped, "Apprehend that man!"

After a brief instant several of the men closest to Will made a grab for him. Will dodged them, lifted the stave, and surged toward his best opening—straight ahead.

Toward Devon and Katrina.

Billy raised the gun that had grown lax in his hand, but Devon snarled, "No!" and went forward to meet his enemy.

When Will tried to bring the stave down on Devon's head, Devon grabbed his wrist and twisted.

Moaning, Will dropped the stave. Devon punched him in a

brutal uppercut that knocked the slighter man to the ground. "Get up, Farrow," Devon gritted through his teeth.

"That's enough, me lord," the magistrate said, rushing back with the length of rope he'd filched from a nearby shop. With the aid of several of his men, the magistrate soon had Will trussed on his feet.

However, as he was led away, he said quietly, "You've not seen the last of me, Cavanaugh." He looked at Katrina. Only then did his face change.

The longing she read there struck Katrina like a blow. She buried her face in Devon's jacket, unable to watch as Will walked proudly away. Why did it have to end thus? Images of Will laughing, doctoring, and teasing Robbie flashed through her head, but they only made the final picture of him more devastating. Katrina was too miserable to pay much attention to what transpired next.

Planting his hands on his hips, the magistrate demanded, "And why have you all come here this morning?" He looked accusingly at the staves several of the men still held.

They were hastily dropped. Shoulders shrugged; hands rose in innocence.

"Why, they came to get the grain I'm dispersing until the crops come in," Devon said mildly, still cradling Katrina. To Billy he whispered, "Go into the miller's and purchase five barrels of corn. My credit should be good."

Smiling, Billy went.

"Eh? What's that?" the magistrate asked, blinking in confusion. His surprise was mild compared with that of Devon's recent antagonists.

They goggled at him in shock. Katrina lifted her head from Devon's chest to listen.

"Only in the nature of an investment, you see," Devon added, forcing a hard note into his voice. Pride couldn't spoil this little charade now. "I want my men hale and hearty when I open the mine. Probably in a few weeks."

No one pointed out that the majority of the men in the crowd worked in other mines, but many thought it.

"And if we all make as much money as I expect, I may expand my enterprise. At the very least I'll be hiring more men," Devon added, neatly circumventing the last excuse for refusing.

When the miller, his expression timid, exited rolling a barrel before him, the men gave a cheer and descended on him en masse. This time, however, joy rather than fury glowed in their weary, tough faces. The miller began the laborious task of sacking up grain.

Devon didn't notice. His eyes were locked with Katrina's. In broad daylight, in the middle of the busiest district of Truro, Katrina planted a kiss full on Devon's lips.

Neither of them heard the teasing catcalls. John beamed like a fond father. Billy grinned. The magistrate sighed a bit enviously and went home to his shrewish wife.

When Katrina at last drew away, Devon said huskily, "After that, you're staying with me. We've some talking to do."

Katrina's luminous eyes went dark. She took a deep breath, accepted his hand, and walked away with him for what she knew would be the last time.

Five streets away Will leaned casually against the rock wall as one of the magistrate's men prepared the cellar into a cell. He was busy pushing straw into a pile and spreading a blanket over it, so he didn't notice that Will's shoulders moved slightly as he rubbed his wrists against the edge of a chipped wedge of stone.

When the frayed ropes snapped, Will waited until he was certain the man hadn't noticed. Silently, he shook the ropes away. He stooped, picked up the longest length, wrapped it about each hand, then tiptoed up behind the guard. The man was just coming to his feet when the rope slipped about his neck.

He hadn't a chance, for Will knew exactly where to exert pressure, and for how long. In but a few minutes he slumped lifelessly to the ground.

Will spared him one regretful look, then he bent to undress the man, who was also tall and slim. After he'd switched clothes, Will dragged the body atop the blanket and turned it on its stomach, facing the wall. He dropped his own hat over the man's darker hair and tied the corpse's hands.

Then, pulling the guard's battered hat down over his features, he climbed the cellar steps.

Katrina was too miserable to speak on the drive to Devon's manor. She sensed tension in the man sitting beside her. He knows, she thought. He knows this will be our last night together.

She stared out the window at the cloudless day, feeling only stygian darkness in her soul. She had no right to keep tormenting him. She had to let him go. Somewhere he'd find a woman he could love, who would give him the fine heirs he deserved. She tried to take comfort from her own nobility, but even the thought of Devon with another woman was devastating. Let the future be hanged.

For one last time she'd live for the present.

She turned to him with a brilliant smile. "And what shall we do when we reach your home, my lord?"

Uncharacteristically, he didn't respond to her teasing. "Talk, Katrina." And he looked out the window again, his expression moody.

After the manservant let them in, Devon led the way into the study. Katrina's steps lagged at his air of decision, but she forced herself to follow.

"Send a luncheon tray in, please," Devon said to the servant, opening the door. He stood back to let Katrina pass, then closed the door.

Katrina was too nervous to sit, so she wandered the room. She felt Devon's penetrating stare, and had to quell the instinct to bolt.

"I shan't eat you, Kat. Come, sit. It's time to pay the piper." Excellent, Devon, he thought to himself. Where's your legendary charm? Never had he needed it more, never had it been less in evidence. He knew why, of course. His nerves felt raw, exposed. This was the most important hour of his life, and he couldn't gamble their future on a false smile. No, only the honesty she'd taught him would serve.

Yet, when she eased down on the settee as far away from him as possible, he had to grin. He scooted across the upholstery to her side.

"Damme, it seems we've played this scene before. Shall I

seduce you all over again?'' He traced the flush staining her lovely face. ''With pleasure, my lady.''

He hovered over her, his lips tingling under her sweet sigh of surrender. ''After you tell me what I want to know.''

Her drowsy eyes widened. Apparently she saw his resolve, for she tried to turn her head away.

Gently he caught her chin. ''No. No more evasions. I can't go on as we are, Kat.'' Devon felt the dam bursting within him, but he no longer had will to fight it. Frustration inundated her in a torrent of words. ''How do you think I feel knowing that last night you might have died? You went on another run, didn't you? That's the only reason you would have been with Jack.''

She bit her lip guiltily, and that was all the assent he needed.

''Damn you to hell. God must have sent you to earth to punish me for my sins.'' He let her go and surged to his feet.

He looked magnificent in his fury, striding about like a caged lion. His hair was rumpled, half-loose from his queue, and his clothes looked as though they'd been slept in, but vigor and determination glowed from every heated pore. All this wonderful power could be hers if she said the word. She clenched her fists, shaking with the effort to stay silent.

''You lied to me! You promised you'd tell me whenever you went on a run. And what the hell were you doing alone with Jack?''

''He was waiting for me near the cottage. He wanted to question me. He'd suspected for some time, I think, that Will was stealing. He was about to name Will when he was shot.''

The prosaic little recital sent a shiver up Devon's spine. Paradoxically, it also made him so furious he thought the top of his head would blow off. He was on her in two great strides to haul her to her feet. ''You could have died, you little fool, don't you know that?'' He shook her once, hard.

She flung back her head proudly. ''Of course. I knew the dangers when I became a smuggler.''

He released her as if she'd burned him. ''And you expect me to wait calmly, unaware if the woman I love will come safely back to me or not?''

''Don't you exaggerate the dangers? Jack is dead, Will is imprisoned.''

"And what of the law, wind, sea, and cliffs? Other smugglers? The French?"

Katrina shrugged. "And smallpox, or ague, or being run over by a wagon. I can die safely in my bed, too." She stepped up to him until her body pressed at all his pleasure points. "But I didn't come here to stir up an old argument. We've other, more pleasurable ways to brangle." And she put her arms about his neck to draw his head down.

At first he resisted, but her coaxing lips soon felt the change from anger to passion. He clutched her to him desperately, his mouth searing hers, and she knew she'd won.

Yet, as he swung her up into his arms, kicked the door open, and carried her toward the stairs, she knew she'd lost, too. It was best this way, she told herself. She didn't want their last memory to be a bitter argument. As he slept she would leave. Tears threatened, but she forced them back. She'd allow nothing to spoil this last memory.

"Leave the tray in my chamber," Devon growled to the approaching servant. The man hustled up the stairs and opened the door for them, set the tray down, then melted away, closing the door behind them.

Devon didn't even set her down; he carried her straight to the bed. Brusquely he unbuttoned her blouse, then yanked off her skirt. She didn't protest, for she understood the forces driving him. Her own hands, working at his shirt, were as frantic.

When they were bare to one another, their eyes met for a lingering moment. His gaze bespoke so much: love, need, passion. Yet it was the desperation she read that made her close her own eyes and reach for him. When he tried to speak, she drew the words into her own lips, transforming them with a kiss. He sighed into her mouth, and let her help him forget.

Big hands traced every precious hollow and treasured cove; smaller hands charted the rugged contours and vast plains. All the while their lips held in a drugging kiss that saved them from the need to think. Primitive urges guided them away from the precipice. Soon they'd have to attempt it, but for now they could pretend only smooth downs lay ahead.

His lips scorched her already heated skin from the hollow of her throat to the soles of her feet. She tried to reciprocate, but he held her still, proving that in this, at least, he was master. Tongue followed the same course, stoking rather than dousing the fire. Katrina soon began to writhe and moan. Ruthlessly he quelled her, one hand on her shoulder, the other on her thigh. He licked and nibbled the most pleasurable areas only a lover knew. Inner thighs, arms, hollow of her back, breasts, and feminine triangle, all knew the power of his possession.

"Come to me, " Katrina begged, trying to reach for him. She felt him, hot and ready against her thigh, but he twitched away from her seeking hands.

He lowered his tousled head to her stomach, rubbing himself against her like a great cat. The growl that escaped him, however, was not contented.

. Katrina's eyes opened at the tormented sound.

"Is *this* all you would grant us?"

"It was enough. Once." Katrina raised her head to pull him back into her arms.

He allowed it, but he held her legs closed with his own. "No longer. If you would have more of me, you must tell me what happened. No, don't look away. I must know, Katrina."

She kissed his trembling mouth and felt blindly. His arousal was so hard she knew he couldn't restrain himself much longer. Her fingers slipped up and down him, eliciting another growl. Sensuously she began to buck beneath him, her breasts aching for his touch, her womanhood unfurling like a bud bathing in the dew.

A tortured sigh escaped him. He couldn't resist her longer. She was his, would always be his even if . . . His thoughts shied away. Only melding with her could ease his fears.

"You're mine, Katrina. Always, always, always—" He repeated the word over and over as he pushed her legs apart and surged into her like the tide. This was no gentle lapping, however; it was a gale driven by elemental needs.

They were no longer Devon and Katrina, or male and female. They were immutable entities of sea and moon. Nothing mattered but the driving urge to connect. Yet even as they surged together, they knew a true meeting was impossible. Sea could reflect moon, but never touch it; moon could attract sea, but never hold it.

The knowledge only made them more desperate. They

crashed together, again and again, and when the upswell took them, they rode it for a brief, buoyant moment when all seemed possible. The seas calmed, reflecting the moon so clearly that its yellow glow seemed surrounded, absorbed. For that tiny instant they were one, the warm golden heat streaming from him to her enough to reify the impossible.

As such instants always do, however, they faded soon enough. Again they became man and woman, seeking to deny their own separateness. Devon slumped against her. Wrapping his arms tightly about her waist, still nestled within her, he slept.

Katrina told herself to leave, but she was so tired. If she moved, she'd wake him. Just for a moment . . . She, too, slept.

The sun was lowering in the sky when she woke. Gingerly she tried to slip away, but when contact was broken, he awoke with a start. She went still.

He drew back to look at her. She was pale, silent. Waiting. And then he knew.

He withdrew abruptly and hovered over her like a thunderclap. "Damn you. Fuck me, good luck to me, was it?" When she flinched, his voice lowered to weary distaste. "I can almost hate you. You intended to leave when I slept, didn't you? And this time you wouldn't come back."

Her silence was answer enough.

He laughed harshly. "More fool you. I've not had more than a catnap in days. Do you know why?" He leaned forward to emphasize his words. "Because you're boxing me into my own private hell, and I can do naught but bruise myself because you won't let me out."

Her face twisted with pain. "I don't want to cause you unhappiness."

"No? Once, I might have believed that. No longer. Your stubborn silence means only one thing: You've avenged yourself upon me. Taunted me by teaching me to appreciate all we have to offer one another, then denying us both." He rose to pace the room, magnificently male in his nakedness.

Katrina knew she had to leave before she fell apart into tiny, irretrievable bits. "No, no, you don't understand." She began to collect her clothes.

He whirled on her. "Then make me understand."

Tears came then, a bucket of them. "Dear God, I'd wed you if I could. Do you think I hold my love so cheaply?"

Coldly he watched the tears track down her cheeks. His voice throbbed with the emotions boiling beneath the ice. "I don't think you love me at all."

Katrina took a step back, her hand to her cheek as if he'd struck her. In her worst nightmares she'd never dreamed it could end this way. Her only consolation had been the knowledge that at least he'd remember her fondly. Was she to be denied even that?

Should she tell him? Then, at least, he'd understand. Her woman's pride recoiled from the thought of admitting the violation she'd endured. What purpose would it serve, save to cause him more pain? She'd suffered enough for the both of them. Yet how could she let him believe that the sacrifice she made out of love was naught but sick revenge?

Her silence seemed damning to Devon. Unable to bear the strain in her face, he turned away to dress. The hope that had kept him sane was flickering; the chasm yawned at his feet. He'd pretended it wasn't there long enough. When he was dressed, he turned to bridge it or fall to his doom.

She still stood quiet, her face far away, one hand to her cheek. Once more, she'd shut him out. He clenched his hands, but forced his voice to calm. "You don't even bother to deny it, I see." He waited tensely, but when she still didn't reply, he affected a shrug. "That's your choice. Go, then. Let me seek whatever happiness I may find."

And he turned away to stare out the window. Run, my one and only love, before I fall to my knees and beg. He heard shuffling footsteps and expected to hear the door opening. He tensed, his nails bringing blood to his palms.

Instead the footsteps paused behind him. He turned.

Hope flickered to life again—until he saw her face. It was frozen in such misery that she looked almost plain. The vitality that gave Katrina such beauty seemed snuffed.

"Very well, Devon. You leave me no choice. I can bear much, but not the thought that you'll remember me so cruelly."

His heart leaped in his bosom. He almost smiled. Thank you,

God, he exulted. Whatever it was couldn't be that bad. Once they had it out in the open, they could seek the future intended for them.

Katrina's glassy eyes stared at a point over his head as she recited, "Sutterfield intended to rape me the night he took me to the brothel. I didn't stop him; the madam did."

Devon frowned, but his confusion deepened when she went on.

"She wasn't motivated by charity, of course. She . . . wanted to make use of me as quickly as possible."

"But that doesn't make sense—"

Her smile was a ghastly thing. "Oh, but it does. You see, I was pregnant."

Gasping, Devon tried to take a step back, but he was against the window. Unable to stay still, he moved sideways. His eyes dropped to her flat stomach. Pregnant. With his child. He waited, examining his own feelings. He found only pleasure. He knew then that his last reservations were gone. He wanted Katrina's children. A passel of them. "But . . . but where's the child? Have you kept it hidden from me?"

Anger stirred at the thought. He moved forward, stopping when she lifted her hands feebly to ward him off.

"He . . . died, Devon. And I'm unable to have more children. That's why I can't wed you." Still without looking at him, she tried to turn away.

He swallowed. Grief made his eyes water, but when she moved to the door, he leaped forward to catch her shoulders. His face, too, had grown pale. "How do you know that? How did you lose it?"

She shook her head.

He pleaded, "Please, Katrina, I must understand. . . ." His voice trailed away under the impact of her eyes. He sucked in his breath as if he'd been punched. Never had he seen such despair. Understanding began to coil in his stomach like an angry snake eager to strike. Nausea grew, but he forced himself to listen to her lifeless whisper.

"Pregnant women do not make good whores. They . . . intended to give me a potion, you see."

He moaned and shook his head violently, but now her voice

was relentless. "It wasn't needed. A rather strong but vacant man was to hold me down so they could give it to me."

Devon inched along the wall, his hands covering his ears. "Oh God, dear God, no . . ."

She followed him, a macabre satisfaction filling her at his obvious distress. He'd ripped the scab away from the wound; now she could only let the puss drain. "I didn't want to lose the child," she droned, "so I fought him." She began to shake as the memories assailed her. She was seeing the past, so she didn't notice Devon's fixated stare, or his working mouth as he tried to swallow his nausea.

"He wasn't quick, so I dodged his blows. He hit the wall and grew enraged. He . . . punched me, then kicked me—"

"Stop it!" Devon blindly moved back, unable to bear any more. He knocked against the table where the untouched tray sat. He stumbled and fell, food flying about him, tea staining his jacket.

Katrina cradled her stomach, rocking on her heels. "Oh God, the pain. But do you know what was worse? Knowing that I hadn't loved the child enough. I . . . hated the way it was conceived. To this day I fear God punished me for not loving the child as I should. By the time I knew I wanted it, it was too late."

Her eyes focused on Devon again. His bright head still shook back and forth, as if denial could stop the horrific pictures in his brain. "No, no," he keened.

Katrina bit her lip so hard she drew blood, and a measure of calm descended. "That's why I can't wed you, Devon. Because of the infection, I can't have children." She turned to go, hoping, praying, that Devon would stop her. He didn't. When she reached the door, she whispered, "Good-bye, my love."

The door closed behind her quietly, like a final whimper of pain.

Vaguely Devon heard the sound through his black torment, but he was unable to move. Spasms gripped his stomach, and he wondered if she'd felt like this when she lost the child. He doubled over and began to retch.

He vomited again and again, still heaving even when his stomach was empty. All the while he barely felt the misery, for he was seeing the past. The bitterness he reaped now was the harvest of the misery he'd sown two years ago. . . .

Why didn't Katrina hate him? At last he understood. No wonder she'd been so wary. Only a good woman of deep feeling could have overcome such a tragedy and accepted the attentions of a man who'd hurt her so. "I'm sorry, I'm sorry," he whispered. Even as he spoke he knew she'd already forgiven him.

Most women would have wanted to watch him squirm. Not Katrina. As always, love guided her. She'd not wanted to hurt him.

He moaned again. The sound made him wince, but still he couldn't rise. How could he seek her out after this? He didn't deserve her.

The child, the child. What would he have looked like? With a certainty that came too late, he knew he would have been beautiful. His careless, selfish past had robbed him of a future. Devon buried his face in his hands and wept.

Katrina stumbled with weariness. The rocky path seemed to stretch infinitely. Did it matter where it led? She'd as soon walk to the sea and keep going, for a life without Devon was no life at all.

The beauty of their relationship had ended with such ugliness. Katrina was blind to the sun lowering in the sky, or the rocks she stubbed her toes on. She saw only Devon's ghastly face. Retribution left an evil taste in her mouth. The fact that he'd demanded it didn't make his agony any less. Or hers, in the telling.

She clutched her stomach again. Shrouded in the dark memories, she didn't hear him until he was upon her. She looked up and saw a spectral figure, rearing like vengeance against the bloody sky.

She gasped and backed away. Before she had time to run, Will dismounted from the stallion, caught her waist, and threw her in the saddle. She managed one scream before he leaped behind her, covered her mouth with his hand, and galloped off. She fought him, but he was far too strong.

In the distance Billy, who was returning from Ellie's, heard the scream. He searched the landscape and glimpsed a woman on horseback fighting against a man. She was too far away for him to see her features, but the sunset burnished her hair to molten gold. Her struggles knocked the rider's hat off, and Billy saw that he, too, was blond.

As the rider gripped Katrina more firmly Billy drew the carriage to a halt and hissed to Robert, whom he'd brought to see the horses, "Run, lad, like the wind. Get Devon and tell him Farrow's taking Katrina north. I'm going to follow." As soon as Robert hit the ground running, Billy picked up the whip and lashed the horses. The curricle was light, pulled by two of Devon's best animals, and Farrow's horse was burdened by two. Billy prayed it would be enough.

At first Katrina didn't hear the pursuit over the stallion's gallops. She was too busy hanging on to struggle, but when the faint sound of clattering carriage wheels caught her ears, she turned her head.

Her hair whipped Will in the face, blinding him, and he slowed. He, too, heard.

Squinting, Katrina discerned a big, shaggy-haired man with indistinguishable features in the gathering gloom. She did, however, recognize the curricle. "Billy!" she screamed. "Help!"

Will crushed her ribs. "Silence. Unless you want your lover's ass-licker shot."

Katrina bit her lip. Her voice trembled only silently when she asked, "Will, why are you doing this?"

"Later." Will sent one last look behind them, then he veered off the trail so fast the stallion stumbled. Will hauled the animal's head up, and he obediently took them up the indicated hill. Large boulders pocked the earth at frequent intervals, so footing was treacherous.

Billy would never be able to follow them there, Katrina knew. Despairing tears came to her eyes, but then a new sound reached them.

Will paused on the hill to listen. Soon the muffled thumping became the distinct sound of riders pounding up the trail toward the manor. When they appeared around the bend, Katrina rejoiced. It was the magistrate and his men! They were probably going to warn Devon that Will was loose. She drew breath to scream, but Will tightened both arms about her middle and squeezed.

Through the haze gathering before her eyes, she saw Billy meet them and point. The five men turned their heads, then urged their own mounts upward.

"Bloody hell," Will cursed viciously, releasing Katrina. He shifted his head indecisively. The mine sprawled before them, the various buildings housing the engine, the stamping works, and the coal house looking bleak and deserted. Assorted chimneys pointed like wearily cocked hats toward the evening sky. All was silent because Watt's engineers worked only during the day.

Will kneed the stallion down the slope. Katrina held on for dear life during the steep descent. The moment they reached level ground, Will jerked on the reins and slithered down. He pulled Katrina off, unlashed his saddlebags, and tossed them over his shoulders, then dragged Katrina after him. He slapped the weary beast on the rump, and it bolted into the gloom.

This time Katrina's screams were more than a cry for help; she realized where he was taking her. Terror echoed off the rocky tors, but Will doggedly dragged her, struggling, into the bowels of the earth.

Billy, who'd untied one of the carriage horses and brought up the rear of the pursuing men, winced at the sound. Devon had told him once of Katrina's fear of containment. "Hang on, lass, we'll come for ye!" he yelled.

Pushing the others aside, he lashed his horse mercilessly down the slope. Riding bareback, he almost fell, but he reached ground in time to see Farrow disappearing down the shaft. Billy vaulted off his animal and ran toward the faint candle-glow.

Farrow hissed at her angrily, but she stayed frozen on the ladder, afraid to move. Blackness lapped at her feet. Only flimsy stays kept her from being consumed.

"Hurry up, damn you, else I'll club you and lower you down on the rope. God knows how badly you'll be bruised and scraped."

Fury rushed through Katrina, washing terror away. How she hated him; how she reviled herself for her own gullibility in trusting this degenerate scoundrel. She'd see that he paid for this. Taking a deep breath, she began to descend.

The further she went into the gloom, the harder it became to stifle fear. The candle on Will's hat barely pierced the vast darkness. She saw lanterns staked into timbers at frequent intervals; she knew why he didn't light them. But she was puzzled by the echoing sound of splintering wood. The ladder seemed firm enough.

Cold, moist air assailed her, and she could only imagine what hell this place must be when the pumps, snaking down alongside her like sleeping serpents, were spitting their steam on the laboring miners. Pungent odors filled her head: sulfur, wet timbers, raw copper ore. The vague nausea that had troubled her earlier returned with a vengeance. When her feet finally reached level ground, she sank down the wet cavern wall and buried her face in her knees.

"Come on, we've got to go deeper," Will growled, pulling on her arm.

She lashed out at him and began to gag. Since she hadn't eaten lunch, however, her stomach was empty. The dry heaves racked her for several minutes, but at least the physical misery abated her emotional fears somewhat.

Watery-eyed, she glared at Will. Only then did she notice what he'd done. The splintering sounds she'd heard . . . Katrina began to shake again. "You're mad," she whispered, staring at the broken remnants of the ladder he'd chopped up with a small ax as they came.

Even as she said it, she knew she was wrong. That was the horror of it: He was quite sane. Coldly, grotesquely sane. "Why?"

A harsh laugh shook Will. He looked about, then dropped comfortably down beside her. "I'd do anything to get you away from him. *Anything.*"

"But I don't love you." When he flinched, her voice softened to regret. "Now I can't even admire you any longer." She shook her head sadly. "I suppose you'll tell me, too, that you murdered Jack for me?"

"I did."

She covered her mouth as more spasms racked her, but she couldn't block out his remorseless voice.

"And I don't regret it. Davie told me he tried to rape you. Besides, I didn't want my identity known just as I was about to get out of smuggling."

"And would you have killed Davie, too?" Katrina dropped her hands limply in her lap.

"Davie's seriously ill with lung disease. If he survives, by the time he talks I intended for you and me to be long gone."

"How?" She looked about them at the tunnels of stone. Will surely hadn't been down here enough to get them safely out of this maze.

"There's a way out, all right. I've no wish for suicide." Will cocked his head as a new voice joined the mumbling up above.

"Katrina! If you're all right, please yell." Devon's voice echoed faintly down the shaft.

Katrina scrambled away from Will and screamed, "I'm here, Devon." She frowned when Will stayed motionless. Why didn't he care that she called to Devon? She gasped. "You *want* him to come, don't you?"

She leaped to her feet, almost banging her head. Will had to crouch, the roof was so low. "Devon, don't come! He has a gun!" She strained to hear, but silence lay as heavily on her as the fathoms of rock above her head.

Grabbing her arm, Will pulled her behind him down an adjacent shaft. The rough passage, lined with timbers, led ever downward. Lanterns lined the walls here, too. If only he would light them . . . But Katrina wouldn't give him the satisfaction of asking. Oh God, it was so dark. So cramped. She began to fight again in earnest, to no avail. She was dizzy with weariness and hunger, so her strength was even punier than usual against Will's.

Katrina cast hunted looks around. The walls were closing in. She . . . couldn't breathe.

Will forced her into a passage so low that they had to crawl. Water seeped down the walls, wetting their clothes. A small canal full of water ran downward shortly past where they hovered, disappearing into solid rock.

Finally Will pushed her into a nook in the stone and planted himself in the passage before her. He pulled the saddlebags off his shoulders, took out his pistol, and began to load it.

The sight cleared Katrina's swimming head. Terror for

Devon became more immediate than her own fear of entrapment. She cast a yearning look at the ax Will had dropped beside him, but it was too far away. Even if she reached it, could she use it?

Her gaze settled on the saddlebags. Guineas and pound notes spilled out of one of the pouches. She picked up a handful of notes. Their crisp crackle made her sick all over again.

"Is it really me you want, or am I just an excuse for your own greed?" She drew a relieved sigh when he paused to slice her a glance. She flicked the notes at his nose. "You've been embezzling from those you took an oath to serve for longer than you've known me."

The insolence worked. He stiffened and put the pistol aside to catch her shoulders and press her into the stone. The candle atop his cap flickered in his eyes.

How could blue eyes scorch with coldness? she wondered dimly.

"What do you know of my years of service? Have you any idea how many people I've saved, often without a penny in recompense? The men pay my wages out of their own, but I've often served their friends and neighbors at no charge. While men like Carrington and your precious earl feed on their despair, I've worked my fingers to the bone, day and night, trying to bring a better life to these people. And some of them don't even thank me, much less appreciate me." Will's voice softened with satisfaction. "That will change when I'm gone and their usual sot of a sawbones is hired."

Katrina heard faint rustling sounds and said loudly, "That's why Jem was so wary of your help, wasn't it? I never understood at the time, but he didn't want to be beholden to you. Like Carrington. You sent him to kill Devon, didn't you? What did you have on him?"

Will shrugged. "He raped a girl of good family. I doctored her. Her parents didn't want a scandal, but I needed help with the distribution among his fancy friends. So I used him." He smiled bitterly. "Over time, those who are used become masters at it themselves."

"I was just another pawn, wasn't I?" Katrina's tears made her eyes soft and luminous in the dim candlelight. "You saved my life. Because of it you think you own me. What a fool I am.

I . . . trusted you. The evidence was damning, but I didn't see it because I didn't want to believe you culpable. Oh Will, how could you?'' Her voice broke as the tears fell in earnest.

Will's hands trembled as he smoothed her shoulders. ''Shh. I never meant to cause you pain. Since the day I first saw you, I've wanted only to make you happy.'' He clutched her shoulders desperately. ''Katrina, I was there, remember? I saw what your love for this . . . demon did to you. Since you don't seem to have strength enough to reject him, it's up to me to protect you.''

She shook her head violently. ''I don't *want* your protection. I'm neither weak-witted nor weak-willed, despite what you may think.'' She covered the hands holding her shoulders with her own. ''Please, Will, let me go and give yourself up.''

His sad sigh rippled down her spine. ''I cannot. Please, come with me. Let me take care of you.'' Then, almost inaudibly, he added, ''You'll . . . need a father for the babe.''

In the midst of her sorrow his words hit her like a slap in the face. She lifted her head and stared at him. ''Pregnant,'' she whispered. Then, with a little squeal of joy, she hugged her abdomen. ''Oh Devon, we've a life after all.''

Will looked at her oddly. ''You didn't know, did you?''

''No. Praise God, my prayers have been answered.'' And then, as the shock of the revelation waned, the full import of his statement took hold. Her beautiful smile flickered and died. Why hadn't she realized this before now? The signs had been there: her tender breasts, her nausea. She'd attributed everything to her emotional state and the events of the last few days. After Will was apprehended, she'd had no time to think. He claimed to love her, yet he'd put her through the greatest torment she'd ever known for his own twisted designs.

Her voice became as hard and chilly as the stone surrounding them. ''You lied, didn't you? All along. You knew I could have children.''

He shrugged. ''Not at all. You yourself said your menses were irregular. The infection could well have harmed you permanently.''

''But you weren't certain. You lied because you knew it was the one thing that would drive me away from Devon.'' He looked away from her accusatory eyes.

The last of Katrina's fear of being buried waned. This master manipulator would have to find another puppet. She had a future to look forward to now. For the babe, and for Devon, she had to keep her wits and find a way out of this.

Katrina couldn't see him, but she knew Devon would come, somehow. She had to distract Will. "It almost worked! I left him tonight never intending to see him again." She beat her fists at his shoulders. "You bastard! Do you know what agony you put me through? I'll not have it, do you hear? You'll not harm him. If you do, I'll kill you myself—"

Will winced, then his face set with such mingled pain and fury that she gasped and shrank away. "Then so be it. Once he's dead, you'll have no one else to turn to save me." He picked up his pistol again, his fingers hurriedly loading the other barrel as a soft footfall whispered in the adjacent shaft.

Katrina's heart leaped in her breast. "Devon, be careful, he has a gun!" she screamed. "Double-barreled!"

The footsteps paused. All was silent save for Katrina's raspy breathing. Then they made out an approaching pinpoint of light. Will eased up on his knees and lifted the pistol, aiming slightly beneath the light. Katrina grabbed for his arm, but he got the shot off.

"Nooo!" Katrina's scream resounded into silence. She strained to see.

Instead of falling, the candle continued relentlessly on. Katrina sighed gratefully as she realized what Devon had done. Knowing the candle would make a perfect target, he carried it high and to the side rather than setting it in his cap.

She saw from the change in Will's aim that he, too, understood Devon's craftiness. She had to stop him before he shot again. She gathered herself into a crouch on her toes and lunged. She connected to his back just as he fired. The shot went wild into the corridor where Devon stood. They heard the shattering of glass, then the strong scent of oil. He'd harmlessly exploded a lantern, Katrina deduced.

She was so relieved that when Will shoved her aside, she made no resistance. Too late, she realized he'd picked up the ax, snuffed his candle, and gone to meet Devon.

"He's got an ax," Katrina yelled, crawling out of the cramped space and standing up in the adjacent corridor.

The wavering candle paused, then it, too, was snuffed. Total blackness descended, velvety, stifling. Katrina stayed frozen, crouched between the two corridors, knowing that doing otherwise would only complicate Devon's task. Her nails bit into her hands under the strain, but all she could do was listen. And pray. The advantage must be Will's, for he was far more accustomed to this hellish place than Devon.

She heard the ax clang as it struck stone. Sparks flashed, but not enough for Katrina to see. Then she heard a soft thud followed by an oof. Devon had hit Will! She was glad, viciously glad. Stomping feet skidded as the men battled over the ax. She heard the ax scraping the shaft walls, breaking several lanterns. The scent of oil grew stronger.

"You fool!" she berated herself. Then, without fear even in the stygian gloom, she crawled back into the small tunnel and felt frantically through Will's things. There it was! She hurried back into the other shaft, felt along the wall until she found a lantern, then struck the flint in the tinderbox. No sparks flew. Was it too damp?

A cry of pain, too deep to be Will's, galvanized her. Breathing deeply, she steadied her shaking fingers and tried again. This time the wick caught. Katrina turned the wick up. The shadows danced away, revealing the life-and-death struggle.

Will still held the ax, but Devon's hand about his wrist kept it from striking. Normally Devon would have been stronger, but he seemed tired from the exhausting climb down the long shaft on the rope Katrina saw snaking behind the struggling men. Katrina also saw scratches and bruises on Devon's face.

"Dear God, please, help him," she prayed aloud.

Unable to force Will's hand down with his arm, Devon used his legs, walking Will backward, trying to throw him off balance. Katrina moved to step out of their path, but she had nowhere to go but back into the crawl space.

Devon slammed Will against the stone next to her, right below the lantern. Then, with a feral growl, Will jammed his knee into Devon's groin.

Devon dodged, but Will's glancing blow slowed him briefly. Will pulled his arm free and swept the ax high to bring it down on Devon's head.

He didn't notice the lantern directly behind him until the ax head smashed the globe. Oil showered all three of them, but only Will stood close to the flame. Will's shirt sleeve flickered, then burst into flames. He screamed, the ax flying wildly as he beat at the blaze.

Devon was doubled over in pain, so Katrina only had to jerk on his arm to pull him flat on the floor, away from Will. The residual oil in the wick kept the lantern lit, briefly.

Even when the flame died, they could still see. . . .

Sitting up, Devon pulled Katrina protectively under his arm and watched Will's gyrations as he tried to put out the flames. The back of his shirt had caught now. Will rotated against the cavern walls, trying to smother the flames, going farther away from them. His burning shirt brushed against the rope Devon had climbed down, which now sagged against the shaft. The hemp caught.

"Shit!" Devon hissed. "That rope was used with the old engine. It's saturated with oil." The rope seared a fiery path upward on his words, igniting the greasy trail where the engineers had installed the new pipes. One of the higher, drier timbers smoked, then burst into feeble flame. An adjacent lantern sizzled, then exploded, feeding the blaze. The men above, understanding the danger of fire, hauled on the rope. The burning fibers swung wildly, igniting more greasy timbers as it moved.

Katrina glanced from the disaster above to Will. He had dropped the ax to remove his shirt. She saw that his arm was red and slick looking. He gritted his teeth and ripped his shirt open, shrugging out of it. The ends of his hair caught but he patted the flames out and threw the garment aside. Then, his chest hair singed but only his arm badly burned, he picked up the ax in his undamaged hand and came toward them, kicking the burning shirt out of his path. The contact was enough to catch his pants leg.

Moisture gleamed at his feet. It looked too thick to be water, Katrina thought. Just as Will stepped into it, Katrina realized what it was. Oil. Pooling in the floor from the other broken lanterns.

"Will, look out!" she screamed an instant too late. His foot had already reached into the slime. His entire pants leg caught.

He leaped forward, jumping over the pool of fire that whooshed into life. More timbers smoldered, igniting as the lanterns on them also caught.

His scream of pain hammered into Katrina's eardrums. He ran toward them and the adit of water that had been dug to help drain the mine. By the time he reached it, however, his breeches were aflame. He dived into the canal. The water hissed and steamed around him. The flames went out.

Will slumped limply back against the stone. His upper body was blotched, his face dark with soot. When his eyes opened to stare at them, unearthly pale and glowing in that blackness, Katrina buried her face in Devon's sweaty shirt. She had respected and admired this man, even loved him, as a friend. She couldn't bear to see him end this way.

Apparently Will couldn't bear it, either.

"Take her," Will said huskily. "Get her away. If we don't get the fire out, the mine will collapse with the timbers."

"What do you plan to do?" Devon asked, pulling Katrina toward the entrance. He looked up, but the roaring blaze licking ever upward was so bright that it hurt his eyes.

"The adit," Will answered wearily. "The water will do the rest."

"But man, you'll be killed."

"Everything I care about is lost to me. I'd rather die here for a reason than swing on a rope or rot in prison." The rigid set of Will's features, the way in which he refused to look at Katrina, told Devon much Will left unspoken. "Give me the ax, Cavanaugh."

"Will, no . . . You can't die this way," Katrina pleaded, lifting her head.

Devon went to the ax and skidded it along the floor until Will could reach it. Before returning to Katrina, he gingerly lit his candle from the blazing pool and set the tallow firmly back in his cap.

Meanwhile, Will had finally met Katrina's eyes. Her lips quivered at what she read there.

"Drowning's a better end than hanging or burning alive." Will's macabre smile faded. "At least you can't call me a manipulator now, Katrina. This is the last thing I can do for my people. And . . . for you." Will closed his eyes as if he'd deny that another man held her. "Cavanaugh, if you aren't good to her, I swear I'll come back to haunt you."

Will said hoarsely, "Go now. Not to the entrance. Come in here. To the left is an opening that will take you to another part of the mine. Take the first right, then the next left. Both lead upward, to another entrance. But hurry. Once the water comes . . ." Will picked up the ax and scooted along the narrow space to the end of the cavern. The blaze behind them allowed them to see clearly even deep inside the crawl space. Katrina glimpsed Will gripping the ax tightly, then drawing it back in the limited space and slamming it against the stone above the canal, where the adit ended.

Then Devon pushed her into the small opening she'd not noticed in the dark. He followed quickly. Katrina was surprised at how big the shaft was. Even Devon could stand upright. They hurried upward, turning as Will had directed.

The ringing echo of ax meeting stone grew fainter. Then they heard a queer, muffled thunk, followed by an ominous roar. Water hissed like an angry dragon, then spewed violently, gathering speed as it came. A garbled scream was abruptly cut off, then came the sounds of water, untold gallons, rushing through every crevice, flattening all in its path. They heard more hissing and smelled smoke and knew the fire was dying.

"Run, Katrina!" Devon cried, pushing her hard. The shaft was too narrow for them to move abreast. Katrina ran as fast as she could, Devon right behind, but still they heard the relentless water gaining on them. When they at last reached the ladders leading upward, Katrina wanted to cry with joy. Her weary feet slipped, and Devon picked her up and set her on the first rung.

"For God's sake, hurry! You can rest soon, but climb for now. If you value my life." Devon looked behind them and spied white curls gushing where they'd recently stood.

Reaching deep within herself, Katrina planted her aching feet on the ladder and climbed. And climbed. And climbed. So urgently that she wouldn't notice until later the splinters lacing her frantic hands. Devon was right behind. Soon the water was slurping at his feet, then wetting his ankles, tasting him.

Katrina turned her head and saw the water's hunger and

scooted faster, her hands and feet flying. Now the water was up to Devon's thighs, dragging at his weight.

Sobbing, Katrina continued the endless climb. The ladders seemed to stretch forever. Finally, just as she spied the stars beckoning at the entrance, the water sullenly receded.

It seemed to sigh with disappointment as it settled back, filling other innumerable nooks and crannies. With a final burst of strength Katrina pulled herself out on a rough ledge of stone near the dark, silent stamping room, and moved aside so Devon could climb out.

They lay flat, gasping with exertion and relief. Devon pulled her to his chest, his frantic heartbeat slowing as he felt her reassuring softness. "Are you all right? I was afraid being so enclosed would . . ." He shuddered.

She squeezed his shoulder. "I was terrified at first, but then fear of you and anger at Will saved me. I don't think I'll ever again be afraid of being trapped."

"Something good's come of this, then, thank God." Devon sat up. Katrina followed suit. Only then did they notice the glow against the sky.

"Oh dear God, the new engine!" Devon scrambled to his feet. He bolted into the darkness.

Every muscle screaming its protest, Katrina sat up to look. Brilliant against the night, the lower part of the three-story engine house was in flames. The ropes and grease the engineers had used had made a perfect wick for the conflagration. They'd not expected danger of fire since the mine was closed.

Katrina forced herself up to follow Devon. Only then did she remember the oil soaking her clothes—and Devon's.

"Devon, wait!" She hurried after him, stumbling with weariness.

By the time she'd clambered over the rough ground, Devon was pulling away from Billy's joyous hug.

"We're both safe." He looked around at the men, who had fetched buckets and were running, one at a time, to fill them at the well some distance away, then splash them on the flames.

"No, no, not that way," Devon exclaimed. "Form a line, and pass the buckets down. It's faster." While the magistrate and his men obeyed, Devon searched for more buckets. He handed one to Billy and kept one himself.

"Help me rig up a pulley. Farrow gave his life to save the mine. He punched through a wall, filling the shaft with water. We can form two lines."

Katrina helped them find rope and staves, then hammer and nails. Devon didn't even notice her until she gave him an armful of wood.

"Go home and wait for me," he growled, his face filthy, his hair straggly with sweat.

She stared at him as if he were the most beautiful man she'd ever seen. "I'm not letting you out of my sight again," she said simply. "Be careful. Remember your clothes are full of oil."

He glared at her. "What do you care! You expect me to believe that when you ran like hell earlier?" He turned away to help Billy set up the wood.

She smiled secretively, feeling wonderful even in her exhaustion. She sat down to watch Devon take command and dreamed of seeing him do the same with the brood they would have.

Soon more men rushed up the hill. Fishermen, smugglers, miners. All who heard of the fire came to help. Katrina watched their hard, tough faces. Some seemed taken aback at seeing the lord looking like the meanest surface worker, groaning with effort as he himself tirelessly pulled buckets up to pass them down the new brigade that had formed. But they gladly joined the line.

Katrina's eyes filled with tears of joy as she watched. For once, men of both classes, lord and laborer, magistrate and menial, worked together. Somehow Katrina knew she was witnessing the event that would change the course of this district's history.

Devon shouted encouragement. "We can do it, if we pull together. Come, let's sing. It will make the rhythm easier." He cleared his throat and sang in a clear baritone, "Rock of ages, cleft for me . . ."

The Cornishmen joined in hesitantly, at first, then louder. The song did help, and soon they were filling, passing, and emptying the buckets like the well-oiled machine they labored to save. The fire, which had been licking greedily at the second floor, subsided under the constant barrage of water.

Devon's voice was hoarse with weariness as he shouted to the tiring lines, "Come on, just a little longer. Faster!"

With redoubled effort the men ignored their aching arms and passed, endlessly passed. The fire flickered, then died.

Everyone waited tensely while Billy slipped inside the charred building to examine the pump. He came out shortly afterward, his grin splitting his dark face. "Seems fine. We did it!"

A jubilant roar climbed to the night sky. Empty buckets were thrown skyward; full ones were emptied on friends. Two of the men standing near Devon exuberantly threw the contents of their buckets at him.

Devon's grin faltered. The men gasped and dropped the buckets, backing away slightly. The other men froze, waiting to see what the lord would do.

Devon looked like a harlequin, for the water had splashed on one side, leaving half of him black. His eyes opened, gleaming like golden guineas.

"Damme," he said into the tense silence. "Can't you do better than that? Do my back, too." And he turned, looking expectantly over his shoulder.

Roaring with laughter, the men filled their buckets again and splashed him. Devon filled his and splashed back, his laughter joining theirs.

A free-for-all ensued. Katrina sat perched on her rock, watching with an indulgent smile.

When he'd calmed, Devon sought her. He filled his bucket again and came toward her.

Her eyes narrowed on his mischievous face, both halves clean now. She stood and backed away, her hands held out. "Oh no, you don't. I'll have my bath in the normal way, thank you."

"Come now, you're enjoying our fun so, don't you want to join us?" He inched nearer.

"I've had enough 'fun' for one evening," she responded tartly.

Billy put down his bucket to watch. Others soon followed suit. The men nudged one another, grinning. It pleasured them to see that this lord was much like them after all. He was just a man with a maid, delighting in teasing his woman. Those who knew Katrina waited expectantly; she'd give as good as she got.

Devon rotated the bucket gently. "Our fun has only just begun, m'dear. You'll wed me, child or no child, if I have to almost drown you to wash your odd notions away. Let me show you. . . ." He hefted the bucket.

Abruptly Katrina halted. She was touched at his generosity. He must love her greatly to be willing to give up all hope of heirs. An odd smile stretched her lips. She knew the others watched, but she didn't care. She wanted to shout her news to the world. She couldn't wait any longer to tell Devon. "No, sir, it's I who will soon be showing you. And everyone else."

Devon paused, his head cocked in confusion. He'd not heard that joyful tone in her voice for a very long time. Indeed, ever since they'd exited the mine, she'd seemed . . . different.

His fading exhilaration left him bone weary. The bucket sagged in his hands. "No more riddles, Kat. My head's spinning."

She stepped up to him. Even streaked with soot, her face was poignantly lovely in the lantern glow. "Very well, my dear lord." She took his free hand and put it to her abdomen. "In a few months the whole world will see at a glance how much we love one another."

Devon's hand jerked against her. "What do you mean?" he whispered. He'd braced himself to lose her too many times. The lightness in his head began to descend through his body.

"I'll wed you whenever you say, Devon. I have to. I'm not barren after all. I . . . carry your child. I'll deliver sometime in the spring."

Congratulations were shouted from the watching men. Devon didn't hear. He knew only that Katrina had let him glimpse heaven again.

The bucket fell from Devon's loose grip. "A baby," he whispered. He blinked, but the roaring in his ears grew louder. "A baby." He sighed again. Then, for the first time in his life, Devon Alexander Tyrone Cavanaugh fainted. Straight into Katrina's arms.

The men roared with laughter and ran forward to help Katrina support his heavy weight. She brushed them away and sat down where she stood. Cradling Devon in her lap, she kissed the top of his head and blessed it with her joyful tears.

Part Six

―――――

"But true love is a durable fire,
  In the mind ever burning,
  Never sick, never old, never dead,
  From itself never turning."

    ―SIR WALTER RALEIGH,
      "As You Came from the
        Holy Land"

Chapter Sixteen

THE EARL OF Brookstone, his handsome face haggard with strain, paced the study. The cigar he carried left a trail of smoke behind him.

Billy, who was sitting next to Ellie on the couch, caught his wife's hand and played with her gold band. "He's so paper-skulled he don't know what he's doing. He hates those things. Only keeps them for me."

Ellie giggled and patted her own rounded belly. "Will you be the same when my time comes?"

Billy pretended to be affronted. "Have you ever seen me less than calm?"

"Yes," Ellie said complacently. "Many times." She looked significantly down at herself and smiled when her stalwart husband blushed.

"What are you two muttering about?" Devon snarled, saving Billy from a reply. "Something at my expense, I daresay."

"Lad, why don't you go on up? You're run ragged with worry." And you're running me ragged, too, Billy said with his eyes.

Devon didn't even notice. He was staring blindly up the stairs. "She told me to stay here. She doesn't want me."

Snorting indelicately, Ellie retorted, "Nonsense! She's only trying to save you worry. The way you've hovered over her these last eight months, she was afraid you'd faint again if you were forced to watch her pain."

Billy rolled his eyes. "A reasonable expectation, lad, ye must admit."

Devon glared at him. "I'll never live that down. You won't let me."

Innocently, Billy stared back at him.

Growling in frustration, Devon whirled to pace again, lifting the cigar back to his mouth—the lighted end first. He cursed and licked his burned lip. "If this is a taste of what fatherhood will be like, then I can't anticipate the experience."

Ellie rose and walked over to him, snatching the cigar away. "There's only one way to find out." She stubbed the cigar out in the ashtray on the desk, then gave him a small push. "Go and see her. She wants you there, truly."

Devon sent a longing look up the stairs. Then: "Bloody hell, I'm damned if I do and damned if I don't." And he clambered up the stairs, taking them three at a time.

He'd expected chaos in the bedchamber; what he found was calm. Katrina was breathing as Rachel instructed. Her face was drawn with the long labor, and her fingers combed through the coverlet, but she didn't groan.

John had stayed with Robert at the cottage to keep him out of the way, but he'd asked to be informed as soon as the child arrived. Devon had left orders that his servants were to travel the district with the news. So many people wanted to know. Especially Davie, who had recovered to become the headman of Devon's other mine. They'd already found one new vein of copper and believed they were on the verge of discovering another.

Collecting his frightened thoughts, Devon inched toward the bed. "Katrina, are you all right?" He drank in the sight of her tired face. It had been fifteen hours. How much more could she bear?

Her eyes popped open. "What are you doing here?"

He stepped back, his face tightening. "If you don't want me . . ."

She gasped and groped for his hand. "Stay."

"She's been trying not to scream so she wouldn't alarm you," Rachel said, swiping Katrina's damp brow.

Devon's eyes filled with tears. If he lost her now . . . He clutched her hand so tightly his knuckles whitened. "Scream away, my love. Anything that will make this go faster." He smiled wanly. "If I faint, I promise to do so out of Rachel's way."

Katrina smiled weakly at the joke and returned his clasp.

Rachel smiled at him sympathetically. "It won't be long now. You can help her push."

Only another hour passed, this time with Devon holding Katrina's hand, urging her on according to Rachel's commands.

"It's coming," Rachel cried. "Once more, Katrina!"

Groaning, Katrina arched against the great bed. A tiny body slipped into Rachel's waiting hands. "It's a boy, Katrina."

Devon barely spared the child a glance. Katrina was the one who'd worried the whole eight months that she'd fail him.

His breath stopped as he watched Katrina fall back limply. He patted her cheek. "Kat? Kat, speak to me!"

"Let me see him," she whispered. "Is he . . . handsome?"

Devon took the blanket-wrapped bundle. He glanced at the tiny face, then stared. The best of himself and Katrina looked back at him. The boy had Katrina's large, slanted eyes and golden hair. He had Devon's square chin and slashing eyebrows. The tiny fist grabbed at his questing finger, and missed. Devon helped. The lad gripped strongly.

Smiling proudly, Devon took the child to his wife. "You've done as well in this as you do in everything else, my love. He's beautiful." He set the baby, who was still crying lustily, in his wife's arms.

He sat down next to her and watched as she turned the blanket back to investigate. A bemused smile stretched Devon's face as he watched her count the fingers and toes. "See, he's all there. Just as I told you he would be."

Katrina sighed her relief and hugged the tiny body close. "Thank God." She opened her bodice and put the baby to her breast. His howls stopped abruptly.

Going to the armoire, Devon fetched a small gaily wrapped box and carried it to the bed. "Here you are, my love."

"Oh Devon, not another present. The Brookstone jewels are more than I'll ever wear."

"This one isn't ostentatious. I know your tastes better now, my love. I saw this on my last trip to London and knew you must have it."

He tore off the wrapping for her, then opened the box and spread out the protective paper. Katrina reached inside.

Her breath caught as he turned up the lamp so she could see clearly. Her eyes drank in the object in her hand. "Oh Devon, it's beautiful." She held a porcelain unicorn. Its mane flowed wildly, its feet pranced proudly, but its head butted with affection against the side of the girl who stood beside it, her arm about its neck. Their posture was such that the viewer couldn't tell who was leading whom; they seemed one lovely entity, each incomplete without the other. Flowers were strewn on the lush grass that seemed to beckon them to a golden future.

Only the girl's long hair and the unicorn's horn were gilded; the rest of the statue was white, all the more striking in its purity. The girl's features seemed familiar. Katrina turned the statue about. "Why, it looks like me."

Devon dropped down beside her to lift her and the child into his arms. "It is you," he said huskily. "The girl I'll carry always in my heart, even when we're very, very old." He hesitated, then asked, "Can you dream with me now, my love? Do you still believe, as you told me after our first meeting, that Eden doesn't exist?"

She cupped his cheek, her tears falling hot and fast. "I've no need to dream any longer. Reality is all the joy I'd ever hoped to find."

The unicorn fell unheeded to the coverlet.

The child suckled on, knowing his first taste of the security that its parents had so lately found, blissfully unaware of the tortuous road that had led to his birth, or of the many happy years still to come. . . .